REGINA PORTER

The Travelers

VINTAGE

1 3 5 7 9 10 8 6 4 2

Vintage
20 Vauxhall Bridge Road,
London SW1V 2SA

Vintage is part of the Penguin Random House group
of companies whose addresses can be found
at global.penguinrandomhouse.com

Penguin
Random House
UK

First published by Vintage in 2020
First published in the UK by Jonathan Cape in 2019

penguin.co.uk/vintage

A CIP catalogue record for this book is available
from the British Library

ISBN 9781784708863

Printed and bound in Great Britain by Clays Ltd, Elcograf S.p.A.

For my mother and father
and
the everyday storytellers who entered their house

REGINA PORTER

Regina Porter is an award-winning playwright and a graduate of the Iowa Writers' Workshop, where she was an Iowa Arts Fellow. She was born in Savannah, Georgia and lives in Brooklyn. *The Travelers* is her first novel.

CAST OF CHARACTERS

JIMMY VINCENT, SR., *a fireman from rural Maine*

NANCY VINCENT, *Jimmy Sr.'s librarian wife*

JAMES SAMUEL VINCENT, JR., *a Manhattan lawyer, also known as the man James*

SIGRID VINCENT, *the man James's first wife, a casting agent*

RUFUS VINCENT, *the man James's legitimate son, a Joyce scholar*

ELIJAH AND WINONA VINCENT, *Rufus Vincent and Claudia Christie's five-year-old twins*

ADELE PRANSKY, *the man James's second wife, an artist*

AGNES CHRISTIE, *wife to Eddie Christie, an urban planner*

EDDIE CHRISTIE, *husband to Agnes Christie, a Navy vet*

BEVERLY CHRISTIE, *Agnes and Eddie's eldest daughter, a registered nurse*

CLAUDIA CHRISTIE, *Agnes and Eddie's younger daughter, a Shakespeare scholar, wife to Rufus Vincent; mother to Elijah and Winona Vincent*

MINERVA C. PARKER, *Beverly's teenage daughter*

PETER "PEANUT" PARKER, *Beverly's teenage son*

KEISHA AND LAMAR, *Beverly's four-year-old twins*

KEVIN PARKER, *Beverly's ex-husband, a former cop*

CHICO, *Beverly's roti-selling boyfriend*

BARBARA CAMPHOR, *married to Charles Camphor, lover to the man James*

CHARLES CAMPHOR, *banker, husband to Barbara Camphor*

HANK CAMPHOR, *Barbara and Charles's dark-haired son*

SUSAN WEATHERBY CAMPHOR, *Hank's wife*

TESS CAMPHOR, *Hank and Susan's three-year-old daughter*

BIG SEAMUS CAMPHOR, *Charles Camphor's burly first cousin*

CHARLES JOHNSON, *Agnes Christie's lover and Eloise Delaney's distant cousin, an engineer*

ELOISE DELANEY, *Agnes Christie's childhood friend and lover, an adventurer*

HERBERT DELANEY, *Eloise's father, a cannery worker*

DELORES DELANEY, *Eloise's mother, a cannery worker*

KING TYRONE, *Eloise's one good cousin (on her mother's side), a fisherman*

SARAH AND DEIDRE, *King Tyrone's wife and daughter, a fisherwoman and a marine biologist, respectively*

FLORA APPLEWOOD, *Eloise Delaney's friend and lover, a retired social worker*

JEBEDIAH APPLEWOOD, *Eddie Christie's cousin, a Navy vet and moving man*

REUBEN APPLEWOOD, *Eddie Christie's first cousin, a naval officer*

LEVI APPLEWOOD, *Eddie Christie's first cousin and Reuben's younger brother*

TIME

This novel travels from the mid-fifties to the first year of President Obama's first term.

SETTINGS OF NOTE

Amagansett, Long Island; Buckner County, Georgia; Manhattan; Memphis, Tennessee; Portsmouth, New Hampshire; Brittany, France; Berlin, Germany; and Vietnam

BACKGROUND

Tom Stoppard's *Rosencrantz and Guildenstern Are Dead* premiered at the Edinburgh Fringe Festival on August 24, 1966. The existential comedy is told from the perspectives of Rosencrantz and Guildenstern, Hamlet's ill-fated comrades, as they journey on board a ship to England.

THE TRAVELERS

PASS IT ON

W HEN THE BOY WAS FOUR, HE ASKED HIS FATHER WHY people needed sleep. His father said, "So God could unfuck all the things people fuck up."

WHEN THE BOY was twelve, he asked his mother why his father had left. The mother said, "So he could fuck anything that moves."

WHEN THE BOY was thirteen, he wanted to know why his father was back in their house again. His mother told him, "At forty-one, I can't be bothered to go out and find anyone to fuck."

AT FOURTEEN, when profanity seemed to roll off his friends' tongues like water down a leaky pipe, the word *fuck* held no allure for the boy. None. What. So. Ever.

AT EIGHTEEN, the boy (Jimmy Vincent, Jr.) left his hometown of Huntington, Long Island, to attend the University of Michigan.

Jimmy was, by all accounts, a very good student and handsome to the point of distraction. He could have had any girl he wanted, but as these things often go, he pivoted toward a wonderfully plain girl named Alice. Jimmy convinced himself that he loved Alice, and the two freshmen enjoyed tipsy, acrobatic sex. Delighted by her good fortune, Alice would hug Jimmy close to her with gratitude and say, "Oh God. Oh, me. *Me?* Fuck, fuck, fuck."

AFTER MICHIGAN, Jimmy returned to the East Coast. He landed a job as a paralegal at a white-shoe law firm and met a tall New England girl. Jane was a medical student who could pass for a runway model. She didn't talk dirty and people stared whenever they entered a room. Here was a girl Jimmy might have not only married but loved, even at the tender age of twenty-two. He took Jane to his parents' house on Christmas Eve, which also happened to be the anniversary of their first year as a couple.

AFTER A LOVELY dinner that Jimmy's mother had spent all day preparing from her favorite cookbook, Jimmy's father strolled into the living room and sat between Jimmy and Jane. He sipped Madeira port and reminisced about his childhood in rural Maine. "A hot potato will heal a stye. A raw potato under the arms works better than deodorant. Put a potato in your shoe and kiss a cold good-bye. That's the farm boy's dictionary right there. I left one row of potato fields for another. Long Island used to be full of potatoes, if you didn't know." When Jane dipped into the kitchen to check in on Jimmy's mother, his father turned to him and said, "Son, are you blasting that? Hold on to that. Don't fuck that up. Jimmy boy, what I could do with that." Jimmy, who had always been called Jimmy Jr., decided instantly that he preferred the name James. When James was admitted to Columbia Law School, he drifted away from Jane.

Nancy Vincent's Christmas Menu

"Rib-Roast Splurge"

Merrie Roast of Beef, Roast Potatoes, French-Fried Onion
Rings, Broccoli with Easy Hollandaise, Salad Apple Rings,
Brown-and-Serve Fantans, Candle Cake, Hot Coffee,
Mugs of Milk

—*Better Homes and Gardens: Special Occasions*
(New York: Meredith Press, 1959)

WHEN JAMES WAS thirty-one, he made partner at his firm. He was wealthy, though not shockingly rich. James had seen heart attacks give two partners, not much older than him, the old heave-ho, so he carved out time to travel at home and abroad. It was his pleasure to date an impressive array of women. He married a pretty Middlebury girl not far from her college on a rolling blueberry hill in Vermont. James and Sigrid bought a three-bedroom apartment overlooking Central Park. His lovely wife had one flaw, a scar on her nose, a gift from a random stranger who had knocked Sigrid off her pink Schwinn bike while she was cycling with her parents in Prospect Park. "Move the fuck out the way," the spandexed stranger had said, zipping past her on suede roller skates. This story seemed somehow prophetic to James. He loved Sigrid as much as she loved him. Sigrid gave good laughter. They had one son. They named him Rufus. And called him Ruff. Sigrid told James she would have no more. After a one-year leave of absence, Sigrid returned to her career as a copy editor.

WHEN HE WAS forty, nothing stirred in James. He had read somewhere that people in their forties were miserable, but James was content to take his Ruff to baseball games at Yankee Stadium and to put the dull but profitable work of the office on hold from Friday to Monday. He found himself teaching at his alma mater, Columbia, and liking it more than the practice of law.

WHEN HE WAS forty-two, everything stirred in James—especially after he saw his elderly father interred in a family grave in Cabot, Maine. A colleague from the law firm pulled James aside before the funeral and said, "You're lucky you got to know your dad as a grown man. Not all of us make it to eighty-one." James wanted to say, *Fuck you. I didn't know my dad at all.* Instead, he said, "Thank you for traveling to Maine. Thank you so much."

WHEN JAMES WAS forty-five, Sigrid told him he spent too much time alone in their apartment and she required a change. They were on their annual trip to Vermont, a few yards from the blueberry hill ski resort where he had first proposed to her. It proved a lackluster weekend. James consulted the same colleague who had attended his father's funeral. "Menopause is a problem," his colleague said. "Time to trade her in." James thought this seemed a bit premature and asked his mother to weigh in. She sent James a recipe from *Better Homes and Gardens.* Over a plate of homemade mushroom risotto that he had spent most of the afternoon preparing, James told Sigrid, "The change of life can be your enemy or it can be your best friend." Sigrid took their son, Rufus, and moved across the country to a Spanish-style apartment in Los Angeles. These days, she jogs most mornings on the beach and drinks Sapporo beer in the evening with her boyfriend.

WHEN JAMES WAS fifty and sleeping with Akemi, his much-younger Japanese assistant, Rufus called crying from Venice Beach. "Dad, some serious shit just went down. Would you come to L.A. and get me, please?" James was not prepared for his son's bad news. He hung up on Rufus, but not before telling him, "I'm sorry, Ruff, but I'm trying to sleep—so I can unfuck all the things that God has fucked up."

Akemi, which means "great beauty" in Japanese, watched James reach for the V&T pizza box on the nightstand. She noticed that he had taken to snacking in bed lately. She pulled the covers over her shoulders and would not pretend to love him. "You don't know how to grow old here." James told her he needed some time alone. And when Akemi left, he called Rufus.

WHEN JAMES WAS fifty-eight and happily married to fifty-six-year-old Adele, whom he loved because neither of them needed to talk much, he went to visit his aged mother at the retirement facility she now called home. His mother had white hair and white dentures and he was astonished by how vibrant her fake smile was. He had never told his mother that she was beautiful. She was the kind of woman who wouldn't have appreciated the compliment. "How are you doing, Mom?"

His mother looked at him and said, "Enough is enough." This statement struck James as necessary but oblique. He wondered if she was thinking about checking out. It was a coward's way, but one he would never rule out himself. She gestured toward an old man in a shabby silk bathrobe two tables down. The old turtle was thick in conversation with a plump middle-aged female visitor who might have been his daughter or a much-younger wife. "I can't get any peace. That old geezer is always hitting on me."

"You still got it going on, Mom," James said. His mother smiled and pinched his cheek. It wasn't the same as telling her she was beautiful. But enough was enough. She pushed her chair back and told James she looked forward to seeing him the following Sunday.

WHEN JAMES WAS sixty and Rufus, now married for several years and with twins of his own, called to ask, "How do I keep my marriage together, Dad?" James told him simply, "By not getting a divorce." Rufus had married a black woman named Claudia Christie, which meant that James's grandchildren, Elijah and Winona, were multiracial, biracial, *part black*. Everywhere James went in Manhattan, there were *half-and-halves*. He had once made the mistake of using the term *mulatto*. Rufus took him aside and explained to James that the word was verboten. Say it again and he would see his grandkids nevermore. Still, when James walked down the street with Elijah and Winona, his feelings were as mixed as their skin. "They are so stunning," people would say. *But they don't look the first thing like me*, he confessed to Adele.

ONE SUNNY AFTERNOON in August, James was tossing a softball in the backyard with Elijah. He spent most of the summer and autumn months now with Adele at their beach house in Amagansett. They were looking after the grandkids for the week while Rufus and Claudia attended a Joyce conference in Dublin. James and Adele liked to sip their martinis at noon. Noon martinis had become a ritual in Amagansett, but not golfing. Never golfing. It concerned James when Adele emerged from the kitchen in a 1940s Mildred Pierce swimsuit and deposited Winona in the ancient floating donut. The donut was blue and white and decorated with red crabs, but you could tell it was biblical in age because the crabs were now a rusty pink. James split his attention between Winona in the pool and Elijah, who was throwing the softball with a mean, mean curve. The boy had a good arm. And, in the right light—now wasn't this a funny thing—the kid looked just like him.

"Grandpa," Elijah said, gearing up for another throw—a throw that smacked the palm of James's hand with a sharp sting. "Why do people need sleep?"

They were on the expansive green lawn. They were both in swim trunks. Their swim trunks were the same aqua color. Adele liked everything in her beach house color-coordinated and bright, like the Caribbean. The idea that everything in a beach house should be white was obscene. Speaking of Adele. Where was Adele? Winona was in the floating donut singing. Kicking and singing. Splashing and kicking. For a moment, James was confused. Growing old wasn't easy. Sometimes he tried to trace time backward to 1942, the year he was born.

"What did you say, Elijah?"

"How come, Grandpa, we all need sleep?"

James could see Adele through the patio windows. She was pouring another martini. She was talking on the phone, probably to one of her artist friends about where they would take the kids for dinner tonight. Now that they all had grandkids, dinner was part of their routine. Dinner and martinis.

"Elijah," James said, turning toward the pool. Winona was dozing. Winona was asleep. Her body was slumped over the floating donut and she was drifting into the deep end of the pool.

"No one knows why people need sleep," James heard himself tell his grandson. "Sleep is a mystery."

DAMASCUS ROAD

1966   1976   1977   1988   1999   **2010**

A WEEK AFTER THEY FINISHED BUILDING DAMASCUS PREP, that school for rich kids who couldn't get in anywhere else, an eighteen-foot alligator crawled out of the swamp to inspect his former home. In the first-floor hallway between the Science Laboratory and the Art Studio, the nearsighted principal and the eighteen-foot alligator crossed paths. The principal, a transplant from the North and a former Latin professor at Amherst, recalled reading somewhere that if you encountered a snake in a tunnel or an alligator on the ground, you should run crisscross. He wagered a bet that sideways might be too slow and bolted into the nearby Art Studio, where he took out his cell phone and called Animal Control.

When Animal Control failed to show, the principal called the local sheriff. Fifteen minutes later, a retired officer and one of the county's best marksmen arrived in his Ford pickup and shot the alligator dead. The officer, still towheaded in his old age, declined payment in cash. He and some of his retired officer buddies hauled the carcass away. On any given night now, Agnes heard, you can go up to the Great Byrd Lodge, where the alligator is stuffed and mounted. You can guess how long the alligator was in his prime and how much he weighed. There is a barn wood chalkboard on a corner wall and a piece of chalk attached to twine string. The first customer each night who comes closest to guessing the alligator's weight and length wins a complimentary slice of pecan pie or a pint of locally brewed beer. Agnes M. Christie, senior citizen and prodigal daughter of Buckner County, Georgia, has not dined at the Great Byrd Lodge. She prefers wine to beer, and pecan pie is too sweet for her palate anyway. Nor has Agnes ventured out to Damascus Prep, though she knows the road that leads to the school all too well.

"YOU DRINKING THAT Coca-Cola like you have to be somewhere."

The year was 1966. Agnes Miller was nineteen, a majorette in her second year at Buckner County College. She wore a powder-blue shirtdress and a bubbly bouffant in the fashion of Diana Ross and the Supremes. To be a majorette, you had to have nice legs. Agnes's legs were so long they could skip across the Nile. Her hemline was modest. She worked part-time in the college library. Whenever anyone asked Agnes what she wanted to be when she grew up, she would tell him or her automatically that she wanted to be a teacher. It did not matter if Agnes liked the profession. The answer was suitable and pleasing.

"I happen to have a busy schedule." Agnes smiled at the dark brown, well-dressed man sitting on the opposite end of the counter at Kress Five & Dime. Really, she had no place to go but home and nothing to do but homework. Classes were over and majorette practice had ended two hours before. Agnes was rewarding herself with her daily glass of Coca-Cola. She sat next to her childhood friend Eloise, who never wore a dress when she could wear pants. It was the late afternoon and the counter was eerily quiet. The protests and sit-ins in Buckner County had come and gone with tension, restraint, and a willfulness not to notice. Whites had reacted first with anger and then with cool logic: turning their attention to the suburbs, opening restaurants and shops and building split-level, ranch-style houses in new neighborhoods that Negroes dare not enter.

"Well, I'm Claude and I happen to have time on my hands." Claude Johnson slid nimbly from stool to stool and stopped at the one beside Agnes. He was an engineer, he said. And had just been hired to work at Southeast Aviation. He wore neat gray pants and a twill blazer with leather patches on the elbows and a shirt and tie. He wore them easily and well, despite his farm boy neck and shoulders. Claude treated Agnes and Eloise to a second round of Coca-Colas. His attention was clearly trained on Agnes, but he did his level best to include Eloise in their conversation. Everything about Eloise screamed *back off*, especially the way she leaned into Agnes whenever Claude was speaking.

"I'm not pushy but I'm going to call you tonight," Claude promised, as the three of them left Kress. He told the young women that he was from a little town called Tuxedo, Georgia, and had attended Morehouse College. Eloise, in her first attempt at civility, mentioned she had people from Tuxedo, but then she added, "Tuxedo's a hick town. My poor relations have poor relations in Tuxedo that they don't want to know."

CLAUDE CALLED that night. He called before Agnes did her evening calisthenics. And before Agnes's mother and father turned out the light in their upstairs bedroom. He called before Eloise, who resided in Agnes's house, brushed her teeth for meanness with Agnes's toothbrush and opened the drawers to Agnes's claw-footed chifforobe.

"Is that you, Agnes?" he said.

"It's me, Claude. Though I suppose if I'm to be an English teacher, I should say *I*."

"Sweetie, when you are in the comfort of your own home, I think you should say whatever you please."

"This isn't my home; it's my parents' home."

"Are you happy there?"

"Well. It's not something I stop and think about all that much.

But I suppose I could be happy anywhere," Agnes laughed, and was startled by the velvet in her voice.

"I wish you would be happy with me," said Claude.

"I don't know you, Claude."

"We can work on that. How about a movie this Saturday? I'll pick you up for dinner around six?"

"That's a start."

Agnes hung up the phone and only afterward realized that Claude didn't have her address. She counted. It took sixty seconds for him to call back again. Eloise stood in Agnes's bedroom doorway. She had on one of Agnes's nightgowns.

"I hope someone doesn't kill that big man," Eloise said. Agnes rolled her eyes at Eloise. Didn't Eloise know that pettiness was stale? Pettiness made your teeth fall out prematurely. Pettiness made your breath bad.

"Why do you say such things?"

Eloise shook her head. "He just has that look about him."

IT WAS NOT unusual on autumn nights in 1966 for Eloise to reach across her pillow and lower the sheets on Agnes's side of the bed. Sometimes, Eloise's thighs would drift onto Agnes's legs and Agnes would stare out the bedroom window at the moon and the star-spangled sky, stroking the back of Eloise's head and the nape of her neck and the slender line of her firm back and all the other parts of Eloise's body that turned her on. They moved quietly and efficiently—for they could not risk utterances or words. Deacon and Lady Miller's bedroom was just across the hallway.

The next morning the girls rose in the best of spirits, poised for a new day.

CLAUDE TOOK AGNES to see *Nothing but a Man* at the local colored theater on the outskirts of town. They ate popcorn with extra butter poured on top. After, Agnes said, "My God, I'd like to look like Abbey Lincoln."

"You look better than Abbey Lincoln," Claude said.

"Claude, you are a liar. Where'd you learn to be so smooth?"

"Now, listen, I didn't say you *sing* better than Abbey Lincoln. Then I'd be a liar."

"It's true. I can't carry a tune." Agnes giggled. "They kicked me out of the choir at church and my daddy's a head deacon there."

"That's bad."

"I haven't been back since."

"You're prideful."

"You don't exactly strike me as a humble man."

"Let me hear you sing for myself."

Agnes opened her mouth and sang "Baby Love" as they walked toward Claude's gray 1961 Chevrolet Impala. It was not a new car like she had expected, but it was clean and had running heat. A minute into her singing, Claude took her hand.

"Now, Agnes, you're not doing anybody any favors with that voice of yours, least of all the Lord."

She nudged him. "I am a falsetto. It's rare for a woman to be a falsetto."

He nudged her back. "You know what they say about pride, right? Pride cometh before the fall."

CLAUDE JOHNSON RENTED a garage apartment about two miles south of the more affluent colored neighborhood. Where Agnes lived, the front doors of houses were painted red to indicate who owned their homes outright. Claude rented his apartment from Mr. Gilbert, the proprietor of the town's only colored furniture store. Agnes walked about the two rooms of Claude's place, noting the freshly painted white walls and bookshelves; most of his books were on engineering or nonfiction: *A Thousand Days: John F. Kennedy in the White House*, *The Autobiography of Malcolm X*, and *The Structure of Scientific Revolutions*. His degrees from Morehouse College and Hampton Institute hung on the living room wall. On one of the end tables, there were several photographs of what seemed to Agnes to be a large extended family, composed mostly of women and children. There were fresh flowers on the walnut coffee table.

Agnes picked up one of his family photographs and turned it toward Claude. "How many of you are there?"

"Asked the only child." He smiled. "Enough to keep the women-folk busy."

"Womenfolk?" She ruffled her nose and sniffed the flowers before returning the photograph to the bookshelf. "Three, most likely two, is my limit."

"That seems reasonable and fair."

In the background, Abbey Lincoln began to sing and Agnes allowed her body to sway. She nodded to Claude appreciatively and snapped her fingers.

"You're right. She can sing."

Claude was sitting on a tan-colored couch, which, like most of the furniture in the apartment, had been supplied by Mr. Gilbert. Claude had touched up the room with a few bright throw pillows from Sears and a shag rug.

"I have to tell you, Agnes," he said. "I don't intend to stay here."

She continued to snap her fingers. "Claude, you decorated this place yourself?"

"I'm giving myself two, three years, tops. Then it's California or New York."

"They're not treating you well out there at Southeast Aviation?"

"Don't ask a question if you aren't prepared to hear the answer."

She stopped snapping her fingers. Of course, Claude had to have his struggles. He was tall and big and brown. He spoke well and did not wear shabby clothes. "That bad?"

Claude sat forward. "We will never beat our children, Agnes. You hold me to that, you hear? My father believed in the whipping switch. He'd grab one in a heartbeat. I suppose he didn't know any other way. I was a little black boy with a sharp tongue. He'd say, 'Son, this is the South. Why can't you talk sensible like your brothers and sisters? We got to take the edge off that voice of yours or you won't make it in this world.' Here's the thing, Agnes. I hated the man for the longest time, but I understand him now. Monday through Friday, I go to work, and I shave the edge off my own voice."

"Just you?" she said, raising her brow.

"My options are better elsewhere. I'm educated. And I've maintained close ties with my Morehouse and Hampton brothers. New York, New Jersey, Washington, D.C. Even Massachusetts. I won't rule them out. But it's my time now to build my résumé and help my family as best I can."

"I see," Agnes said. She noticed his honey-colored eyes had softened.

Claude patted a spot beside him on the sofa. "But enough of me. Tell me what *you* want, Agnes."

For a moment, Agnes was stumped. Claude was the first man to sit back and listen while she fumbled to carve out a dream for herself. "Something other than being a teacher."

"HE IS MY COUSIN, three times removed," said Eloise, the last night she slept in Agnes's bed. Agnes had rolled away and whispered to Eloise, "Isn't it time you found a man of your own?"

Eloise persisted. "He is my cousin on my mother's side. All my mother's people die young."

Agnes climbed out of Eloise's twin bed. "I can't do this anymore."

Eloise didn't reach out for Agnes, though Agnes sensed she had wanted to. Eloise was stuck on Agnes's words and the idea, the idea that she could or should find herself a man. "What man?" Eloise asked Agnes. "Does Claude do for you what I do for you?" Agnes had rushed out of the bedroom, a flash flood of tears on her pretty face, but by the time she came down for breakfast the next morning, she and Eloise were the best of friends again. Both girls enjoyed scrambled eggs and bacon, orange juice, milk, and green apples, sliced the way Eloise liked them.

"You have been awfully good to me," Eloise said to Agnes's mother, Lady Miller. Lady Miller was a baker. She rose before dawn most mornings to work at the Jewish bakery on Jefferson Street. This morning, she had called in sick. The spirit had told her she should stay at home. Lady had been a young woman like her daughter once, and though not book smart, she was neither deaf nor blind nor dumb.

Lady put together a care package for Eloise but turned away when Agnes asked her childhood friend, "Where will you go now?"

"To my cousin, King Tyrone. He's 'bout the only decent one."

AGNES'S PARENTS did not say anything the first night she slept over at Claude's house, but the following evening after supper her father, a stonemason who'd helped erect a quarter of the buildings in Buckner County, pulled Claude aside and asked the young man what were his intentions toward his daughter. Claude called Agnes over and said he would not talk about his intentions without consulting his girlfriend first, in case their intentions were mismatched. Agnes said she wanted to finish college. She was in her junior year. Claude said he would reside in Buckner County until Agnes completed her degree. Agnes's mother said until Claude put a ring on their daughter's finger, Agnes should not sleep out anymore. That same night, Claude parked outside Jackson Quick Convenience Store while Agnes went inside to purchase a dozen boxes of Cracker Jacks. It was from the sixth box burrowed beneath the caramel kernels that they ferreted out a small plastic ring with a faux magenta stone. They threw the remaining boxes away.

THERE IS A little town thirty miles west of Damascus Prep that used to know hard times. The town lost a third of its population to manufacturing jobs in American cities during the two world wars. But in the 1990s, when they filled in the swamp and built the dorm and the campus and the tennis courts and the housing for faculty, a good number of the town's citizens found employment maintaining the campus grounds or working in the cafeteria or as custodians, security guards, and landscapers. Real estate was still affordable. The ambiance was nice. Applications to the boarding school spiked and so did tuition. Proprietors of the shops on Main Street could now afford to hire salesclerks full-time. There was a constant demand for small goods and high-end merchandise. The local barber, a spirited preacher and sometimes drunk, took to working every other Sunday to accommodate Damascus Prep students and staff. They enjoyed the bluegrass music he played in his shop and the Grover tambourine he rattled while trimming their hair. The movie house, at least a century old and rumored to have belonged to one ghoul and two ghosts, now played art films to capacity crowds. It doubled as a music venue as well. And since privilege is often coupled with a desire for fresh produce and lean, quality meat, a health food store and gourmet market were opened to appease Damascus Prep students and the county's more health-conscious residents. The tackle shop began carrying designer fishing rods, and the local fishermen now offered morning and evening boat tours of the swamps. At the end of the school year, families chartered boats from Georgia to coastal Maine. One little prep school on what used to be a dark and lonely road with scarcely a streetlight and only the rubbing together of grasshoppers' legs and the *ribbit-ribbit* of Georgia bullfrogs had revitalized an entire town. Of course, Agnes M. Christie doesn't know about this renaissance firsthand. She reads up on Damascus Prep during lulls at the Buckner County Library, where she volunteers three days a week since returning south. Sometimes, you let things go in old age. Other times, you hold them close.

DURING AGNES'S senior year at Buckner County College, Claude told her that Abbey Lincoln was coming to Atlanta. He was excited because it would be a perfect opportunity to stop over at his parents' and to introduce Agnes to some of his Morehouse brothers and their lovely wives and girlfriends. Lady Miller kissed the Cracker Jack ring and gave Agnes and Claude her blessing. Deacon Miller slipped Claude a crisp fifty-dollar bill and asked if he had enough gas for the road. The needle on the gas gauge of Claude's Chevrolet pointed to full, but Agnes's father put an extra gallon of gas in the trunk anyway. "You'd be foolish to smoke," he told them as they drove away.

———

THE STOP IN Tuxedo, a rural town you could walk through in five minutes, was direct and to the point. Claude's parents were quiet folk who put out their one best tablecloth and mismatched pieces of silverware. They served a simple roast that was juicy but had none of Lady Miller's devotion to pitted fruit or Mediterranean herbs. There was no centerpiece or garnish on the table. Claude's mother served iced tea in mason jars. And during their visit, two hours timed to Claude's watch, a welcoming committee of burly brothers and sisters flocked in to say hello. It was clear that they had placed not just their hopes but some of their savings on their baby brother. Claude managed to hug each of them and promised that on the next visit home he and Agnes would stay longer. "The work, Mama," he said as he slipped an envelope on the table that Agnes knew was his hard-earned money. "I have yet to take a sick day or go on vacation. I'm saving all that up for when I can enjoy it."

IT WAS ON the drive home from Atlanta—after the Abbey Lincoln concert, which ran an hour late, and after Agnes had met most of Claude's friends, that the couple ran into a mess of traffic on U.S. 80, the Dixie Overland Highway. Claude and Agnes were listening to the radio and laughing and dissecting the evening's events, from the songs that Abbey had sung to the way Claude's friends had freely scrutinized Agnes and offered their opinions. "Well, Claude, the wrapping paper is lovely and the contents are equally fine." Agnes had gone from feeling superior around Claude's family to feeling shallow and stupid around Claude's friends, who were far more active in the civil rights movement than she or her parents had ever been. Agnes made a silent promise to herself to read some of Claude's nonfiction books with more than a passing interest.

"You did well," Claude said.

"I thought some of them were awfully pretentious," Agnes said. "I don't know how you managed."

"If you wait long enough, people will show you who they really are," Claude said. "I just waited for them to reveal their real selves."

———

IT WAS TWO in the morning when Claude turned onto Damascus Road, a long and desolate stretch that he would have normally avoided, except that it provided a shortcut to Buckner County. He was most mindful of the speed limit, even though his foot was pressed harder than normal on the gas. Neither Claude nor Agnes noticed the police car until it pulled onto the road and the officer turned on the blue lights and the siren. Immediately, Claude slowed down and parked along the shoulder of the road. The moon was high and the sky was black as obsidian and they were surrounded by low-slung trees crippled by marsh and swamp. When the police officer leaned into the driver's seat and turned on a flashlight, Claude already had his license out.

"Evening, officer," Claude said, neither looking at the officer nor looking away.

"You chasing the moon?" the officer asked.

"I'm sorry?" said Claude.

"Seems like you have some place to go?" The officer was a thin man, as thin as Claude was big. His ash-brown hair was going bald up top, but he had a full handlebar mustache that curved along the edges.

"Was I speeding, officer?" Claude asked neutrally.

The officer took the license. "I do believe you were."

Agnes, like Claude, stared straight ahead.

The officer leaned deeper into the car and seemed just on the verge of returning Claude's license. He tipped his hat to Agnes. "I suppose with *that* kind of cargo, I'd be speeding too."

Agnes could see Claude flinch. She put her left hand on his elbow. The officer gave Claude's driver's license a long second look. "I'm going to run this through. You sit tight."

As the officer made his way to the patrol car, a low whistle escaped Claude. It was a cool night. Cooler than usual, and Claude could see his own breath.

"I am going to start this car, Agnes," Claude said.

"Claude, he wants you to do something. That's what he wants."

"I don't like the look of him."

"Just be polite. Just be still."

"What was I thinking?" Claude gripped the steering wheel. "Turning on the road here."

Officer Jamie Haig called for backup. It took about fifteen minutes for William Byrd, a fellow officer and the county's best marksman, to arrive on the scene. William Byrd was broad-shouldered and clean-shaven and his eyes were peacock blue when he smiled, which he rarely did. He had blazing red cheeks and flaxen hair that, even in old age, he would cling to. Lean Officer Haig conferred with broad Officer Byrd, and the two men decided that Claude and Agnes should step out of the car while they searched it. When Claude, in the most civil voice he could muster, asked what exactly they were looking for, Officer Byrd put his thick hand on his rifle and told Claude he'd do well not to disrupt their search. The officers looked in the trunk, and between the cushions in the front and back seat of the Chevrolet. They tore through the glove compartment and poked their heads under the hood before telling Claude to get back in his car. Claude waited for Agnes to climb in the passenger seat first.

Officer William Byrd shook his head decisively. "We need to take a peek inside her purse."

Agnes opened her elegant black clutch bag, a recent gift from her mother. *A new dress and bag. Something nice to wear to the Abbey Lincoln concert.* Agnes watched, a knot starting to twist her stomach, as the officer's clumsy fingers rifled through her personal belongings.

"Jamie," Officer William Byrd said to his narrow partner, "I think we need to pull this young lady aside for more questioning."

"What kind of questioning?" Claude said, moving involuntarily toward Agnes.

Officer William Byrd pointed at the purse. "There is contraband in this bag."

Agnes started, her own anger soaring. "There is no contraband. Why, there's just lipstick and perfume and my identification card!"

"Jamie," said Officer Byrd, with casual assurance, "I think we might need to call for more backup."

"Now look here," said Officer Haig, turning to Agnes. "This isn't anything that can't be resolved in a few minutes. We can clear this up with a walk down that there lane." He pointed to a curving lane, buffeted by weeping willow trees and swamp.

"Her fella"—Officer William Byrd nodded toward Claude, whose fists were coiled—"he's a bit anxious."

"You love this man?" said Officer Jamie Haig.

Agnes looked at Claude. She thought about Eloise's words. *The men in my family all die young.* She thought about the burly officer whose fingers were even now tickling his rifle.

"That is our personal business," Claude said, his body rocking with controlled fury.

Agnes nodded. "Yes, I . . . *love*."

Towheaded Officer William Byrd started down the road and took Agnes with him into the swamp and trees. It was a quarter of an hour later before he showed his pale face, and he approached without Agnes. There was a deep night blush on his already red cheeks and he smiled at Claude in an easy, cheerful way. He took out a whiskey flask from his shirt pocket and held it up high, taking a few swigs. "Jamie, I don't think the gal has contraband, but you know my eyes are bad."

Claude was now in handcuffs. A slow stream of blood was inching down the back of his head, which had collided most violently with Officer Jamie Haig's billy club. Before Officer Haig excused himself, he whispered to Claude, "Don't you try on Willie what you tried on me. I would in no way advise it." Officer Haig ran his fingers through his thinning hair as he moved around the car into the darkness.

"You'll feel better after a drink." Officer William Byrd sidled over to Claude, kicking Claude's feet from underneath him. He tilted the flask to Claude's mouth and poured the whiskey onto Claude's face. Claude turned his head away, locking his lips. He would not drink the liquid that burned like hot soup on his face.

Not long after, Officer Haig walked back down the road alongside Agnes. Officer Haig opened the passenger door for Agnes, and

Agnes, still looking straight ahead, climbed into the car. Officer Haig eased Agnes's purse onto her lap. The flip in Agnes's bouncy bouffant was flat.

"I want you two to get home safe," said Officer William Byrd, removing Claude's handcuffs and pressing him into the driver's seat of the Chevrolet. "It's been a long evening for all of us. And as these things go, it could've been a lot worse."

Claude cranked up the ignition and peeled off. He did not know it, but he was crying. Agnes retained her composure, blinking when Claude asked if he should take her to the hospital. Blinking when he asked her if they should stop by Mrs. Francine's house, the town's colored midwife, who was used to being woken up at ungodly hours. He asked her if she was all right, and that was when Agnes stared down at her hands and noticed the Cracker Jack ring was no longer on her finger. She turned to Claude, screaming and hysterical, begging him to turn around.

"Agnes," Claude said. "I will buy you a thousand Cracker Jack rings, baby. But those men will kill us if we go back. I can't turn around."

"Take me home, then," Agnes said. "Take me home now."

THE FOLLOWING DAYS, when Agnes did not come to the phone or return Claude's calls, Lady Miller assumed that the meeting with Claude's family hadn't gone well. Deacon Miller, a Booker T. Washington cloak of a man, had been viciously chided for his dark skin as a child. He suspected that the light-skinned educated crowd in Atlanta had snubbed his only daughter and that Agnes was putting the best on the outside and snubbing them right back.

One Sunday morning before church, Claude appeared on their doorstep. He had not been there in two weeks. Deacon Miller did not welcome him into the house, but Agnes consented to step outside on the front porch. Claude knelt before her, on bended knee, and proposed, showing her a sparkling engagement ring with the largest diamond she had ever seen. It must have eaten up his life's savings to buy such a ring.

"Claude," she told him. "It's not your fault."

"Agnes," Claude said, repeating her name over and over again.

But she would not consent to marry him. To ensure that Claude would not come near her and that she would not relent, Agnes surveyed her options. The next month at her first cousin Charlotte's wedding reception, she met Edward Christie, a gregarious, sturdy little man. Agnes was a good foot taller than Eddie Christie, who proposed to her on their first date. There wasn't even time for a church wedding. Lady and Deacon Miller were baffled, heartbroken witnesses to their only daughter's courthouse wedding. Agnes packed her bags and moved north to live with her husband's people. Eddie went off to Vietnam six weeks after they were married.

EDDIE'S FAMILY OWNED a brick house a few blocks away from Little Italy in the South Bronx. For a Southern girl whose world was steeped in black and white, Little Italy was something new. The Bronx Riots had not yet occurred. Agnes, pretty and charming, learned to speak Italian from the Italians, who took a liking to the tall young woman who always said *please* and *thank you* and *how are you today*. Agnes enrolled at Fordham University, where she completed the degree that Damascus Road had interrupted.

AGNES DID NOT become an English teacher. Her first job was for the city, as a project assistant. What began as a safe government job with a good pension would eventually turn into a rewarding career in urban development. Agnes and Eddie named their first child (born nine months after they married) Beverly, after Eddie's grandmother. As soon as Beverly could crawl, she followed Agnes everywhere. Beverly's clinginess filled Agnes with doubt and disappointment, but she was a good child overall, happy of nature like Eddie.

EDDIE CHRISTIE'S entrances and exits made it easier to remain a happily married couple. When her husband came home, Agnes did not have to feign love. Love was a muscle. You used it. You worked it out, and love rewarded you with flexibility and strength.

———

THE SPRING OF 1969, a year after Dr. King was assassinated in Memphis, Agnes received a midnight call from Eloise, who was visiting family in Buckner County.

"Agnes," Eloise said, "I had to just about kill that mother of yours to get your number."

Agnes put a protective hand to her stomach at the sound of Eloise's voice. She was expecting her second child, in her third trimester.

"How are you, Eloise?" Agnes heard herself say.

"You know me, Agnes. Give me something to latch onto and I thrive."

"You are well, then?"

There was a pause. "Most days, I am."

"Good."

"Listen," Eloise spoke quickly. "Claude was found shot dead in his apartment in Dorchester, Massachusetts. They think it might have been an armed robbery. One of his coworkers found him."

"Claude?" Agnes heard herself say. She had not spoken his name in three years. "Claude? Dead?" Massachusetts wasn't even five hours from where she lived.

"I'm sorry, Agnes," said Eloise. "Some of us aren't cut out for life in big cities."

Agnes put down the phone and took to her bed. Eddie's mother called the doctor. When the doctor asked Agnes what was the matter, she told him there were a thousand and one sharp pains coursing beneath her skin. The doctor said she had acute bursitis, which sometimes happens to pregnant women. Lady and Deacon Miller came up to look after their only daughter, but the clutter of the Bronx and New York City itself assaulted their senses. After two weeks in the Bronx, they retreated to Buckner County.

A BABY GIRL was born to Agnes and Eddie Christie four weeks early. She came into the world in the maternity ward of Columbia Presbyterian. This time, Agnes longed to hold her baby girl, to rescue the child from her incubator and the hospital's unnatural light. She was happy to coo to this new daughter and sing lullabies and happier still when she took the child home. She named her daughter Claudia, and when Eddie, recently home from the war, mentioned that Claudia was not a family name, Agnes massaged the calluses on her husband's hand and said, "I just like the sound of it."

A HOSPITAL IS NO PLACE FOR CIGARETTES

2009

AM A REGISTERED NURSE IN EMERGENCY MEDICINE AT Columbia Presbyterian Hospital. My official title is Resource Co-ordinator. There are four other RNs who work beneath me: four other RNs who follow my lead. I could walk around here being a dictator—if I wanted to. Walk around here like one of these surgeons, acting all knowy-and-showy, like God put the power of healing in their fingertips. But when I come to work I understand that it's not about me. It's not about my coworkers either. It's about these people up here in this hospital. I might be the last face somebody sees. And that's a blessing. An honor. That's sobering.

I could have been a doctor myself. But I never got around to applying to medical school. In my nursing classes, I always made straight As. My fifteen-year-old son, Peanut, would proofread my homework. He'd look up from a paper I had written and say, "Dag, Mom, you are smart."

And I'd just smile and shake my head. "What makes you think you got all your smart genes from your dad?"

My kids' father, Kevin, is a policeman—correct that—*was* a policeman. He's out west in the Arizona desert now running immigration checks with Border Patrol, sending desperate people back to Mexico. It's a good thing we learned Spanish in high school. We grew up in the South Bronx, a few blocks east of what used to be Little Italy. Back then the Bronx was full of Puerto Ricans, and we just picked up Spanish naturally and took it as an easy language requirement in high school. That's what I tell my kids: you're learning one minute, and the next minute that learning is carrying you. You can't see the end in the beginning. So play it safe and get the beginning right. Of course, Kevin used to tease me, say I picked up Spanish easy 'cause my grandpa was Cuban, but he was from the generation that only spoke English.

After having the kids—I've got four of them—my medical school applications never left my dresser drawer. Kevin and I were just trying to stay ahead of the bills. Maybe I'll go to nurse practitioner school one day. I'd make a good nurse practitioner. They keep saner hours. The way I see it, these doctors don't have time no more. And they're not making money like they used to, anyhow. With doctors, it's in and out, out and in. I heard one doctor yelling at his supervisor the other day. This supervisor is always trolling, breathing down his neck. "How am I supposed to examine twenty-five patients in one day? What if I miss something? I'm a doctor. Not a circus magician." Six days out of the week, I hate his snooty ass. But right then, I was feeling him.

So, this is the man James. That's what my sister Claudia calls her father-in-law: the man James. The first time she told me about him I said, "Why you preface his name with *man* like that? Is he prejudiced or something?" Claudia just shook her head. "He's not prejudiced," she said. "He's lost."

The man James is stranded here in the Neurological Intensive Care Unit. I promised Claudia I'd check in on him during my break. She and her husband, Rufus, are somewhere in the South of France. First, a conference in Dublin. Then a vacation in France. Some of us get to live the life. They're headed back to the States now because this old dude bumped his head on the deck of his Olympic-sized swimming pool while trying to rescue my niece Winona, who nearly drowned. I don't know this for a fact, but I put the pieces together like a jigsaw puzzle. When I saw Winona's brother Elijah, I took him aside and said, "Elijah, what happened?"

Five-year-old Elijah said, "The floatie thingamajig tipped over and Winnie had to swim."

Hearing that made me mad. Turned me from worried to foul. Brought up all kinds of we've-got-bile energy with my sister, Claudia. I could have looked after Winona and Elijah. I've got a prewar apartment in Washington Heights with three bedrooms and a deluxe sofa couch. I could have made it work. The cousins would have gotten to see each other, which they rarely do. We would have *all* had fun. I would have taken them for pizza and to the Victorian Gardens or up to the Bronx Zoo. I own a family pass and the kids could have seen those scary-ass Siberian tigers. They could have gone to the butterfly observatory or ridden the monorail. Claudia thinks my son Peanut is smart by default, by accident, but here's the thing: I *do* shit with my kids. I don't abandon them. Never have. Never will. I don't always feel like being bothered, but what mother does? What mother goes from day to day saying, *You are mine. I love you kids.* And doesn't have a moment when she cries out, *FUCK THIS FUCK THIS FUCK THIS.*

Now, this here James Samuel Vincent is sitting up in Neural ICU halfway comatose with a busted-up head, and his ladylove wife, Adele, has carried *my* niece and nephew off to FAO Schwarz and Dylan's Candy Bar on 60th Street because they nearly drowned. And instead of smoking a cigarette like I want to be doing, I'm checking in on the man James because I *promised* Claudia I would. One way or another, I always keep my promises.

If Claudia took the time to ask, she'd know I have my own problems: a super-sized plate full of headaches. I called Miss Lydia, my twins' babysitter, to see if my daughter Minerva had picked them up, because Minerva never answers her cell phone and then, while I'm calling Miss Lydia, Peanut's texting me: *Do I need to go to robotics? Do I need to pick up Keisha and Lamar?* And I'm like, *Chill a motherfucking minute.* Please. *Peanut. Chill?*

But Minerva showed. Miss Lydia called me and told me as much. And I got this happy little skip in my heart. Maybe Minerva is going to turn out all right. I can't wait to tell her that James and his drunken second wife nearly drowned her cousin. I can't wait to tell her that Adele is making amends at Dylan's Candy Bar. Minerva *hates* Dylan's Candy Bar, despite being a fanatic for chocolate and sweets.

Here's the thing: I knew Minerva was going to be trouble when she was ten, and I took her to Serendipity's on the Upper East Side for a mommy-and-daughter treat. I wanted to take her to Serendipity's because I read somewhere that Diana Ross had a limousine take her and her daughters there on their birthdays for a bowl of hot chocolate ice cream. I thought I'd show Minerva how the fabulous people live. But when we got there, Serendipity's was closed. They weren't in business anymore; I hadn't thought to call in advance. I was feeling real stupid, but Minerva just shrugged and said, "Where to now, Mom?" And I reeled myself in from stupid to *I got this* fast. I wasn't about to disappoint my girl. And we started walking, like I knew where we were going. We're walking around the Upper East Side, and I'm feeling the yoke of the poor around my neck with every fucking step we take. The Upper East Side can assault you like that. From the high-end nail salons to the little boutiques with the silver bells you have to ring to enter, to the fancy big windowed cafés that look like modern works of art. We came to Dylan's Candy Bar, and it was crowded with young people and old people getting their candy joneses on. We stood outside for a minute watching the people pouring in and out of the store.

I said, *"Let's go there."* We followed the masses. And Minerva was beyond happy. She got busy pouring candy out of plastic bins into little bags with red strings to cinch them together. Whoppers and Hershey's kisses and gummy bears and peanut butter cups and caramel clusters and black licorice. And Skittles. Lots of Skittles. And Minerva's like, "Mom, who is Dylan to give us all this candy?"

Someone next to us whispered that Dylan is the daughter of Ralph Lauren. And Minerva was like, "Ralph Lauren? His real name isn't Lauren. His real name is Ralph Lifshitz and he's from the Bronx—like us. He's just fronting. Fronting for status."

And that was when I thought, *Gee, she's smart. Trouble's coming. Keep her busy.* For a while, I did. There was gymnastics. Swim lessons. Spanish. The viola. I even splurged on lacrosse equipment. But then my marriage fell apart, and so did Minerva.

Right now, I want a cigarette bad enough to kill. But I'm going to hang tight with the man James until my next shift. Claudia will ride me for a lifetime if I don't keep my promise. It's quiet and peaceful up in here. How much quiet and peaceful do I get? Something about this quiet makes me miss Kevin. I should reach out and tell him to come get Minerva. His ass needs to know that his daughter's unspooling. Of course, he'll think I want him back. Kevin will think the call is about sex. Men always think the call is about sex. It's funny—the things we get wrong in a relationship. We got so many things wrong. But we mostly same-paged it with the kids. It's the shit we got right that's hard to protect. You feel what I'm saying, James? You hear me in there? I hope you hear me. You better hear me. Fuck, you *might not* hear me. Don't veg out. Stay in the game, James Vincent. Why is it, God, that a hospital is no place for cigarettes?

LET THERE BE SALT

1954   1969   1979   1989   **2009**

OR A MOMENT IN THE HOSPITAL ROOM, JAMES SAMUEL Vincent's heart nearly stopped. The sensation came with the realization, and the dread, that God was not only a woman, but lo and behold, the Savior of the world was black. James was high on painkillers and Her image came to him fuzzy, like something out of a dream. He found himself straining for words that would not come, struggling to move his arms as if to declare, *Before you judge me.* But then his thoughts swam back to a bright blue day and an aqua pool and that granddaughter of his, Winona, slipping through the hole of the donut-shaped flotation device and sinking down, her reddish-brown curls twirling in the deep end of the pool. James had turned then, dropping the mitt in his hand, telling Elijah to stay where he was, and he had rushed toward the pool, as fast as his sixty-seven-year-old legs would take him, which was relatively fast, moving off the perfectly manicured lawn and onto the slippery edge of the bluestone deck, where, just before he dived in, the wet ground beneath him gave way and the man James fell into murkiness.

———

JIMMY JR. He was little Jimmy Jr., a twelve-year-old boy all over again, standing under the kitchen ceiling fan watching his mother break the fine-bone china, the teacups and saucers, the eight-piece dinner and salad plates, the crystal flutes. There had been a disagreement between Jimmy's parents. There was always a disagreement between Jimmy's parents, but this one had boiled over into a full-fledged row. Ugly words were spoken that neither could wipe away or take back.

His father, Jimmy Senior, had accepted a new job with the fire department in Fresno without consulting his wife. A new job meant moving three years straight, but Nancy Vincent loved Portsmouth. Yes, Portsmouth was expensive (especially for a one-income family), but it was also a good place to put down roots and raise their boy.

"They need firemen in Fresno. They'll even pay for our house." Jimmy Senior was a fireman, but firemen were being laid off left and right, thanks to recent budget cuts in Portsmouth.

Nancy Vincent roared like a lion that Sunday morning. She was a redhead, but not prone to bouts of anger or foul temper unless genuinely provoked. "I went to Fresno once for a librarians' convention. Fresno is hell. We're not taking Jimmy anywhere near Fresno."

Their last home, just one year before, was in Hartford, Connecticut. Nancy had not complained when they left Hartford for Portsmouth. Promises were made. They would stay put in their new town until Jimmy graduated from high school.

"When we move to Fresno," Jimmy Senior said, "we'll get a dog."

"Jimmy wants a cat," said Nancy.

Jimmy Senior shook his head. "What boy wants a cat?"

Jimmy wanted to stay in Portsmouth. "Please, I'll take a dog or a cat if we can stay here." At twelve pushing thirteen, he was already taller than his father. The boy could not know that one day he would have two sons of his own: one son in a marriage and the other in a dalliance. The dallied son would possess his father's looks, manner, and temperament.

"The movers are coming next month. The last day of school," Jimmy Senior said, finally. "It's settled. Get packing."

His father put on a new suede coat. Sometimes on summer evenings in Portsmouth a breeze rolled in off the ocean and a jacket was the best defense. Jimmy Senior headed to the neighborhood pub to drink Guinness with his friends.

"I'm going to visit my family," Nancy yelled after her husband.

"You don't have family."

"I've got my uncle Monroe."

"And where's the money going to come from, kiddo?"

Nancy had been out of work for three months. The economy was also rough on librarians in Portsmouth, with its restaurants, shops, and museums. But Nancy had an eye for bargains. She and Jimmy Jr. were suckers for the Trading Post in nearby Kittery.

JIMMY SENIOR FLEW to Fresno a week ahead of them for orientation. Nancy went from room to room in their three-decker apartment singing "Bye, Bye Love" and picking out the tokens that mattered most to her.

"There's been a change of plans," she told Jimmy.

He was shocked by his mother's efficiency, perhaps a skill developed as a librarian. She piled his baby pictures into a leather suitcase. She left her wedding photos behind. She gathered Jimmy's birth certificate and social security card, their winter coats, rain boots, a few pants, shorts, and shirts, and said, "Who says women don't travel light?"

They each packed one box with their favorite books. Jimmy liked Dickens and Poe and Melville. He could read *Moby-Dick* all night long.

JIMMY BARELY HAD time to say good-bye to his best friends. Lukas and Boone were acne-prone, active boys who also liked to read late into the night. They pedaled over on Schwinn Deluxe Racer bikes. Jimmy could not know it then but Lukas Fall's B-52 would be shot down during a mission in Vietnam. Boone McAllister would become a conscientious objector and open a health food store for vets in Portsmouth. The only thing Jimmy knew sitting on the steps of his apartment building that evening was how much he would miss them. Nancy Vincent never corrected Jimmy when he told people that Boone and Lukas were his cousins. She said it was only natural to latch onto a new family when your own family was disjointed and small. Both of Jimmy's parents were only children. Or at least Jimmy's mother was. Jimmy Senior never talked about his family unless he was drunk. *Maine people* was the most he would offer. *Southern folk*, Nancy Vincent said of her relations. The kind of white Southern folk who couldn't stomach the prejudice in their hometown, she added, as if words could make up for grandparents Jimmy didn't know. Uncle Monroe was the only living uncle she had left. Until recently, Jimmy had thought he was the stuff of fables—as real as a cartoon character or a mermaid or merman.

"BE PREPARED. Southern people are strange," Boone warned Jimmy. But it seemed to Jimmy that anywhere he went—at rest stops and filling stations and diners and motel lobbies on the thirty-two-hour road trip to Tybee Island, Georgia—people were sufficiently strange. They smeared ketchup on French fries angrily, asked for random directions they did not follow, came up and made small talk like they were catching up with long-lost friends. Sometimes, Jimmy would sit in the car while his mother rushed into the bathroom for "a bit of freshness." He'd sit with his long legs propped like a tent in the passenger seat eating Fritos and looking at the people coming and going, traveling but somehow frozen, stock-still. Freshness was a phone call to his dad. Freshness was his mom rushing out of the rest stop and not even looking as she crossed the street to the parking lot. (She had nearly been hit twice.) Freshness was too much silence and his mother's small feet begging for a speeding ticket, as she pressed down hard on the gas. Freshness was the brittle look that came across her face when Jimmy dared to ask after his dad.

THE DRIVE TO Tybee lasted a minor lifetime, with a stop in Manhattan to see a free outdoor revival of the musical *You Can't Take It with You*, which was something Jimmy thought neither he nor his mother needed to be told. In Washington, D.C., they stopped to admire the Lincoln Memorial. They stayed in a Holiday Inn in Maryland and enjoyed the complimentary breakfast with coupons.

"If breakfast is complimentary, why do we need coupons?" Jimmy asked his mother irritably.

Nancy refused to entertain his frustration. "Uncle Monroe is a nice man."

"When was the last time you saw him?" Jimmy said.

"Oh, I must have been five. I remember he owned a fish market."

"Great. I can sell fish. I can grow up and become a fisherman."

"Sounds like a dandy plan to me." Jimmy's mother took life young. And maybe she would be forever young. The troubles of married life didn't play out on her face the way they did on some women's. It took a pretty woman to pull off a pixie cut: features open to the world with close-cropped hair. She had shorn her hair just before they left Portsmouth with metal scissors. Left a mound of red tresses on the black and white tiles in the kitchen. She had also left behind dreams of retiring in Portsmouth. A Cape Cod cottage house. The perfect scale for a family of three.

"Well, I paid for this with my hard-earned money," Nancy said, when they drove off in the 1951 pink Cadillac Coupe de Ville, which was the sole piece of property in her name. "Your father wouldn't be caught dead in anything this pink. Hell, maybe that's why I bought it."

UNCLE MONROE WELCOMED them into his shaky, two-bedroom bungalow with a nod and a smile and a shit-happens grin. He wore a grizzled beard on a long hangdog face. *Well, Dad said I wanted a dog and now here I am living with one. You can't get much more doglike than Uncle Monroe.* It was a mean thought, but a slow acidity had taken root in Jimmy since they'd left Portsmouth. He had yet to see one rainbow, and rainbows had been fixtures in his life. There was a lot of sunshine and clouds in his Portsmouth, which made for colors coming at him from nowhere and bursting up the sky.

It was a good thing that Nancy hadn't brought much with her. Uncle Monroe kept a man's house. His fish-selling days were over, but his house was full of plastic fish heads and newspaper rolled over tables and old pots and pans and hard beds and a scratchy plaid sofa and a small TV with basic reception so he could watch the morning news and hear if a storm was coming.

"You don't believe in comfort, Uncle," Jimmy's mom told Uncle Monroe as she limped out of the bedroom after her first night's sleep on the rock-hard mattress.

"Comfort isn't functional" was Uncle Monroe's reply

"I like your brand of comfort," Jimmy's mother said, when the hot water turned stone cold five seconds after she stepped into the shower.

"Water rots iron and sinks battleships," said Uncle Monroe.

"This from a man who sells fish."

"I sold it, darling. I *ain't* no fisherman."

Nancy laughed. "Is this a ruse or are we related?" The next week, he went out and ordered two new mattresses from Sears and set them up in the bedroom that Jimmy and his mother shared. He also brought home a bouquet of sea lavender and asters from Piggly Wiggly's.

NANCY VINCENT LOST some of her zest two weeks into their stay. She went for long strolls on the salt-colored beach, but in the evenings—without Jimmy. And she'd taken to mumbling to herself, sudden outbursts that made Jimmy want to put a stopper in his ears: "Jerk. Stupid. Jackass. What was I thinking all these years?"

"When are we going back to Portsmouth?" Jimmy asked his mother three Sundays into their stay.

"In due time."

"What does that mean?"

Uncle Monroe interrupted. "It means your old man was a pain in the ass. And Portsmouth's a memory."

"Watch the language, Uncle," Nancy said.

Uncle Monroe threw up his hands. "My friend King Tyrone just pulled in a boat full of crabs. You ever held a blue crab?" Uncle Monroe looked at Jimmy.

"I like lobster," Jimmy said.

"He wouldn't know a blue crab if it pinched him on his nose," Nancy admitted.

Uncle Monroe's face dropped so long Jimmy thought it might graze the floor. "Now that's a sin. And a shame."

TYBEE MEANS SALT in Euchee, his mother cooed to him. *The Euchee Indians founded Tybee Island. They were the first people to live here.* And where are they now, Jimmy wanted to know? A pretty beach might mean something to someone else—but not to Jimmy Vincent. First off, he preferred his beaches untamed, wild with rocks and crags and perilous jetties that you scraped your knees raw on. He liked the frigid beaches of Maine, his *father's* beaches, and the chill that hit a nerve ending when you took that first plunge. Jimmy's summers in Portsmouth had never been this gooey or sticky. Tybee Island was an entirely new measure of humidity and heat. Since the heat took "some getting used to," his uncle Monroe's pet phrase, Jimmy got into the habit of rising at the crack of dawn, before the beach dwellers took over the beach and the sun took over the day.

One morning, after declining Uncle Monroe's invitation to go crabbing for nearly two weeks, Jimmy decided he had nothing to lose by tagging along. Otherwise he would have to endure another lecture on the history of Tybee Island from his mother. Nancy Vincent was determined to pique her son's interest. *I know it might not look like much to you, Jimmy, but this island used to be a destination. Taking the salt, they called it. People would come from all over for the fresh air when they were sick.*

Uncle Monroe drove his truck a short six blocks to King Tyrone's house. King Tyrone owned a shack on a pier facing the marsh. He was a skinny, dark-hued man of about forty. Jimmy was surprised to see how many years Uncle Monroe had on the fisherman. He was also surprised by the abundance of sea lavender and aster flowers bordering King Tyrone's property.

"Piggly Wiggly, my foot," Jimmy said.

Uncle Monroe shrugged. "Don't bring confusion with you here."

They wasted no time getting out on the water. King Tyrone did not care for company that wasn't related to him. And sometimes, he didn't much want to be bothered with relatives.

"They call this the dead man." He cracked a crab open and showed Jimmy the fleshy innards. "That's how we tell a female crab from a male one. The bright orange means this she-crab was carrying eggs."

They stood in King Tyrone's fishing dinghy with crabs crawling all around them. Jimmy looked at the blue crabs pulling and crawling over themselves on the deck of the little gray-and-white fishing boat and wanted to cry. Something about them was beautiful and sad.

"Good eating tonight." Uncle Monroe slapped Jimmy heartily on the back.

Jimmy watched King Tyrone pluck up a dozen or more blue crabs with his bare hands and drop them in a wooden barrel. His hands were callused all over and he seemed indifferent to their pinchers.

"That doesn't hurt?" asked Jimmy.

"You get used to it after a while." Sometimes when he was out on the water, King Tyrone thought it might be nice to have a wife and kids waiting for him on shore. But the ocean was unpredictable. And bad luck ran in his family. "Pinchers don't faze me no more."

LATER THAT EVENING, while his mother rolled out extra newspaper on the backyard picnic table, Jimmy watched Uncle Monroe drop the crabs into a red lobster pot of boiling water in the kitchen.

He watched their frantic dancing and their slow drag to color change. Jimmy did not think he could eat the crabs, but his appetite betrayed him. He ate well that night.

The following morning, his mother went with Uncle Monroe over to Stingray's, a local seafood joint, and filled out an application for a waitressing job.

"Best start somewhere," she said. "No point in waiting."

The day after his mother started working at Stingray's, Jimmy took his uncle Monroe's old rickety bike and cycled six miles to Fort Pulaski. He didn't tell Nancy for fear she'd worry about the traffic he'd encounter on Highway 80. He paid the price of admission and took pictures of the fort to send to Boone McAllister and Lukas Fall. His friends had written to tell him they were reading *All Quiet on the Western Front*. He responded with a letter about the Confederate soldier whose ghost was said to roam Fort Pulaski at night in search of his head. After the tour, Jimmy pedaled along the dirt paths surrounding the fort. He cycled past plants and flowers and birds whose songs seemed tropical, foreign. *They do not have these species of birds in Portsmouth*, he wrote to Lukas and Boone. He biked the whole way home in an old fisherman's straw hat that belonged to his uncle Monroe, and for the first time, the afternoon heat didn't bother him.

IN PORTSMOUTH, one evening shortly before he and his mother had left, Jimmy was heading home from Boone's house and heard a voice that he recognized as his father's. He had turned around and there was Jimmy Senior and his firemen cronies ambling down the street, joy and liquor and every kind of corruption jumping off their skin. *The scattering*, he heard his father say, slapping one of his friends on the back, *keep your woman scattered and she will always come back. Some other gal's stray hair, a number that means next to nothing to you and everything to them. All their confidence is blubber. I never met a woman who didn't doubt herself.* Even as Jimmy Senior spoke, he had a woman on his arm, another redhead, a woman who, for half a second, Jimmy tried to believe was his mother. Except that her clothes were younger, tighter. A red sweater to match her hair and ski pants. Jimmy had looked around and then up in the air, almost expecting to find a ski lift, but there were no ski lifts in Portsmouth.

JIMMY SENIOR CALLED once from Fresno. "Fresno is hell," he admitted to Nancy. "I got the desert. You got the beach."

Jimmy's father did not say he wanted to get back together with his mother. Jimmy's mother did not say she wanted a divorce. "Tybee Island is pretty," Nancy said. "I like this part of the Atlantic. People are easy and friendly."

"You're still in the honeymoon phase. Wait till you get to know them."

"I think that's exactly what I will do. Wait." She gave herself permission to drawl.

"Put my boy on the phone, please."

"*Your* boy? The stretch marks are on *me*," she laughed.

"Well, Nancy, when you come back to me, I'll be ready with the cocoa butter cream."

"Who says I'm coming back?"

Jimmy's father chuckled then, and when Jimmy came to the phone, he said, "Jimmy, remember this: the world will take a bully over a fool any day of the week. And your mama's a fool."

"I miss you, Dad." Jimmy looked at his mother. Her expression told him that he was Judas. And she was Christ. He could not know that within a year's time his father would relocate to Huntington, Long Island, and bring them along with him. It would be Jimmy Senior's longest period of gainful employment. Jimmy Jr. would graduate from Huntington High School and attend the University of Michigan on a scholarship.

"Jimmy boy, I think I need a nap," James Senior said. "Time to unfuck all the things that I have fucked up."

THE EVENING TIDE was coming in and Jimmy rolled up his khaki shorts and waded knee-deep into the Atlantic. He had not swum in this ocean since they arrived on Tybee Island. The beach was flat with soft fine sand. Jimmy tiptoed and waded farther out into the water, and the lukewarm ocean responded by sending a bright wave that knocked him clear off his feet, wheeling him right into an undertow and daring him to gasp for air. In the bowels of the Tybee Island undertow, Jimmy refused the dare. He willed his muscles to relax and his mind to calm the fuck down, until the ocean released him. He came up to the surface and inhaled fresh air. Forgotten. He'd forgotten what a good swimmer he was. How good it felt to— *swim.*

JAMES SAMUEL VINCENT opened his eyes and was back in Columbia Presbyterian's Neurological Intensive Care Unit. "My granddaughter?" he tried to say to Beverly, the dark God. But his words came out muddled: "MEGEDEEE."

God's fuzzy face leaned close to his. Everything smelled vaguely of cigarettes. So, God smoked cigarettes, he thought.

"We've been worried," Beverly said.

So God was worried. Did this mean that he, James Samuel Vincent, was headed for heaven or hell? He blinked again, trying to grasp the countenance of this alien God's face. She would not come clear to him. She was as shifty as his thoughts. The room seemed to levitate around James, alternating between a shimmering blue and a harsh white light.

"MEGEEDEE," James tried again.

Beverly Christie, who was used to the crazy things painkillers did to old people, leaned in closer and replied. "Rufus and Claudia are on their way."

Ruff, James's mind said, *my boy Ruff.* But his mouth said. "Woof Woof." It was then that James understood that his mouth was covered. Smothered in plastic. He was on a ventilator. This sudden knowledge made James struggle and kick.

"You took a bad fall," said Beverly. "You hit your head."

So he was alive. But what about his limbs? Why couldn't he move his limbs?

"You were transferred to Columbia Presbyterian," Beverly said. "Adele is with the kids."

James felt something. A prickling. A sting. *Jesus. Lord. Christ.* Tears were beyond him. He hadn't cried in over thirty years. Who was he crying for, anyway? Was he crying for himself?

"Winnnnn," the man James said.

And Beverly understood him. She stroked his silver hair and whispered, "Winona and Elijah will be so happy. They've been asking after you. We told them their bubby was sleeping like Rip Van Winkle, only not for a hundred years."

ACT ONE

1971 1980 1990 2000 **2009**

POKEN IN OUR BACKYARD IN THE SOUTH BRONX, OUR little piece of corner land with plum tomatoes in a pot and little leaf cucumbers growing along the trellis fence we shared with our Italian neighbor, Alfredo "Freddie" Maddalone. *Toss the coins. Where are Rosencrantz and Guildenstern?* My mother, Agnes, swears that my first sentence in English was *Where are the coins?* I was on my knees and she had just returned from basting the Sunday roast in our teal-blue galley kitchen. Beverly and I were beating pots and pans when I said: *Where are the coins? Toss the coins, Rosencrantz and Guildenstern.* I was not yet two years old, and she said it terrified her to hear me speak these words so clearly. And that being Southern, which is to say superstitious from her first breath, she thought, *Lord, something is wrong with my baby. It's unnatural for a child to string words together like this.* But then she remembered that my father, who was once again at sea, had read the play to Beverly and me instead of *Ferdinand* or *Goodnight Moon.*

I'm going to have to talk to Eddie when he gets home, my mother said. My father was on a Navy aircraft carrier in the South China Sea. He was on his final tour in Vietnam.

My mother called Mr. Maddalone over to hear me repeat the words because she *just knew* her friends would think she was boasting. Mr. Maddalone and his late wife had taught Agnes to speak Italian and how to prepare *pasta e fagioli* and Venetian-style lobster sauce (a pinch of nutmeg, they swore) and pizzelle wafer cookies on a waffle iron. After his wife's death, Mr. Maddalone continued to make pizzelles every Sunday and bring them over wrapped in crisp wax paper.

Speak, Claudia, my mother said. *Say it. Again. Claudia, speak.* But I didn't say a word. It was Beverly who stood up in the plastic turtle sandbox and tore off her summer frock and bloomers. She shook her baby hips and patted her baby thighs and sang "Ride Captain Ride" while Mr. Maddalone laughed and my mother ran to replace my sister's clothes.

"Well, Agnes," laughed Mr. Maddalone, "you've got your work cut out for you. One girl's a poet. And the other's surely an exhibitionist."

I DID NOT become a poet. I became an academic. I traffic in Shakespeare and the Everyday Man. I have tenure, and there is a waiting list to attend my class. My seminars routinely open with a profile of William Henry Brown, the retired steamship owner from the West Indies who, in 1816, founded the first African Grove Theatre in downtown Manhattan. It is accompanied by a slideshow of the Globe Theatre and the South Bank. I pose the question: "Who has the right to Shakespeare?" I re-create Shakespeare's world for my students as best I can. That *other* London. Divided by the river

Thames. Rich men cross by waterboat. Regular citizens let their feet carry them over London Bridge. Theater artists. To my mind, exiles, really. Working for meager wages. Against impossible odds to hone their craft. Free, Bankside, from the government's sharp gaze. Consider the pollution. The seediness. And stench. Gambling. Bear-baiting. Prostitution. Death lurking in dark alleyways. Thank God for the taverns. It's the only place where a working man or woman can get their fill of food and drink. Or have a good laugh. Such riffraff, you say? But aha! This is where the action is. *This* is where our Bard's quill takes ink. Where his players play. Shakespeare can't afford to bury his head in the sand. The show really must go on. There is a constant deadline. He learns to work fast. His audience arrives—most with no education at all—expecting a good show. They bring rotten fruit and rancid meat. Come now. Entertain us. We've been standing on our feet all day. We'll stand some more. Bring out the fool. The murderous king. The wretched prince. The coldhearted queen. God help you, if we're bored. An agreement has been made between Shakespeare and his audience. He is, after all, a fur trader's son. He will take anyone with him who is willing to travel. At the very least, he will meet you halfway. I learned in my formative years that there is something in Shakespeare for everyone. Of course, Rufus favors the "coins" story. His version always goes over well with our more academic friends. But we've crossed the Atlantic for winter break in a remote part of Brittany. Here, my husband's anecdotes do not take root or land. They lack topsoil. And topsoil is important—we're told—a source of water and nutrients that fends against erosion. So that new crops might grow.

WE ARE IN a little town in northwest Brittany, in the department of Le Finistère. We have come to research Gaelic folktales and Celtic lore. We are guests on a modest seventeenth-century farm with narrow corridors and small windows and doors meant to save on electricity and keep the farmhouse warm. We're here to listen to Rufus's cousins, Guy and Estern LeComte, speak the old language. My husband has set out to write a modern interpretation of Walter Y. Evans-Wentz's *The Fairy-Faith in Celtic Countries* and nineteenth-century folklorist Paul Sébillot's *Contes populaires de la Haute-Bretagne*. But there's been precious little writing and a great deal of mise-en-scene. Rufus trails the wizened farmers everywhere they go with an eight-millimeter video camera.

When we first arrived in Le Finistère, I glanced to the left and to the right, across the impressive expanse of moorland, and whispered in Rufus's ear: *Lock me up in a room and I'll soon cut off my hair.* The French definition of *Le Finistère* is "the end of the world," and by God, it felt that way.

"Give the place a chance, Claudie!" Rufus whispered back. "It's not as bleak as all that. We'll have plenty of time to eat and sleep and fuck."

There isn't a problem in the world that Rufus believes cannot be solved by cunnilingus. The act for him is rumination, relaxation— distraction. Thigh as pillow, after. A place to lay his head and nap.

"And who will look after Winnie and Elijah?" The question is pointed. A dig—though not completely unwarranted. Lately I am full of digs. They catch me off-guard. Like a vitamin D deficiency.

"We will look after our own damn children," Rufus says, color flushing into his pale cheeks and face. "*We* will."

IN AUGUST, OUR five-year-old daughter, Winnie, nearly drowned in Rufus's father's swimming pool in Amagansett. Paramedics performed mouth-to-mouth resuscitation to revive her. Rufus and I were unwinding in the South of France after a Joyce seminar in Dublin. We were eating *socca* (chickpea pancakes) when Rufus received the call from his stepmother. I will never eat *socca* again. We caught an evening flight to JFK. On the plane I sat fuming, thinking if my father were still alive, my mother wouldn't have retired in Buckner County, Georgia. If cancer hadn't whittled my dad into a straw man, we would have taught his grandkids Rosencrantz and Guildenstern. *Winona? Elijah? Where are the coins? Toss your grand-daddy the coins?!* At Columbia Presbyterian my sister Beverly—a registered nurse and something of an exhibitionist—greeted us with prompt rage: *That's what you get. You chose them over us*, she said: *You and your overtime status thing. Elijah hipped me to the shadiness. While Winnie was lapping up pool water, your in-laws were slurping martinis.*

Now Winnie wakes up at night screaming and flailing for a "pinkpinkpink donut thingamajigie!" She won't go near a swimming pool. Was it an accident? Absolutely. *For sure.* But Rufus and I had to explain to his father and stepmother, Adele, that martinis and pools and children don't mix. Lately, we carry tension. The kind of tension that—I have watched my friends—inspires lesser couples to split.

LE FINISTÈRE IN January is not usually so unforgiving, we're told. During the summer months, this is the part of Brittany where the tourists come to frolic, romp, and enjoy the mild temperatures. To date, I've found no mildness here. Am I in a mood? You bet I am. My moods run bleak these days like the clouds above my head. I bundle Winona and Elijah in hats, scarves, thick wool sweaters beneath their down coats. We stalk the barren fields, whose spring harvest will yield green artichokes and cauliflower. Our twins are energetic and require exercise. They dash ahead of me christening random clouds.

Owl

Deer

Whale

Unicorn

Man

No more than enough snow to brush off your coat as you walk. This is what the old cousins told us when the first snow came. The snow didn't stay, but the cold lingered and threatened to damage Guy and Estern's crops. I glance over my shoulder. And where is my husband? Rufus has fallen behind and become a tiny black dot in the fields. He strolls in animated conversation with the two old men. His arms swing up and down. Are Guy and Estern LeComte really my husband's cousins? I'm certain they're lovers, but because I've refused to speak a word of French since we stepped foot in Le Finistère, there is no polite way to broach sexuality with them.

DURING THE WINTER months, Estern prepares meals in the fireplace. A fireworks display in their hearth. Tonight's meal is leg of lamb on a spit. We crowd together and watch the wood burn brilliant red, blue, and orange sparks. Winona and Elijah pretend they are camping in Maine and beg Estern and Guy for s'mores and folktales that Rufus records with his video camera. I remind our kids, *No s'mores here*. Farm food is no-fuss elegant. The lamb's succulent juices drip into a cast-iron pan to flavor our rutabagas, potatoes, and chard. I am in charge of dessert and try my hand at *petit pommes* topped with currants and sugar and brown butter. I sit at the end of the dining room table peeling and coring hard green apples while Rufus interviews Guy and Estern. To keep the children entertained, Guy ties a kerchief around his eyes and becomes Saint Hervé, the blind monk who loved animals and tamed a wolf to plow his fields. Rufus translates, looking so youthful leaning across the splintered dining table from his newfound cousins, trying not to invade their space. Elijah and Winnie toss lamb bones to the four mutts they've nicknamed All Dogs, much to the delight of the two old men.

Rufus's kin make every effort to include me in their conversations. They slow their French. I respond in English. When I look at them—yes, yes, my own bit of jealousy here—I think of my late father, Edward Christie, and my "uncles" Levi, Reuben, and Jeb: men who grew up in the Jim Crow South but made homes in large American cities. They would not have wanted Guy and Estern's life for all the money in the world, but it's possible Guy and Estern will outlive them all.

BRITTANY HAS BEEN depopulating for years. Young people who don't want to become farmers leave and go elsewhere. Old people who have been farmers all their lives stay and then die. And when the children sell, the elegant stone farms are increasingly becoming vacation homes.

———

"WE COULD BUY the farm," Rufus announces after dinner. We are in Guy and Estern's kitchen washing dishes.

"Have you ever milked a cow?"

"Yes," says Rufus. "In Vermont on a summer camp farm. I milked cows for eight weeks."

"That was make-believe."

Rufus plunges a plate into the water and it makes waves. He rinses away the suds and delivers the plate to my hands for drying. As I dry, I make a mental note of practical things Guy and Estern need in their kitchen. An electric can opener. New pot holders and dishrags. A decent set of silverware too. I will send them a care package when we return to New York. The farmers lease a booth at the village farmer's market during the summer months. They sell artichokes in small mason jars, pickled carrots and cauliflower, and fresh butter with thick salt crystals to the tourists who swarm the English Channel. They barter to stay abreast of property taxes on their dilapidated three-room farmhouse.

"Have *you* ever milked a cow, Claudie?"

"I eat them. Must I take their milk too?"

"Cheeky thing." He leans over and pecks me on the cheek. "Do you want to go upstairs and fool around?"

"This is why we can't own a farm," I tell him. "We would drown in our own distractions." The word *drown* makes Rufus wince, and I realize that without even trying I've made another dig.

I AM AN ONLY CHILD, Rufus says. *When Mom and Dad go, aside from you and the kids, I won't have any family. I won't know my people.* Sometimes I tell Rufus: *But I don't know where my people are from, only that they are from Africa and could be from almost anywhere on that continent.* I once had a friend who went to Ghana and stood on the shore of one of the forty castles where slaves were sold and carried off in chains across the Atlantic. My friend, who had traveled with a church group, recalled lining up on the harbor while a local historian looked them up and down and said: "You are from the east and you, your people are from the north and your people are from the south, and you, your people are from the west." But I have not been to Africa. I have not had my mouth swabbed with Q-tips, no DNA sample taken that will point me vaguely there. Nothing about Africa has solidified in me yet.

WE MET RUFUS'S father at V&T's in December, a pizza joint two blocks from our Columbia University apartment. We ordered two large pepperoni pies and watched the cheese and sauce run off the thin crust.

"Adele and I miss the kids," James said, throwing his arms around Elijah and Winona. The twins had wasted no time climbing into the booth beside him.

"How's AA going for Adele, Dad?" Rufus asked.

"You shouldn't punish us for an honest accident," said the man James. "Claudia, be the voice of reason here. There has been a punishing."

"James," I said. "I'd rather not have this conversation in front of the kids."

"Nowadays"—he shook his head—"people treat children like paper. Children don't tear."

"Says you." I smiled and cut my pizza with a knife and fork. James is a killer in the looks department. Gregory Peck in old age. A shock of just-gray hair and steel-blue eyes that undress women in a way that is not displeasing because of the face undressing them. I've felt him once or twice undressing me. He offered Winona an oversized Putumayo African coloring book and chunky wax crayons in colors like aubergine. Children rode the backs of giraffes in the savanna. Zebras grazed. Exotically clad natives strummed guitars and beat drums. Winnie was delighted and engrossed. Winnie is a coloring fiend.

"Tickets for you." James turned to Elijah. "We'll see the basketball game at Columbia."

Grandfather's and grandson's hands arched into a fluid high five.

"Dad," Elijah said. "Gramps got tickets for us to see the Columbia-Princeton game."

"Great. That's great." Rufus changed the subject. "You know Mom had a scare?"

The man James never talks about his first wife, Sigrid. "Well, will she die or will she live? Is she gone or is she still here?"

"I think she'll live, James," I said. *Love*—it was my husband's love for his mother that made me marry him, though nowadays I love Rufus less frequently. I could love Rufus more.

"She'll live," Rufus inserted. "*Scare* by its very definition implies that she's come through the worst of it—survive—unless, of course, you're posing an existential question?"

"Don't Joyce me, boy," the man James said. Rufus is a Joyce scholar. The man James taught law for many years at Columbia, where he also attended law school. On more than one occasion he has implied rather strongly that we owe our tenured status to his professorship and legacy. He gnawed his pizza the old way, turning the crust inward like a sandwich.

"Elijah, Winona," I sighed. "Napkins in lap. *Napkins.*"

Rufus signaled for Elijah and Winona to squeeze into the booth between us. But Winona was engrossed in coloring and Elijah twisted his head: *no.*

"See?" the man James said. "They love their grandpa." He leaned forward and pinched Elijah on the cheek. Elijah looks like the man James. He walks like the man James and talks like him too.

"We were hoping, Adele and I, that you could come over to our house Christmas morning. Open presents with Winnie and Elijah."

The kids are quiet. The kids are attentive. They have missed the man James. My sister's words hit me again with blunt force. I've made the mistake of letting Winnie and Elijah bond more with Rufus's parents than my own.

"We're spending Christmas morning with Claudia's sister and mother this year," Rufus said. He reached for my hand and I gave it to him gladly.

"Christmas afternoon, then," James persisted.

"Do you know about this project I have with Mom?" Rufus sprinkled oregano onto his pizza. "Mom and I are putting together our family tree. Thanks to her, I've tracked down distant cousins in Brittany. She's flying in from California for Christmas to join us as well."

"So I'm shut out. No Thanksgiving? No Christmas?"

"Dad, we're here now. Let's enjoy it?"

"Adele misses the kids, a house without kids on Christmas—"

"Isn't Adele Jewish?"

"Is that a slight, Rufus? I raised you better." James's face reddened. "Plenty of Jews celebrate Christmas. We're celebrating Chanukah and Christmas this year."

"This is not about Adele being Jewish."

"Then why did you mention it?"

Rufus dabbed at the oil on his pizza with a napkin. "I don't want to celebrate Christmas with *you*. Now you want to be the doting granddad? And we're supposed to be pleased. I left you in charge of our kids and Winnie nearly drowned."

For a moment, there was silence. The pizza congealed. "Maybe the day after Christmas, Rufus?" I suggested.

Adele adores Elijah and Winona. Adele's first husband—she has told me stories—was a bruiser. All things considered, she has rebounded well. And the man James is not without kindness.

"I'll have to see what Mom wants to do." Rufus chewed his pizza slowly.

"Well, it's settled then," the man James said. "I can't speak for Brittany, but you know the French are renowned for being anti-Semitic. When Adele and I went to Paris, she said she never felt more Jewish. She is not religious, but we found ourselves wandering the old Le Marais to cope with the French."

"I'm sorry, Claudie," said Rufus. "But I can't believe this asshole who called our kids mulattoes is accusing me of being anti-Semitic."

"What's a mulatto, Dad?" Elijah is five, older than his sister Winnie by seventeen minutes. Race has not figured into his equation. Yet. Whenever I look back on that evening at V&T's, I think: One day Elijah won't be so innocent.

"Nothing," Rufus said.

"Grandpa called us *nothing*?" Elijah asked. Winnie looked up from her coloring book and the tip of her crayon spilled outside the margins of the giraffe she was coloring.

"Elijah," I whispered. "We'll talk about this when we get home. Okay?"

The man James turned to Elijah. "*Mulatto* is an old way of describing people who are of mixed heritage. It's a word I had to learn not to use. It's—outdated. Offensive. Something I didn't know."

"Can we get the check?" Rufus asked.

"The kids are still eating," said the man James. "Let the kids eat."

I squeezed Rufus's hand tight with my left hand and made eye contact with the waitress who was clearing off the booth in front of ours. Later that night, Rufus will ball up into a knot on our bedroom floor. He will say he's lactose intolerant and shouldn't have eaten the pizza. I will put a hot water bottle on his stomach and move it around in circles. I will tell him that anything is possible. This is the age of allergies and autoimmune diseases. This is the millennium of anxiety.

"You think you have to go to France for your heritage? You're *also* Irish."

"Isn't it enough that I'm a Joyce scholar, Dad? How much Irish do you want?'

"Just you remember, I wound up in the ER saving Winnie. I didn't let her drown. I *saved* my granddaughter."

"Kudos to James Samuel Vincent." This time I chimed in alongside my husband. "If I hadn't already had two glasses of wine, I'd propose a toast. But unlike some people, I know when to stop."

The man James seemed momentarily stumped. "Even the best men among us drop their pants every now and again," he said loudly.

The waitress came over. She tossed a sideward glance at the man James.

"That wasn't directed at you, young lady," James said.

I sat on the outside of the booth. Rufus was almost pushing to get me out. "Claudie, let's go. Please."

"I dropped my pants some forty years ago."

Winnie slapped her hand on the table and laughed. "Grandpa dropped his pants!" Her explosive laughter was like music to our ears. Rufus and I smiled. It was the smile of worried parents. The waitress moved away quickly with the check.

"Meaning *what*, exactly, Dad?"

"You go to enough conferences, you'll drop your pants too—if you haven't already."

"No shit?" Rufus said. "In front of my wife and kids. You say *this*?"

"Kids. Claudia. Cover your ears." The man James stepped out of the booth and placed both hands on Rufus's shoulder. Through the storefront window, Columbia students loped up and down the side-walk. Christmas lights twinkled. "You don't have to trek to Brittany to meet cousins you don't know. Ruff, you have a half brother in Raleigh, North Carolina. Hank Camphor's his name. Hank."

It took Rufus a few seconds to process what the man James was saying. He crossed to the storefront window and pressed his face against the glass. When he turned around, he was laughing. He laughed his way out of V&T's, saying, "Stay away from my family, Dad. Stay away from me."

AND SO, WE'VE come to Le Finistère. My husband will not speak of Hank Camphor from North Carolina, nor will he return his father's calls. I climb out of bed most mornings when it's still pitch-black outside and stoke the remnants of Estern's lavish fire. I wait for Winnie to scream. Her screams herald morning and set All Dogs to baying. Her screams disorient the rooster. There is no peace when Winnie screams on the farm. Rufus is always the first one to bolt into Winnie and Elijah's room. He bolts. I stall.

"Winnie. Winnie. It's *all right*," Rufus says desperately. When I finally summon the courage to enter the children's room, I sit on the opposite side of Winona's bed, away from my husband. But together, together, we rock Winona gently back and forth. Elijah sleeps through it all. Somehow. Or is he a great pretender? Estern and Guy make a brief appearance in their long flannel pajamas. I wonder what they make of their middle-aged American relatives. Rufus tells the two men that everything is all right. Winnie's just had another nightmare.

"Everything's not all right," I snap at Rufus when Guy and Estern leave.

"I don't know what to do," Rufus says. Winnie will fall asleep just as quickly as she awoke. She will fall asleep huddled between our chests and not remember her nightmares in the morning.

"Claudie, *what* can we do to fix this?"

Rufus and I are considerably older than our parents were when they started families. They were babies compared to us. Like most of our friends, we waited to have children. We waited—so we could make money. We waited—so we could focus on our promising careers. We waited—*for what?* I tell myself our parents would have been on top of the situation with Winona. I tell myself they would have tackled their troubles head-on. I tell myself we're tired. And tired people can tell themselves anything—when they're on the run.

"Rufus," I hear myself say. "This isn't our home. We've been here long enough."

ROSEN-CRANTZ and GUILDEN-STERN are DEAD

by Tom Stoppard

INTERMISSION

1969

T HIS IS THE PLAY THAT BELONGED TO CLAUDIA'S FATHER, Eddie Christie. The play that Eddie lifted from an officer while on shore leave at Subic Bay. The play that Eddie Christie carried in his back pocket when he returned home from Vietnam in 1971. The play that he read as bedtime stories to Claudia and Beverly. The play that Claudia—by then a three-year-old smarting over the indignity of an afternoon nap—grabbed, ripping the front cover right down the center. A rip so fresh and raw that Eddie Christie's normally cheerful face went flat and he turned Claudia upside down in the backyard so that her head was one with the dirt and grass and ants searching for crumbs from Mr. Maddalone's pizzelles. Claudia felt the ants surging up her ponytails and patrolling her scalp. They stung or perhaps there was only the sensation of stinging. Claudia couldn't help but scream. Her cries brought Agnes out of the house, followed by her sister Beverly, who had just gone down for her afternoon nap.

Beverly pointed: *Claudia, Claudia tore Daddy's book.*

It's just a book, Eddie, Agnes said, tears springing to her eyes. Eddie had never raised his voice to anyone in their modest brick house. He had survived the war. He had returned home in one piece and in his right mind. Mostly. He talked to walls sometimes. But mostly, mostly . . . Eddie Christie was a man of reason.

I will help you tape the pages, Eddie, Agnes said. *The girls and I will help you, but first you need to give me our child.* Eddie turned Claudia right side up, and the four of them retreated to the kitchen and sat on the bright red vinyl chairs and mended the cover of Tom Stoppard's *Rosencrantz and Guildenstern Are Dead*, so that it was almost as good as new. Eddie Christie smiled and kissed his wife and girls. "Well, isn't that something?" he said. "Ladies, would you look at that!"

ACT ~~TWO~~

1969

W HAT IS EDDIE READING?
 You'd think he was an educated man.
 I joined the Navy in 1966. My sophomore year in
Bronx community college.
 Eddie, are you a poet?
 No, I just like to read.
 Shakespeare. Look at Eddie read Shakespeare.

I STOLE THE play from an officer while in port at Subic Bay. It is the
only thing I ever stole in my life. The officer was carrying on about
his wife this and his wife that and how *his* wife had seen *Rosencrantz
and Guildenstern Are Dead* in the West End of London and sent over
a copy for him to read. He sat there at the bar drinking scotch and
bragging a mile a minute. All that bragging strained my ears and
got me to missing Agnes. Some of our wives were busy raising children or working and couldn't afford trips of leisure. Some of our
wives were pregnant with our second kid. When the officer wasn't

looking, I just walked over and lifted the play off his stool. Big sins start small.

I JOINED THE Navy to get away from the Bronx, for I loved it too much: the salsa clubs and the women and the thrill of speeding down Fordham Avenue after midnight with the top down in my old man's Buick Skylark. I like to laugh a lot. There's always a smile on my face about something because I learned early that shit gets in the way. And God help you if you can't laugh. I'd drop an entire paycheck on a new suit and shoes to party at the Palladium, the Embassy, or the Tropicoro. You couldn't take a girl out for a night on the town dressed like a bum in those days. You had to put it together right. I put it together so right I flunked out of community college my second year. My old man never spoke Spanish but, brother, he had a mouthful for me then. I went from paying one utility bill to paying rent. And Pops had already paid off the mortgage. I took his point. And when a recruiter approached me, I joined the Navy.

MY FATHER WAS a components man at Sokolov & Brothers, a piano factory in the Mott Haven section of the Bronx. For over twenty-nine years he rubbed elbows with German and Italian immigrants who thought he was white like them. But Dad was Cuban from Havana. Shortly after he came to America, he took a black American wife and an American name. Eduardo Christonelli-Garcia became Eddie Christie. Then he bought a single-family house in the South Bronx. His job was supposed to pass down to me, but by the time I came around people weren't buying pianos anymore. They'd rather catch a movie or sit in front of their TV or spend time at the nightclubs. My old man had the statistics down. *Once, you could've counted sixty piano factories in the Bronx alone. That's just how it was. The Bronx was the piano manufacturing capital of the world.* People come at you with so much attitude about the Bronx. But that was his livelihood. Something he was proud of. When I hit manhood, the piano industry was a done deal. Factories were going out of business left and right. Sokolov & Brothers was one of the last holdouts. My pops got an upright piano and a modest pension when they shut down in 1959. Then he took a part-time gig as the custodian at my school.

MY FIRST DEPLOYMENT, I was assigned to the boiler room as a seaman's apprentice (pay grade E-2). It didn't take much training for me to figure my way around. Or to realize that it wasn't a good fit for me. Snipes, they called us. Working below deck. Trolling the bottom of the ship. I like blue skies and fresh ocean air. But I had better sense than to complain because at least I was receiving technical training, skills that could open the door for me to move up in rank. I signed on as an A-4. In civilian-speak, that's four years. I was thinking big picture. Glad not to be a steward in the mess hall. They used to do that to black and, later, Filipino sailors. Put us in the galley and scullery, assign us cooking and cleaning detail as mess hall attendants. My cousin Reuben Applewood had joined the Navy a year ahead of me and told me what to expect, so I was prepared for a certain amount of prejudice. Maybe because I was prepared for it, that's why it didn't happen. That first deployment in '67, I got by okay. The black and white crewmen weren't exactly buddies, but we weren't rolling in the hate either. We just kept separate, did our own thing. My biggest concern was staying on top of my duties so fuel wouldn't leak and the ship wouldn't explode. That's a bad way to go. And it's more common than you'd think. My second deployment, things veered ugly. The whole vibe changed. James Earl Ray slaughtered Dr. King. Aimed a Remington .30-06 rifle at his neck and head. The timing made an impression too. Dr. King was no fan of the war. He had started making noise about our presence in Vietnam. Noise not everyone wanted to hear. When word spread that King was shot, some white sailors lit up crosses. Hauled out beer for keg parties too. *Communist. King's a Communist* was the catchphrase. Brother, them's fighting words. You didn't need to be a Black Panther to lose it over that shit. Life on the USS *Olympus* went from hot and sweaty to sweaty and tense. Sometimes, I found myself caught between white men sneering and black men fuming. Like Rosencrantz and Guildenstern, I knew the beginning but I couldn't call the end. I'd sit in my bunk with the play on my lap and tune shit out. Funny. I'd taken the small paperback for spite with no intention of reading it during my first cruise, but magazines and books were hard to come by on the USS *Olympus*. Wouldn't you know Rosencrantz and Guildenstern kept me laughing?

ROS: *Half of what he said meant something else, and the other half didn't mean anything at all.*

That was just what it sounded like when our politicians tried to justify the war. Old President Johnson had us in over our heads.

ONE EVENING MY COUSIN Jebediah Applewood came into our berthing quarters spitting fire. You would have thought he was a bull. Jeb and Reuben and Levi (Reuben's little brother), they all grew up in the same house. We're related on my mother's side—a fact we kept quiet in the Navy for fear the officers would assign us details where we'd never see each other.

"We need to do something about this motherfucking chief petty officer," Jeb said.

I knew all about Chief Petty Officer Nelson "Nelly" Mammoth. Most sailors get mellow when they drink, but Chief Mammoth al-

ways became, what was the word, pugilistic. We called him Nelly
behind his back because he had two distinct personalities rolled into
one. In his duties as chief boatswain's mate, the fool had no equal.
He was responsible for supervising the ship's deck maintenance
crew, and he did so with a firm hand. There was no part of the USS
Olympus that Nelly wasn't familiar with. He monitored and trained
deckhands, saw that ammunitions and missiles were loaded properly in the massive ship elevators that traveled between the hangar
and flight decks. The scuttlebutt was that he could operate almost
any piece of equipment on the USS *Olympus*. And his duties seemed
to give him genuine pleasure. But Chief Petty Officer Nelson Mammoth was something else. He rejoiced in riding the black seamen
about Project 100,000. Liked to ask what year you enlisted and if
you enlisted before, during, or after Project 100,000—when they'd
let just about any dumb ass in. Nelly would make you take an IQ
test on the spot and call you every racial slur in the book. It didn't
matter that the program to recruit 100,000 *soldiers* was limited to
the Army and Marines. Five percent of the sailors in the Navy were
black. I guess that was too many for him. When he approached me,
reeking of bourbon—his drink of choice—I'd speak to Nelly in
a babble chorus of Italian, Greek, and Spanish. He'd whistle and
say, "Let me guess. You came in early?" I never answered him. For
eighteen months, Chief Mammoth kept tabs on every black sailor
aboard the USS *Olympus*. We were in a war. And we were losing.
You'd think he'd have better things to do with his time. Color shaded
Nelly's perspective, but water ended it.

"What do you think, Eddie?"

I stopped reading and smiled at Jeb. "I think Rosencrantz and
Guildenstern need to be stealthier. Hamlet's not buying their act."

"No, Eddie—about Nelly Mammoth."

I thought about our cousin Reuben. He would know just the
thing to say to Jeb. "I don't think he's worth the trouble. I mean, in
the larger scheme of things, we'll get over him."

Jeb stood over my bed. I took the low bunk to avoid banging my
head on the ceiling.

"Last night Nelly broke the steward's nose. That crazy mother-fucker broke the damn boy's nose because he forgot to serve ketchup. And the kid's too scared to report him," Jeb said.

"Why you got to call Nelly a motherfucker. Why you got to disgrace his mother? We don't know the woman. She might be all right," I said. I wanted Jeb to leave me alone so I could get back to reading my play.

Jeb sighed. He was used to me carrying on about *R&G*. "You with me, or what?"

"That depends," I said. "I'm always with you, but none of this is new, Jeb. What *exactly* are we talking about here? The steward will complete his tour, just like the rest of us. And then he'll put this shit behind him. I'm not sure what you hope to accomplish."

Jeb opened the aluminum locker next to our racks and took out his stash of *Jet* magazines. He read the articles but mostly eyed the centerfolds. I could tell he was giving me the silent treatment. And that it would go on that way for the rest of the night. We were like brothers on the USS *Olympus*. Nowadays, we don't talk much. After the war, I headed home to the Bronx and Jeb returned to Georgia. Last I heard he was working as a moving man and had settled some-where in New Hampshire. I did get one postcard from Jeb: *I thought Norway was cold but winter in New Hampshire is one cold motherfucker.*

Still cussing, I thought. Still cussing. "What are you laughing about, Eddie?" my wife asked.

WE WERE OPEN-SEA sailors on the USS *Olympus*, an 1,056-foot aircraft carrier on Yankee Station in the Gulf of Tonkin. An air-craft carrier is a big ship. It can glide through the deepest parts of the ocean like nobody's business. There were times when I'd roam the different stations and gape at the machinery. Seeing how it all came together helped me sleep better at night. My second tour, I was assigned to the flight deck crew. We were the offshore support team for the Navy pilots who ran surveillance and launched daily air raids against the North Vietnamese.

THE USS *OLYMPUS* held over four thousand sailors. In some berthing quarters, they bunked eight men in one room, head to head. You heard them snore and cry and jack off. Occasionally, if they didn't mind putting their lives at risk, you heard them fuck. And it was never the ones you would think either. People just got in a mood—and if the wrong mood caught them, they'd do damn near anything. Like Jeb and I did. When we grew tired of Chief Petty Officer Nelson Mammoth.

IF REUBEN HAD BEEN on the USS *Olympus* with us, things might've turned out different. Summers, my mother would send me down South. *To know my people*, she'd say. I'd vacation with Reuben, Jeb, and Levi and play baseball and get up into all kinds of mischief. Reuben was the oldest by two years, so even back then he was the "sergeant," tagged with keeping us out of trouble. Growing up in the Bronx I had all kinds of neighbors, and I wasn't so stuck in the black and white of things, but when I went south my mother, she always gave the same lecture about Emmett Till. Everything was shorthand for Emmett Till. *I don't want to have to come down there and look at your face in a coffin, you hear?* We would talk about it, you know, Reuben, Jeb, Levi, and me. And laugh—not at Emmett, but at how half the things we couldn't do had no rhyme or reason to them, like swim with kids in a pool full of chlorine. We laughed because when you come from somewhere else and see colored that and white this, it doesn't make sense, and you see how ridiculous the whole thing is. Reuben would tell us, *Whenever white folk come at you shady, choose your ocean. Arctic. Atlantic. Indian. Pacific. Southern. And keep your cool on it.* Every week we got an allowance to go downtown to buy a brand-new comic book. Us four boys had to share one comic. We'd read it together, and then we'd take turns reading it on our own. But to buy our comics, we had to go to this bookstore on Main Street. The owner of the bookstore, Sadie's Fine Books and Whatnots, had this old tan bulldog that would prop itself in the store's doorway. The bulldog would drool and growl and show his yellow teeth and block the path and Miss Sadie, a tall thin white woman who looked like some rare bird, would laugh and say, *Oh, now, you boys want your comics, come on, come on*. And Reuben would say, *Time to travel. Choose your ocean*. He would be the first one to go. And that bulldog would leap and snap when Reuben crossed the threshold to the store and Reuben would do what he could to distract it, so we could get across unharmed. More than once that bulldog nipped Reuben's ankles and shins and drew blood. And Miss Sadie would whistle and say, *Come, boy, come*, to her dog and then she would give Reuben his comic free of charge and he would limp home ahead of us, holding that week's *Flash Gordon*.

IT'S A FACT: I don't sleep so well lately.

———

I've got the jitters.

———

When did I become this—*jittery* bug?

———

Chief Mammoth had a wife. Do you know that's what bothers me the most? His wife and his kids. I think about birthdays and holidays that grew large and empty after we did what we did and Chief Mammoth went under.

I think about the fog and how it covered the ship. And how he smiled when he saw me on the deck smoking a cigarette. He should have known that I don't smoke. He should've taken time to know more about me. "Substandard New Standard Man," he said. There were coffee stains on his teeth. "What are you doing out here tonight?"

———

His yellow teeth shimmered in the fog.

———

"The deep blue sea isn't blue at all," I said. Those were the last words Chief Petty Officer Mammoth ever heard.

———

Lately, I sit up in my lower bunk at night and listen to the voices calling out to me. Who's calling out to me? I see and hear the strangest things. . . .

———

LISTEN, LISTEN, TO ME NOW. Rosencrantz and Guildenstern are dead. I've seen them strolling the flight deck of the USS Olympus *in the South China Sea. I've seen them tossing coins and talking all manner of crazy shit. They ask me what they did to Hamlet to make him treat them so? I tell them the truth, between loading bombs on A-4 attack jets—bombs that will kill civilians and Viet Cong in almost equal numbers. You colluded with King Claudius. You cats were rats. Prince Hamlet was your best friend. You cats were supposed to have his back. And that's when they get disgruntled and call me a surly Moor. Moor? Well, that's news to me. Last I heard I was just another black man in Vietnam. Black man in Vietnam, steer us to London, they say. Trust me, brothers, you don't want to go anywhere near London. You're ripe to lose your heads if you tarry there, but Rosencrantz and Guildenstern just toss their coins and shake their heads and say, Moor, you can't be trusted. We saw you throw Chief Mammoth overboard. You are a murderer. You and that other Moor murdered a man. You oughtn't have done this thing. And I say, don't you think I know it? And then I count the minutes to lunch break and rush off to the laundry room to find Jeb.*

"Jeb," I say. "Rosencrantz and Guildenstern are messing with me again."

Jeb likes working laundry detail. He says clean laundry reminds him of Buckner County, Georgia. He grabs me by the arm and looks around to make sure nobody is listening. He tells me to wait for him outside the black canteen. We don't eat with the white sailors unless we have to these days. We mostly keep to ourselves, Jeb and me.

"What the fuck is wrong with you, Eddie?" Jeb finds me drinking cold coffee ten minutes later. "You aiming to get us court-martialed? You can't come in the laundry room talking loud like that 'bout Chuck."

Chuck is the nickname black soldiers sometimes give whites. They sent a search-and-rescue mission out for Nelly, but no one knows when he first went missing. Only that he didn't show up in the petty officers' mess for dinner or that night's movie.

Man overboard, they said. Chief Mammoth had taken to drinking heavily. He was becoming a first-class lush.

"I'm just saying, Jeb . . ." My voice trails off. "They're *in* my head."

"You need to give me that damn play, Eddie. Hand over that motherfucking play and pick up a *Jet* or *Ebony*. I mean it now."

"That's not happening."

I want to tell Jeb how sometimes Rosencrantz and Guildenstern sneak up behind me and whisper that Chuck is swimming back. I say Chuck. They say Nelly? I say Nelly. They say Chuck? It's like the war. Circles within circles. But this bit of information falls under a long list of things JEB DOESN'T NEED TO KNOW. Every evening after dinner the captain of the USS *Olympus* announces over the loudspeaker how many bombs we've dropped, men we've lost, and targets we've destroyed. Jeb puts a pillow over his head and points to the wall where he keeps his list: JEB DOESN'T NEED TO KNOW. Like most of the sailors on this carrier, we've never set foot in Vietnam. But I've seen grunts and pilots coming back in body bags or with missing limbs. I've seen the beyond-dead look on the faces of some soldiers who don't understand their own good luck. And don't want it. And it makes me glad I've not seen combat.

"Maybe you need a little dope to take the edge off." Jeb considers me.

"I don't want dope, Jeb. I don't want to be strung out where I can't even stand up straight."

"What *do* you want, Eddie?" Jeb says. "You confuse and bedevil me with this shit."

I nod. "I want to see Agnes and the girls again. I want to get back to the Bronx. I want a home-cooked meal. I want to sit on my front porch and think about nothing."

"Then keep it together. Otherwise we're both fucked," said Jeb.

ROSENCRANTZ AND GUILDENSTERN are dead. Listen, listen, to me now. I have seen them adrift on a riverboat in the Gulf of Tonkin.

Come back, come back, I say. *That's not the way to London.* But they shake their heads and toss their coins and shout: *Moor, we must leave this place. This is not our war. We cannot stay.* They bid me come with them, but nothing good happens in the Gulf of Tonkin. Ros and Guil will be lucky to make it through the day. Jeb tells me that their departure was a gift from the gods. A goddamn blessing. Thank the Sweet Lord Jesus those two meddlesome motherfuckers went away. Jeb says there's been a general cooling down of my senses since they departed, but I didn't know my senses were hot. Only my morality. Jeb says morality can kiss his black ass and when we get to Subic Bay, he and I are catching all the sex shows in Olongapo. We're going to find a dozen prostitutes and get ourselves laid. But I miss Ros and Guil. There's no one to talk to or tell certain things. Like how Chief Petty Officer Mammoth hurled his racial slurs and

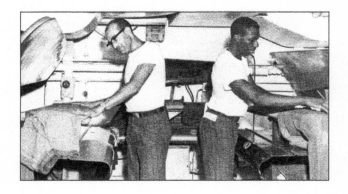

pounded the steward viciously upside the head with his blunt fists because the steward, a wan boy of sixteen from a New England town, had a twist in his wrists that could not be bent right and a sway in his walk that would not be forced straight. And how in the thick of a storm that same Chief Mammoth roamed the ship like a caged demon, high on the jolly juice and paranoid about everything. He sought out the steward boy for his weekly round of beatings and threw him down a flight of stairs, leaving him like a small ball of knitting wool. And all the crewmen, Jeb and I included, hated Chief Mammoth, but we could not bring ourselves to stand up for the boy. The boy stirred something in us that made us hate him more.

It could be you, Jeb said, finally.

It could be us, I said.

Tomorrow, we both agreed.

And that is how we did the thing.

ACT THREE

1995

T HIS IS THE LONDON REVIVAL OF *ROSENCRANTZ AND Guildenstern Are Dead* that Claudia and her then-boyfriend Rufus flew her father and mother to see for Eddie Christie's fiftieth birthday. This is the revival of *Rosencrantz and Guildenstern Are Dead* after which Rufus asked Eddie Christie if he could have his daughter's hand in marriage. This is the revival of *Rosencrantz and Guildenstern Are Dead* during which Eddie Christie, now a chubby middle-aged man in a black tuxedo and top hat, closed his eyes and recited the words, for he knew them all by heart, and by experience. So that when Claudia turned to him later and asked, "Well, Dad, did you like the play?"

Eddie Christie nodded and rolled the playbill in his hand. It was the first play he had ever seen, but he did not think it would be his last.

WHEN SHE WAS little, Claudia bounced from room to room in the Christie house talking to walls and acting out scenes from

Rosencrantz and Guildenstern Are Dead. Sometimes, in the talking, she would look up and see her father studying her.

Claudia. Claudius, he would say. King Claudius killed Prince Hamlet's father. Why on earth did Agnes name our child Claudia?

The way Eddie said this made Claudia fret for fear of being turned upside down on her head again, but then her father would pick her up and carry her around gently on his shoulders. *Where are the coins? Claudia, Claudia, help me find the coins.*

There is a dog-eared copy of *Rosencrantz and Guildenstern Are Dead* on Claudia's desk at home. She has not read the play in years, but during her travels she carries it as a good-luck talisman. In her haste to pack, she did not bring the play to Brittany.

POST-NAM EDDIE

1972

HIS FIRST FEW MONTHS HOME, EDDIE CHRISTIE SEEMED happy to look after his two girls. He let them run up and down the stairs and all about the house, playing countless games of hide-and-seek. They reminded him of small squabs—little birds that were fast to fly away. He could imagine their birdlike arms changing into wings. He could imagine the girls soaring out the windows of their brick house and never coming home again, if he upset them. And so, whenever some recollection of the war compelled Eddie, he would spin away from his daughters in search of some corner to sort himself out.

It was three-year-old Claudia who caught Eddie Christie conversing with the living room wall. She asked her father who he was talking to.

He told her he was breaking the fourth wall.

"What's on the other side of the wall?" she said.

"A stage."

"And what's on the stage?"

"Why, naturally, a play."

And that was how he began to act out *Rosencrantz and Guilden-stern Are Dead* with his girls. And how Claudia began to give the walls words and to believe in Hamlet's friends the way most children believe in Santa Claus. And how, sometimes, when the walls roared and rumbled in Eddie Christie's head, Claudia would sneak up behind him and whisper, "What are Rosencrantz and Guilden-stern doing today?"

"They're just tossing coins."

"Heads!" she would laugh.

"Tails!" And he would nod, unloading spare change—nickels, quarters, pennies, and dimes—from his jeans pockets onto the parquet floor. How the change jangled. The noise his change made.

He knew that in the best of situations he probably shouldn't talk to himself or to walls, but so long as he had something to hook his thoughts on, he was one up on most vets. His girls let him know when he was out of whack. They plied him for laughter or said something so stupid, stupid cornball ludicrous—*Oh, look, Daddy, we just gave you the moon*—to tickle his mind and itch his heart with absurdity, so that he would forget the wall for a brief time to hold their moon in the palm of his hand.

AT SIX O'CLOCK every night Eddie sat in the living room to watch Walter Cronkite on the *CBS Evening News*. He made himself triple-decker mortadella sandwiches with pickles and mustard and peppers on crusty semolina bread. He sucked on hard butterscotch candy as predinner treats, depositing the silver wrappers into a candy dish on the round glass coffee table. Eddie was hefty by nature, but the exercise regimen in the Navy had kept his heft firm. While tracking the news of Nixon's war, Eddie developed a paunch that would lead him into old age.

"Agnes," Eddie announced one night while sitting on the foot of their full-sized canopy bed, "it's about time I did something with myself."

"What do you have in mind?" Agnes didn't think it was her place to find her man a job. She thought he might resent her later.

"I don't know," he said.

Agnes stopped brushing her teeth and came out of the bathroom to sit on the bed alongside her husband. She brushed her teeth according to the alphabet, from A to Z and then backward, the way she had been taught as a child. "It will come to you," she said. "I'm just grateful you're here with the girls."

"Really?" he said.

Agnes nodded. "Of course, Eddie. Really." They almost never ate seafood, and Agnes could only afford to buy roast beef or a steak every other week. But in the grand scheme of things, red meat seemed minor.

Eddie reached out to touch her black slip. Agnes preferred fitted slips to negligees. When he touched her, Agnes's body tensed but she did not pull away. They had tried sex his first week home, but he'd made a mess of things. Maybe it was the prostitutes he'd slept with in Olongapo. Eddie wanted to believe he hadn't enjoyed the sex and that the women were little more than a distraction, but he had taken pleasure in his carnal sins.

"Not tonight," said Agnes. She dimmed the light on her nightstand.

"Another night, then." They had married quickly. And young. Sometimes, Eddie believed the cork in their bottle was missing and the wine might turn to vinegar.

WHEN AGNES WENT to work, Eddie did not touch the chores or errands she left behind: the baskets of laundry to be washed, dried, and folded; the grocery list and errands during the day that might necessitate run-ins with mouthy moms and screaming children; the vacuuming, sweeping, and mopping of floors. He found chores that pleased him.

He built a tree house on a gnarly birch in their backyard. He adorned the birch with scrap wood scavenged from trashcans and vacant lots. Eddie wore thick workman gloves and warned the girls: *Look but don't touch or you'll need tetanus shots.* Beverly and Claudia were deathly afraid of needles. If the spirit moved them, Eddie and his girls performed random scenes from *Rosencrantz and Guildenstern* while combing through trash heaps. Neighborhood kids would stop to gawk at the little brown man and his fly daughters reciting what sounded like a foreign language.

"WHAT'S THE FORECAST today, Alfred?" Eddie would yell across the attached front porch to his old neighbor, Alfred Maddalone.

"Simmering to fair."

While the girls taught themselves how to hula hoop and double Dutch on the crooked sidewalk, Eddie and Alfred Maddalone passed the time heckling the occasional junkies making off with their neighbors' television sets, toilets, and Maytag refrigerators. They stood on their porches clutching the railings with the fervor of fans at Yankee Stadium. They played judge and jury—calling out Riker's prison sentences and threatening to snap pictures if a junkie didn't put their neighbor's lawn chairs back. Sometimes they got as good as they gave. A royal cussing. A triumphant finger. A few stray rocks that narrowly missed Claudia's and Beverly's heads. The threat of a nighttime visit served with Molotov cocktails. The two men always stood their ground, so the junkies might know there would be consequences if anyone broke into their homes or made off with their shit.

It was rumored that Alfred had ties with the mafia, though as far as Eddie knew, the old man had always been on the up-and-up. He had owned a local pharmacy on a side street off Arthur Avenue and would climb out of bed at three in the morning for a young mother-to-be in the throes of morning sickness or some poor uncle wrestling with kidney stones. Shortly after retiring, he sold the business to finance his son's college tuition.

"Talk some sense into Pa," Nicky Maddalone pleaded with Eddie. He was now a successful dentist on Madison Avenue and visited his father every other Sunday. He did well enough to run ads on the subway. The three men would lounge on Alfred's porch dipping amaretto biscotti into strong black coffee. "I got a big house in Nyack. He doesn't have to put up with this. Look what they did to our neighborhood. These Puerto Ricans, they aren't human. They got the *why bother* about them."

Eddie wanted to ask Nicholas, *What am* I *if they are* they? *A moulinyan?* He and Nicky had eaten gnocchi from the same bowl as boys, running in and out of each other's houses tracking mud all over the place and nearly giving Bella Maddalone, who swept and mopped her kitchen three times a day, multiple heart attacks. They had boasted about the girls they wanted to do at Our Lady of St. Claremont's Catholic School when their own hands were the only action their penises were receiving.

"There's always a *they*," Eddie said. "Every decade or so, a new *they*. Once your grandparents were *they*." The Maddalones were from Puglia, Italy's heel. They burned brown in the summer. Eddie said this to Nicky in massacred Italian, but his friend no longer spoke his father's language. How to talk to Nicky now?

Nicky finished off his coffee. "You need me to vouch for a loan, Eddie? You move and he'll move."

"This is my home," Eddie said.

Nicky stood up on the front porch. He still did his grocery shopping on Arthur Avenue most Sundays. "Yeah? And how's that working out for you, Eddie? All the good people are gone. There's nobody left."

ON SUMMER EVENINGS when the heat from the cement, the buildings, and the sidewalks had cooled down and there was something like fresh air, Eddie loved to climb the ladder to the tree house with his wife and children and squeeze in tight, rubbing elbows together for an unmolested view of the Bronx sky. In Vietnam, the sky had taken on the vast blueness of the South China Sea, shape shifting with astonishing ease. Eddie was always aware that he was at the mercy of nature: water below him and heaven above. And it was a relief that he could still count the stars and peer past the smog on certain nights in the Bronx.

He took the girls to Crotona Park and threw them in the pool. Beverly and Claudia learned fast how to swim. When Agnes complained about the damage the pool water did to their tresses, despite the swimming caps, Eddie shrugged. "No one looks at a drowned man and comments on his hair. The water takes it all."

AGNES BAKED SPARINGLY: on birthdays and anniversaries, for the holidays, a mandatory sweet potato pie. She had witnessed first-hand the energy her mother put into baking and decided at a young age that baking could eat up a married woman's life. But when she grew homesick for something or fretted over the monthly bills, out sprang the mixing bowls and sifters and measuring cups—a batch of lavender cookies or a hummingbird cake to appease Eddie and the girls.

"Daddy and his friends are so silly," Beverly whispered in the teal-blue galley kitchen. She knelt on a stool at the kitchen counter watching her mother roll out lavender cookie dough with a wooden rolling pin.

"Really?" Agnes was puzzled. Eddie didn't seem to have many friends these days. Once or twice she had nudged him to call his cousin Jeb or go out for drinks with Nicky Maddalone or some of his buddies from before the war, but Eddie's response was always the same. "I'll get around to it."

"What did Daddy tell you?" Agnes said in a voice full of brightness. "About his friends?"

"Mommy, I've never seen them myself, but there's these two white men who talk funny. Daddy says they come out of the wall and throw coins at him. Sometimes, we throw coins back at them."

Over dinner that night Agnes was animated and affectionate with Eddie. Instead of going directly to work the next morning, she ran errands and returned home. Agnes made her way quietly inside the house. She found Eddie and the girls in the kitchen. The girls sat in chairs on top of the kitchen table, and Eddie stood on the table beside them. Beverly held a paper towel tube—a telescope? Claudia beat two frying pan lids. The pans clanged like wedding bells. Eddie reared forward, stomping on the kitchen table, so that it rocked from side to side like a dinghy on the ocean. Polka-dot bedsheets dangled from the kitchen walls on a clothesline strung up with masking tape. The sheets formed a moat around the kitchen table. Water flowed freely from the kitchen sink onto the linoleum. The burners on the kitchen stove were lit. And on each burner, water boiled.

"*Well, gentlemen, it's more or less like we told you,*" Eddie said, peeking over the curtains at the kitchen walls. "*Sometimes, you've got to shit or get off the pot.*"

"*Never, ever, never,*" shouted the girls in clipped British accents. Their ponytails swinging, their sandaled feet tapping the table, hands on their slim hips.

"*You're nothing but a pair of fools.*" Eddie shrugged. "*On a ghost ship.*"

"*Guildenstern is a fool,*" said Claudia.

"*No, Rosencrantz is the fool,*" said Beverly.

"*But Ros always wins!*" squealed Claudia with delight. She jumped up, did a little dance, and nearly fell off the table.

"Is this what you do while I'm working all day, Eddie?" Agnes entered the kitchen and turned the burners off one at a time. She stared into the bubbling pots of water.

Eddie and the girls froze. "What are you doing home?"

"Last time I checked, I live here too."

Eddie leapt off the table. He looked around the kitchen and tried to see the room from Agnes's perspective. "The girls and I were just—playing."

"You play dangerous." She squinted. She had to know. How hadn't she known?

"I thought you trusted me."

"Beverly, Claudia. Get off that table and help your father clean up this mess," Agnes said. "There's a point after which I don't trust anyone, Eddie. Neither should you. Clearly you have too much time on your hands."

For the first time in their marriage, the air was frosty between Eddie and Agnes. Their tension ran straight to the girls. Beverly and Claudia bickered over who was too old for a plastic cup or who cheated at Operation or what happened to the Ken doll's head.

EDDIE ATTENDED THE eleven-fifteen mass on Sunday mornings at Our Lady of Claremont Catholic Church. Agnes and Claudia preferred the comfort of home. Church meant that Beverly got Eddie all to herself. She would clutch her father's hand as he walked past the abandoned sand-colored buildings telling stories about people who no longer lived there. During mass, Eddie let Beverly fill a small plastic container with holy water to bathe her Barbie dolls. They called this concoction Holy Water Perfume.

The priest sought Eddie out during coffee hour in the parish hall. Over coffee and day-old pastry donated by fellow parishioners, he said, "Eddie, I hear they're looking for a custodian at Claremont's Catholic School. It would be our pleasure to have you."

Eddie had never gotten used to seeing his old man lugging a mop and broom. Where was the forward momentum in accepting the same damn job?

"What happened to your old janitor?" said Eddie, not wanting to appear upset.

"He was a difficult personality."

Eddie investigated the matter with Alfred Maddalone. "Active hands," Mr. Maddalone reported. "They caught him feeling up one of the girls in the broom closet."

Eddie began to calculate the things he could do with the extra income. The money would be for family vacations. When he shared the news with Agnes, he came bearing a map of the United States. He unfolded the map on the four-leaf kitchen table that sometimes nicked his skin. He circled Niagara Falls and campsites in the Adirondacks. Maybe, next year, the Hoover Dam or the Grand Canyon? Surely, a trip to Washington, D.C.?

Agnes paused between putting frozen garden peas in the fridge and pouring two glasses of cold milk for her girls. Beverly and Claudia were required to drink a glass of milk every day. Strong bones allowed you to stand on your own two feet and, if necessary, to flee.

"Eddie." Agnes leaned into her husband. "I didn't mean what I said about not trusting you. Please don't take the job because of me." She hated the idea of Eddie going from one uniform to another. It took daily effort not to compare him to Claude Johnson unfavorably.

HE STARTED THE Tuesday after Labor Day. Agnes arranged her schedule so that she could drop the girls off to daycare. It was Eddie's responsibility to pick them up. He did not wear his uniform to work but arrived early enough to change in the faculty locker room. He switched out of his uniform before leaving work, so that the girls recognized him as their father first.

The logistics ran smoothly for the most part, but there were the occasional evenings when Agnes joined her colleagues in the Urban Planning office for happy hour. She always had a smile for Eddie when she came home late. It pleased her to see him in nice slacks, shirt, and loafers.

THAT SAME YEAR, Our Lady of Claremont Catholic School hired a visiting theater artist to direct a student production of *Twelfth Night*. In addition to an impressive collection of costumes from past productions, Barrett Bass came wearing an English tweed suit and black leather sneakers so shiny and new, Eddie whiffed around for their cow.

EDDIE'S SWEEPING WAS compact and brisk. If he paced himself and worked up a sweat, an hour might pass in fifteen minutes. And if he worked his way from the top of the six-story building down to the first floor, he ended up in the auditorium, where Barrett Bass rehearsed with his students in the afternoon.

"My dear young thespians," Bass said. "Right now, your intentions are mired in confusing dialects that point away from Elizabethan times to Bronx playgrounds. We must rebel against these dialects on stage. This is one of Shakespeare's oft-produced plays. Endeavor to ease your tongues and do Sir William justice."

Eddie went down to the school library and checked out a copy of *Twelfth Night*. The librarian, a part-time volunteer and PTA coordinator, found his request touching.

CLAREMONT WAS MOSTLY composed of black and Puerto Rican students. Eddie could walk from classroom to classroom and count the number of Irish and Italian kids on one hand. Many of the students had relatives in Vietnam or somewhere else dodging the draft. Eddie always had a good morning and a good-bye for the students between cleaning the bathroom stalls and emptying the trash cans. While he polished the winding stair rail and replastered a section of the ceiling in the teacher's lounge, Eddie practiced lines from *Twelfth Night* under his breath. He developed a reputation among the kids as the prompter. They would shout out any quote from the play and Eddie would recite the next line. It occurred to Eddie that he was now doing the household chores that Agnes had wanted him to do. He disinfected bathrooms and wiped down the staff kitchen, the tables and chairs in the lunchrooms. The job was enough for two men, but Eddie didn't complain.

THE SEVENTH GRADERS were rehearsing Act I, Scene IV of *Twelfth Night* in the auditorium when Gabriel Ruiz forgot his lines; they had been in rehearsals now for several weeks running, but Gabriel always blanked out on the same scene.

DONNA AS VIOLA

Sure, my noble lord,
If she be so abandoned to her sorrow
As it is spoke, she never will admit me.

GABRIEL AS ORSINO

Be clamorous, and leap all civil bounds,
Rather than make unprofited return.

DONNA AS VIOLA

Say I do speak with her, my lord, what then?

GABRIEL AS ORSINO

O, then unfold the passion of my love,
Surprise her with discourse of my dear faith:
It shall become thee well to act my woes;
She will attend it better in thy youth
Than in a nuncio's of more grave aspect.

DONNA AS VIOLA

I think not so, my lord.

GABRIEL AS ORSINO

Dear lad, believe it.
For they shall yet belie thy happy years
That say thou art a man. Diana's lip
Is not more smooth and rubious. Thy small pipe
Is as the maiden's organ . . . the maiden's organ, the . . . the?

EDDIE WAS IN the auditorium fixing the arm of a chair when Gabriel looked around for someone to help him. Barrett Bass stood with his arms crossed, tapping his feet impatiently.

"*Shrill and sound,*" chimed Eddie from the back of the room. "*And all is semblative a woman's part. I know thy constellation is right apt. For this affair. Some four or five attend him. All, if you will, for I myself am best when least in company. Prosper well in this. And thou shalt live as freely as thy lord, to call his fortunes thine.*"

Barrett Bass laughed and moved downstage. "Well, *someone* knows his lines. Maybe you should have a role in our play?" He had heard of the Shakespearean janitor.

"I have a heater to check." Eddie always ate his lunch in the boiler room, where he could gauge his temper and, if his mood ran hot, talk to the walls.

"Come, just for a minute or two." Barrett smiled. "Indulge us."

Eddie walked down the red aisle with the metal toolbox in his hands. He did not come to the center of the stage.

"Hey, Ruiz," he called, avoiding eye contact with Barrett Bass. "You like football?"

"No." Ruiz, who had a Michael Jackson 'fro and Michael Jackson acne, shrugged.

"Baseball."

"Even better." Eddie smiled. "When the lines fizzle in your head, imagine a baseball carrying them. Roll with the words and you'll hold on to more than you forget."

Eddie left the auditorium. He avoided rehearsals for the rest of the week. It was the most depressing period of his employment at Our Lady of Claremont. The hours crept along like caterpillars.

"HOW MANY PEOPLE did you kill in Vietnam?" Barrett asked.

Eddie was on his knees in the teachers' lounge stripping chipped paint from the molding. The principal was pouring a cup of coffee and two of the teachers were chatting by the blue water cooler.

At first Eddie ignored the question. He had loaded bombs onto airplanes. He had seen men fly away who did not return. He had smelled napalm on some who did.

"I wasn't on the ground," Eddie said.

"But you killed?" Barrett Bass asked.

"Indirectly." Eddie climbed to his feet. "But it's possible that I killed one person directly."

"Only one?"

"One's plenty," Eddie said. "One's enough."

The teachers' lounge went quiet. Barrett Bass smiled dubiously. He had participated in nuclear disarmament protests in London as a graduate student. His modern interpretation of *Richard III* had caused a minor stir in New York and Edinburgh. Now he was in the running for an associate artistic director position at an up-and-coming off-Broadway theater.

It wasn't the smile on the drama teacher's long face that irked Eddie so much as the way Barrett lowered his hand on the shoulder of Eddie's uniform, like he was wiping off a small speck of dust that Eddie had missed. And it wasn't so much that Barrett had wiped off that imaginary speck of dust but that, at that same moment, the principal and two teachers laughed. Not to be mean, but out of nervousness or status or whatever thing makes people behave one way when they should behave another. Eddie grabbed the handle of the broom leaning against the lateral file cabinets and began to sweep. First he swept around the theater director, like he had seen his mother and Bella Maddalone do when he was a kid. He swept around Barrett Bass and then across his leather sneakers. Eddie was trying to sweep a problem away. His sweeping gained momentum and his broom acquired dust as the shiny leather sneakers lost their luster. Barrett Bass backed away with each swipe of Eddie Christie's broom. By the sixth swipe, he fell flat on his ass.

This time the principal and teachers stifled their laughter. As a young man, Eddie had had a thing for nice shoes and clothes. He'd drop a small fortune on his wardrobe. But he wore slip-resistant Oxfords now. Eddie leaned over and offered Barrett Bass his hand, but Barrett rocked back and forth on the hard wood floor. "I think my fucking foot is broken."

THE NEXT MORNING, Eddie showed up for work and found the principal waiting for him outside the faculty locker room.

"Eddie," the principal said, "we're lucky he's not pressing charges."

"The guy's a piece of shit," Eddie said. He had not yet changed into his janitorial uniform. "So, what's the deal?"

The principal blushed. Eddie noticed he was blocking the entrance to the faculty locker room. "On behalf of Saint Claremont's Church, I'm sorry it has to be this way. But the faculty and staff, we lead by example. . . ."

Eddie slipped his hands into his pockets and jingled small change. "Does this mean I won't be seeing *Twelfth Night* at the winter recital?"

The principal nodded. "In light of recent events, I'll have to ask you to skip the play."

ALFRED MADDALONE REACHED out to a cousin who reached out to another cousin and Eddie landed a nine-to-five job at Ronaldo's House of Flowers on Arthur Avenue.

"Eddie," Mr. Maddalone warned, "listen with your ears. These guys, they're connected. And some of them are made. Never borrow money from anyone. No fraternizing. Remember, you're not their friend. The only time you are their friend is for weddings, funerals, or baptisms. And paper, paper doesn't exist. Never write anything down. Many an ass has been offed because of a note someone neglected or left."

When Agnes asked what his new job entailed, Eddie told her he was an assistant manager. They both agreed that it was a step up from janitor.

At first glance, Ronaldo's House of Flowers was nothing to fuss about, but look twice and you might notice a flight of stairs to the rear of the shop. The second floor housed a Sicilian restaurant with frescoes on the wall. Eddie had gone upstairs once—to carry a box of imported Roman-style artichokes to Ronaldo's mother, who doubled as the chef. It was the kind of establishment that did not take reservations.

Above the restaurant was a greenhouse where Ronaldo grew certain plants and flowers throughout the year. Three days a week, he sent Eddie to the flower district in Manhattan to pick up fresh plants. Eddie developed a knack for selecting choice blooms and haggling for a good price. He would come home on Fridays with fresh roses for Agnes and the girls. That summer he planted an herb garden in the backyard and filled it in with pansies and violets and rosemary and fennel.

This was an altogether peaceful time for Eddie, who began to recite *Rosencrantz and Guildenstern* to the flowers because at Ronaldo's there was no time to talk to walls. The roses understood him, and it pleased Eddie when a plant he had nurtured found a home outside the store. The men who pulled up in Cadillacs and Lincoln Town Cars and tailored suits thought that Eddie was touched in the head, a simpleton, dense. He need not do much, other than being a black man, to encourage their misperceptions of him.

IT WAS THE second weekend in June when bullets rained on Ronaldo's House of Flowers. Eddie would remember this for a long time after because in the papers they would mention how crowded Arthur Avenue was that day, a muggy Saturday afternoon with families dining in the outside cafés or doing their weekend grocery shopping. Eddie had just finished hosing down the sidewalk and was using the hose to wash his hands when a group of men stepped out of the shop. He knew that one of them was a capo they called Sal, short for Salvatore Galliano. Salvatore ate at Ronaldo's upstairs restaurant every Saturday, and every Saturday he paused to admire the flowers on display on the sidewalk. He never bought any, not even for the wife and girlfriends who sometimes tagged along with him. But this Saturday, Salvatore stopped to consider the bird-of-paradise.

"How much?" he asked Eddie.

Lately, Ronaldo had begun letting Eddie man the register. Eddie dried his hands and moved over to Salvatore Galliano.

"Three dollars each. Forty for the bouquet," Eddie said.

Salvatore reached in his pocket to take out his wallet and cursed. The wallet was on a table upstairs alongside his second serving of pistachio cheesecake. He motioned for one of his men to go up and fetch it just as a black sedan swung to the curb. There was a moment, a fraction of a second, when time bent backward. A man slid out of the black sedan in a white three-piece suit. Bullets from the gun he held sprayed Salvatore Galliano's men before they had time to cover their boss or protect themselves. Eddie's eyes locked with the shooter. Was it an illusion or was he a black man, a black *hit* man who couldn't have been much older than Eddie. How to explain Eddie's surge of recognition, his swell of pride and loathing, of love and repulsion? Rage confused his body. Adrenaline kicked in. Eddie upturned flowers and knocked them to his left and to his right, pulling himself and Salvatore Galliano to the ground and away from the assassin's bullets.

"I'M A VET," Eddie said later, when the cops and reporters pressed him for details about the shooting. "I've seen so many things go in and out of walls, half the time I don't know if I'm coming or going."

He turned his back abruptly to the cameras and made spirited dialogue with the decimated flowers. Two men were dead. Salvatore Galliano had walked away unharmed, and Eddie was determined to drive home the point that he wasn't a reliable witness. Put him on the witness stand and he'd be a lost cause.

Alfred Maddalone visited to congratulate Eddie on a stellar performance. "I couldn't have played it better myself."

Ronaldo's House of Flowers was shuttered for six months following the shooting. Eddie received $6,000 in severance pay. Eddie and Agnes agreed it would be foolish to decline the hush money. They put it into their rainy-day savings and used it to cover Claudia's room and board at college.

WHEN ALFRED MADDALONE mentioned another job lead, Eddie remembered the saying: *The Lord helps those who help themselves.* The jobless rate in New York City in 1972 was nearly 11 percent. Eddie applied one, three, four times for a position with the MTA. Sixteen months later, he went to work for the Bridges and Tunnels department as a tollbooth clerk on the George Washington Bridge.

He seldom had time to read *Rosencrantz and Guildenstern Are Dead* during the day and was often too exhausted to reach for the small paperback at night. Eddie tried, with varying degrees of success, to put the war and Chief Mammoth behind him. He tried, with more success, falling in love with Agnes again. Sometimes, Eddie talked in his sleep. In this way, Agnes gleaned things about her husband he could not share and she would not question. He kept a spare stack of coins in his tollbooth at work. Whenever a motorist crossed the bridge reasonably short of fare, Eddie would offer a quick bit of trivia—*Did you know it cost sixty million dollars to build this bridge? They finished it in 1931. The lower half, well, it's quite naturally named after Martha Washington*—before smiling and waving them on and tossing coins from his private stash into the register with the other bills and small change.

THE SUMMER SEASON

1983

T HE BLACK FAMILY MOVED IN NEXT DOOR TO HANK AND
his parents on Memorial Day. They arrived at the height of
the afternoon. The sun was brutal, but the wind was in a more
generous mood. A cool breeze came rushing in from the Gulf Coast,
so guests could have some respite from the heat.

Hank's father, Charles Camphor, was holding a brand-new set
of golf clubs. Instead of iron, Charles had opted for wood, persim-
mon to be precise. He was explaining how the solid wood staffs and
heads enhanced his shot. He was exhibiting the golf clubs to his
first cousin, Big Seamus, father to Seamus III. The Camphor cousins had come to gape at Charles's five-bedroom, three-bathroom
gingerbread house with its latticed balcony and wraparound front
porch and automated garage door. The house sat on an acre of land
on Sunset Beach, a gated island community in Buckner County,
Georgia. It had come with majestic weeping willow trees and
strategically placed juniper plants and shrubbery to better absorb
the noise from the marsh, which was bountiful with wildlife. The

coastal soundscapes were subdued during the day but operatic at night.

Charles Camphor's cousins hated the way their women fussed over the bidet Charles had installed especially for his wife, and the chef's kitchen—a kitchen with a marble island at its center—for a woman who couldn't boil a pot of rice. Charles's wife, Barbara Camphor, had snuck away that very morning and driven downtown to Mrs. Trudy's Roadside Restaurant, where the black cooks still wore antebellum uniforms and the ceiling fans didn't do anything but inflame the heat. Barbara spent a good five hundred dollars on an immaculate spread: okra gumbo, Southern red rice, fried chicken, pickled relish, mustard greens, and among other things, home-style potato salad. Savory dishes she hadn't the stamina to prepare, but when layered into the right piece of crockery, Barbara could claim the glory.

Burgers and dogs cooked on the grill. The rest of the food from Mrs. Trudy's was laid out on the wooden picnic table. Barbara came outside and stood beside her husband. She and Charles Camphor were blue-eyed, sandy-haired people who tilted naturally toward the sun. They had bequeathed their good looks to Hank, but Hank's hair tended toward dark waviness. While Charles lollygagged with his cousins, Barbara kicked off her navy-blue espadrilles. In the summer of 1983, espadrilles were a kind of fashion statement, but she wore them solely for comfort. Barbara didn't have to worry about fashion. She would look good gutting fish.

"Who taught Barbara how to boil an egg?" Charlie's cousins and their women were laughing and talking.

"Barbara, who told you the difference between mashed potatoes and potato salad?" Big Seamus's wife asked.

Barbara sipped her Milwaukee beer. "I guess that means I did all right in the kitchen." On the drive home from Mrs. Trudy's she had passed their old townhouse downtown. It had not been large enough to entertain Charles's family, which was a blessing. When she was growing up, her parents, factory workers at Pabst, would invite friends and family over at the spur of the moment. Everyone knew to check their egos at the door. You stopped by because you wanted to be there and you lingered because the company was good. Fellowship was lacking here. She loved their new digs but she missed the townhouse's intimacy.

Barbara assumed the role of hostess and moved about the lawn pouring Charles's people liberal drinks because that was what they had really come for: free meals and her husband's liquor. What they didn't know was that Barbara had transferred the prime whiskey and bourbon and scotch and rye and gin into different decanters the previous night and replaced them with the cheap booze they were now quaffing. Hank had helped her; he loved helping his mother pull a fast one on his father's cousins. It was one of the great pleasures of the summer season.

That Memorial Day, they were laughing and passing the time when one of the cousins—the skinny one with the gaze of a peregrine falcon—asked, "Who lives next door?"

"No one now," Charles said. The yellow Victorian house with the weeping willow tree in the front yard was vacant when Charles and Barbara had bought their house nine months ago.

"Place like this." The peregrine falcon cousin scanned the exterior of Charles's house from top to bottom. "You must be doing well for yourself, huh?"

Charles looked at Barbara: this was the cousin she had advised him not to invite. Every family has one. *Charles, honey, you're too kind. Some people will always be hungry*, Barbara had warned. *Even after the feast.*

"Let's just say the price was right." Charles ribbed this cousin with the hard head of his brand-new golf club. And everyone laughed.

That was when the moving truck came down the quiet street and rolled into the driveway of the yellow Victorian next door. Behind the moving truck in a silver Volvo sat a sextet of people with brown skin.

"Tell me you're not seeing what I'm seeing?" the peregrine falcon said. The other cousins burst out laughing in that mean jovial way that would follow most of their progeny into their own adult lives. Charles himself stood frozen, and so did his brand-new clubs. It was Big Seamus who turned things around.

"*Hush*," Big Seamus snapped. "You don't want Charlie's new neighbors thinking we're ignorant." Hank would remember this kindness thirty years later when he sold Big Seamus his parents' house.

The new neighbors climbed out of their silver Volvo and walked toward the entrance of their new home. For a second, the mother seemed to cast a glance their way, though Hank might have just imagined that she did. She wore a crisp blue summer dress and navy-blue espadrilles exactly like his mother's, only her heels had the height advantage by two or three inches. The woman walked alongside her husband, and behind the woman walked four kids: a dainty teenage girl with curly shoulder-length hair in a purple paisley dress that sashayed when she moved. A short, droopy-eared basset hound strutted to the right of the girl. Then came a boy with a buzz cut and glasses. Hank, who had recently turned thirteen, guessed that the boy was around his age. Last out of the car was a pair of chubby fraternal twins. The twins, a boy and girl, were maybe four or five years old. They were decked out in summer sailor suits, like their father, Reuben Applewood, a recently retired captain in the U.S. Navy.

Hank thought of the family of mallard ducks from the children's book he had loved so much in kindergarten, *Make Way for Ducklings*. The family had the same brown coloring of mallards, only without the green collars around their necks. There's a season when mallards molt and lose their green collars. Molting mallards cannot fly.

"I worked hard cooking this food," Barbara said, steering her husband's family's gaze away from the new neighbors. "Ain't that right, Hank, darling? Now, let's move everything inside before the heat does it and us a disservice. Food poisoning's a thing you don't want but once in life. I have a plane to catch in the a.m., but y'all can sit up in the air-conditioning and drink my husband out of house and home."

At the Buckner County airport the following morning, Barbara kissed Charles almost too passionately before boarding her plane. "Now, don't do anything I wouldn't do," she said. She was on her way to a regional Red Cross conference in Atlanta.

"I'll save it till you get home, babe." Charles slapped Barbara gently on the butt.

Barbara stepped back and gave Hank's hair the finger wave. Sometimes, she would drape her fingers through his lustrous black mane and say, *Baby, it's time to swim.*

"Hank," she said. "Try not to grow too much."

FOR THREE DAYS Hank spied on the neighbor boy, waiting for a time when he could say a natural *hi* or *hello*. The thick tortoiseshell glasses the boy wore made his face look stern and serious. Hank figured the boy's thoughts were always two steps ahead of him and he was angry because the thoughts wouldn't listen. (It was a feeling Hank knew all too well, especially when his mother was away.)

Hank finally met up with him on the way home from sailing lessons at the Sunset Beach Country Club. The neighbor boy was walking the droopy-eared basset hound.

"You not afraid that dog's going to run into the street?" Hank said. The basset hound walked without a leash several yards ahead of the boy, its nose desperate for any secrets the sidewalk had to tell.

"Tipper knows how to cross the street," the boy answered. "And, anyway, there's not much traffic on a cul-de-sac."

"You trained him?" Hank said, feeling suddenly like an idiot.

"No, he's mostly my sister's dog. He doesn't care really about anyone but Lonnie."

"Then how come you're walking him?"

"The twins are positively disconsolate. When they get that way, I don't like to be in the house."

Hank was about to laugh at the boy's haughtiness, but checked himself. "I'm Hank," he said, easily.

"Huck?"

"No, *Hank*—like Hank Williams." He began to yodel.

"That's country music," the boy said, backing away from him with something like scorn and removing a Rubik's Cube from his shirt pocket. He worked the cube deftly, twirling it around in his hands, aligning yellow, green, white, blue, struggling to line up the red.

"What's wrong with country music?" Hank said, noticing the way the boy's Chuck Taylor sneakers curved in slightly. He was pigeon-toed.

"Nothing. But around here people play it all the time." The boy must have noticed Hank staring at his feet because he pointed them outward. For the first time the boy considered Hank. "Some of Elvis Costello's music is kind of like country music. And I like him."

"I like Elvis Costello too," Hank said, relieved to have found common ground.

"You like Blondie?" the boy asked.

Hank nodded.

"The Pretenders?"

Hank nodded again.

"Pink Floyd?"

"Uh-huh." Hank removed his hands from his shorts. He was suddenly feeling more confident. "I like Queen and Black Sabbath too."

The boy lost interest in his Rubik's Cube. "Yeah." The boy shrugged. "But how can Freddie top 'Bohemian Rhapsody'? I'm Gideon..."

Gideon held up his hand for a high five. Hank was already five-eight at thirteen. By the time he entered college he would have grown another eight inches. Gideon, whose legs were waiting to catch up to the rest of his body, barely reached Hank's shoulder.

The two boys walked up and down the block twice with Tipper leading the way. When they stopped, they were in front of Gideon's house again. His sister was on the front porch reading *Teen Beat* magazine. Tipper saw Lonnie and ran up the verandah stairs. Lonnie lowered her book and kissed the dog on the nose. Her hair was pulled up into a curly ballerina bun and she wore a pink beach jumper and sandals.

"She sure likes *Teen Beat*," Hank said. For the past three days, he'd also spied on Lonnie sitting out reading on the front porch.

"Don't let Lonnie fool you. Anything could be behind that magazine. Anaïs Nin. Colette. D. H. Lawrence. Whatever exotica she finds hidden in our mom's bureau."

"Do you think I would like Anaïs Nin?"

"Stick with Black Sabbath. Who says she likes them, anyway? Around here, people need something to do. There's not anything to do around here."

"That's not true," Hank said, suddenly feeling the need to defend his neighborhood. "There's sailing at the country club. There's tennis. And they've got all sorts of activities for different age groups. You can swim or you can take your bike and go off on one of the trails. And on Saturday nights, there's outdoor movies."

"We'll get to the country club, eventually," Gideon said. "In the meantime, I've got my Rubik's Cube and Lonnie's got her *exotica*."

Hank did not like the way Gideon said *exotica*. He did not like the way he said *positively disconsolate* either. He wasn't sure he liked Gideon at all.

Gideon wove his fingers around the Rubik's Cube, twisting and turning again.

Hank's attention drifted back to Lonnie on the verandah. "But she looks so stuck-up and sweet."

"Don't go getting any ideas. Lonnie's going to be a surgeon one day. She says to understand the human anatomy, you must first understand passion. Passion builds and destroys things. Including bodies."

"How old did you say she was again?"

Gideon returned the Rubik's Cube to his shirt pocket. "Would you like to come over to my house some time?" he asked.

"Sure," Hank said.

"Good, then." Gideon walked into his house without looking over his shoulder.

AT NIGHT TIPPER would climb through the little doggie door in the kitchen to go outside and howl. Hank thought the dog might be homesick, like Lonnie and Gideon, then remembered that he hadn't even gotten around to asking Gideon where home was.

"It's the breed," Charles said. Hank and his father were in the backyard stargazing. "It's in a hound dog's blood to bellow and yowl. Of course, that's not a real hound dog, if you ask me: too squat. A dog like that is not good for anything except comic relief."

"Dad?" Hank chose his words carefully. "I was thinking maybe the new boy next door could come over to our house?"

"No, son, I don't think so."

"Why not?"

Charles sat up in the deck chair. He was senior vice president at S&S Bank. The title was not quite as demanding as it seemed, but there were certain stresses. In the 1980s, people who hadn't had money for a long time were starting to see a change. It was the Reagan era, and Reagan believed in giving something back to the common man so that the common man didn't have to stay common for long. During the Reagan years, Charles would see development on the island blow up. He would greenlight a high percentage of new homes. Charles had a healthy son and a five-bedroom house. And a wife who liked helping people so much she wouldn't stay home. It fell on him to teach his son how things were done. "There are no fences between the two yards. You boys can meet in the gazebo and talk as much as you want."

"But it's hot out."

"The gazebo has plenty of shade."

"Dad, it could get kind of awkward if he invites me to his house but he can't come to mine."

"There are other boys. And the timing's not right."

"What does that mean, Dad? It's summer."

Charles smiled at his son. Charles had a nice smile that took up half his face when a day at the bank was behind him.

"We haven't even brought over a welcome plate," said Hank.

"When we moved in, neighbors brought us welcome plates the first day."

"And your mother threw everything away. You know how she is about food with a high caloric content. This is the only house in America without a jar of mayonnaise."

"Well, I'll ask her. I'll ask Mom."

"Do that," Charles said, closing his eyes. "Welcome plates are a woman's job to make and bring."

"Not about the welcome plate. About Gideon."

Charles Camphor's eyes remained closed. Hank couldn't tell if he'd fallen asleep or was bent on ignoring what he'd said.

THAT NIGHT HANK lay on the top tier of his bunk bed with his feet dangling over the edge and fantasized about his new friend's sister. When Gideon had told him that Lonnie read exotica, Hank had come home and looked up the word in his pocket-sized Merriam-Webster dictionary.

> **exotica:** *things excitingly different or unusual;* especially: *literary or artistic items having an exotic theme or nature*

Hank wanted to tell Gideon that he wasn't as naïve as he thought. Charles Camphor kept an impressive collection of pornography in the basement. Hank didn't always get to the videos, because they were too distracting, too easy to lose track of time staring at Seka giving head or getting butt-fucked. But *Playboy* and *Hustler* and *Penthouse*, Hank bothered those issues every month. He developed his own opinions about the world while browsing Bob Guccione's *Penthouse Forum* (for the profiles and the politics). After he finished reading, Hank would unbuckle his pants, arrange the pictures the way he liked, and jerk off to Black Sabbath.

BEFORE BARBARA CAMPHOR flew to her latest conference—after the Camphor cousins had cleared out and left them to clean up everything—Hank had overheard her tell his father, "Charles, I have a happy vagina. You will not make my vagina sad."

If the details hadn't been so personal, Hank might have told Gideon all about them. Better yet, he might have asked Lonnie Applewood, *What makes a vagina happy?* And no doubt, she would've slapped him in the face for asking. The next morning, Hank had confronted his mother.

"Are you and Dad happy?"

Barbara was brushing her teeth. Her plane would take off in two hours. "Hank, darling, I won the lottery when I caught Charles."

"Mom?"

"Why, yes, Hank? What are your troubles? Why do you ask?"

"I thought I heard you arguing last night."

His mother rinsed her toothbrush and began to apply makeup and eye shadow. Hank thought she was pretty enough not to need either. "When we stop arguing," she said, "that's when you should worry."

"So, no divorce, then?"

"Hank." Barbara flashed him a smile. "People are lazy. They get divorced because they accommodate their partners too much or too little. With a marriage, you've got to chart your own course."

But Barbara Camphor hadn't called in three days, not since she left for Atlanta. This was the first time she'd gone out of town and not left a message or checked in on Hank and Charles.

GIDEON APPLEWOOD'S HOUSE smelled like ginger. On the counter in a glass cake pan was a triple-layered coconut cake with candied ginger. Gideon liked pineapple in his cake, but Lonnie was allergic to pineapple, so it wasn't allowed in the house.

"We were on Turks and Caicos for Christmas break, and Lonnie drank this pineapple drink and her throat closed up. Now she never goes anywhere without Benadryl." Hank noticed that Gideon would dangle pieces of information about Lonnie in front of him like a carrot and then sit back to see if he would take the bait.

It was a house that was made for comfort, with furniture you could spill your body into. And books, floor-to-ceiling—books that poured out of the built-in bookshelves left by the previous owners. On his initial visit, Hank only saw Gideon's mother once. She was in the playroom and preoccupied with the twins. Gideon and Hank spent the bulk of their time in the rec room. Hank delved into his second slice of coconut cake and Pink Floyd's "Another Brick in the Wall" blared on the radio and Gideon—who Hank was learning never liked to be still—was jumping up and down. Not dancing but jumping. Instead of depositing quarters in the pinball machine, Gideon had to give the machine a good hard whack every time he wanted to turn it on or play another game. The rec room was the most chaotic place in the house, between the noise from the rec-ord player and the pinball machine and the mountain of toys and bicycles and a shrink-wrapped velvet pool table that made Hank blush because, looking at it, he had a sudden, pornographic vision involving Lonnie.

"How'd you get the pinball table?"

"Bribery."

"No shit?" Hank said.

"Yeah, my dad basically bought us stuff to move here. It was that or—"

"He'd have to deal with you being *positively disconsolate*."

Gideon raised his brow. "More or less."

"What did he promise Lonnie?"

"We're going to New York City over the Christmas break for a cultural trip."

"I guess you probably miss your friends. In Ohio."

Gideon smiled at Hank. His smile took on the universal language of mean. Eventually meanness staked its claim on everyone. "Do you have any friends, Hank?"

CHARLOTTE APPLEWOOD WAS a middle school teacher and would return to work full-time after Labor Day. A cursory review of the test scores of her incoming pupils had confirmed her reservations about returning south. The academic year was bound to be long and tedious. Charlotte was bent on giving the twins one-on-one time now, because she would not always have the time or energy when the school year commenced. Like Barbara Camphor, she was neither a cook nor a baker. And so, her aunt Lady Miller, chief baker at Gottlieb's Bakery, would send over chocolate chewies, raisin-clad gingerbread men, and whatever cake she was inspired to bake every few days. Lady Miller had once believed the lie that daughters never venture far away from home, so to see her niece Charlotte return to Buckner County while her own daughter Agnes stayed north was bitter medicine.

"It's 1983. Things are not like they used to be," Lady Miller was fond of saying on quiet evenings when her niece would call with grumblings about returning to Ohio. Charlotte had attended three different Mommy-and-me groups in Buckner County, but there was always this energy, *something* she couldn't quite put her finger on, that made her want to circle the wagons and shelter her children.

Charlotte told her husband as soon as he came home from work that Gideon had a new friend. They were in the rec room.

"Did you get out today?" Reuben Applewood asked. He was the newly appointed dean of Buckner County's historic black college.

"I went downtown. I walked the twins around Robert E. Lee Park."

"That's a lot of work for you. Why didn't you just go up to the country club?"

Charlotte bounced the twins on her knees. "We are not in Shaker Heights anymore, Reuben. So I'm going to say this once. For the sake of body and soul, no child of mine's going to that country club."

"Charlotte, they need to continue their swim lessons. They're good swimmers, but not good enough to make it if they fall off a boat into the middle of the ocean. I want them to be comfortable when they take sailing lessons."

"Well." Charlotte shrugged. "I guess they'll have to go downtown to the Y and tread water with the rough element."

———

IN SHAKER HEIGHTS, the liberal and integrated neighborhood outside Cleveland, Ohio, Gideon Applewood left behind these things:

1. Best friend
2. A tree house (which his father built on his sixth birthday)
3. A red View-Master that he gave to his best friend's baby brother (who followed them around everywhere they went)
4. Milkshakes at Tommy's
5. Hot dogs slathered with chili con carne
6. The Cleveland Indians and ballpark hot dogs slathered with chili con carne and stadium mustard
7. Mrs. Frost, his seventh-grade English teacher, who maimed his book reports with her red marker but always wrote in parentheses: *Be yourself, Gideon, and keep smart.*
8. The Pretenders LP from 1979 that he left on the bedroom floor
9. The love letter inside the jacket of the Pretenders LP from Cassidy, the first girl to kiss him
10. The phone number on the back of the letter from Cassidy. They had hatched this crazy scheme to run off to Vancouver together—a scheme that involved backpacks and hitchhiking and rides on Mennonite carriages.
11. The threat to jump headfirst into traffic on Highway 77 if his parents did not turn around to retrieve his Pretenders LP

Years later, in 1990 at the ticker tape parade in downtown Manhattan for a recently freed Nelson Mandela, Gideon and his first girlfriend would spot each other, lower their Free South Africa placards, and pull away from the crowd, their bodies jumping, their heads swaying, propelled backward and forward by the momentum of the day and their love for Chrissie Hynde and the Pretenders.

"I'm a lesbian," Cassidy would whisper.

"That's cool," Gideon Applewood would say. "I'm gay."

———

BARBARA CAMPHOR RETURNED home the first Sunday in June bearing gifts: a case of peach-infused beer for her husband and a red bicycle light with the Georgia Bulldogs insignia engraved on the side for Hank. After a dinner of grilled grouper, Hank's parents retreated promptly to their bedroom, leaving him to watch summer reruns of *M*A*S*H*. They emerged toward the end of the second episode and sprawled out on the living room couch. They wore a fresh change of clothes. Barbara rested her head in Charles's lap.

Hank was sitting on the floor. He turned off the TV and looked at his parents. "So, when are we going on a cultural trip?"

"A cultural trip!" Barbara sat up and yawned. "What a nice idea. Why didn't I think of that?"

Charles stroked Barbara's hair, which smelled like Sea Breeze and cigarettes and maybe just a hint of marijuana.

"Barb," he said. "Have you taken up smoking again?"

"Hank, honey." Barbara yawned. "What kind of cultural trip did you have in mind?"

"Well, I was thinking maybe New York. Over Christmas."

"Son, you know that's family time at the cabin," Charles said.

Barbara smiled at her husband. "They have Van Gogh at MOMA, Charles. Don't you think Hank should see *Starry Night*?"

Charles took a sip of his scotch. "Van Gogh cut off his ear."

Barbara laughed. "It made his eyes better and his hands generous."

Charles bent down and gave his wife a kiss. "Come here, darling, I love the way you look at the world. In fact, I love the way you look."

"Then, it's settled. A week at the cabin and a long weekend in Manhattan." She winked at Hank. "All right by you, big shot?"

IN MID-JUNE BARBARA went on another Red Cross mission. Charles delivered her to the airport and, to ease his mind, went to the country club for a round of morning golf. He then went home and roused his son, who was giving in to the teenage habit of midday naps.

"Hank, let's go and see your friend," Charles said, removing a set of car keys from the pocket of his plaid golf pants.

"Where's Mom?" Hank cleared sleep from his eyes.

Charles pointed toward the heavens. "Among the clouds."

"Why didn't you wake me?"

"I'm waking you now, son. Hop in the shower. Our girl will be home soon enough."

WHEN THEY CROSSED the bridge, leaving behind Sunset Beach Island for the mainland, any hope Hank entertained of Charles Camphor inviting Gideon to join them faded. Charles drove west down Magnolia Avenue. Plantation-era mansions with azaleas past their bloom gave way to modern brick and frame houses, some that had seen better days. Charles took a narrow right down an unpaved lane with a row of shotgun shacks. The shacks were attached and laundry hung from clotheslines on the slanted front porches. Jerome Jenkins and his mother sat on the top step of their porch. Jerome Jenkins was the only black boy in Hank's grade at Sunset Beach School. All the kids knew Jerome was there on scholarship. The school had had difficulty recruiting minority students. It didn't help Jerome's situation much that he was heavy and came to school with deep-dish-pizza-style crud in his eyes and a fine film of what he called "ash" on his skin.

"Mr. Camphor," Jerome's mother said, coming toward the car in a printed housedress that Hank thought Charlotte Applewood would never wear. "'Round what time you think you'll bring Jerome here back home?"

"Tomorrow morning after breakfast, if that's okay, Mavis?" Charles said, adjusting his rearview mirror.

"I didn't pack no overnight clothes, Mr. Camphor."

Charles smiled. "You just gave us a reason to drop by some stores." Charles winked at Jerome. "What you say, Jerome?"

Jerome never looked Hank's father in the eyes, if he could help it. "That's fine, Mr. Camphor."

"Mavis, I'll get your boy back in one piece. Don't you worry now."

CHARLES ASKED JEROME where he wanted to eat and Jerome said he liked the Morrison's downtown. The franchise would eventually close its Historic District location and open a new one in the Southside mall. But in the summer of 1983, you could still grab a tray and go down the buffet line for a home-style breakfast, lunch, or dinner. Charles selected baked ham and a side dish of hush puppies and turnip greens. Hank and Jerome went for the fried chicken and thick, beanpole string beans with macaroni and cheese, which the cooks always managed to make just the right side of creamy. They were sitting in their booth sipping sweet tea when Gideon and his family made their way through the Sunday buffet line. Hank saw Gideon and jumped up instinctively, nearly capsizing his drink. He eased out of the booth to say hello, leaving his father alone with Jerome.

Jerome had a small triangle of Mexican cornbread in his mouth. He made a point of chewing before he spoke. That was the first thing Mavis would ask when he got home. *Did you chew before you spoke? Did you flush their toilet? Did you wash your hands? Did they try the freaky-deaky on you 'cause you know they like to freak?*

"What do you want to be when you grow up, Jerome?" asked Charles Camphor, casually.

"I like wires," Jerome said.

Charles nodded. "So you want to be an electrician, then?"

"Well, sir . . ." Jerome was thinking that he really wanted to eat his Mexican cornbread and leave off on the small talk.

"Jerome, you don't have to call me sir."

Jerome smiled. "I just like to stand sometimes and look at wires."

"Don't look at wires too long." Charles sipped his sweet tea. "You might stand under the wrong one and electrocute yourself. There's a lot of folks going to the electric chair these days. It's good you want to be an electrician."

Hank brought Gideon and his family over to their booth.

"I think we are neighbors," Reuben said.

"That we are." Charles did not stand up.

"Well, this is my wife, Charlotte, and our daughter Lauren, and our son Gideon."

"You have some other children, I'm told?" Charles asked.

"We have *twins*, Mr. Camphor. And they are at home with my aunt." Charlotte looked at her watch and directed Gideon and Lonnie toward an empty booth.

"Fine Sunday," Charles said. "Where you folk coming from?"

"We just finished church," said Reuben Applewood.

"Yes, there's many a good Baptist church around here."

"Thank you for the recommendation, but we're Catholic."

"I'm Methodist myself," Charles whispered. "But that's our dirty little secret." And then he grabbed Jerome's hand. "Did you meet Jerome here? Jerome here is Hank's best friend."

Hank looked at his father. He liked Jerome well enough, but best friend? His best friend was . . . He didn't really have a best friend.

Charles waited for his son to say something to confirm his close bond with Jerome, but Hank just stared off into space.

"Well, gentlemen," Reuben said. "It's been a pleasure." He gave Jerome a sailor's salute and tilted smoothly away from them.

When Hank sat down, Charles offered his son a hard stare.

"That girl," Jerome said, gesturing toward Lonnie Applewood in her tangerine summer dress. "She real pretty."

"Lauren?" Hank laughed and brushed Lonnie's birth name upside down with his tongue before running it across his lips. *"She sure is."*

"THIS IS HOW you tie a knot," said Charles, in and out, out and in. Jerome tried to pay attention, but the rocking motion of the sailboat on water had him desperately seasick.

Jerome fumbled with the knot and paused to consider the greatness of the ocean. He was glad he had on a life vest, for he could not swim. "That's a good job you're doing there, Jerome," Charles said. Four times it had taken Jerome to master the knot. But on the fourth try, his knot was perfect.

"Some more of those oyster crackers," Jerome said, rising and wobbling and wondering if the food he had eaten would come tumbling out of his stomach. The oyster crackers were supposed to help him with the motion sickness.

"Pop the wristband," Charles yelled.

"What, sir?"

"When you eat the crackers, pop the motion bands."

Hank was at the helm, steering the sailboat. Here was the thing about the ocean, no matter what problems Hank had or how mad he was, whenever he got on water, things dropped away and became food for the fish. His father came up alongside Hank and threw his arms around him.

"He's doing all right," Charles said.

They were heading back to shore and the wind was against them. Jerome moved around the boat holding on to whatever he could find, like someone at a roller-skating rink. Hank continued to steer the boat, the wind moving through his hair, and the water blue like he imagined the water to be on Turks and Caicos.

"Dad, I don't think Jerome likes sailing."

"He likes it just fine. Adjusting is all. A new experience."

"Why did you say he was my best friend?" Hank asked, trying to modulate his voice in a tone that was not disrespectful but that his father might hear. "I don't have a best friend."

Charles had played football at Clemson. He was a running back. He had pledged Phi Kappa Delta—and once a year attended a reunion with his old friends. Hank, this boy, was such a mystery. Charles had craved brothers as a child and run amok with neighbors and cousins, but Hank could make do with Barbara as his best friend. "That's not a thing you should be proud of," Charles said, his voice rising above the ocean. "You want to be some lonely dipshit jerking off in your bedroom? You'll never catch a good woman that way."

"You're an asshole," Hank blurted out. "Who are *your* friends, Dad?"

Hank's father tendered his face with a slap.

———

ON THE WAY to the boat, they had stopped by Parker's, the clothing store where Hank and Jerome were both fitted for their school uniforms. The salesclerk always left the hem long, and then a week before school, she'd call the clients to come in, make alterations, and measure how much the children had grown. Charles ordered three uniforms each for Hank and Jerome, pushing his American Express card toward the salesclerk. "You understand now that when Mavis comes in, she has good credit. Her credit is long."

Charles did this discreetly, so that neither Jerome nor Mavis had to say thank you. The same was true of the tuition payments. If Mavis fell short, there was a trust fund for Jerome Jenkins.

JEROME THREW UP as soon as they reached shore. Despite Charles's protestations, the boy asked to go home. If he had heard Hank and Charles's argument, Jerome was smart enough not to let on.

"Mr. Camphor," Jerome said, offering his hand to Charles before climbing the stairs to the shotgun shack. "Thank you. I'm hoping we can go sailing again."

"Anytime, son," Charles said. "That's the spirit."

Hank's senior year in college, Charles Pierre Camphor would die in a boating accident, and Jerome Jenkins would fly in from Denver, Colorado, to speak at his funeral. A successful manufacturer of high-end wire toys, Jerome would recall his first sailing adventure, and Charles Pierre Camphor's unwavering generosity toward him.

IN FRONT OF his dad, Hank wore the puffiness on his face like a badge of honor. *Wait until Mom sees the bruise*, he thought. *Just wait.* But on the day of her return, Barbara telephoned to say she had been detained in New York.

"What do you mean, 'detained'?"

"Well, I can't get a flight out of here," she said. "There was a layover in New York. We girls thought we might as well make a weekend of it. I can do some groundwork for our Christmas trip."

"Barb, I want you on the next plane home."

"That's not possible, Charles."

"Make it happen."

There was a pause on the phone. "I was offered a promotion."

"Where? In New York?"

"Of course not."

"Let's talk about it when you get home."

"You're not listening." Barbara breathed deeply into the phone. "I've accepted already, and now I'm going to take some time to network."

"Are you drinking?"

"Heavens, no."

It was the inhalation of a cigarette. *Heavens*, he thought. Such highfalutin language. "Barb, are you drunk?"

"We haven't worked out a job title yet, but, Charles, if I play my cards right, two years from now I'll be the Southeast executive director."

Charles laughed. "On whose authority?"

"Charles, I've been with the Red Cross for nearly four years. My background as a registered nurse made me a natural at disaster relief. I'm good at what I do. I thought you'd be happy for me."

Dead silence. "How many men did you blow, Barb? Which supervisor did you sleep with?"

On the other end, Barbara moved the phone away from her ear. She had met Charles when she was a teller at S&S Bank and he was fresh out of business school. Once they had started dating, she had transferred to a different bank to avoid tongues wagging. She understood that dating in a work environment always puts one party at a disadvantage. The money from her teller job went toward nursing school. Two years out of nursing school, she married Charles and worked at Saint Joseph's Hospital three years before having Hank. After Hank was born, she took close to a decade off before going to work for the Red Cross. It had been hell moving up the ladder after staying home for so many years. She hadn't been trusted to commit fully to her new job, but she had worked harder than some of the younger Red Cross nurses. With this new position, she would be required to deal with a different type of domestic disaster. There was this new disease. The virus. AIDS. There would be questionnaires and literature on delicate subjects, including sexual preferences. It wasn't what you said, in Barbara's opinion, but how you framed the question. She tried to reach through the telephone wires and connect with her husband by softening her voice. "And how are things going at home, Charles, darling? How's my boy?"

"Well, let's see," Charles said, looking toward the bedroom where Hank had mostly shut himself in for the past two days. "Great, Barb. Things are great."

THIS WAS THE first time Hank had stolen money from his father's wallet: twenty-five bucks from Charles's neatly folded wad of cash. Hank was extra careful to ease the money clip back on the same way he'd found it.

"At Star Castle, they have Donkey Kong, Centipede, and Pac-Man." Hank was standing in the Applewoods' kitchen, holding a bag of navel oranges.

"That's very nice of your mother," Charlotte Applewood said, accepting the oranges that Hank told her were a belated house-warming gift. "But this isn't necessary. She brought over a plate of potato salad our first night here. I've been meaning to ask her for the recipe. It was delicious."

Hank blushed with ignorance. He had cycled to the store and bought oranges. They were something he could afford and still have money to treat Gideon and Lonnie to an afternoon at the arcade.

"Mom, can I go?" asked Gideon.

"I don't know, Gideon. I just put the twins down for their nap."

"There's the Island Shuttle," Hank said. "It stops at the Island Center. It's a twenty-minute ride from there to Star Castle."

Lonnie peeked over her magazine. She was reading her mother's copy of *Mademoiselle*. "My," she said. "You've thought of everything."

Charlotte tossed her daughter a leave-him-alone look. Gideon was lacing his Chuck Taylors.

"It's noon. I expect you boys back here by five. Does that seem fair?"

"Yes, ma'am," Hank said.

Charlotte crossed to the kitchen counter and unearthed some cash from the bottom of her handbag. "In case you come up short."

She kissed Gideon on the forehead and reached out to touch Hank's cheek. "A boo-boo?"

"He's not a baby, Mom," Gideon said. "Boo-boos are for babies."

"Well, Gideon, you'll always be my babies. All of you."

"Sailing accident," Hank said. He hesitated before going over to Lonnie. Tipper dozed on the ground next to her high chair. Hank reached down to pet Tipper, trying not to let himself become overly distracted by the sight of Lonnie's long legs.

"You coming?" he asked.

Lonnie stared down at Hank. "I've outgrown the arcade." Hank was crestfallen but tried not to show it. Lonnie slipped down from the chair and sat on the kitchen floor. They patted Tipper together in silence. This was the most she'd ever said to Hank Camphor. The closest Lauren Applewood and Hank would ever sit.

"Thank you for asking, though," she said. Lonnie reached over and touched Hank's face dramatically. "Try Tylenol, dear boy."

HANK AND GIDEON lost track of time at Star Castle that day. Maybe it was the red lights pitched so brightly against the dark. Or the other kids. And their laughter. Hank laughed so much his stomach hurt. It didn't even matter that he was losing. Lonnie Applewood had flirted with him, hadn't she? Placed her perfect fingers on his face. He couldn't help but believe that somewhere in her heart, Lonnie had feelings for him. Hank replayed the scene over in his head and it gave him a wicked adrenaline rush. One minute he and Gideon were taking turns chasing pellets with Pac-Man. The next minute they were slobbering down Fresca, stale popcorn, and hot dogs. Gideon ordered hot dogs with canned chili. "The poor man's version of chili con carne."

"Why poor?" Hank said.

"*Consider*, the meager helping of meat, the beans smashed together like a hash, the aroma of dog food instead of cilantro and cinnamon."

"I see you're had a lot of time to think about this, Gideon."

"Yo-yo-yo, you trying to say something?"

"Yo-yo-yo, maybe."

During the summer of 1983, there was a heat wave in Buckner County. The cool dampness of the arcade with its central air-conditioning unit was a haven for nerdy kids with nothing to do. The darkness blurred racial lines easily.

"I wish your sister had come," Hank said.

"Man." Gideon shook his head. "Can't you just hang with me? Lonnie's out of your league. Anyway, she has a boyfriend. Back in Cleveland."

"Is it—serious?"

Gideon turned away from Hank. "Donkey Kong."

"Gideon, come on, I need to know."

"So, Hank," Gideon said. "How come you never invite me over to your house?"

Hank stalled in front of Donkey Kong. "It just—never came up."

"Huh," Gideon said.

"Maybe when my mom is back in town."

"Okie-doke." Gideon smiled. "Lonnie and her beau. They've done the deed. I walked in on them once."

Hank closed his eyes. "I don't believe you."

"We're even," Gideon said, after a pause. "I don't believe you'll have me over either."

Hank and Gideon missed the six o'clock Island Shuttle and had to rely on the city bus to get home. The city bus made a serpentine crawl through what felt like every poor neighborhood in the county. By the time the boys arrived on their respective doorsteps, it was half past nine and the sun had turned its back on the island. Gideon's mother was waiting on the front porch. Hank stood on the sidewalk as Charlotte Applewood admonished and hugged Gideon. *Are you out of your mind? I almost called your father.*

The whole bus ride home the two friends had sat in silence. Hank could not refute Gideon's claim. Gideon neglected to say good-bye when they parted ways.

"WHERE WERE YOU, SON?" Charles Camphor was in the living room. The decanter next to his glass was empty.

"At the arcade."

"That woman. Your friend's mom. She came over here. You boys put the worry in her."

"Her name's Mrs. Applewood. Charlotte."

"Well, *Charlotte* wasn't a happy camper."

Hank went into his room and shut his door.

"You took money out of my wallet, Hank." Charles followed Hank to his bedroom door.

"Borrowed. I borrowed it," said Hank. He locked the door to his room. "I'll pay you back when Mom gets home. Out of my allowance."

"Why do you have to be such a little shit?"

Outside there was a crescent moon, and Tipper was howling.

"I honestly don't know," said Hank.

Charles leaned his forehead on the bedroom door. "When I was your age, my parents didn't have to stay up on me like this. I had to hold up my end of the burlap sack and fill it with whatever I could get. Sometimes, Big Seamus and I, we'd take my old BB gun and go hunting rabbits, squirrels, and opossum. And my mother would gather up some dandelion greens and cook up a stew. Other times she'd stretch out meals with grits. Boiled grits. Fried grits. Baked grits with molasses, for dripping. She had grits for every season. Polenta, they call it in restaurants now. But it was just grits to us, Hank."

Hank opened his bedroom door. "I want a basset hound."

"What?" Charles looked confused.

"Like Lonnie and Gideon."

"No."

"They're a good breed: basset hounds."

"That's a matter of opinion."

"And gentle. The brochures say they're gentle with kids."

"Okay, so here's what we'll do. We'll find some common ground. There's bound to be a dog that our family will be happy with."

"Family?" Hank laughed. "What family?"

"Keep it in bounds, son."

"You're not my family."

"Since when?"

"Mom can't even stand to be here."

"Your mother's a modern woman. And God knows it scares me, but I love her for it, Hank."

"Well, I want a basset hound."

"Not happening."

"And a different family. Like the family next door." Hank crossed his arms. "I want a family that's brown."

"What are you going to do when you get 'em, Hank? You think their life's perfect? You think they don't have their own storehouse of shit?"

"I think, I think"—Hank made a display of exerting brain-power—"they rise above it somehow. It's easy—easier—when you have a midget dog for—ha—*comic relief* and a mom who notices your swollen face and a sister your new friend wants to kiss and a dad who works all the time but when he comes home doesn't slap you in the face or say to his wife, 'Darling, who did you screw today. How was that blow job?'" Hank stomped. "So, give me a basset hound and a house full of brown people to live with. I don't care about your burlap sack full of grits."

Charles dropped his whiskey glass, and Hank threw up his hands reflexively to ward off the coming blow.

Charles stared down at the broken glass and, making no effort to pick it up, backed away from Hank's bedroom and moved deliberately toward the front door. On his way out the door, Charles

Camphor pulled a golf club from his brand-new case. He lifted the wooden staff in the air and gave a good long whistle as he practiced his aim. Hank followed his father into the front yard, but at a safe distance. He watched his father practice his aim, blowing off steam.

Outside, Tipper had given up his yodeling and baying. When he saw Charles and Hank, Tipper ran toward Hank, wagging his tail. Hank started to brush past, no, to *move and insert himself in front* of his father then, but Charles grabbed Hank by his shirt collar and pushed him aside. Hank went tumbling down on the grass as Charles raised his golf club and broke it over Tipper's back with one glancing blow. The impact came as such a shock to the dog that it neither yelped nor whimpered. Hank would later convince himself Tipper hadn't had time to feel a thing. Of course, this wasn't true. One second Tipper was full of life and breath and air. And the next, he lay limp on the ground.

"Well, Hank," Charles said, lowering the staff and staggering back toward the house. "Bury your dead."

Hank sat on the grass next to Tipper's body and howled.

BARBARA CAMPHOR STEPPED out of a taxicab two hours later and noticed that all the lights were on in the Camphor house. She found Charles fast asleep on the living room sofa. She noticed the broken glass in the hallway next to Hank's bedroom. She searched the rooms of the house and when she could not find her son or wake Charles, she went outside and searched the part of their backyard that abutted the marsh. Hank was there digging in the moonlight. To his left was a small mound of dirt. Barbara hurried over to her son and looked into the hole he was digging. Barbara held her breath and faltered momentarily. She took the shovel away from Hank.

"No."

"Dad broke Tipper's back."

"Hush."

"He's a bad man, Mom."

"Who?" Barbara spun around.

"Dad." Hank muttered. "Why does he hate them?"

Barbara stared past Hank toward the neighbors' house. "Your father grew up hard, Hank. It'll take two lifetimes to rub the hardness off him. We only get one."

Hank shook his head. "You didn't see—"

"Tell me later, Hank. I can't stomach it right now," Barbara said. She motioned Hank away, but he didn't budge, as she rolled up the sleeves of her green silk blouse. A recent gift from a man she had been seeing for over a decade. A married man, James Samuel Vincent, whom she'd seen recently in New York City. They had both agreed their love affair was through. Barbara started digging. "I'll take over from here."

LATER THAT NIGHT Reuben Applewood stepped outside in his pajamas and slippers, allowed himself a few leisurely puffs on his Cuban cigar, and turned on his flashlight. This was Tipper's cue to show Reuben where he'd done his business, so that Reuben could retire for the evening and the dog could come in. But instead of Tipper, every firefly in the neighborhood seemed to dance around him. The nocturnal chorus of marsh life was in full swing. Reuben Applewood was neither a superstitious man nor without mother wit. When on his third try, Tipper did not respond to his call, Reuben muttered under his breath: *These shady motherfuckers have killed my children's pet.* He began to construct the narrative that he and Charlotte would replay for their kids. For they were still of an age where certain truths could break them. And he would never permit this to happen. *Choose your ocean. Choose your ocean. Choose your ocean.*

IT WAS HANK'S honest intention to find Lonnie and Gideon another dog, but then his mother surprised him by staying put until August when she attended a Red Cross convention in Los Angeles. She returned with a preponderance of gifts. In her super-sized duffel bags were mini corn tortillas from a Mexican food shop, towels from Venice Beach printed with images of palm trees, flip-flops, and beach bum surfers. She had a trio of autographed Dodger jerseys in small, medium, and large. And for Hank, specifically, an autographed baseball with signatures from the entire Los Angeles Dodgers team, who had kindly treated the Red Cross delegates to a complimentary game at Dodger Stadium. Charles's gift was an elegant pair of gold-plated golf markers, monogrammed with the initials *C.C.* Charles blanched when he opened them. "Maybe I'll take up running," he said.

After the convention, Barbara stuck close to home with Hank and Charles, and the Camphor house was peaceful and quiet. There was boating and detailed plans for the Christmas trip to New York City, and Barbara Camphor convinced her son to join Charles on his runs, and running was a good thing because Hank begrudgingly, which is to say, over time, met other kids who liked to run— kids like him—with similar interests.

GIDEON APPLEWOOD'S NOTEBOOK ON FRIENDSHIP

Me: Dad thinks Tipper ran away.
Hank: I'm sorry.
Me: My sister thinks he tried to go back to Cleveland.
Hank: Has he run away before?
Me: Never.
Hank: Gideon . . . Well, I guess there's a first time for everything.
Me: I think a car got him.
Hank: I bet you're right.
Me: I keep expecting to see Tipper on the road, but Lonnie says stare straight and look ahead.

(P.S. Hank doesn't ask about Lonnie anymore. Hank ALWAYS asks about Lonnie. I smashed my Rubik's Cube tonight.)

THE MOVING MAN STANDS STILL

1971

HOME /HŌM/ *NOUN*

- the place where one lives permanently, especially as a member of a family or household.
- an institution for people needing professional care or supervision.
- the goal or end point.

JEBEDIAH APPLEWOOD HAD NOT HAD A HARD-ON IN ninety-two days. He had fucked one hundred sixty-three women in Vietnam, a modest number by some estimates. There were some soldiers who had fucked twice that number in half the time. Jeb was a devout list keeper and documented his exaltations, not to brag or boast but because occasionally his head got foggy and he couldn't always keep track of time. He had been taking a cocktail of medicine for venereal diseases—chancroid, gonorrhea, and chlamydia. Jeb had managed somehow to avoid herpes and syphilis. In this way, he thought his mother's and aunties' good prayers had interceded on his behalf.

———

SOMETIMES HE WOKE up in the middle of the night in a cold sweat and examined his body the way an anxious parent examines a newborn baby. The pieces were all intact, but Jeb was certain some vital part of him was slipping away. He installed a love altar on his bedroom mantelpiece, unfurled a swath of purple velvet there and adorned it with movie posters of Pam Grier and Brenda Sykes and Vonetta McGee. He framed his altar with frosted acrylic beads and sandalwood incense and thick red wax candles in homage to his foxy brown sisters. Jebediah was twenty-four years old. He would sit on his bed and study Vonetta's, Pam's, and Brenda's faces intently—*such lovely, lovely faces*—before stepping back for a fuller view of their magnificent Afros, asses, and tits. Then Jeb would sink to his knees and ask these goddesses to release him from nightly dreams of drowning and death.

JEB'S MOTHER AND his aunt Flora prepared a feast to welcome him back to Buckner County, Georgia: a buffet of soul food in the house of his youth. Jeb looked at the platters of good things and knew he would find no satisfaction in them, but he picked up a paper plate and fork and ate not just one serving but two, so that his mother's friends would not have their dishes or time offended. He did not want to hurt the congregation of church women who had helped to raise him, protecting him like hawks protect their young. Jeb noticed that they all referred to his time in the Navy as *off* or *over there*. They never said *Vietnam*.

Ruby Dennis brought her potato salad made with celery pressed in a mortar because the juice cut down the need for heavy mayonnaise. Martha brought her fried chicken dipped in cold water and barely dusted with flour, so that the meat was tender on the inside and the skin was crispy on the outside. Lullabelle made smothered shrimp with whole peppercorns and creamy grits. Stella cooked red rice with bell peppers and stewed tomatoes and andouille sausage. Josephine baked macaroni and cheese in a trio of colors, expensive Gouda, cheddar, and Edam cheeses she could not afford; at the end of every month she had to borrow money from family and friends.

———

DURING HIS TOUR, he had seen prostitutes catch Ping-Pong balls with their vaginas, enticing soldiers to ferret them out for entertainment. Bars where only white soldiers gathered and bars that catered exclusively to black military men. There had been brothels devoted to every kind of debauchery a soul could imagine. And drugs to stoke those imaginings with. The women in Subic Bay—and later, Bangkok—had expected nothing of Jeb. Not even friendship. He could cross the bridge to Olongapo City for an hour or two, fuck them silly, and forget that he was killing their Asian brothers. Sex, how good it felt, *sex*, when he could still feel sex. You could occupy a country with guns and sex. Open your wallet. Pull out a five, ten, a little extra when you're black. And know that the women had seen enough to welcome you and expect nothing. But in Buckner County—his mother and aunties and, Sweet Lord Jesus, the girlfriends they were itching to set him up with, didn't they know he had nothing to give? *Yes, you've been over there. But now you're back here.* Sometimes Jeb pinched himself. He wasn't convinced. Sometimes he stared down between his legs and nothing was stirring. It struck him suddenly that in Buckner County there were not many men. He felt the sharp absence of uncles and cousins. When had this happened? He walked around downtown and saw that a lot of the brothers were idling and broken. Or missing. His first cousin Reuben Applewood had encouraged him to enlist in the Navy. *There are not many of us in this branch of the military*, Reuben had written, crouched over his bunk bed on the USS *New Jersey*. *When the draft comes, you will have no say. You will be a grunt on the front lines. You will be infantry.* All around him, Jeb saw women and children and old men.

LET'S GO FISHING, the handful of old men Jeb knew would say. He would reel in a croaker, take one look at its eyes, and unhook it. The old men said: *Jeb, let's go bowling*, and Jeb would slip two fingers into the hole of a glazed ball and watch the ball go hurtling down the long lane. When the ball made contact with the pins—*strike*—

there would be such a sound—an explosion?—and Jeb would duck and squint and up the lane would swim Chief Mammoth, spitting up water like he had done when Jeb and Eddie Christie threw him overboard the USS *Olympus*. That ended it for bowling.

Jeb considered calling Eddie in the Bronx but talked himself out of it. In Nam, Eddie had nearly lost his shit. He had pushed Eddie to do something they both regretted. Now Eddie's head was back on straight, and Jeb didn't want to do, or say, anything that might loosen his screws again. *Deal*, Jeb told himself. He'd just have to deal.

"JEBEDIAH," HIS MOTHER asked. "Would you like to join us at church?" Jeb said no, but he gave his mother and Aunt Flora a ride to St. Paul's of the Redemption Catholic Church and then went to the movies. He saw *Dirty Harry*, *The Last Picture Show*, *The French Connection*, and *Willy Wonka and the Chocolate Factory*.

JEB WENT TO the veterans' clinic, thinking a doctor might prescribe medication for his insomnia. In the waiting room, a gaunt soldier with a strikingly bald head—Jeb thought of the bowling alley—started to freak out over the volume of paperwork the staff had placed on a clipboard for him to fill out. *I will wipe the slate clean*, the soldier muttered. In these words, Jeb heard no immediate threat, but a security alarm sounded. Attendants came with straps and restraints and carted the soldier off. Jebediah backed out of the clinic and went two blocks away to buy some marijuana. He slept soundly for two days straight.

HE WAS NOT someone to linger inside indefinitely, so after three months of moseying, he pruned the oak tree in his mother's backyard because he didn't want the folks from the city to do it. Sometimes they cut down whole trees in black people's yards. Jeb climbed the oak tree and avoided the lice in the Spanish moss. He tightened the leaking pipes under the kitchen sink and caulked the roof and cleaned the gutters and put a new drain in the garden so that water would not gather and flood the laundry room. He varnished the floors, and laid new mats under the oriental carpets, so as not to stain the original chestnut floors, and he polished the stairway and swept the chimney and put wood in the fireplace and bought new screens for the windows and he took down the vinyl siding on the Craftsman house, despite his mother's complaint that the vinyl siding was cheap and the wood would only rot from the humidity. Jeb could not tell her why the vinyl depressed him, so he said: *I will paint the house yellow.* Both his mother and Aunt Flora liked the idea of a yellow house.

BY THE TIME the house was done in mid-November, restlessness stirred in Jeb again but the insomnia was gone. He went to Sears and bought two long-sleeve white shirts, two short-sleeve white shirts, two pairs of navy shorts, two pairs of khaki pants, and a blue jacket and a pair of brown suede loafers from Thom's Shoe Store on Main Street. He wore the khaki pants and white shirt to visit the local all-black university. He hoped to attend college on the GI Bill in the spring. As he strolled around the nineteenth-century campus, which was surrounded by bluegrass and salt marsh, it did his heart good to see young brothers and sisters engaged in conversation. *All the young people are here.* For about five minutes, he caught the youthful vibe too and strutted about nonchalantly thinking that at twenty-four, he was still young and had every right to be happy.

Jeb was in good spirits on the elevator ride up to the admissions office, but when the doors opened, ambivalence stepped out with him. Happy? Was this a joke? *Happy?* He posed the question to the guidance counselor. How can I possibly be happy when there is a war going on? The guidance counselor told Jeb that happiness was an existential question. Perfect for Philosophy 101. In Nietzsche, he said, you might find a kindred spirit. Jeb, once he understood the general drift of Nietzsche's worldview, told the guidance counselor that it wouldn't do him the least damn bit of good to sit in a classroom full of happy people discussing the meaning of nothingness.

Well then, let's start with your field of expertise, said the guidance counselor. What are your interests?

Jeb said: I know a thing about bodies of water. But he did not say how water fills the lungs. Stamps out your oxygen. Plugs up your nostrils and ears. He did not describe the fight a drowning body gives. When the water assaults a human body, the body wants to return the favor and assault the water back. Sometimes, drowning men tear muscles on the way under before they lose consciousness.

I like water sports, Jeb said.

The guidance counselor was impressed. He leaned over his desk. Brother, just between the two of us, given how clean our people are and how much we delight in bathing ourselves—don't you ever wonder why most of us can't swim?

Jeb had noticed since he returned from the war that people were short-circuiting. They talked, but seldom listened. No, he said. I have no opinion.

The guidance counselor relaxed once more into the seat behind his desk: Every group has got its bogeyman. The Middle Passage, that's our bogeyman. Why don't we put you down for physical education? You can start with a swimming refresher. You're a Vietnam vet, yes? Swimming is a great way to reduce stress.

Jeb decided he was not ready for college just yet. He checked the back of the *Penny Saver*. There was an opening for "An On-the-Go Type" moving man at Axelrod Movers. Jeb drove to the Southside, where the moving company was located. After a five-minute interview with the owner, Jeb received his first long-distance assignment. His driving partner would be Big Seamus Camphor, a fellow vet and former sergeant in the U.S. Army. They were to transport

furniture from Memphis to Boston and then make a final drop-off
in Portsmouth, New Hampshire.

BIG SEAMUS CAMPHOR was about as burly as a white man could
get. He said he was between jobs and desperate for money. Jeb sidled into the passenger seat of the moving truck and let Seamus
have the keys. It seemed, based on first impression, the tactful way
to go.

Big Seamus was a talker and his talk veered straight to hunting.
Hunting was a sport Jeb happened to know a thing or two about
from the days when he and his cousins would go out in search of the
pigeons the French called squab. Seamus perked up when he heard
this. Both men agreed that squirrel tasted more than fine on a grill.

Big Seamus recounted a recent lunch with his cousin Charles
Camphor: *Twelve dollars for the saddest plate of shrimp and grits I ever
did see. Afterward, we're walking in the park and the damn park's run
amok with brazen squirrels that dared to stand on their hind legs like
they expected me to give them acorns. And Charles was laughing. "Seamus, aren't they cute?" That just about did me in. "What's cute about
them?" I said. "If only I had my old BB gun. Come here, little squirrels."
But Charles walked ahead of me and said: "You oughtn't to eat squirrels anymore, Seamus. And you damn sure oughtn't to tell people I ate
them."*

I still shoot squirrels when no one's looking, Seamus confided
to Jeb. And possum. And rabbits. And turtles. God wouldn't have
given men guns if he didn't intend for us to use them. But I aim my
gun at moving targets. I won't shoot anything that stands still.

JEB LEARNED QUICKLY that his coworker did not have much love
for large cities or highways. If time had been theirs to grasp, Seamus told Jeb, they would do better taking the scenic route. Jeb was
glad that time was not theirs. Small Southern towns did not inspire
curiosity or affection in Jeb.

Marriage troubles, Big Seamus said to Jeb an hour into their
drive: I need to get away from my woman.

In truth, fire was what Big Seamus Camphor was running from. During a candle-spawned house fire a mile shy of town, he had sat down on a little boy's bedroom floor to bow before the flames. Seamus did not like fires, had spent his life fighting fires, but after his time in Nam, he could no longer be a good fireman.

IT WAS UNDERSTOOD that Jeb and Big Seamus would not share a hotel room when they reached Memphis, even though in 1971 the option was readily available to them. They parked the moving truck at a prearranged storage site and agreed to meet up at noon the next day for their one p.m. pickup. Big Seamus had a buddy from Nam he wanted to check up on. He would sleep over at his friend's place, and use his per diem to fatten his meager wallet. Jeb took out the *Green Book* his aunt Flora had coaxed onto his lap and roamed its pages until he came across the name Myrtle Hendricks of Memphis, Tennessee.

MYRTLE HENDRICKS LIVED in the Orange Mound section of Memphis, in an all-black neighborhood said to be the oldest in the country. Myrtle's white frame house had belonged to her parents. During Jim Crow, the house had sometimes doubled as a B&B or, when desperate times called for desperate measures, a long-term occupancy.

She cracked open the screen door so that Jeb caught one brown eye.

Traveler? Myrtle asked.

Traveling through, Jeb said.

Through to where? She opened the door a tad more. There was nothing extraordinary about Myrtle Hendricks, at first. Her legs were too thin, her hair was too kinky, and Myrtle did not wear lipstick to suggest exotic places, promises, or possibilities.

Right now, to Boston and New Hampshire. Who knows, after that?

Jeb had on a one-piece denim moving-man jumper that made him feel like a little kid in a long-sleeved romper. Myrtle looked him up and down. He could see her wagering the cost of letting him rent for a night versus the cost of telling him to go his own way.

It's fifteen dollars for the night and that includes breakfast, she said.

JEB TOOK OFF his moving uniform and laid it out on the full-sized wrought-iron bed with its polyester spread. He began to unpack the handful of clothes he had brought with him. Everything about the room said *Don't get comfortable here*, especially the spread. Jeb was a man accustomed to quilts. The lack of one made him long for his own bed in Georgia. His aunt Flora had promised Jeb that his room would go undisturbed. Jeb could not know the joy that his altar of chocolate nudity gave his aunt Flora, who was a first-class lesbian born too early in the game to live her life openly.

Myrtle asked Jeb if he had any clothes he needed starched, ironed, or pressed for the clubs. He told her he wasn't in town for music. Or clubs.

This is the home of the blues, she said. Beale Street. Stax Records. Seems like you'd want to hear *something* while you're here?

Jeb announced where his heart and mind tilted: the Lorraine Motel.

Why you want to go there? Myrtle said. She had noticed Jeb's disdain for his bedspread and brought him a better one.

I want to see, Jeb said.

Seems to me like anything there is to be seen was seen before James Earl Ray pointed that rifle. You coming after the fact.

Jeb thanked her for the spread. She watched as he unmade and remade the bed in a manner that suggested military training.

It's amazing to me, he said: that no one torched this whole city.

How you know people didn't try? We tried.

I just want to have a look at the place for myself.

It could be a rumor. Rumors abound, sighed Myrtle: But I heard some folks dipped handkerchiefs into his blood. Lord help me. The things that people do: bloody handkerchiefs as souvenirs from a King.

They're called trophies, Mrs. Hendricks.

Don't you do that, Mr. Applewood. Don't you call me Mrs. Hendricks.

Jeb noticed that she kept her pink terry-cloth bathrobe closed tight.

Early the next morning before Jeb had to report to work, he went walking down South Main toward the Lorraine Motel and caught sight of Myrtle Hendricks walking north on the same sidewalk. He

did not recognize her at first without the pink robe. Her kinky hair had been picked into a sassy little Afro with an autumn rose on one side and she wore an elegant jade dress and taupe pumps and carried a matching taupe handbag. As she strolled past, she smiled and said, Good morning, and Jeb thought, My God her teeth are white and her eyes are bright and he turned but Myrtle had already disappeared around the corner.

HE STOOD OUTSIDE the Lorraine Motel and wept. He was certain he would be the only one, but there were other travelers who, three years after King's death, had made the journey. The motel had fallen into disrepair since its heyday, when it was a destination for musicians who wanted a comfortable place to rest their heads after long recording sessions at Stax or performances on Beale Street, and other well-heeled clientele who appreciated the amenities offered by Lorraine (the hotel's namesake) and her husband, Walter. The neighborhood surrounding the motel was its own sad affair, made sadder by the history and hope that had preceded it. On the second floor, encased in glass, sat the balcony with the green door to room 306. Some of the travelers would go home and play the number 306 forward, backward, and inverted. Some would have good luck. Most wouldn't. A few would splurge for wreaths and send them to keep company with the other flowers, real and artificial, visitors left there. Jebediah stood on the cracked sidewalk and corkscrewed his body in a northerly direction. His fellow travelers twisted their bodies in sync with his. This was their pilgrimage, and as such, they reenacted in their heads and some in their gestures the final moments of King's life. Someone asked where the bullet had come from and someone else whispered that James Earl Ray's bullet exploded from a north-facing window in the boarded up rooming house across the street from the hotel. North was the direction of freedom, *wasn't it?* Jeb's face became a sponge, sopping wet. He stood there, falling, falling, falling to pieces and thought of naval ships on the China Sea. How below deck in his bunk his ears sometimes farted and popped. And how once he had looked out one of the ship's many portholes and seen a gigantic squid and there was Chief Petty Officer Nelson Mammoth bouncing from the squid's tentacles like a trapeze artist in a circus act. That night he had torn the list of THINGS JEB DOESN'T NEED TO KNOW from his bunk wall. He had ripped the list into confetti threads. But the next day, the list was there again. Rewritten in Eddie Christie's neat handwriting. Eddie knew the list by heart. Maybe that was what it meant to be cousins, brothers—friends? Jeb wept for Dr. King all over again.

DURING HER LUNCH HOUR, Myrtle rescued Jeb from the sidewalk of the Lorraine Motel. She worked the cologne and cosmetics counters at one of the large department stores in downtown Memphis. The position was just fine by her, though she always removed the makeup from her face when she arrived home. Some women went for Pond's and others splurged on expensive products. Myrtle used witch hazel to clean and olive oil to moisturize. Her position as a counter girl was an accomplishment because she was not fair and there had been interviews and meetings and it had been decided that a light-skinned black woman, while more physically pleasing, might prove too much of a distraction for the white men who sometimes came to buy cologne for their wives or alternately too threatening for the white women to whom they might even be related.

Why'd they have to do it? Jeb asked Myrtle: Why'd they have to kill him? Myrtle took Jeb by the arm and led him away.

SHE KNEW HE would go to the Lorraine Motel before he opened his mouth. Sometimes they swore it wasn't on their mind, but their feet would lead them there anyway. Jeb was not the first one she had found trembling on the sidewalk like a leaf. When the men came with that look, Myrtle always told herself that she would turn them away. *You think there's only death in Memphis, death is everywhere*, she wanted to say, but something in her, or them, always changed her mind. The men might end up locked up or in a hospital, hurt because someone didn't understand the nature of their wounds. They all had wounds.

She told Jeb this while setting his bath. She told him this as she poured Epsom salts: I'm sorry but I'm going to have to charge you for the salt.

She told him this when she closed the door to the bathroom and left a chair for him to sit on and deposit his clothes. She told him this an hour later when he emerged from his bath buck naked, having forgotten his towel, and Myrtle screamed, thinking he had come to force himself on her. And the scream startled Jeb into an erection. And he covered himself and said: Myrtle, it's not like that.

And she had retreated into the living room with the plastic wrapped tight over the burgundy love seat and sat down to light a cigarette. Jeb had not guessed she smoked. He had not smelled smoke on her.

He dressed himself quickly and offered to leave.

Myrtle made a dinner of Salisbury steak with canned mixed vegetables and powdered mashed potatoes.

I'm sorry, she said. I'm not a cook. And I don't have children. Two things my husband saw fit to leave me for. *What kind of woman are you?* he said. *You can't cook. You can't bring no babies into this world.* I'm Hannah, I told him. I'm Sarah.

She cooked while smoking cigarettes. Ashes fell into the pot. Jeb wondered if nicotine would enhance the food's flavor.

That's three strikes against you, he said to me. *You quote the Bible. And everybody knows Bible-quoting women can't fuck*. Now, who do you think told him that? Myrtle asked Jeb.

I don't know.

Tell me something: do you know anything?

Jeb knew when somebody wanted an argument out of him: I know I was supposed to report to work two hours ago.

LATER, IN BED, Jeb would draw dove-shaped loop-de-loops around Myrtle's small perky breasts. She would giggle and slap his hands away.

Myrtle, he would whisper, pulling her close to him: That husband of yours was a fool. I'll be more than sad to go.

Down at the department store, everyone knows when someone's uprooting round here, she said. What's the address of the person you're moving again? I like your company, but honest work's not easy to come by these days.

JEB WATCHED NANCY VINCENT open a small oval container of China Blue eye shadow. Myrtle had given it to him to take as a peace offering. Nancy used the application pad to rub a liberal amount onto her eyelids in her dining room. She told Jeb and Seamus that she wanted the Colonial-era dining room table and chairs that belonged to her ex-husband dropped off in Boston on the way to her new home in Portsmouth, New Hampshire. Her soon-to-be-ex-husband was now living in Boston after losing his job as a fire captain in Huntington and, more recently, here in Memphis. There was always something with Jimmy Sr. She had stayed put to sell the house, but now she was homesick for the East Coast.

There wasn't much for Jeb to do. Seamus had packed the entire house on his own. They busied themselves trekking from room to room in Nancy's bungalow, carrying out everything she owned.

I didn't mean to leave you stranded, Jeb said.

Seamus shrugged. Where you been?

I had some business I had to take care of.

Well, it must feel *nice* to be the keeper of your own time.

Jeb didn't want any stuff. Not when he was in a good mood.

Take my pay for the work you did without me, Jeb said: Last night's per diem too. That way we're even.

Aren't you generous? Seamus laughed. His eyes were bloodshot. Seamus had been down on Beale Street partying all night with his friend. He nudged Jeb: Look at you, coming in here with pussy written all over you.

During his tour, Jeb wouldn't have blinked twice at Seamus's choice of words. He had been low-down and dirty with the best of them. But since coming home to his mother's house he'd had to brush his teeth and his tongue.

I did all right, he said.

Seamus winked. That makes two of us.

WHEN JEB AND SEAMUS were done packing up the fringes of her life, Nancy Vincent picked up her Samsonite suitcase and sailed out the door.

Well, she said, applying bright red lipstick to contrast the blue eye shadow, and climbing into a pink Cadillac that could hold half a dozen men: We move in circles in this life. I'll see you in Portsmouth. Try to get my belongings and yourselves there in one piece.

Seamus commented when Nancy drove off that she was damn well preserved for an old chick. He had returned home from Nam and his wife's tits were sagging like day-after party balloons. And he couldn't help but wonder why she had not maintained herself better and how her body could go to hell without giving him the first son. Jeb listened but made no comment because he knew that to comment on a white woman's beauty might arouse discomfiting thoughts in Seamus's head that Seamus might hold him accountable for later. They had 1364.7 miles ahead of them on the drive to Portsmouth, New Hampshire.

———

THEY STOPPED IN front of a truck stop in rural Ohio. Seamus took out a bong and lit it. He wanted to sleep right there in the truck and save money on a motel room. Jeb didn't feel cool sleeping on anybody's side road or out in anybody's elements. There was a nip in the night air. It was close to Thanksgiving.

Jeb and Seamus's recreational drug of choice was marijuana, though neither man would turn down mushrooms, amphetamines, or barbiturates. They climbed into the back of the moving truck, so as not to draw attention to themselves, and took turns inhaling. After a few tokes, Seamus started laughing and Jeb wanted to laugh but no laughter would escape him because he was too busy scratching and itching. Jeb, Seamus said: Either there's some critters in here or you've got the cooties.

But even before Seamus finished his sentence, he also began to itch and scratch. They rose, searching the truck for the source of their troubles. (Seamus would later identify the culprit as the upholstery cleaner used to disinfect the moving truck.) But just then, at that moment, darkness overtook them. The Colonial-era dining room furniture that had belonged to an aunt of Jimmy Vincent Sr.'s from Cabot, Maine, began to weep for the woman Nancy who polished it with lemon oil every Sunday morning. The dining room chairs began to buckle under the weight of the dining room table's tears and Seamus said: What kind of shit is this?

Jeb, who sometimes saw the ghost of one dead man, did not question if furniture could talk but threw open the moving truck's door and rolled onto the gravel like a dog trying to rub off fleas. The fresh air cleared Jeb's head instantly and he lay on the ground taking in long whiffs of oxygen. Above him, the sky opened and he could see not just the world but the universe stretched out before him and he wanted to laugh and he wanted to sing and he wanted to go running in the desert because his heart told him that Myrtle Hendricks was waiting to love him there.

We strung-out, Jeb yelled to Seamus, who stumbled from the back of the truck and was now up front, rummaging through the glove compartment.

The Colonial-era dining room table and the four Colonial chairs burst out of the Axelrod moving truck and took off. Seamus looked at Jeb and Jeb looked at Seamus and Seamus started to run because he wanted to bring the furniture back. Jeb stood up and small pebbles fell away from him. He chased after Seamus. It took longer than he expected to catch up to the burly vet.

Seamus, Jeb said as he continued to scratch himself: They got rattlesnakes and scorpions out here in this motherfucker. There's probably coyotes out here too.

Seamus removed a gun from his uniform. It was a .357 Magnum, the first investment Seamus had made upon returning to the United States. Unemployment was at an all-time high—everywhere. And Seamus could no longer combat fires. If a fireman couldn't combat fire, then the world was surely a dangerous place.

Seamus waved his gun in Jebediah Applewood's face: I'm not afraid of *them*. They got questions. I got answers.

Jeb put his hands up and backed away. Seamus, he said, in a voice that was not quite his: Put that motherfucking gun down. You're high as hell.

I have done some of my best hunting with dope in my system. That damn furniture better come back here.

Seamus began to shoot at the furniture flying above his head. He disappeared into the darkness, removing his uniform as he ran. Jeb watched Seamus's crazy ass flap in the wind.

Reason. Jeb reasoned that it would not look good if the cops showed up and found Seamus Camphor running in the opposite direction from him. *Reason.* Jeb reasoned that if he left Seamus to perish in the desert, foul play would be assumed and he would be the prime suspect. And so, for the second time that evening, he caught up with Seamus, who had run out of ammunition.

Jeb remembered his uncle telling him there was no such thing as a dirty fight if you were losing. Jeb tendered a vicious kick to Seamus's Achilles tendon. When the big man fell, his gun fell with him. At which point Jeb seized the weapon and knocked Seamus out cold. He lay down and fell fast asleep by Seamus's side.

There is no desert on the drive from Memphis to Portsmouth, but this is how tall tales are told. How fiction becomes fact and false memories become legend.

IN NOVEMBER 1971, Jeb and Seamus listened to these songs on the radio as they drove into Boston.

> The Carpenters, "Superstar"
> Isaac Hayes, "Shaft"
> Led Zeppelin, "When the Levee Breaks"
> Marvin Gaye, "What's Going On"
> The Rolling Stones, "Brown Sugar"
> Rod Stewart, "Maggie May"
> Bill Withers, "Ain't No Sunshine"
> Three Dog Night, "Joy to the World"
> Jean Knight, "Mr. Big Stuff"
> The Osmonds, "One Bad Apple"
> The Undisputed Truth, "Smiling Faces"
> Paul Revere and the Raiders, "Indian Reservation"
> Al Green, "I'm So Tired of Being Alone"

The Boston skyline was smaller in scale than Jeb had expected. In 1971, three days before Thanksgiving, he and Seamus encountered veterans shaking paper cups or standing on sidewalks with *Help a Vet* signs scribbled on cardboard boxes. The hippie era, which both men had missed during the war, was on its way out, and glancing from the passenger's and driver's seats of the moving truck, the two men were greatly discomfited by the number of homeless people straddling the streets. *A hard city, Boston*, Jeb thought, but if he had gone to New York, San Francisco, Los Angeles, or Chicago, he might have found a similar hardness.

ARE YOU JIMMY VINCENT? Jeb called out from the passenger seat of the moving truck. Jeb and Seamus had waited an hour in front of Jimmy Vincent's brick house in South Boston before the retired fireman finally made an appearance.

Maybe? Who wants to know? Jimmy Vincent scrutinized them. His face was leather. It had been human once, but bad habits had done something drastic to his forehead and chin. Jimmy wore a skinny brunette on his arm. If the girl was twenty, she was nineteen. If she was nineteen, she was seventeen. Or younger.

We have some furniture that belongs to you in the truck, said Jeb.

I told Nancy to keep it, Jimmy Vincent said.

She thought you might change your mind later, Jeb insisted. As Jeb spoke, Seamus swung the truck doors open and began to unload the dining room table and chairs. Jeb left Jimmy Vincent holding the papers and moved to help Seamus.

The girl crossed to the truck and poked at the padding on the dining table. She clapped her hands happily: All of this—*for us?*

Jimmy Vincent shook his head: Anything Nancy gives me is bad luck.

Where you want us to put it? asked Jeb.

Jimmy Vincent lit a cigarette: Leave it on the curb.

Seamus was horrified by the man's disregard for his inanimate legacy: This furniture belonged to your *people*.

The girl ran her hands along the back of the tall wood chairs and went back to the curb to whisper something in Jimmy Vincent's ear. Jimmy Vincent shrugged: The girl clapped her hands happily again and said: Park it on the front porch. We can sell it tomorrow.

See this? Jimmy puffed smoke, pointing but not looking the girl's way: I just met this a month ago. She's already planning the rest of my life and assuming I want her in it.

Jeb and Seamus left the furniture on the front porch with the brunette playing musical chairs and Jimmy Vincent leaning against the dining table smoking Pall Malls and talking about his ex-wife. How much he hated her. And how miserable the future would be without the hate he had grown into like an old overcoat. Maybe he didn't hate her at all? Maybe he just hated the two of them together. Together they were a blizzard.

Jeb was learning something about being a moving man. Being a moving man was not about the stuff. It was about the history around the stuff. The mistakes that happen when you put too much stock in people, places, or things. Stuff had history. All that history made him glad he traveled light.

THE TWENTY-FOUR-HOUR DINER had a blinking neon sign. When Jeb and Seamus entered, the rectangular counter and pedestal chairs reminded them of Krispy Kreme Doughnuts back home. The glazed donuts in the display case made their mouths water, and the waitresses wore green and white uniforms with nametags just like the waitresses at Kress in Buckner County, Georgia. A placard said, *Best Burgers in Boston*. They sat down at the counter. Seamus rapped his fingers on the counter and asked Jeb to order him a cup of coffee while he went to take a leak. A waitress in a uniform that matched her green eyes came over. She looked around the restaurant before placing napkins, a knife, and a fork in front of Seamus's empty seat. And then Jeb. Several eyes were on the waitress. Jeb, who was sensitive to these things, felt the eyes before he spun around on the counter stool and saw them. The diner was percolating with people. He looked for a face that might mirror his own. There were none. Jeb spun back around easily, hands cupped in his thin jacket. Outside, baby powder snow was shifting to ice and sleet.

Two coffees, please, Jeb said. The waitress smiled and moved quickly, pouring Seamus's coffee. When she lowered the coffeepot over Jeb's cup, an elderly waitress who had been quietly observing them from a distance came over, arms crossed.

I'm sorry. We don't have coffee, the elderly waitress said. Her eyes were on the waitress, but her words were on Jeb.

What's that she's holding in her hand? There was no complaint in Jeb's voice. Just fact.

It's not coffee, the elderly waitress said. The waitress had a bun like Jeb's aunt Flora. Jeb sighed: You got tea?

The elderly waitress shook her head: No tea either.

How about water?

She turned to Jeb and did not blink. If you drink it quick and leave.

We have been driving a long time, Jeb said, appealing to the older woman's humanity. The ponytailed waitress's face was as red as a Christmas ornament. She poured Jeb a glass of water. He was thirsty but pride would not let him touch the glass. There was not that much thirst in the world.

A lot of people drinking coffee and you don't have any? Jeb had done sit-ins in Buckner County, Georgia. He had not anticipated a sit-in up north. Sleep-addled and with traveler's funk shrouding him, he did not know if he had the stamina for a protest.

The older waitress turned to the younger waitress: Now, you see what you started? You know the rules. *Fix this.*

She marched off. And the young waitress whispered: Don't do this to me. I just been here a week. And I need this job.

Jeb responded, louder than he had intended: I'm a Vietnam veteran. I am an American.

The young waitress sighed. Seamus stepped out of the restroom. He climbed into his seat and sipped his coffee. Where's your coffee? Seamus asked, noticing for the first time the waitress and the silence and Jeb's empty cup.

They don't have coffee, Seamus.

Seamus continued to enjoy his drink. He was still processing and taking his sweet time about it. That sign says, *Best Burgers.* Lord I could use a burger with an extra serving of fried onions on top of it. They got Vidalia onions down where we live. You think they got Vidalia onions here?

Jeb wanted to smack Seamus: How the fuck am I supposed to know when they don't even have coffee? Eat what you need to eat. Do what you need to do.

Jeb stood up and left the restaurant. Seamus slurped the last of his coffee slowly and rose. Well, I don't think I'll be paying for this here coffee. Only a fool pays for things that don't exist.

Seamus followed Jeb outside. They climbed into the moving truck. Jeb took the driver's seat. Seamus tossed him the keys. If they had known the area or if Jeb had thought to leaf through the *Green Book*, they could have driven to the black section of Dorchester in South Boston. Of course, in that neighborhood, the tables might be turned, and Seamus might have found himself unwelcome. Like many American cities in 1971, Boston was divided along racial lines and tides. Three years after Jeb was denied service in the diner, the Boston busing crisis would make national news. And more than a few Southerners would snicker at Northern hypocrisy.

They were just pulling off when the ponytailed waitress with the green eyes hurried out of the diner hugging a grease-stained paper bag. She approached Jeb's side of the truck: It's not much. A burger and fries for you to share.

Thank you, Jeb said.

She rushed back toward the diner and paused at the door: My baby brother's fighting over there.

THE THANKSGIVING SNOWSTORM of 1971 left thousands of people stranded. Jebediah Applewood and Seamus Camphor were snowed in for five days in Portsmouth, New Hampshire. Nancy Vincent apologized for the hardwood floors and threw blankets and pillows and sleeping bags down for their comfort. They survived on turkey sandwiches and somebody's idea of turkey soup. The soup was filling but other than that Nancy Vincent mostly ignored them and read books sent by her son, who was a successful lawyer in New York City. Seamus said he could see why her ex-husband had gone younger because Nancy did nothing to accommodate a man other than giving him his daily bread. Daily bread made Jeb think of Myrtle.

Jeb looked at the snow and went out to help Nancy Vincent shovel the driveway. He donned an extra layer of clothing: flannel car jacket, suede gloves, and lined jeans that hung loosely from his frame. Nancy had kept some of her ex-husband's clothes that she could not bear to part with. Jimmy Jr., she said. One day Jimmy Jr. might want them. They forged a path through the snowdrifts. Nancy stopped to catch her breath: There's no shaking his scent.

When the storm broke, Seamus walked seven blocks to the neighborhood pub and Jeb walked nine blocks in the opposite direction to the local health food store. It was a barebones establishment owned by Boone McAllister, the childhood friend of Nancy Vincent's son. The store didn't stock much: plastic bins with nuts and soybeans and a big machine for grinding grains, legumes, and beans into flour and nut butters. Jeb did not know this, but he was witnessing the evolution of the macrobiotic movement founded by Japanese physician George Ohsawa. Boone McAllister had taken Ohsawa's beliefs on nutrition and diet and put them into practice in his store.

Boone McAllister told Jeb that the meeting had been canceled because of the storm, but if he needed a place to crash there was some space in the basement and the back room.

The basement was a dirt floor with low ceilings. There were folding chairs and tables like the ones people played cards on down South. About half a dozen men. Some had the odor of soapless days clinging to their skin and clothes. They came for the soup and sandwiches that Boone McAllister provided every week. Jeb learned from these Vietnam vets that there was an Air Force base nearby and affordable housing in Seacrest but the lack of insulation left chills in your bones. The Navy had mixed up the blueprints for Seacrest with housing they built down in Virginia.

The vets talked about war. The vets talked about conspiracy theories. They all had ideas about the CIA. Some swore they had seen planes being flown out of Nam with heroin. They talked about LSD experiments. And tough choices. Fragging an officer to save their platoons.

Jeb had not been on the ground in Vietnam and mostly kept quiet. In general, he believed that it was better to listen than to speak, and he was surprised when he finally did have something to say that it all made sense. He described his visit to the VA clinic in Buckner County, Georgia, and the angry soldier with the sparkling bald head who couldn't seem to frame his thoughts right. He told the men how the soldier had been hauled away kicking and screaming over papers he was now certain the soldier could not read. He did not mention Chief Petty Officer Nelson Mammoth.

THE DAY BEFORE Jeb and Seamus were scheduled to leave, Boone McAllister offered Jeb a job at the health food store. He had noticed how Jeb hung back and then moved forward. How he folded the chairs and tables after a meeting and was always reading pamphlets. He had noticed Jeb poring over the macrobiotic cookbooks.

I'm thinking about giving up the pork, Jeb told him.

You're on your way to becoming a vegetarian.

I don't know about that.

So Boone McAllister said: We need someone here to help open and close the store. You think you could work the register?

ON THE WAY back to Nancy's house, Jeb thought he saw a woman in the distance climbing into a car who looked like Myrtle. He had not seen another black person since he had arrived in Portsmouth (though he would later learn that blacks had lived in Portsmouth as early as the American Revolution). He called out to the woman and she turned around with a gap in her front teeth and a don't-think-I-know-you stare. She looked nothing like Myrtle and clipped her stride away from Jeb. Still, the thought of Myrtle made Jeb's body respond in a most delightful way. He got a hard-on.

Jeb searched for a telephone booth and found one caked in snow. When his body had relaxed back into itself, he called Myrtle Hendricks collect. On the third try, Myrtle accepted Jeb's long-distance call.

What would you think of living in New Hampshire?

Myrtle had been waiting for his call without hoping for it. She did not let herself hope.

I never been there, she said.

Maybe you should come?

New Hampshire's a whole state.

Jeb spoke into the receiver: We'll start with Portsmouth. See how we do.

Myrtle spoke after a long pause: I'll need an address.

Jeb shifted from one foot to the next: I'll call you soon as I have one.

SEAMUS CAMPHOR KNEW there was no talking Jeb into returning to Buckner County. The two men shook hands briskly, for neither was comfortable with good-byes. Seamus climbed into the Axelrod moving truck and acknowledged that it was going to be a boring-ass drive back. He would never have another black friend nor would he go out of his way to cause black people misery. And years later—long after Jebediah Applewood had become a therapist in the employ of Pease Air Force Base in Portsmouth—Seamus Camphor would grumble about his internment up north. He would say that he developed arthritis from the cold he endured that Thanksgiving. He would say that the cold wrestled with his body and mind. He would say he lost the battle but won the war and rekindled his gift for fighting fires.

THE PORTSMOUTH BUS depot was located next to a hotel. Jeb rented a room for him and Myrtle for the night. Nancy Vincent loaned Jeb her pink Cadillac to pick Myrtle up in. *Romance*, Nancy said: *I am a sucker for romance. That's half my problem.*

Myrtle stepped out of the Greyhound bus with one suitcase because she hadn't trusted her heart to bring all her things, knowing how fickle men could be. She had locked the doors to her house and given the keys to her cousins and told them she would keep them posted.

She stood inside the bus depot looking both ways, left and right. Even indoors, Myrtle was genuinely shocked by the cold. But she had kept track of the weather report and she had come with a peacoat for herself and a peacoat for Jeb. When Jeb saw her, he went over and picked up her luggage.

You must be tired, Myrtle, he said.

You too, she said.

They moved through the bus station arm in arm.

Together.

ELOISE TAKES FLIGHT

1947   1958   1968

BESSIE COLEMAN WAS THE FIRST WOMAN ELOISE DELANEY loved—before she knew love meant anything. There is a rectangular photograph cropped from the *Buckner County Register*, a local Negro paper, of Coleman standing atop the left tire of her Curtiss JN-4 "Jenny" biplane. Her gloved right hand hugs the cockpit. She is decked out in tailored aviation gear and stares directly into the camera. The photograph is at least thirty years old and dates back to 1926, the year of the brown aviatrix's untimely death, but for Eloise's parents the crash might have happened yesterday. They were the town drunks and time played on them murky.

"Man wasn't meant to have wings," Herbert Delaney said.

"Wasn't that a play or something?" Delores Delaney snapped her fingers. *"All God's Chillun Got Wings"*?

Herbert shrugged. "She getting ahead of herself. Wanting to take flight."

"What you saying, Herbert?" Delores Delaney kissed her

husband's long thin hands. "You saying God wanted her plane to crash? God wanted Bessie to die?"

"Well, He sure as hell didn't want her to live. Otherwise, that damn plane wouldn't have malfunctioned."

BESSIE COLEMAN'S PLANE had crashed during a barnstorming exhibition in Orlando, Florida. Delores Delaney liked to brag that she stood right smack-dab in the middle of the crowd the morning "Brave Bessie" was catapulted two thousand feet to the ground, but Eloise knew better than to place stock in anything a drunk said, especially when that drunk was her mother.

NEVERTHELESS, ELOISE WOULD remember these rare evenings from her childhood when she sat at the kitchen table on a broken stool between her mother and father and the three of them peered down together at the newspaper clipping and she did not have to vie for their attention with beer, bourbon, scotch, or gin.

ELOISE'S PARENTS WORKED at the seafood-processing factory two miles out of town. They had grown up shucking oysters and picking crabs and gutting fish. Getting paid for doing something that was second nature to them was like being given money to go on vacation. They could pick crabs with their eyes shut and lose nothing in speed. Sometimes their anxious fingers moved in their sleep, discarding the dead man and the pregnant she-crab belly and flicking out the tender white meat. Every so often, the manager of the seafood factory was forced to make an example of Herbert and Delores for coming to work inebriated or late or not at all. He would let them sweat their imbibing out and Eloise would go hungry until they managed to sidle back through the factory door.

THE SEAFOOD FACTORY was situated in a warehouse overlooking a salt marsh. When the picking season was high, Herbert and Delores would take their daughter to work with them. She would peer out the tall windows at the herons and seagulls and pelicans and ospreys and charcoal-black cormorants scouring the marsh for feed.

MY PARENTS KEPT *me more than they left me.* This was the half-truth Eloise would recollect to female friends. If she recited these words loud enough, she could almost believe they were true. But as a child of nine, ten, eleven, skinny and long with elbows that jutted out hard, she would jab someone deep in the groin if he said anything mean about her parents or her hand-me-down clothes.

That's one hand-me-down child, remarked the neighborhood chorus.

Hello. Good-bye. Kindly kiss my black ass, Eloise Delaney said.

You hear that? Poor thing. That's 'cause her folks don't teach her nothing. And so went the neighborhood refrain.

MONDAY THROUGH FRIDAY: Eloise walked to school five days a week. Rain or shine. When it rained she took a piece of plastic and fashioned it into a raincoat. Later, when she was older and went shopping with her girlfriends, Eloise would look at the brightly colored raincoats priced at forty dollars or more and shake her head. *No wonder young people don't have anything. What kind of flimsy fabric is this?* She would mutter and complain and buy the raincoat for her girlfriend anyway, because Eloise Delaney took care of her women.

ELOISE DID NOT travel a country mile to school when she was little. She did not see cows or pigs grazing on her journey. The school she walked to every day was not a one-room schoolhouse in the middle of nowhere. St. Paul's of the Redemption was an all-black Catholic school, grades K–12, run by nuns with faces the color of unpasteurized milk. They required parasols in the afternoon to shield them from the sun's harsh glare.

IN 1958, ON Eloise's first day in sixth grade, she lived three blocks from St. Paul's of the Redemption, but those three blocks might as well have been three miles because she walked to school with a hungry stomach and a high head. A hungry stomach tells a high head, *You act uppity if you want to, but I am going to growl.* A hungry stomach tells a high head, *You arch those skinny shoulders like they propping up the world if you want to, but I'm serving out a stomach cramp.* A hungry stomach tells a high head, *I am deeply offended that you did not feed me this morning, now you look what just happened? You have given me gas.* A hungry stomach tells a high head, *Bend down and clutch me before I send the emptiness pouring out on the first day of school. I will throw up on your thrift store dress.*

SHE DID NOT CRY, ELOISE. Though her lap was wet. She put a napkin over the wetness and followed the lesson as best she could, but it was only a matter of time before she became undone, distracted. Do I smell like puke? Eloise wiggled in her seat. She could not keep still. Her teacher, Sister Mary Laranski, a young nun who had only recently taken her vows, could have reached for a ruler to raw Eloise's hands. Instead she surveyed her class: colored, some uniformed, some not, mostly poor. Her voice trembled as she addressed her new students.

"Do you boys and girls know Shakespeare?"

Reuben Applewood raised his hand. "We heard of him."

"Well," said Sister Mary Laranski, "what did you hear?"

Reuben kept his eyes glued to the desk. "He was English. And wrote plays. 'To be or not to be: that is the question.'"

Sister Mary Laranski smiled. Reuben Applewood was the smartest boy in his class. By the end of the year, she would recommend that he skip a grade.

"I'm of the opinion," she said, "that a life without Shakespeare is no life at all. Abraham Lincoln received a perfectly fine education reading Shakespeare and the Bible. Some of you will not make it to school every day or, for that matter, every week but if you can hold on to just a little Shakespeare, all will not be lost."

She spoke with a hint of an accent. The accent came out more when she was nervous. The children caught this, and they were curious.

"Where are you from, Sister Mary?" asked one of the students.

"Some place you probably don't know." There wasn't a map on the wall and Sister Mary Laranski made a mental note to buy one. She picked up a piece of chalk and sketched a map on the blackboard. The sketching calmed her nerves.

"I am originally from Budapest. A city in Hungary."

"Do you miss where you come from?" a second student inquired.

"I would if I could remember. Grow up and you will remember everything backward."

Sister Mary, they would soon discover, was always weeping in the bathroom stalls of St. Paul's of the Redemption for the family who had sent her off to the nunnery. The students nicknamed her Sister Mary Weeping because she taught them Shakespeare and wept like Ophelia. But Eloise did not give a damn about anything Sister Mary Weeping said the first day of class. She now understood the thing called love. It seized Eloise—took firm hold when Agnes Miller sat at the desk across from her and opened a pencil case.

AGNES MILLER'S HAIR was styled in two moist ponytails, with perfect bangs. To look at her you would have thought that she had plundered young Natalie Cole's closet. Yes, it seemed to Eloise that the daughter of Nat King Cole had strolled into St. Paul's of the Redemption Catholic School like the place was hers. Now wasn't this some shit? Eloise listened to her heart go *boom boom bang bang boom* like the engine in her parents' sometimey Buick that would run just fine for a while and suddenly stop, so they all had to climb out and push it down a hill until the engine caught again or, worse, stand along the lip of the road and wait for some stranger to give them a ride. This Agnes Miller didn't look at Eloise even once. She didn't cut her eyes or wrinkle her nose or laugh or smile sadly at her secondhand clothes the way the other kids did. The worst insult Agnes Miller paid her was to sit there with her hands folded nonchalantly in her lap, like Eloise didn't exist. Eloise wondered if Agnes caught the whiff of vomit coming off her dress. During lunch break, which they took in the classroom, she watched as Agnes nibbled on what seemed like half a dozen miniature lavender cookies. Agnes licked the pale purple frosting off all the cookies but one before pausing to offer Eloise a cookie she had just licked. Eloise shook her head: *No thank you.* She resolved that this particular bit of haughtiness could not be tolerated. On the walk home, when Reuben Applewood and all the other do-gooders were gone, Eloise told some of her classmates: *Listen up; watch this.* She snapped a branch from a mulberry tree and cleared it of leaves. She followed Agnes Miller down the sidewalk and set to whipping Agnes on her glistening black legs, but Agnes surprised Eloise by adjusting her book bag on her shoulders and clawing at Eloise's face like an alley cat, so that Eloise went home in her smelly thrift store dress with scratch marks all over her face.

"WHO DID THIS?" Delores Delaney wanted to know.

"Girl named Agnes," said Eloise. Her mother cleaned her face with a wet washcloth and witch hazel. She used cocoa butter on the scratches.

"Who her people?" asked Herbert Delaney. "What's her last name?"

"I don't know," Eloise said.

"Is she an Applewood?" her father asked. Eloise couldn't stand it when her parents mentioned the Applewoods. They were the town's oldest black family and there was one in every grade.

"No," Eloise said. "Her last name's Miller."

Delores Delaney frowned for a few seconds and then whacked Eloise on the ear. "You fool girl," she said. "That's Lady Miller and

Deacon Miller's daughter. Her pa is a mason. They something. Don't you know what happens when nothing messes with something?"

DELORES AND HERBERT DELANEY marched Eloise over to Agnes Miller's house and made her apologize to Agnes and Agnes's parents. Eloise routinely hated her parents, but at that moment, she could not have hated them more. When they returned to their bungalow, Eloise retreated to the kitchen and stood in front of the Bessie Coleman clipping. She lifted her arms like the wings of a Curtiss JN-4 "Jenny" biplane and pretended to soar.

THE FIRE LEAPT across the front porch and made its home in the kitchen, where the curtains serviced it with extra fuel, as did the tins of grease for frying fish and chicken. Eloise's parents were asleep, arms and legs intertwined, on the living room couch. Eloise in her bedroom beside the kitchen woke with a tornado of smoke in her nostrils. She called out for her mother and father but heard only the whistle of the fire. They had left a cigarette burning on the front porch and the burner on beneath the aluminum frying pan in which, for supper, they had fried thick slices of store-bought ham.

SHE CALLED OUT AGAIN—*Ma? Pa?*—and slithered down on her belly like something reptilian to avoid the rush of smoke. She found them snoring on the sofa. For a moment, she watched the flames licking the living room walls and thought: *Maybe I would be better off.* Then she rushed down the hallway covering her mouth against the smoke with her mother's tossed-aside dress. She retrieved the Bessie Coleman clipping from the kitchen wall. It was a little singed around the edges, but the fire had not consumed it. Eloise dashed out of the kitchen and back down the hallway toward the front door. But as she stepped forward, her heart would not let her leave them. She crossed over a second time to the sofa and kicked and cussed at them.

"Get out now," Eloise said. "Get your goddamn good-for-nothing black asses off the goddamn couch."

They left as the roof came down.

ALL-WHITE FIREMEN manned the Buckner County Fire Department. They came after the blaze had consumed everything but early enough so that the surrounding houses did not go down in flames. The firemen fought the fire with buckets of water and two long hoses. The fire chief, known as the First Seamus, grandfather to Big Seamus, who would beget Seamus III, who would beget Fat Seamus IV, was a Camphor. The Camphor men had been stamping out fires since the Civil War, except for Charles Camphor, who would become a banker.

ELOISE TRACED THE outline of what used to be her home, illuminated by fire against a sky that hung so close to the ground she thought she saw the moon reaching down to touch the embers. This was another shame-faced moment for Eloise, with her father outside in his dingy long johns and her mother in a dirty, torn slip and the neighbors crowding around them, trying to throw a shawl over her mother's shoulders to cover her and her mother being drunk-drunk and waving them off and her parents arguing about who left the cigarettes burning or the burner on and Eloise thinking: *I should have let them die.*

"This ain't no spectacle," said Seamus the First, and he motioned for his men to push everyone back. He understood that every fire brings with it an outrage against privacy. There was nothing to be retrieved here. The fire had supped. And supped well.

———

IT WAS LADY MILLER, Agnes's mother, who stopped by the neighbors' house the following morning with a suitcase of dresses and underwear for Eloise. Lady received monthly hand-me-downs from the owners of Gottlieb's Bakery. The hand-me-downs were, in most cases, as good as new, but she did not put them on her child. She and her husband were thrifty people but they only had Agnes. Lady didn't want her treasured daughter to wear hand-me-downs, so she saved them for other less fortunate children.

THE NEIGHBORS WHO took the Delaneys in the night of the fire were catching it themselves. They already had four mouths to feed with three rooms to share, including the kitchen. On sight of all seven of them piled up like sardines in a can, Lady knew she had to be an honest Christian and at least offer to help.

"Eloise shouldn't miss one day of school, if she can help it," Lady Miller said to Herbert and Delores Delaney. "Every time a child misses a day of school, they miss something important."

She knew through Flora Applewood's gossip mill that Eloise had been accepted to St. Paul's the year before on a partial scholarship. Lady conversed with the Delaneys in the privacy of the neighbors' back porch, and it was decided that Eloise would come to the Millers for a week or two. Herbert and Delores would ask their supervisor if they could hole up in the cannery until they found something more permanent.

TWO WEEKS AFTER their house burned down, Herbert Delaney told his wife the fire was not an accident. They were in the one-room apartment they now rented behind the cannery. Delores, who had often thought Herbert was a shade paranoid, told him he should have a beer and rethink the subject. He had a beer or two and then he told Delores that he was done drinking. She laughed. On more than one occasion, they had made a pact to quit drinking. But their pact never stuck. They were absentminded, mostly happy drunks, and the rest of the world, including their daughter Eloise, orbited around them. So naturally, when Herbert said he was going to give temperance another go, Delores shrugged.

Five weeks into being sober, Herbert decided to go and see his people. They were fishermen, in New Orleans. He took a sip of bourbon and swirled it around in his mouth like mouthwash. He swallowed the bourbon and was relieved to find that it did not stir a desire for a second drink or a fifth. That night, they lay together, arm in arm. But the next morning Herbert snuck out at the crack of dawn and walked the nine miles to the Millers' house. He carried a large brown paper bag with freshly picked blackberries, three pounds of shrimp, and two cans of lump crabmeat. The shrimp and crabmeat he had stolen to thank the Millers for taking care of his daughter, a practice his wife would continue. Deacon and Lady Miller were on their second cup of Maxwell House coffee when the doorbell rang. At the sound of her father's voice, Eloise ran into the living room wearing a long white nightgown and looking for the first time in her life like a little girl. Herbert had come to take Eloise with him, but when he saw her in that nightgown, he decided against it.

"Eloise," Herbert said, after a pause. "You come from hell-raising people. Don't you burn down these people's house in a fit of temper, you hear?"

"But I didn't," Eloise said. "I didn't burn down our house."

"No," Herbert squinted. "But a spell can't be cast without intent. There's power in the tongue and in the head. In New Orleans, we know this."

Eloise cast her eyes away from her father. "I won't burn down their house."

Herbert Delaney wanted to tell Eloise that he loved her. But the best he could offer was a hug and brief kiss on the forehead. If he told her how much he loved her, there would have been tears, recriminations, regrets.

"You can be something. Or you can be a disappointment," Herbert said. Then he put on his bowler hat and left.

Eloise would never see him again.

AGNES MILLER TREATED Eloise with quiet indifference. So much so that whatever interest Eloise had held for Agnes was greatly diminished when she saw how little they had in common. Both girls were eleven years old, but Agnes drew doodles and studied fashion and spent hours on the bedroom floor cutting out McCormick's dress patterns and laying them all over the room, including Eloise's bed. She played dead white people's music on an upright mahogany piano. She sang church hymns for her parents in an off-key voice that burned Eloise's ears. Agnes was shepherded Monday through Friday from piano lessons to dance class to manners school to gymnastics and Bible study, and it shocked Eloise that Agnes did not roll her eyes or protest at all. Her book bag and her smile were always ready when Lady or Deacon Miller picked her up from school. Oftentimes Eloise would ride along with them and sit in the waiting room, reading or doing homework during Agnes's lessons. The Millers asked Eloise on more than one occasion if she would also like to take up piano or dance, but Eloise knew they were feeling sorry for her.

SISTER MARY WEEPING continued to weep for her Hungarian family in Kingston, New Jersey, but as time passed she wept considerably less. During recess one afternoon, she overheard her students gossiping about Eloise being a thorn in Agnes's parents' side. The next day Sister Mary Weeping approached Lady Miller to see if Eloise might help her out in the classroom after school. Lady and Deacon Miller were saving for their daughter's first home and college. They were saving for their retirement and a golden anniversary vacation in Hawaii. It was a relief to have something to occupy Eloise's time that would not upset their wallets.

FIRST, ELOISE AND Sister Mary planted a variety of beans in egg cartons and placed them on the windowsill facing the sun. Then they decorated a calendar with each student's name on it, so that the entire class would be able to chart the beans' growth. They tacked the Bill of Rights to the wall and untacked the calcified chewing gum from beneath the desks. They organized the Shakespeare plays by title and category: comedies, tragedies, historical plays, and sonnets. They beat out the dusty erasers and reglued the seams of the worn *Encyclopedia Britannica*, reading passages that interested them as they went along. They paused briefly to snack on peanut brittle, which was a sweet that Sister Mary Laranski loved. And when all of this was done, they rolled out a wall-length map of the world that Sister Mary had ordered from the Teachers' Store in New York and, with great care, taped it next to the blackboard.

IT WAS SISTER MARY WEEPING who noticed Eloise's gift for math. "Well," she said one afternoon after Eloise had raced through her fraction and long division exercises with total ease. "If you are good at math, it stands to reason that you might have an ear for languages."

She escorted Eloise over to the map of the world and rested her hand on Hungary. She had highlighted Lake Balaton, the longest lake in Europe. "Repeat after me . . . Eloise."

Welcome	*Isten hozta*
Hello	*Jo napot kivanok*
How are you?	*Hogy van?*
What is your name?	*Mi a neve?*
My name is Eloise	*A nevem Eloise*

In this way, Eloise learned Hungarian. And Sister Mary Weeping's assessment was correct: the child possessed a fine ear for languages. Later, as an adult, Eloise would travel the world and pick up snippets of languages the way some people pick up French fries in a fast-food restaurant. She would remember always Sister Mary Laranski, who in the four years that she stayed at St. Paul's of the Redemption Catholic School confessed to Eloise about the Turkish medical student she had fallen in love with at Rutgers University against her parents' wishes. *Off to the nunnery with you*, Sister Mary said in Hungarian. *Turks and Hungarians do not mix.*

THE ANCIENT HUNGARIAN ALPHABET

"Well, if it isn't Black Agnes with her pretty long hair!" If Sister Mary Weeping was sugar, the Mother Superior was turpentine. She would stop Agnes Miller in the hallway or on the stairs.

"Good morning, Mother Superior," Agnes always said sweetly.

"You have such charming manners, Agnes," said the Mother Superior. "Tell me, how does a girl as dark as you end up with such lovely long hair?"

Agnes would stare down at her black-and-white oxford shoes and when she did not answer, the Mother Superior would tug at her ponytail. It was in this same manner that the Mother Superior tugged at Sister Mary Weeping's habit or turned off the lights in the convent minutes before the sisters were expected to retire or chastised them for staring too long in the mirror or for their unbidden laughter during movie night or Scrabble.

ONE AFTERNOON ELOISE was drinking water at the water fountain. She had just finished a round of softball with the boys and was quite out of breath. Agnes came over and waited in line for a drink. The two girls did not socialize at school or share the same friends. Other than *good morning* or *good night*, they seldom spoke at all. The Mother Superior appeared alongside Agnes and yanked her hair so hard that Agnes shrieked.

"This hair," said Mother Superior. "What's a black girl like you doing with such pretty long hair?"

Eloise froze at the water fountain. She looked the Mother Superior up and down. "It won't be pretty or long if you keep pulling on it like that. Maybe her hair *pretty* cause her mama gives it a hundred and one brushstrokes every night."

ELOISE HAD CRIED the first time she saw Lady Miller undo Agnes's braids. The way Lady washed her daughter's thick hair with water of rosemary and sage, making her own shampoos and soaps because she thought the store-bought ones too harsh. Lady would leave the comb and brush out for Eloise to do her own hair and Eloise would pretend that Bessie Coleman—stylish, meticulous Bessie Coleman, who was savvy not only about how she flew but about every detail of her image, including her perfect mane—was helping her do the brushing and the combing and the parting.

Of course, the Mother Superior did not know any of this when she grabbed Eloise by the ear and led her to the main office, where she took out a long yardstick and serviced her hands with three sharp thwacks, one for impertinence and the other two for bad grammar and syntax.

No one will ever know the lengths the Mother Superior went to keep St. Paul's of the Redemption Catholic Church running. In 1976, when the all-black school finally closed its doors, despite the Mother Superior's efforts, and the African American students were dispersed into the traditionally all-white Catholic schools in Buckner County, the gray-haired and stone-eyed Mother Superior made a hundred and seventeen personal calls with her liver-spotted hands. She pleaded, threatened, and cajoled on behalf of the pupils she hated to love and loved to hate. But in 1958, she was a terror.

AGNES WAITED FOR Eloise outside the Mother Superior's office.

"What'd you talk back to her for?" Agnes said in a furious whisper. "Her old yanks don't hurt me. When she yanks my hair I just count to three and think something mean about her mama."

"Like what?" asked Eloise, rubbing her right hand, which was tender, inflamed.

Agnes led Eloise away from the Mother Superior's office. "Her mama so fat, you say it's chilly outside and she'll grab a bowl."

Eloise looked over her shoulder in the direction she had come from and frowned. "*Her* mama so fat, when she takes a shower she can't see her toes."

Agnes whispered, "Her mama so dumb, if she spoke her mind, she'd be speechless."

Eloise giggled. "Her mama so dumb, when she speaks her mind, her mind says gone fishing."

Agnes laughed. "Her mama so ugly, when she gets up, the sun goes down."

Eloise nodded. "Her mama so ugly, the devil saw her coming and told God he was ready to come back to heaven."

Agnes shook her head. "Her mama so ugly, she looked in the mirror and the mirror cried, 'Oh, mercy me. You ugly bitch. No more.'"

FOR THE REMAINDER of recess Eloise and Agnes played the dozens and were joined by half the kids in the schoolyard. Reuben Applewood and his younger brother, Levi, and their rangy cousin Jebediah were the referees because any game about somebody's mama could disintegrate into fisticuffs fast and where would they be but right back in the Mother Superior's office for another thwack on the hand or, if the Spirit dictated, on the rear end.

FROM THAT POINT ON, the two girls were inseparable. Eloise slept on the lower tier of Agnes's trundle bed, where it was her nightly ritual to study the singed newspaper clipping of Bessie Coleman before falling asleep. She would read aloud to Agnes, recounting

Bessie Coleman's adventures in France and Germany, where she had to travel to learn to fly airplanes because American aviation schools would not train women or people of color. Amelia Earhart and the handful of white aviatrixes from Bessie's era had been born into wealthy families who could afford to buy planes for them or provide private instruction. But Bessie would become the first African American to earn an international pilot's license. She would study with some of the best pilots in Europe, including Anthony Fokker, the Flying Dutchman, and master daring aerial stunts. She would pilot one of the first commercial planes in Friedrichshafen, Germany, and soar above the Kaiser's palace in Berlin. She would return to America a minor celebrity and perform death-defying air shows around the country to raise money for a colored aviation school.

THE BESSIE COLEMAN clipping became a favorite bedtime story for Agnes, who always listened quietly while Eloise read and then closed her eyes. Eloise recounted Bessie's adventures well into their teenage years. She never permitted herself to fall asleep first. She lay in bed inhaling the peppermint soap from the bath that Agnes took every night. There was even a slab of wood on the tub with a nook to place a book and read, if Agnes desired. Sometimes Lady Miller would place a bowl of sliced apples on the slab of wood. She dipped the apples in elderberry syrup to ward off colds.

AT FIFTEEN THE girls continued to share a room but slept in separate twin beds. Eloise inhaled the sweet fragrance but resisted the urge to climb into Agnes's bed. Her heart continued its beat: *bang bang boom boom BANG* like the engine in her parents' doubtful Buick. She had hoped the engine would stall permanently, but when she reached the teenage years and both girls still slept in the same room but in separate beds, Eloise's heart began to beat so strongly that one night she sat upright in bed and went over to Agnes, who slept with a sleeping cap to keep her hair from getting matted. Eloise saw that Agnes's eyes were wide open and she saw that they were relaxed on her. Eloise knelt down as if in prayer and kissed Agnes on the lips, which had just the hint of minty toothpaste. Agnes did not resist the kiss; she only seemed puzzled by its abruptness and pulled Eloise's lips to hers for a fuller one.

Later, when Agnes went for men, she would say to Eloise, "You did this to me."

And Eloise would tell her, "I gave you a kiss. You were the one who added the tongue. The tongue bears witness."

And Agnes would tilt her swan-line neck to one side. She would bat her eyes sheepishly. "Don't knock it till you've tried it, Eloise. I can't believe you aren't the least bit curious."

Eloise would say, "Agnes, I'd rather die than be a living hypocrite." Being penetrated by a man was Eloise's idea of being nailed to a cross. She could not see the logic in that kind of suffering.

THEY WERE IN sophomore year at Buckner County College when Agnes met Claude Johnson. Claude was an engineer employed by Southeast Aviation. And to make matters worse, he was Eloise's third cousin on her mother's side. Eloise hated him instantly. The afternoon he sat down next to Agnes at the Kress counter, Eloise asked the devil to take him. And that same night, on what would be the last night Eloise and Agnes made love, she told Agnes the hard truth.

"It won't last, Agnes," Eloise said.

"Neither will we," snapped Agnes. The next morning Agnes treated Eloise with total indifference.

Eloise could not say whether Lady and Deacon Miller were ignorant of Agnes's interests. Daughters are often above their father's reproach, and so it was possible that Deacon Miller had no idea what went on between the two young women. But even before Agnes brought Claude Johnson home to meet her folks, Lady Miller had packed Eloise's suitcase.

"It's been a pleasure having you here," Lady Miller said, pressing money into Eloise's hand.

Eloise did not count the money. Her heart was a great orange bundle of flames. She closed her eyes. "Where am I supposed to go?"

"I was married when I was your age. The road is yours." As far as Lady Miller was concerned, Eloise had outstayed her welcome by two years.

Eloise's mother still lived next to the seafood factory. It was rumored that she was "seeing" the owner. Delores Delaney would drop in once a month with shrimp, crabmeat, or fresh fish. Once she came toting an impressive chunk of mako shark, and Lady Miller marinated and grilled the meat on skewers. Eloise knew that sharks slept with their eyes open. It was one of the many things that Sister Mary Weeping had taught her. But Sister Mary Weeping had renounced her holy vows and returned to New Jersey to marry the Turk when Eloise was in ninth grade. Eloise was certain that she would never hear from her mentor again. She could write, speak, and read Hungarian, but what was the point? She never ran into any Hungarians. People either kicked you out or they ran away.

"I will find my cousin King Tyrone on Tybee Island," said Eloise finally. "He is the only decent one of my kin."

"Well, it's been a pleasure having you here," Lady repeated.

Lady prepared Eloise's favorite food for breakfast: maple-cured bacon, scrambled eggs, freshly squeezed orange juice, and apple slices with elderberry syrup layered on top. Agnes came late to the breakfast table that morning and barely tossed Eloise a glance. When Eloise rose to leave for good, Agnes followed her as far as the front door and asked if Eloise would mind leaving the Bessie Coleman clipping as a souvenir.

"Agnes," said Eloise, "I want to leave this house on a nice note. But truly, truly, you can kiss my black ass."

Agnes sighed and waved herself with an invisible fan. If her mother had not been present, she would have purred, "But, Eloise, I already have."

ELOISE'S COUSIN King Tyrone said, "Seems like it'd be easier if you liked someone whose body parts run counter to your own."

Eloise had laughed at King Tyrone because that was something she'd thought of herself, but to hear it put that way out of King Tyrone's mouth called to mind the complication of things she was sick and tired of wrestling with. They sat on his back porch overlooking the marsh, cleaning greens. To her left, she had a pail of salt water to soak the greens in and draw out the worms and, to her right, a brown paper bag for the rough edges that could not be salvaged. In the middle was a wooden bowl full of greens she had recently picked and torn apart by hand, so that they might simmer long and cook tender.

"Tyrone, when you ever known a damn thing in this world to be what it seems?"

"Well," King Tyrone said, after a beat, "there's a room here with your name on it for as long as you need one."

Eloise wanted to ask King Tyrone how he'd arrived at his cool temperament, but she already knew that a life on the water was the sum total of his happiness. King Tyrone was a fisherman like his parents. His mother and father had mostly kept to themselves, shunning family gatherings and hell-raising, Saturday night parties and churchgoing affairs. Nothing animated them more than talk of the weather, for the weather influenced the day's catch. And the day's catch influenced the day. King Tyrone was fifteen when the ocean took his parents.

"That's awfully good of you, cousin. I will sleep me well tonight."

But the stillness of island life only reminded Eloise how restless she was. Her first week there, she took to smoking Pall Mall cigarettes. Her second week, she kissed King Tyrone good-bye and used the cash that Lady Miller had given her to take a bus back into town. She went into Anderson Fine Tailors, a men's clothing store, and emerged with an assortment of stylish men's pants, shirts, vests, and blazers. She crossed the street and peered into the window of a haberdashery. The bowler hat she'd bought was in the style her father had worn. Eloise tipped the hat at a slight angle. She was certain she wore hers better.

————

ELOISE AND AGNES were enrolled in the same classes at Buckner County College, but Eloise could no longer trust her heart in Agnes's presence. She took a leave of absence and found a job as a cashier at a downtown grocery store. She was a handsome woman, especially in shirts and slacks, and it did not take long for her to win the favor of the single and married women who approached the counter with cartons of milk and eggs and baby formula and Tide. She gave easy compliments and made small talk with them and directed them down the aisles where the bargains were and away from the pieces of tainted stew beef that had sat behind the butcher's counter for too long.

Her first girlfriend after Agnes was a married woman named Grace Bell. Grace was a poor facsimile of Agnes but she was similar in her disengaged approach to the world. *It must be a pretty-girl thing*, Eloise thought. *Only pretty women can afford to be so carefree and careless.* Grace's husband was a Pullman porter. He made good money riding Seaboard Air Line Railroad up and down the Eastern Seaboard, which meant he was away for weeks at a time.

ELOISE WENT ONE Sunday to visit her mother, who was still taking shrimp and crabmeat to Agnes's family every week.

"About the shrimp," said Eloise. "You need to stop carrying food to those people. My time there is done."

Delores Delaney was nursing a can of Miller beer. She had once had the best figure in town. But the drink was turning her body from sugar to shit.

Delores looked away from Eloise and grunted. "I didn't know I'd given birth to a son. Maybe I should have named you Earl."

"That's all you got to say to me after being a lousy mother all these years?"

"Well," Delores said, helping herself to one of Eloise's cigarettes, which lay on the table between them. "Did I beat you?"

"No."

"Did I ever eat and not let you eat first?"

Eloise laughed. "Not that I can remember. But sometimes you let me starve."

"I starved too."

"Not for drink."

"Sweetie, even in that I was good. You can never say I handed you a drink."

Eloise considered what her mother had said: "Maybe you should quit."

"This is my *disease*, Eloise."

The truth of her mother's words made Eloise's brain rattle.

"Pa quit," she offered.

"And left. You become sober, you have to leave behind all your regrets."

Eloise lit herself a cigarette. "You never said you loved me."

"Is that why you running round here decked out like a man?"

"No, Ma, it's just one of those things good parents tell their children. It's something *I* would tell kids, if I had them."

Delores puffed cigarette smoke her daughter's way. "Well, I'm sorry for my love's absence." She rose and walked over to the economy refrigerator.

Eloise stood up and circled around the studio apartment. Her eyes scanned everything to see if there was any evidence of a boyfriend, or the owner of the seafood factory. Her mother's place was surprisingly tidy. In a corner against a red brick wall she kept a stack of beer cans and corkscrews. There was some method to the stacking. During the 1980s in Berlin, Eloise would see art installations stacked the same way and think of her mother.

"You keep the shrimp." Delores shoved a bag into Eloise's hand. "They the jumbo ones with the heads still on."

Eloise gave the shrimp to Grace, who made a first-rate pot of gumbo.

ELOISE LIVED IN a furnished one-bedroom apartment on the end of a dirt road where neighborhood children were always outside playing. The children liked her because she cussed them something awful when they called her Butch Eloise and after work she would sometimes play dodgeball with them. She was sucking on an Orange Creamsicle pushup pop and playing hopscotch with the kids when Grace's husband showed up with his cowboy belt. At first she thought, *Someone's kid's about to get an ass kicking.* But then Grace's husband moved through the kids and came toward her. He held the belt so that the golden buckle swung in her direction and before she could duck, he grabbed her by the arm and began to beat her with the buckle, starting up her pants legs and working to the hips, the breast, the neck, and the face. It was the belt his wife had ordered as an anniversary present from Dallas, Texas, tailor-made to his measurements.

The neighborhood kids took umbrage at the well-heeled man beating one of their own on their home turf and jumped on Grace's husband. He knocked them off like they were stale wind but nonetheless stopped. The neighborhood kids in all likelihood saved Eloise's life because Grace's husband did not want to hurt children, even by accident. Eloise was the one he had come to kill.

He left Eloise buckle-bloody-prone on the street. Just two hours earlier, his wife had feasted him with some of the best shrimp gumbo he'd ever tasted. But as they lay in bed afterward, Grace had cried out Eloise Delaney's name.

FLORA APPLEWOOD USED herbs from her garden to pull out the swelling in Eloise's face. She opened tall stalks of aloe vera plants and spread the gel over the young woman's bottom lip, where the belt buckle had split it in two. She circled the low-slung four-post bed with the swiftness of a hawk, swooping down and peeling away the clothes that clung to Eloise's body dirt. *Gingerly*, she had admonished her nephews Reuben, Levi, and Jebediah Applewood, as they carried Eloise up the three flights of stairs into Eloise's apartment. The young men took great care because Eloise Delaney had attended Catholic school with them and because it was considered anathema in the Applewood family to lay a cruel hand on a woman.

Aunt Flora spoke out loud to keep Eloise conscious and to steel her own taut nerves. When her nephews left, Flora told Eloise how at sixteen she had traveled to New York to live with her cousin. And how she found that cousin living in a filthy one-room apartment with a metal tub in the kitchen. And how people were always moving north and exaggerating their living conditions for pride's sake or to lure more family there. But if you want to do bad in this world, you can do bad by yourself.

You know something, Eloise, Flora said. *I hope you heal okay cause you got light skin and the bruises might show more if they shift to scars.* And Eloise, who had never thought of herself as light-skinned, stared at her arms. How could it be that she did not know this about herself or had trained herself not to care? Skin is skin, she told herself.

During Eloise's convalescence, she had not heard from her mother, her girlfriend Grace, or Agnes Miller. The news of her beating would not reach King Tyrone until well after the fact. It was Flora who sat rigidly on the edge of her bed and listened to her breathing. It was Flora who read the article about Bessie Coleman for Eloise in the same way that she had once read it to Agnes. It was Flora who ran a hot comb through her hair. It was Flora who was telling Eloise, in so many words, to escape.

ELOISE ENLISTED IN the WAF (Women in the Air Force) branch of the military. The day before she reported for duty, she gave Flora a present. She untied Flora's upswept bun and removed the faint rouge from her lips and brushed her hair, and she unclasped the neatly pinned dress and unrolled her beige stockings and put the heels in a neat row at the foot of her low-slung bed. She unhinged the white bra strap and slipped down the white panties and told her to lie down and be still, and Aunt Flora, who had shown her kindness without any expectation of favor, did not protest because she had been young once and on the receiving end of brutality and tenderness.

———

THEY SENT ELOISE to Lackland Air Force Base in San Antonio, Texas, where she excelled at basic training and gave up cigarettes. There were two or three women with whom she might have become romantically involved, but during those eight weeks of boot camp she barely had time to catch her breath. Eloise ran twelve to fifteen miles a day, morning and afternoon, according to the drill sergeant's whim. She was a natural on the obstacle course and did not flinch during hand-to-hand combat. M16s and M14s made her hands sweaty, but she grew accustomed to manipulating them. The female soldiers were under constant supervision, but despite bouts of intense loneliness, Eloise opted for professional camaraderie. She didn't want to provide anyone with an excuse to summarily dismiss her intelligence or question her ethics. Flora Applewood had also coached her on the power of discernment. *Look but don't touch, Eloise. And if you do touch, touch at your own risk*: a homespun precursor to *Don't ask, don't tell.*

The East Room of the White House, November 8, 1967,
President Lyndon B. Johnson signing H.R. 5894.

SPECIALIZED TRAINING FOLLOWED boot camp. Eloise could already type ninety-eight words a minute because at Catholic school girls were required to take typing and home economics. In addition to a proficiency in math, she spoke Latin and Hungarian, considered by some to be the most difficult language to learn. Eloise did not have the temperament to become a nurse, nor had she joined the war effort to work as a secretary. Another recruit suggested the Air Force Defense Language Institute.

ELOISE TOOK THE Bessie Coleman clipping to the institute and tucked it under her pillow at night. Her heroine had learned to fly planes with French fliers and German ace pilots. Her heroine had dabbled in German and French. Why the hell not? Eloise stayed focused and busy—and would not let herself think about Agnes, who had moved on from Claude Johnson to a man named Eddie Christie, a distant relative to the Applewoods. She didn't know what hurt her more: Agnes's inclination toward men or the swiftness with which she bounced between them. Two days after she received her certificate from the DLI in French and German with the second highest scores in her class, Eloise heard from Flora Applewood that Agnes had married Eddie Christie. She put in a request for an immediate transfer to Vietnam.

ON JANUARY 29, 1968, she arrived for duty at Tan Son Nhut Airbase near Saigon—two days shy of the Tet Offensive. Tan Son Nhut Airbase was the busiest airport in Southeast Asia—some said the world—and it was about to become one of the hardest hit targets during attacks by the Viet Cong and the North Vietnamese Army against American military forces and their allies in South Vietnam. The attacks overlapped with the Vietnamese New Year and were accompanied by missiles, rockets, and twilight sniper fire. Eloise, jetlagged from her sixteen-hour flight across the Pacific, woke up in the midst of what she swore was a shitty dream. Then she felt the women's barracks quake beneath her. And spied through her bunk window one-hundred-and-twenty-two-millimeter rockets streaking across the sky. There were tremors and starbursts when the incoming rounds made impact. Eloise thought of her childhood home. When a house burns, everyone loses and no one wins.

SHE WAS ASSIGNED to the command headquarters as a special intelligence analyst. Her responsibilities included poring over raw data from commanding officers and American reconnaissance: men who worked ahead of the front lines. She pinpointed discrepancies in intelligence reports to avert casualties, analyzed local geography and transportation, planned supply lines through mountain passes. Later, she would say that intelligence officers ran either hot or cold, and the seemingly mundane, case-sensitive attention to detail exacted much from them. Eloise resumed her pack-a-day cigarette habit. She spent ten- and twelve-hour days listening to recordings, parsing out interviews from the Montagnards, indigenous people who lived in the mountains of Laos, Cambodia, and Vietnam and were American allies. The Montagnards did not have a written language. They relied on oral tradition, not unlike Eloise's ancestors in low-country Georgia.

ALL FOUR BRANCHES of the military—Army, Navy, Air Force, Marines—were stationed at Tan Son Nhut. At the nightclubs in Saigon and the beer bars on base, Eloise socialized with the black lieutenants. She employed due wit to keep their relationships close, honest, and platonic. Because she had developed a reputation for being quick on her feet, she convinced her supervisors to let her go into combat for intelligence surveillance. It thrilled her to participate in these missions. She was convinced that under different circumstances she would have made a solid lieutenant, or even a commander, but during the Vietnam War, women were not allowed to participate in active duty, nor were they allowed to use weapons. The nurses had been the first WAFs deployed in Southeast Asia due to a shortage of male nurses. Their ability to save lives and navigate the emotional and physical casualties of war (for their patients and themselves) had opened the door for enlisted women like Eloise to go to Vietnam.

In letters to Eloise, Flora Applewood would often ask if she had run into Reuben or Jebediah Applewood on their tours of duty in the Navy. Eloise wrote back no, but in truth, she had encountered Jebediah Applewood at a nightclub in Subic Bay. She came up to him; Jebediah was slugging down martinis and his eyes glowed devil red. He had his arms draped over two women, one of whom Eloise immediately summed up as an American hooker flown in to keep the soldiers happy and a Filipino girl dressed like Marilyn Monroe. It unnerved Eloise to see Jebediah Applewood carelessly pawing the women. She knew that soldiers carried on this way, but she had not played in the school playground with them. They had not carried her up three flights of stairs after she was beaten within an inch of her life.

"What's up, cousin?" Eloise said.

Jebediah was not high enough to think they were related. When he was young, he had had a crush on Eloise Delaney, who ran so freely with the boys. He let his dope eyes roam over her masculine frame and was not the least bit deterred by the possibilities. At the other end of the circular bar sat Eloise's current girlfriend, who did administrative work at Tan Son Nhut Airbase. Eloise signaled that this might take a minute.

"You want a drink?" Jeb turned to the bartender, not waiting for Eloise's response.

"I stick to one." Eloise took Jeb by the arm. "Why don't you come outside with me?"

"I don't want to leave Eddie," said Jeb, nodding toward the back of the bar where a makeshift stage was set up and a stout man stood in the center of a sprinkling of soldiers acting out what looked to be some strange variation of Shakespeare's *Hamlet*. The little man stood on a wooden ladder. He had taken brightly colored silk curtains and cut them into costumes. His cast consisted of a motley crew of soldiers and civilians. Some sat in a circle, like small children, their legs crisscross applesauce. Others swayed in a silent dance, as if the play, *Rosencrantz and Guildenstern Are Dead*, were slow drag music. The room was a stir of blue smoke and Eddie Christie squinted to make out the words in the playbook clutched by his chubby fingers.

EDDIE

Tragedy, sir. Deaths and disclosures, universal and particular, Denouements both unexpected and inexorable, transvestite melodrama on all levels, including the suggestive. We transport you into a world of intrigue and illusion . . .

Outside the bar, Jebediah leaned against a side wall.

"How you doing, Jeb?" Eloise said, studying the sailor. Jeb had been the scraggliest of the Applewood men. Narrow shoulders hunched in; limbs too long for his body. Now there was stubble on his face. He had grown something close to handsome.

Jeb lit a cigarette. "I been better."

"Haven't we all?" she said. "You know your aunt and I stay in touch?"

"Yeah? That's good. So what? What about it?"

Eloise boxed Jeb on his ear. "I'm not gon' tell her I saw you like this. I won't tell her the precise nature of your being precisely fucked up."

Jebediah took a deep breath in and let a deep breath out. "The war suits you, Eloise. But for some of us, this shit ain't real." He leaned in close and Eloise was appalled by the foulness of his breath, the smell of drugs and alcohol coming off his skin. "It *can't* be real."

"Who's that short dude on the ladder?" Even before she asked the question, Eloise knew the answer.

"That's my *blood* cousin. Eddie Christie," Jeb said, and then laughed. "He's married to your girl, Agnes. They got two kids."

Eloise boxed Jeb on his other ear. "Shut up."

"What you want to do that for?" Jeb said, covering his ear.

"'Cause I can." She turned to go back into the bar.

Jeb called after her. "Eloise, come back here. Eloise, you know... maybe we could. Maybe I could . . . enjoy a bit of Southern comfort?" He let the question linger so that the meaning took.

"Jebediah Applewood"—Eloise smiled—"I hope you get home in one piece. In the meantime, kiss my natural black ass."

SIX MONTHS LATER her military vehicle came under enemy fire on a late-night drive from downtown Saigon to Tan Son Nhut Airbase. Eloise and two officers were thrown from the jeep. Shrapnel caught Eloise on her right knee and barreled through another lieutenant's shoulder. Eloise had no weapon to defend herself. While the four male officers returned fire, Eloise dragged the wounded airmen with her and took shelter underneath the jeep. As she lay on the ground with Dragonfly fighter jets overhead, Eloise thought of Brown Bessie—the nickname her mother and father had called Bessie Coleman—in her Curtiss JN-4 "Jenny," performing loop-de-loops and ground dips and figure eights high in the sky, where nothing could touch her and no one could hurt her.

I KNOW WHERE THE POISON LIVES

2008

DIOXIN KILLED OUR DADDY, I TELL CLAUDIA WHEN DADDY gives up the ghost at Riverside Hospice. My sister looks at me like I'm talking some hypercrazy la-di-da, zip-a-dee-doo-dah-ay-level shit. I repeat, for her sole benefit, that dioxin is highly toxic. The main ingredient in Agent Orange. That shit ate up our daddy's intestines. I show her clippings, nicotine-stained articles, my folder of testimonials from other Blue Water vets who served on aircraft carriers in Vietnam. But Claudia shrinks back and juts out that chin of hers like she did when we were little girls pretending to be those lame-ass British dudes on Shakespeare's ship.

"Everything is not a goddamn play," I mutter. "Sometimes the goddamn play is not the thing."

"You talk like a sailor."

"I'm a sailor's daughter. So are you."

"This is not the way to do it." She shrugs. "This is not how we should honor our father. Why can't you allow yourself to mourn, Bev? Simply feel what you need to feel."

I feel. Angry. 'Cause the Daddy I know will be buried in three days. After that, his body will collapse, bloat, and split wide open in a six-foot grave. Maggots will crop up to do their dark work, aiding, abetting the transformation of his remains. Skin, our daddy's beautiful chestnut skin, will drop away from its skeleton. Even as I bathed him this afternoon, putrefaction, intestinal rot had already started. Liver cancer makes a body septic. The more septic a body is, the quicker it rots. Embalming stalls the process, but the process is already in motion. Happening. Edward Christie's death certificate will say *septic failure*. These are things I'd rather not think the fuck about. Things I tried to shut out of my head while I performed my last act of kindness, which was to wash Daddy. I couldn't let the hospice nurses clean his cold body, as wonderful as they have been. It was mine to do. My way of saying good-bye, adios, *arrivederci, baby*.

Claudia will speak at his funeral. She will wax philosophical despite her sorrow and eulogize him, but I saw his lips turn pale and his brown eyes lose their light. Claudia was singing on his deathbed, "Okay, Daddy. It's okay, Daddy. Please, *go home*." She was reading fucking *Rosencrantz and Guildenstern*.

TWO HOURS AFTER Daddy dies, the sheets have been stripped and his body carried off to the funeral home. His metal bed is empty now. My eyes hug the lavender walls—a designer would call these walls *mauve*. When his health took a turn for the worse and the doctors said he had six months to live, I reached out to my friend Shirley. We were running buddies back in the day. Shirley used to skip class to snort coke with me downtown in the bathroom stalls at Nell's and the Limelight. She was hot, but I was hotter. Maybe we were destined to become teenage moms together. The nuns at Our Lady of Claremont Catholic School looked the other way when we showed up in thick cable-knit sweaters and cardigans in June. Our classmates didn't. Their ridicule was vicious. Our attitude was fierce. But we were girls—scared-shitless girls—trying to act like grown women. Before I told Kevin, I went in for an AIDS test, more for the baby's sake than anything else. The Red Cross had started this AIDS awareness program. They were giving free tests all over the city. When the white nurse stuck the needle in, I was trembling.

"You look like a smart girl." Her name tag said Barbara Camphor.

"I'm going to keep it." This was the first time I let myself speak these words out loud.

"Well, all right. That's one way to do it."

I thought the way she said it was rude. "You don't think I should do it?"

"You already done it, honey. That train has left the station and off she goes."

I remember laughing but wanting to smack her. But she held the needle. And she was taking my blood. "You think I should keep this baby?" I had fucked around but I was sure the baby was Kevin's.

"Between thyself and thy God."

"You're not very helpful."

"I'm helping you find out if you have the virus that causes AIDS. I'm hoping you don't, but if you do, you've got to find a way to live. Understood?"

She had found a vein and only tapped me with the needle once. A pinch. Then nothing.

"You make a good living?"

"Now, that's the kind of question I like to hear a girl in your predicament ask. That's the kind of question *I* would ask." I watched her put the vials of blood on a tray and write something down.

"I could do better," she said. "But I do well. And sometimes well has to be enough."

I WAS THE ONE who told Shirley about nursing school. We got our diplomas but skipped graduation. We'd hang out and study at my house. Studying was the only time our parents helped us out because, after we finally told them, they wanted us to know we'd fucked up and they weren't having it. I watched the way my mom's and dad's faces lit up when Claudia got into Columbia. That was when I moved into a studio apartment with Kevin rather than be there to see her attend college first. Seeing my little sister go to Columbia hurt. If I couldn't be special, fuck it then: I'd be independent. I went the ER route. Shirley went geriatric before becoming a hospice nurse. She arranged for me to take a private tour at Riverdale.

"We'll see to it that your father transitions with dignity," she said.

As hospices go, it was a decent establishment. "He won't be able to afford it, Shirley," I said. Daddy's insurance didn't cover a private room.

"Bev," said Shirley. "It's taken care of. I've got this."

Shirley set Daddy up in a private room with a spare bed and a comfortable green chair so that Claudia, Mom, and I could stay overnight with him. The room had a garden view. In the garden there were small hard pears that you could lift from a tree, and tulips and peonies and hot pink azaleas that vexed me with their greedy bloom.

TWENTY-FOUR HOURS BEFORE Daddy died, we thought he might bounce back. He'd been down for the count several times over the last two years but always rallied himself around the bend. Mom had fallen asleep next to his bed. The metal railing doubled as her pillow. I'd gone downstairs to smoke a cigarette. Claudia was snoozing in that green leather chair that resembled a La-Z-Boy wannabe. When I came back in the room Daddy was sitting up with his eyes open and saying in a voice so strong you wouldn't have known he was down to a hundred and fifteen pounds, "Where is the strawberry ice cream?" And I just turned right around in my knock-off clogs and found the hospice nurse and they brought him two scoops of strawberry ice cream in a disposable cup. Mom spoon-fed Daddy, and he gobbled up the ice cream and started talking with those British dudes like they were right there in the hospice room with us.

"Well, if it isn't old Ros and Guil," Daddy said. "How'd you cats find me here? I see you boys have finally touched shore. Yes, I've seen better days myself."

We had grown up with Daddy mouthing off and tipping his hat around the house to these British dudes that no one else could see.

And Mom said, "Well, it's like old times in here."

And when Claudia heard Daddy speaking, she jumped up like Sleeping Beauty from a too-long nap and rummaged through her purse for her copy of *Rosencrantz and Guildenstern Are Dead*. Claudia read to Daddy whenever she couldn't think of anything else to do. She went over to his bed and recited the first lines her eyes fell on.

"*Foul! No synonyms. One-all!*" Claudia said. Instantly, she was Rosencrantz. Daddy smiled. So, I followed her cue and became Guildenstern. I didn't need to look at the lines to play the part. None of us did, except maybe Mom, who never learned the words 'cause someone in the family had to be a spectator and reel in the madness.

ME AS GUILDENSTERN: *Statement: Two—all. Game point.*

CLAUDIA AS ROSENCRANTZ: *What's the matter with you today?*

ME AS GUILDENSTERN: *When?*

CLAUDIA AS ROSENCRANTZ: *What?*

ME AS GUILDENSTERN: *Are you deaf?*

CLAUDIA AS ROSENCRANTZ: *Am I dead?*

ME AS GUILDENSTERN: *Yes or no?*

CLAUDIA AS ROSENCRANTZ: *Is there a choice?*

ME AS GUILDENSTERN: *Is there a God?*

Daddy was laughing so hard. We were his British fools on a ship to death that couldn't be stopped, and the harder he laughed the more we carried on. We could have been four and five, or nine- and ten-year-old girls again, preening in front of our father, hamming up our performances. But when I glanced at Daddy again, his face had become a death mask. Before I could stop myself, I ripped the book out of Claudia's hands and tore it open, right down the middle, where it had been bound and taped back together years ago. I would have torn that damn book to pieces, except that Claudia screamed and her hands provoked her curly hair: "Beverly, please. *No*," she cried.

"Girls, girls!" our mother shouted.

But Daddy was still laughing, high on morphine. As far as he was concerned the British dudes were in top form. That was when Minerva and Peanut came in. Minerva gave me a look like, *Not here*.

Mom turned to Peanut. "Take your mother some place with you, *please*?" And Minerva, who was wearing a spaghetti-string summer dress in early spring with too much summer in it, traded places with Mom and kissed her grandfather. Claudia knelt on the floor by the bed on all fours, trying to hold together the cover of the book.

"Claudia," Mom said. "We fixed it once and we can fix it again."

Claudia looked up at me. "There's a name for women who move through the world like you do."

I shrugged. "An angry bitch?"

"An indignant black woman."

Daddy stopped laughing. My kids were watching me. "What's wrong with being indignant when the situation warrants it?" I asked.

Minerva cast a sideward glance at me. "People come here to rest. In peace."

Claudia rose and acknowledged Peanut, who was content to stand in the doorway. He loved his grandfather, but dying people unnerved him. "Apologies, nephew," Claudia said, "it's a tad boisterous in here."

I wanted to tell her to kill the euphemisms. *You act just like white folk. When white folks say* boisterous *they mean there's color in the room. When you tell white folk something they don't want to hear, they look at you like you aren't there and ask you to repeat yourself like they can't follow what you're saying. That's supposed to trip you up and make you think you're incoherent. And when white folk say there's been a change of plans, it usually means someone's about to get fired, or dropped, or left at the curb.* I work in the medical profession and I'm goddamn invisible to most of the doctors until they need something, and Claudia's coming at me with more white people logic? There's no strain or putting on airs when Claudia speaks, and that's what sets me off every time. I know damn well that we both grew up in the South Bronx, but whenever I look at Claudia, I start wondering if maybe I'm crazy. Maybe we weren't working-class after all. Maybe we were born with silver spoons in our mouths and SAT tutors to ensure we stayed upper-middle class. *Maybe* we grew up in a doorman building on the Upper West Side or on some posh block downtown—because Claudia speaks and wills it so.

But I held my tongue and my dregs of peace and followed Peanut out of the room into the hallway. I turned to my son. "Peanut, what do people mean when they say go home? How are you going to tell a dying person to go home if this is the only place they've ever known?"

"I don't know."

"He's dying," I told my son. "Plain and simple."

"Mom, I feel you"—Peanut clutched my shoulder—"but you need to chill."

"I know I got my bitch on. It's been working all morning up the sleeve of my shirt. I need a cigarette."

"I'll go get you some cigarettes," he said, anxious to find an excuse to leave the hospice.

"No, Peanut, I'm fully equipped to get my own cigarettes. You go on in there and say good-bye to your grandpa."

FIRST THING I did when I arrived at the hospice this morning was switch into scrubs. I don't believe in signs, but in retrospect, maybe that was a sign Daddy would die today. I made myself a promise when we found out he was terminally ill not to confuse my professional self with my life self. I didn't want to numb out or fall into nurse mode around Daddy. I wanted to be his daughter first and a nurse second. When I leave work, I never bring it home with me. And when I go to work, I go clean. That's one of the many tips I picked up from my father. He was strict about changing out of his uniform before he got home. He had two uniforms that he brought home in a nylon laundry bag for Mom to wash and press. There should be a policy in this country about how nurses go to work. I don't get how you prance in off the street wearing a nurse's uniform after riding the subway and wash your hands and care for someone. I don't do that. I change and clean up at work. I don't believe in God, but I pray for me and my patients—the ones I know and the ones going out and coming through.

THERE'S THIS SONG about the birds and the bees and the bees in the trees. And that's kind of what my childhood was like. The butterflies and the birds and maybe the fucking bees too ran away with the lies the teachers were telling us in school. They ran with that shit and dropped it down on our neighborhood, where real people like my parents were just trying to find their way. And hoping we would find our way too.

I AM ONE YEAR older than my baby sister. There are things she can't remember or wants to forget. I remember Daddy eating salami sandwiches and watching the *CBS Evening News*. I remember Daddy talking back to Tricky Dick. I remember how still the room was when he died. How the air just left him and there was no difference between his corpse and the metal bed that held it.

MY DADDY WAS not drafted in the war. He enlisted. My daddy celebrated the Fourth of July every year. And Memorial Day and Veterans Day too. My daddy sang the national anthem during Yankee games. He was smart, but he could have been smarter. He was not poor, but he could have been rich. He wasn't the first father to tell his girls we were his riches—or the last. There was no complaint in my daddy. And it makes me sad as shit. Maybe the fumes from the exhaust on the George Washington Bridge really killed him. But I'm sticking with dioxin. I will not sugarcoat the ugliness. People are dead who should be alive. People die every fucking day. And I know where the poison lives.

MINERVA, ALL OVER THE PLACE

2009

W HEN THEY POSTED THE SIGN FOR THE PLAYWRITING contest, I didn't think much about it. I was on academic probation because my grades had slipped to mostly Cs and a D and I'd been kicked out of the school orchestra for not showing up for rehearsals and my viola sat in a corner by the TV collecting dust because my mom was hoping that I would take an interest in it again. There was the Suzuki synthesizer too, a gift from Dad when he learned that I quit the viola because his thing is when you get stuck, try something else to unstick yourself. The first week I got the synthesizer I tinkered around with it. I wanted to make Mom feel like shit because it's more or less basically all her fault that our dad walked. When Dad slipped the way men just do, instead of her going off and slipping herself, Mom calls a confessional session in the living room so we can talk shit out. Like I want to hear Dad fucked some bitch. And it's one of those sessions where everyone's supposed to stay calm and speak in turn but then, of course, we're all taking sides. My brother Peanut, he's like you did what? And Dad looks at Peanut cause he wonders like I do sometimes if maybe Peanut's half a fag, not that I care, some of my best friends are fags at LaGuardia, and I'm like, now what? Now what? And Mom makes Dad feel all bad and Dad explains that he's not going to do it again. She was a fellow officer and they were bonding over the stresses of being cops, and Mom's nodding and then we're all making up and keeping happy-go-lucky time, and for a while, everybody and everything is chill, but then Mom starts getting perked up, she comes home and she's not wearing the dark-ass lipstick that our cousin Gladys used to ride her about and Mom cuts the dead hair off her split ends and then she actually puts in a texturizer and her curls hang natural like Aunty Claudia's and she's wearing Elizabeth Arden perfume, and I say, loud enough to start a tsunami in our living room, *Dad, did you buy Mom Elizabeth Arden perfume?* And I get a kick saying this and Mom's cussing me out for messing with her swag and Dad says but you've never liked perfume. Perfume gives you a headache. Maybe my hormones are in flux, Mom says. 'Cause now I can tolerate the scent. But Dad's too sharp for that. He catches her one day at the food truck near Columbia Presbyterian sharing a cigarette with this old dude. She admits to having a fling with this old-ass dude with a bad leg named Chico who sells roti and other food out of a food truck 'cause he got priced out of Bed-Stuy, and Mom is like we mostly just talk, well, maybe we kissed once. Dad knew all the ways a man and woman could kiss. And that's when Dad starts cutting his eyes at Mom and skipping dinner and then he starts going out and hanging with the crew at work he'd always called a whoring-ass bunch of men and Dad's coming home late like every night and Mom's working and cooking dinner and putting the twins to bed and then they begin fighting all the time and Peanut and I get in the middle and it's poor people's drama, Jerry Springer–level drama, and Dad says how does he even know the twins are his. The twins don't look the first damn thing like him, which is total bullshit. He says maybe Keisha and Lamar are the food truck guy's kids. And Mom says that's ridiculous because Chico still had a store in Bed-Stuy then.

And Dad says how she knows what Chico had. That's not all Chico had. And Dad left and Mama threatened to take out a restraining order on him and Peanut and I are like Mom, you can't do that. Dad will lose his job. And Dad's like, she would do that to me? Damn. That's low. And he moves to Arizona cause he knows some other cops out there. He makes a big deal about moving to Phoenix and I think he's expecting Mom to beg him not to go. It's like once he says he's leaving he's got to follow through and they are both stuck on stubborn. I wish they would get back together but then Mom, she can't be alone or lonely, so she falls into something with Chico. And there's no turning back. Dad's out and Chico's in, I'm like, fuck this. And she's like watch your mouth and show adults respect. I pay the rent here. So I start staying out with my friends and skipping school just 'cause I feel like it and my teachers say, oh yeah, well here's to your grades plummeting, and then I'm like, so what, and then they say one more semester and it's over, you're so out of here, and I'm like shit, no, they'll send me to school with remedial kids. My little brother Peanut is gloating cause he's at Bronx Science and thinks he's the next Steve Jobs. That's when I hit the books and school again. I cannot, will not, be showed up by Peanut. And that's when I see the poster about the playwriting contest and Professor Bass, who is too old to be teaching high school but the damn union can't fire him, says, you could probably write something decent if you weren't so arrogant. He says half the students in the school don't deserve to be here. And I roll my eyes and say well what, if you were me and you weren't supposed to be here what would you write about for a fifteen-minute play contest? And Professor Bass says, not about hiking in Madagascar or fly-fishing in Mongolia. Write about something that comes from the old ticker. And that's when I ask my stupid-ass Mom questions while she's lapping her coffee and eating Dunkin' Donuts 'cause now that Dad's gone she's picked up a few pounds again. She says, Minerva, there's a lot of people who if they had come up in a different time they might have done great things. Your gramps was one of them. And I'm like, how is this new information? She tells me to call Grams. And Grams, she's just glad I picked up the phone. Grams tells me about the play Gramps found on the boat in Vietnam, *Rosencrantz and Guildenstern Are Dead*. The one Aunty Claudia kept. I get mad with Mom all over again for being such a second-class citizen. I write a play about a man on a boat reading Shakespeare and then cut to his daughters reading the same play later while he is dying and I win second prize, and when I show Professor Bass the play, he spills his coffee on the raggedy-ass suit he always wears and bursts out crying. I brace for another lecture on the sorry state of the arts in New York City and the artist's struggle for dignity in the face of adversity. Or how maybe if he had stayed in Europe when he was younger things would be different. But Professor Bass wipes his eyes with a handkerchief. Nicely done, he says. And I get a ribbon and twenty-five dollars for my second-place prize, and I have Peanut meet me at the Drama Bookshop in Times Square, and we pick up *Rosencrantz and Guildenstern Are Dead*. They wrap it in nice navy-blue wrapping paper and we head home. I show Mom my second-place ribbon and give her the play. I am pissed at her for not having bought her own copy years ago. Mom tries to hug me but I step out of arm's reach. I have somewhere to be. But Mom's not having it. She grabs hold of me tight. And we stand there like that for a hot minute. And I don't fight it 'cause maybe she needs the hug more than I do. Maybe. And when she's holding me, I remember being little and how she used to read to me all the time. When I leave, Mom's still in the living room leafing through the play.

And I know just for once, I got it right.

WRITING EXERCISES/PROF. BASS LANGUAGE STRUCTURES

MINERVA C. PARKER

(Dialogue)

MINERVA'S DAD

Minnie, you would like the desert. It's not all brown like I was expecting. The desert in Arizona has a lot of brown, for sure, but there's these beautiful parts too up in the mountains where it's green and blue and silver. I can almost see what people like about it. I took a friend with me for a few days up in—

MINERVA

Who you dating? You dating someone? Already?

MINERVA'S DAD

It's pretty in the desert. I have a friend.

MINERVA

You said you were never going to get married again.

MINERVA'S DAD

Did I say that? I mailed you guys a postcard of the station where I work. It's one of the oldest buildings in Arizona. Now, why do you keep sending me these inappropriate postcards of half-nude women?

MINERVA

They're free. I grab them at Two Boots Pizza and the Strand.

MINERVA'S DAD

Seems like your mom should have money enough to front for stationery and stamps. I pay child support.

MINERVA

Is she black?

MINERVA'S DAD

You sound like your mom. Estrella's Navajo. And Spanish.

MINERVA

We killed the Navajos. Buffalo Soldiers. Herded them. Like you running Mexicans back over the border, Dad. Or should I call you Custer? You're going to be responsible for a whole generation of Mexicans hating blacks.

MINERVA'S DAD

And you're making Cs in history. So, what's wrong with this picture, Minnie? Anyway, Custer was in Wyoming. Little Big Horn. Get your geography straight.

MINERVA

I don't give a shit.

MINERVA'S DAD

Watch your mouth. Bev tells me you been sleeping over at someone's house? I'll come there. Do I have to come there?

MINERVA

And stay?

MINERVA'S DAD

No, Minnie. To visit. And there'll be no pleasure in it.

MINERVA

IT'S THREE WEEKS SOMETIMES BEFORE WE GOT A LETTER. Why can't you use FACEBOOK or text like a normal person?

MINERVA'S DAD

I don't believe in it.

MINERVA

But you're in a different state.

MINERVA'S DAD

People used to write letters. Back in the day, the dumbest fool could write a solid letter. There was this documentary on the Civil War—

MINERVA

Why can't I come live with you?

MINERVA'S DAD

There's too much sprawl—and too many drunk drivers with no regard for speed limits.

MINERVA

You said the desert was beautiful.

MINERVA'S DAD

Maybe when I get more settled.

MINERVA

Do you still love Mom?

MINERVA'S DAD

Doesn't matter.

MINERVA

Mom still loves you.

MINERVA'S DAD

Some things just don't matter.

MINERVA

Dad?

MINERVA'S DAD

Minerva, be a good girl. Kiss the twins. Peanut. That brother of yours, tell him life's a beast out here. He needs to man up.

(Poetry)

CUSTER BE KILLING MOTHERFUCKERS

My Da out in the desert
Say it's brown then it blooms
He Custer all over
In a border patrol uniform

Disappear
Fast fade to zero
And not look back
What's supposed to happen?
Say, Minnie, be a good girl
When good girls go to hell
I'd rather be a bad girl
Heard bad girls go upstairs
What can you tell me?
When you free to disappear
And I'm still here
And we still here
Ain't seen you in six months
Check this: that's half a year

STEAM

1971   1986   1996   **2010**

RUFUS, WHERE ARE YOU FROM, SON? *I WAS BORN IN NEW York City. Not far from here. Columbia Presbyterian.* And your folks? What do they do? *My dad's an attorney. James Vincent. My mother, Sigrid, is a casting agent in L.A.* Huh. Product of divorce. *Yes, sir.* Big family? *No, sir, I'm an only child.* Oh, so is my wife here. So is Agnes.

Claudia and I were seated on the camel-back sofa in the L-shaped living room with the glass coffee table and stucco walls that reminded me of my mom's first apartment in Venice Beach. Eddie Christie kept nudging a tray of sopressata and assorted cheeses and breads our way. The breads were from his favorite Italian bakery in the neighborhood; semolina rolls and seeded loaves and ciabatta that he encouraged us to layer with various cheeses. Cheeses that he insisted were not available in most markets in New York City. Stinky Italian cheeses that he had got special. The way he said "got special" was the only incentive I needed to eat them. Mrs. Christie seemed content to let her husband drive the conversation. She leaned against him on a leather love seat with her long legs crossed. "I always wanted a sister or brother," she said, "but I guess things worked out. I have my husband and daughters now."

"TELL ME A SECRET?" I said to Claudia Christie. Junior year. Three weeks into our relationship at Columbia University, and I knew I would ask Claudia Christie to marry me. I lived off-campus in Morningside Heights with a philosophy major who stayed at his girlfriend's place every other night. I lived off-campus because I've always been a light sleeper. It runs in the family. Sleep eludes me. Back then, I'd climb out of bed at three in the morning and play my saxophone. I had no real ear for it, but the music did wonders for my sleep. By second semester, my roommate had moved downtown to the West Village. He slinked out on a Saturday and Claudia moved in within a week. We holed up like bandits in our apartment those first sex-crazed weeks of the winter semester. We were young and nimble and awed by the constant pleasure our bodies could give. It's the nature of the college years for students to have intense . . . hook-ups, as they say now, and become partners overnight. Friends nick-named us *the disappearing act* because we only stepped out of our apartment to attend classes or for food, mostly inexpensive takeout. Pizza at V&T's. Rice and beans at Tom's. Rotisserie chicken and the falafel–baba ganoush combo at Rainbow Chicken. The Mediterranean food made our breath smelly, but even garlic comes with fringe benefits. Manipulate a glove of garlic the right way and your senses will excite you. (A woman named Parsnip taught me that trick.)

"Ruff," said Claudia. "There are no secrets anymore." She was propped up on our knotty futon with Goethe's "Der Prokurator" in her lap. We were taking a class on the birth of the novella form in literature. Pretty thrilling stuff for English majors.

"The name is Rufus." Only my mother and father called me Ruff. But I liked that Claudia had taken immediately to using my nickname.

"I can't take you seriously as Rufus. I hear Rufus and I think of Rufus and Chaka Khan."

"Damn, you hurt my feelings."

"*C'est dommage.* You'll live."

College dating can scare you. I had woken up with some girls I didn't want to see again and probably wouldn't have touched in the first place if I hadn't been at the wrong party at the wrong time. It's a minor miracle to roll over the morning after a dorm party happy to see the person you climbed in bed with the night before. But I liked waking up with Claudia next to me. I am white. Claudia is black. Most of our time together, we've haven't had an issue with race. This world, though, we've found this world has issues enough for both of us.

"Maybe secrets are now the province of Victorian melodramas," I said. "But come on, there must be something deep, dark, and personal in your past? Give me your best shame."

"If I take you home, you might catch fire." And then she laughed. I didn't know it at the time, but this was her father's laughter, raspy and warm, laughter that suggested August summers and cigarettes, though she did not smoke. I call this Claudia's nervous laughter: her laughter before the truth. And if you can pick up habits from your partner, I would say that I picked up laughter from Claudia, except that my mother courts the world's laughter too.

"Seriously," Claudia said. "My mom's usually a very cool customer. She keeps her own counsel about most things. But my last boyfriend ended up at Columbia Presbyterian with first-degree burns on his shoulder. They used nail clippers to unpeel his shirt from his shoulder. I thought his family might sue."

AGNES CHRISTIE TRIED to burn me with an iron the first time Claudia took me home. I don't remember the iron, only the steam and the way it bubbled from the little spigot on top of the flat chrome handle. I want to say the iron was Venetian red, but it might have been blue or silver or gray. Things were going well enough. Or so I thought. Mrs. Christie yawned and excused herself. When she returned I initially mistook the piping hot iron she was carrying for a decanter of Chianti. I smiled at the pretty brown woman with my future wife's oval face and held my ground. She approached and I extended my arms and hands out to confront her heat. This gesture, my fingers dancing forward and not pulling away, made Agnes Christie pause and glance down at the iron.

"Why, *Mrs. Christie*," I said. "You won't burn me without burning yourself."

Mr. Christie came up alongside his wife. "Agnes," he said. "It's all right."

"Forgive me," Agnes Christie said. And turned off the hot iron. "Where I come from, it's seldom a good thing when strange white men show up at your house."

"Well, I promise to devote myself to being less of a stranger somehow. But my whiteness, that's something I can't do anything about."

CLAUDIA PREPARED ME for her mother's iron. We had rehearsed together the best way to respond if she came at me.

I was surprised by the dearth of books in the Christie household initially. In the living room, the only books on display were the *Encyclopedia Britannica* and a collection of Shakespeare plays that Mrs. Christie had purchased during an auction at the Catholic school she attended as a child. This blew my mind. Perhaps, if you knew Claudia—you'd have to know Claudia to understand. Or, perhaps, it all comes down to personal privilege and expectations? I had grown up in an apartment overlooking Central Park West with a study. I would spend hours making forts out of the books that lined the walls there. When I visited Claudia's house, I was sure she would throw open a door and there would be evidence, a secret cave of books that revealed how she had arrived at Columbia. Some trace of a budding scholar's nook. But there was only a twin-sized bed and a chest of drawers and a desk, above which hung a *Purple Rain* poster. The Christie house didn't lack material things. There just wasn't much room to spare. Everything was functional. It was one of those moments, and I've had a few of them as a white man married to a black woman, when I understood my own privilege.

You can talk about privilege until you're blue in the face but you'll never understand it until you've lived with someone who has had to do more with less.

"She's not crazy," I said, speaking above the loud hum of the 5 train on the ride back to our apartment. We would take the 4 to 125th and then catch a cab the rest of the way home.

"What?"

"Your folks exist in shutdown mode. So do mine."

Claudia looked away. "Please don't judge my family based on your parents. It's unproductive. They're from a different generation. Shit happened. We—Beverly and I—can't ask."

"Why?"

"It's *theirs*, Rufus."

"But we inherit it. Don't you want to know what makes them tick?"

Claudia sighed. "Not really. It's enough that they loved me."

OUR FIRST CHRISTMAS, I bought Claudia's mother a vintage iron. I found it at a thrift shop on Venice Beach while on holiday with my mom. When Mrs. Christie unwrapped the present, I wasn't sure how she or Claudia or Mr. Christie would react. I wasn't sure if they'd appreciate the joke or if it was a joke or my passive-aggressive stance, my way of saying, *If you burn me, I will keep coming, I will not give up and I will come back for your daughter again and again.*

But she smiled—and a flush showed on her dark cheeks. "My gift's a bit more—pedestrian. A Yankees cap from Eddie and me."

IRON GIVING HAS become a tradition between us. Every Christmas, I buy Mrs. Christie an antique iron. She collects them like artifacts in a museum—flatirons, box irons, sadirons. Now that she doesn't have Mr. Christie to iron for anymore, I'm not sure how much she irons in Buckner County, Georgia. During her Sunday chats with Claudia, I've been tempted to ask her if she still owns them.

———

EVEN NOW, TWENTY years later, Claudia likes to work in bed. She will take a plastic food tray and prop it in her lap to grade student papers. We live in university housing, a ten-minute walk from the apartment we first shared. History surrounds us. Evidence of how we came into being, mutated, had children. When people say that New York has changed, I'm not always sure what they mean. Changed, for whom? I can chart our evolution in city blocks and miles. Of course, the stores and restaurants come and go. Rainbow Chicken is long gone. Gotham Cabinets, where I bought my first futon, hangs on, but I'm not sure the new generation digs futons. The vibe is different uptown and downtown. We used to escape to the Lower East Side for a gritty counterculture experience, but it's all blonds with trust funds on Ludlow now. When you have kids, you don't miss these things in the same way. You don't have time.

MY NAME IS Rufus Noel Vincent. I am forty years old. These days, three times a week, you'll find my wife and me at the pool in our building taking swimming therapy with our daughter Winona. The best way to overcome a fear is to revisit it, according to Winnie's therapist. And so, Claudia, Winona, and I—during this time Elijah gets one-on-one time with his grandfather, my dad—swim like amphibians from one end of the pool to the other. Winona loves the crawl and when I'm crawling through the water alongside her, quite often I think about Hank Camphor, the half brother I do not know. I think about my father and my mother and all the shit from my past that I've worked overtime to forget: *one little fish; two little fish; three little fish.* I can't tell if I'm swimming away from the past or headfirst toward it.

MY MOTHER PULLED me out of Trinity Prep my freshman year in high school. She thought the environment was too incestuous. I had attended Trinity with the same kids since pre-K, played in the same softball and soccer leagues in Central Park, gotten stoned at the same birthday parties, and attended the same sleepover camps in Vermont and coastal Maine. Mom regretted that I had not tested into Hunter College High School in sixth grade. That she and Dad had not pushed me to be more academic. She was certain that we needed a change. And recently, recently, I had developed this annoying vocal tic: habitually clearing my throat. There was something lodged in my larynx that wouldn't come up.

"It's Scotch-tape sticky in there," I'd often say.

My mother and father took me to Manhattan Eye, Ear, and Throat Hospital. The best specialists in New York examined me, but none of them could find anything lodged in my throat. Nor did I test positive for allergies. I was in perfect health. A healthy teenage boy.

"It's in his head," one doctor said, finally. "What's happening in your home?"

Up until that point, I toyed with the piano, an instrument for which I displayed little talent and fleeting interest. Everyone at Trinity played an instrument. Mom, who was of European extraction, often played our Steinway baby grand piano in the evening after work. She believed playing the piano might relax me, if nothing else. My dad had grown up in a household without musical instruments, but he loved jazz, Miles Davis everything. "So What?" He bought me a secondhand saxophone from a jazz musician who claimed to have jammed with the greats. Dad paid a small fortune for that saxophone even though, he admitted later, his gut told him he would've done better with a new one.

"Use this to clear your pipes," he said. "If you make progress, I know a pro who'll give you lessons."

His tone toward my mother was not as kind. "What were you thinking taking Ruff out of Trinity? He has a built-in community there."

"That's not the only place I'm going to take him," Mom said. When she first asked my father for a divorce, they were in a yellow taxicab on Fifth Avenue, returning home from a fiftieth birthday party bash for a senior partner at his firm. The prospect of divorce came as a shock to my father. In the following weeks, he simply ignored Mom's request.

"Maybe you were right to send him to a new school," Dad said one night at the dinner table. He put his hand over Mom's.

"The Pacific!" She looked away and removed his hand.

"You lost me there, Sigrid."

"I've always wanted to live near the Pacific Ocean."

Dad understood immediately. "You can't take my son out west."

"He's fifteen," Mom said, not confident but putting on a show. "The decision is his."

"A divorce?" I asked, and cleared my throat. I performed little circular movements, my three fingers waxing and waning over my Adam's apple. I didn't know this at the time, but these small massages were practice for the belly massages I would give Claudia years later while singing to our unborn twins. They were practice for the massages Claudia would give me after I'd eaten pizza or some dish with dairy that my stomach couldn't tolerate.

"Why don't you get up and get Ruff some water, Sigrid?" Dad said. "The boy sounds like a broken vacuum cleaner."

"I was waiting for you to ask me to get water!" Mom shook her head. "Tell me, should I get water because I'm a woman?"

"I love you because you're a woman."

"That's the problem. You love *all* women," she said.

Dad whistled. "Ruff, it might be a good time for you to practice your saxophone."

There was a breeze blowing into the dining room from the terrace deck. The deck overlooked Central Park West. I could smell cheap roasting peanuts and hot dogs from vendors eleven floors down. I could hear the hooves of horse-drawn carriages.

"Rufus." Mom smiled. "It was good of your dad to buy you a saxophone. Out west you could be near the ocean and play in a marching band."

"New York is an island," Dad said. "It's surrounded by water on all sides. California is a desert. One day, the Pacific will rise up and say California's too damn thirsty. The Pacific will do what you have no reason to do, Sigrid. Throw up your hands and walk away."

"Are you saying Dad cheated on you?" I hesitated, torn between going to my room to practice and remaining at the dining room table.

Mom laughed and laughed and laughed. Her laughter made Dad blush. He looked like he was performing some mathematical breakdown of the times he might have cheated on Mom.

"You think I slept with women at Trinity?" he said, finding the idea both insulting and preposterous. "You don't use the lavatory where your kid lives. School is where Ruff lives. His second home."

And with this one statement, Mom and I understood that Dad had cheated, though the locality was in question.

"Tell me I'm not a good father, Sigrid?" he said. "In every way that counts, I've been a solid, hands-on dad."

I was seeing my father in a new light. Dad had taught me how to pitch a tent in the rain during a thunderstorm. He had taught me to throw a softball in Central Park. Dad had shown me how to build a fort of bungee cords and a fort of books with Robinson Crusoe and Huckleberry Finn in our study. But Mom had taught me how to ride a bike. And Mom had taken me to Benihana. There were a lot of evenings when Dad was out of town that Mom and I had eaten alone. I started thinking about the Scotch tape in my throat that wouldn't go away and how its stickiness intensified when I was in the same room with both of my parents.

"California has sunshine." Mom nodded. "It's the Sunshine State."

Neither Dad nor I had the heart to tell Mom that Florida was the Sunshine State. Mom was an intelligent woman but she flustered easily. I went in search of my saxophone. I didn't want to go to California. But I was pissed at Dad.

Walkin' in L.A.
Walkin' in L.A., nobody walks in L.A.
Walkin' in L.A.
Walkin' in L.A., nobody walks in L.A.

—Missing Persons, Spring Session M, 1982

———

EVERYONE KNOWS L.A. has palm trees. Lights that flicker and twinkle neon in the night. Five-lane highways gorged with traffic. And pollution decorating azure skies. In Venice, we walked. It's never been true that nobody walks in L.A.

"Two legs will carry you any number of places," Mom said. "If you are curious and on the lookout for swatches." And Mom was curious.

"Like the watch?" I asked.

"No, swatches of neighborhoods." She landed a job as the assistant to a casting agent two weeks after we moved into our apartment.

"Explore L.A. firsthand," Bruce the casting agent told her. He was the only man I'd ever met with more hair than my father. He pulled his tawny mane back into a ponytail.

Mom enrolled me in Venice Senior High. There was no marching band, and about this, she apologized more than once, profusely, several times—even enlisting Bruce's help to enroll me in Beverly Hills High.

"No thanks," I said. "Find me a tutor. I'll stick with private lessons."

"Is that a question or a command?" She regarded me with her raised brows knitting.

Mom rented a two-bedroom apartment in a Spanish-style villa with an interior courtyard and wisteria working its way up the faded balconies. There were bougainvillea and hibiscus plants, orange and intense and persistent in the August heat. There was dryness. We lived two blocks from the beach. Bruce lived in the West Hollywood Hills. Sometimes on the ride to his estate in Mom's Volkswagen Bug, a car that catered to her petite frame but was dwarfed by mine, I'd look at the white letters jutting out of the hay-colored hills. The hills reminded me of Bruce's hair. I was certain that he wanted to do Mom, but there was a lot of doing in the laid-back California air.

We moved to Venice Beach in July 1986. The vibe was raw and seedy and scary, but then again, so was New York. Years later, people would ask me how did I get by in L.A., and I would say, *It's not some place you go to get by.* I was fifteen and two blocks from the beach and girls with bikini-clad bodies. You could look like Frankenstein on Venice Beach in 1986 and still fit in and get laid. I would walk out on the boardwalk and sometimes it would feel like half the homeless people in New York had found new digs in Venice Beach. As community-driven as the vibe was, there was a good bit of protest about the homeless taking up shelter on the beach. If Mom had come to Venice hoping to find some kind of utopia, she was disappointed. We landed on cut glass and rank canals with hypodermic needles.

"Look out on the Pacific and nothing else matters," Mom said. She told me the Pacific had spent half its life calling her and she hadn't even known it.

Our apartment building was full of women with names like Sage and Parsnip and Jasmine. All of them had been actresses or models or professional dancers at some point but moved on to jobs as flight attendants and administrative assistants or catalog models. At least one, Sage, had lost custody of her two-year-old daughter. She didn't know where her husband had taken the girl or if she would see her again. Mom made friends with these women, who acted younger than they were. Later, during the sex I would have with them, I rummaged through their purses and found their birthdates on their driver's licenses: an old thirty-six, a taut forty-one. I waited for Mom to reach back to seventeen or twenty-one. I waited for her to dye her hair blond. And she waited for me to stop waiting, monitoring the cough that no longer seemed to exist out of the corner of her eyes. Even though she was a third-generation American she exaggerated her European accent. People said she looked like Nastassja Kinski, which wasn't the least bit true, but she took the compliment and milked it.

"My people are from Brittany," she would say. Mom wore these little scarves crisscrossed around her neck, tied in the French style.

"Rufus," Sage or Parsnip or Jasmine would ask me. "Do you like the boardwalk?"

I looked at them and they looked at me. *You don't use the bathroom where you live*, I heard my father's voice in my head. I went to the beach, down to the breakwaters where the surfers hung out and got stoned. I got stoned with them pretty much every day. That's how I fell in with a surfer named Herb. Herb was a musky white guy with dreadlocks. *Herb sells the herb* was the running joke. He asked if I wanted to go into business with him. I didn't.

"You're a wholesome kid. People like wholesome kids." Herb probably had three years on me.

In the morning, I surfed, and in the afternoon, I played my saxophone on the boardwalk for small change. To my amazement, I did all right. And I wasn't even that good. There was this old woman, a barfly who wore the same red corduroy jumpsuit every day and lived in one of the SRO hotels. She'd show up in the early evening and belt out the same verse from the Platters' "Only You" repeatedly:

Only you, can make this world seem right
Only you, can make the darkness bright
Only you and you alone . . .

Then she would disappear with the day's earnings.

If Mom knew I was smoking weed, she didn't let on. She worked fourteen-hour days with Bruce because the casting business was brutal and it had its seasons and Bruce worked with what he called cutting-edge independent directors and actors from New York. Mom had New York literary cachet and a French pedigree. It did not matter that in New York she had shared a corner office in a cubby facing a small window. In Los Angeles, she had floor-length windows and hanging plants and doors that slid open and furniture that looked like it was built for a boat.

BRUCE SOMETIMES CAME over for bouillabaisse at our apartment. "Sig," he called my mother. "Honestly, what are you doing living here?"

Mom kept her conversations with Bruce professional, at least around me. She loved talking shop. I noticed her scarves were longer and looser and the soft pastel colors were now vibrant purples.

"Copyediting is not that different from casting. Copy editors look for flaws and perfect them. Casting agents look for that perfect actor who is committed to unraveling his flaws."

Dad shipped me books from New York. He sent looping handwritten notes: *A boy's never too old to build forts. I build them in my head all the time.*

I told Herb about Dad and he said, "What an awesome fucking father you've got."

I felt a flicker of pride then. I told him stories about the women in our apartment building. He convinced me to make introductions. Herb dropped by one evening. Mom gave him a suspicious look but said nothing. She was on her way out the door to meet Bruce at the Mark Taper Forum. A young actress from New York giving a "star-making turn" in August Strindberg's *Miss Julie*. When Mom left, Parsnip invited us downstairs to her apartment.

I slept with Parsnip that same night. I remember it clearly because the bed squeaked and seemed achingly small but it was king-size. Maybe it was more that I felt small. Herb was there in the beginning. Cheering us on. He kept saying he wanted to watch. His observations made me fumble, so that I stopped like I did when I was a little kid trying to avoid urinating on the toilet seat. Herb evoked primal shame in me.

I held my privates and wanted to say, *May I have privacy, please?* I didn't want Herb to know that I had just lost my virginity.

When we were done, Herb took a turn with Parsnip, who liked to mimic celebrity voices while she fucked. She had a voice for every character on TV: Betty White from the *Golden Girls*; Kelsey Grammer from *Cheers*; Markie Post from *Night Court*. She watched a lot of TV, and it was challenging trying to fuck her and her random voices. Our second time around, I must have put my hand over her mouth because later, after Herb had left, Parsnip climbed out of bed and pointed to her bathroom. "Go take a shower, Rufus," she said.

I was lounging on her sofa in the living room watching MTV

videos: the Bangles' "Walking Down Your Street." Parsnip kept an aquarium full of goldfish in the living room. They were all the same color and so crowded together in their ocean I was claustrophobic for them.

"It was your first time. So I'm obliged to teach you a thing or two. A boy could get in a lifetime of trouble putting his hands over a girl's mouth in the act. Get my drift? That kind of action brings up the wrong stuff. And some women might get off on some guy's dirty cock, but I never met one who didn't prefer good hygiene."

"I like having your smell on me. You didn't tell Herb to take a shower."

Parsnip sat down beside me. "Herb will never be clean. He will *never* be clean."

MY FATHER CAME to Los Angeles for a surprise visit. He didn't book a hotel, so Mom booked one for him. But that night, after dinner in Hollywood, a vegan restaurant where Dad kept moving the miso shiitake mushrooms around on his plate, Mom and Dad came back to the apartment and slept in the same bed. Parsnip and Sage and Jasmine made appearances the following evening to meet Dad. Mom made dirty martinis. (I didn't invite Herb.)

"Ruff, who do you think you're fooling?" Dad said, rustling my hair and pulling me aside in the living room.

"Which one's the hottest?" I asked proudly. "Sage or Jasmine or Parsnip?"

"I lost my virginity in college," my father said. "A girl named Alice. You got this thing all wrong. And they should know better. Technically, you're a minor."

"Dad, it's the eighties. And I'm really into Parsnip."

"Somehow, I thought this decade would be different." He brought me a box of condoms and told me to always take precautions. I showed Dad where I played my sax on the boardwalk. I muddled though "So What?" And he applauded. When the barfly showed up and cried through "Only You," Dad gave her fifty bucks.

"Jesus Christ," he said, after she departed. "Life is mean."

"Mom's happy here." We hadn't talked about Mom. I was convinced now that she was into Bruce.

"What's happy?" Dad said.

I waited for him to ask me to come back with him, but he didn't. He flew to San Francisco the following morning to meet Barbara Camphor at a conference. They met seasonally. Four times a year. Theirs was the kind of affair that wouldn't give. Of course, I knew none of this at fifteen.

AFTER DAD'S VISIT, Mom gave Parsnip the cold shoulder. She made Jasmine and Sage coq au vin and beef bourguignon. Parsnip was exiled from my mother's clique, even though, in Parsnip's own crazy way, she was the best of all of them, except my mother, of course. Sage had confusion. And Jasmine didn't know if she was on the planet half the time. She was always on a plane between New York and Los Angeles. I learned at a young age that a flight attendant's life is anything but glamorous. I am always polite to them when traveling.

MY FIRST-SEMESTER report card came in riddled with Cs.

"I had hoped that being a small fish in a big pond would make you more academic."

"Mom, I'm average."

"No, I don't think so. I won't believe this."

She found a musician in Venice Beach who gave me saxophone lessons. She put an end to my hustle on the boardwalk. "*Up* your grades and then we'll talk."

The sax teacher owned a house facing the canal. He was on the committee for a cleaner Venice Beach. He was a recovering heroin addict. He was also a dour black man with no patience for white teenage boys who wanted to play jazz. "Don't waste my time. And I won't waste yours," he said. "The saxophone requires discipline."

To keep me busy, my mom also gave me a part-time job as her assistant. She made popcorn on Sunday evenings and we watched old films: *All About Eve* and *The Apartment*; *Metropolis* and *Casablanca*.

For pocket money, she had me compile a list of films either shot in L.A. or about L.A. Sometimes, we went around scouting old set locations.

"We did this when we first got here," I reminded her.

"We were aimless," she said. "Now we have a mission."

"And our mission is?"

"There's nothing new," Mom said. "Everything that can be done has been done already. The best we can do is reimagine our way through existence."

We walked home from my lessons on Thursday evenings and would stop by our favorite diner and share an order of miraculously thin, hand-cut French fries. It made Mom happy when I mentioned on our walk that Orson Welles had fallen into one of the canals and nearly drowned while filming *A Touch of Evil* or that Thomas Mann had lived two blocks away from Bruce's apartment in the West Hollywood Hills.

"These are little details I can drop during casting calls," she laughed. "I'll seem smarter than I am."

Things were good between us. Mom and me. I cut back on my weed intake, and Herb moved to Oakland with some people he had met. There was this new girl in my third-period biology class I was thinking about asking out on a date. I didn't have any friends yet. My people had been the surfers and slackers on Venice Beach. Herb's people, mostly. I still slept with Parsnip. Sometimes I thought Parsnip slept with me to get back at Mom.

In October, Mom and I were on our way to dinner when a guy pulled up in a black Ford Mustang alongside the sidewalk.

"Need a ride?" he said. He lowered the window. His chin had folds in it and was beginning to double.

"No thank you," my mother said in her Nastassja Kinski–inspired accent.

"Beautiful night out here," he said.

"That it is." My mother smiled. She paused and the Ford Mustang paused too.

"What are you up to?" the man asked.

"We're enjoying the quiet time—to ourselves," Mom said.

"I could use a sandwich," said the man, unfazed.

"Dude," I said. "There are plenty of restaurants around here."

He leaned over. "You didn't ask what kind."

The guy had big rings on his fingers. Men with rings on their fingers have always given me the creeps. "That's 'cause we don't give a fuck," I said.

Mom put her hand on my shoulder: the shoulder that held my saxophone case.

"What kind of sandwich?" she asked.

"The kind that gives satisfaction."

She cussed him out in French but in English she said, "Did you not hear the Stones song? There's no such thing."

The man, he must have been drunk or on some kind of drugs, looking back on the situation now. He stuck his head out of the driver's-side window to address my mother.

"How about you climb in the backseat and let this young man and me make a sandwich out of you?"

Maybe it was the fact that Herb and I had made a sandwich out of Parsnip and I could visualize fully what the sandwich he proposed would look like. Maybe it was the fact that his words undressed my mother before I could put her clothes back on. Maybe it was the way my mom's face turned red so that mine grew red too. I could feel steam blowing out of my ears.

"What are we doing here, Mom?" It's the question I had wanted to ask since we had first arrived in L.A. What I really meant was, *What am I doing here?* Mom was fine. She loved L.A. I had told Dad this, but now every bone in my body shook with the reality of it. I pulled my saxophone case off my shoulder and smashed it in the double-chinned man's face. His nose and mouth spawned red blood. My mother shrieked. She shrieked and I gripped her arm.

"Just keep walking," I told her. I made myself walk. We walked fast.

"Rufus, you could have killed him."

"Pervert."

"Rufus, we should go back."

I flung my saxophone case over my shoulder. "No."

"I could have handled it."

"The way you handled being married to Dad?"

"You don't get to do this. Not here, not now. You can't go hitting people when they say something you disapprove of."

"It wasn't what he said. It was his intentions."

"When you speak like that you sound just like—"

"Say it!"

"James Samuel Vincent."

There are moments when you look at your parents and wonder. Since the news of the divorce hit, I'd had lots of those, but gone was the coughing. There was Scotch tape on the shelves and in desks all over L.A. but none in my throat. I did not cough in L.A. I sneezed sometimes, but what's a sneeze? All you have to do is wipe your nose. Mom had made me choose. Her or Dad. The problem was, I loved both of them.

WHEN WE RETURNED to our apartment, I climbed into the shower and washed. There had been a preponderance of blood on the man's face but only splotches on my clothes and saxophone case. After I showered, I retreated to my room and took out all the books from Dad that I hadn't unpacked yet: *The Last of the Mohicans*; *Moby-Dick*; *The Call of the Wild*. I made a small fort and squeezed myself into it. I pretended to sleep, but sleep laughed at me. I didn't play my saxophone for months.

Mom turned on the evening news, expecting to find something about the Venice Beach pervert, but there was nothing. I look back on that day and think that in this era—the era of video cameras and cell phones—there's no way we would have walked away so easily. No way *I* would have walked away so easily. Someone would have videoed me in the act. I would have been on YouTube within five minutes.

———

I CALLED DAD and he didn't take the news so well initially. Mom called Dad and he was in Los Angeles twenty-four hours later. She told James Samuel Vincent the whole story. He didn't say a word. The first thing we did was to repack the books he'd mailed me. We repacked them in alphabetical order so that we would unpack them easily when I returned to New York. We took them to the post office and sent them book rate. I needed something to read on the plane and Dad pulled out James Joyce's *Portrait of the Artist as a Young Man*.

"Did you read this?" I asked.

"Joyce," he said, "isn't for everyone."

Neither is California, I thought. We never talked about what happened on Venice Beach again. Not me. Not my dad. And not my mom. I don't know if it's a secret because we don't talk about it or we don't talk about it because there's so much other baggage attached to it. That's just to say, I've never been that angry before or since in my life. The day Mrs. Christie came toward me with that iron, I remembered what it was like to feel threatened or to act on a violent impulse to hurt someone. To want to protect the ones you love. More steam was coming off her body than the iron she held. I've been there. Our bodies carry steam for us.

YOU ARE NO LEE KRASNER

1960 **1970** **1980** **1990**

T HERE ARE FEW THINGS WORSE THAN BEING A PLAIN GIRL born to a lovely mother. Adele Pransky was standing at the soda fountain spritzing cherry pop into a glass mug when Yan Sokolov, Seth's new gambling buddy, strolled into Dean's Beachside Bar & Grill alongside him. Years later, Adele would recall how the breeze from the ocean had licked away the sweat on Yan and Seth's white shirts as they slipped off the Coney Island boardwalk into the bustling bar like the best of friends. They were strangers in fact, these two men, come together after a few drinks of sour whiskey, cigars, and cards at a wobbly table in a whorehouse in Hell's Kitchen.

ADELE'S MOTHER, Rachel Pransky, tolerated Seth's love of cards as long as he didn't lose too much money. Her money. And on that balmy evening, Rachel was busy tending the register. Seth kissed Rachel and motioned for Yan to make himself comfortable at the bar.

"Adele," Seth yelled, waving her over. "Bring my friend here a deluxe plate of haddock and chips."

Adele made her way over to them. "How do you know he likes haddock?" she asked.

Yan nodded. "Indeed, I'll eat your haddock, but phooey on your shellfish."

Adele considered the man, who introduced himself as Yan Sokolov. He was more spiffily dressed than the other men at the bar, a showboat of gray silk and gabardine. Adele liked that he'd discarded his blazer and rolled up the sleeves of his white shirt to blend in with the working-class crowd. She thought him striking in an expressionistic, upside-down way. His mien could be thirty or fifty with all its creases and rock crevices.

"Who is he?" Rachel asked.

"An acquaintance." Seth told Rachel how that very evening Yan had pulled him away from the poker table before all his earnings were lost.

"What's the hurry to be poor, my friend," Yan had said. "Slow down. You can go to the poorhouse any day."

Seth dropped two coins into the jukebox. "I started to tell him to mind his own damn business. But then I remembered you, Rachel, and the portion of my wallet not yet spent. And, of course, I remembered Adele."

Seth slipped his arms around Rachel's waist and navigated her away from the register for a spin on the dance floor. Sawdust kicked up around their feet as Sinatra crooned "I've Got You under My Skin." Seth's Rachel—that was what the regulars at Dean's Beachside Bar & Grill called them. Seth had proposed to Rachel many times, but Rachel refused to marry him until her daughter found a husband. They had been a long time waiting. The bar was the closest thing Rachel had to offer Adele as an inheritance. And the bar was their sole livelihood.

While they danced Rachel and Seth stole glances at Adele and Yan. Adele had removed her apron. She never went apronless in

Dean's Beachside Bar & Grill. Whatever Yan was saying had won Adele's full attention. They were leaning forward, elbows touching on the counter. It was like waves on sand the way Adele lapped to Yan and Yan lapped to Adele.

"I was lucky," Rachel said more than once to Seth. "An arranged marriage with a man I could love. I don't want to marry Adele off. I want Adele to be happy."

Seth never told Rachel this, but Adele didn't have the kind of face that married happy or, for that matter, stayed happily married. Adele's brown hair went frizzy where her mother's dark tresses entertained loose curls. Adele's skin freckled where Rachel's was alabaster white. She had, mercifully, inherited her mother's vibrant green eyes and a nose that commanded attention, a nose that might not work on another face but represented in Rachel a stone-cold beauty and in Adele, something akin to grace. It was usually after a fight and mad sex, never to be confused with lovemaking, that Seth and Rachel agreed to disagree that Adele was treading water in the marriage department. And only then could they make love.

THEY NICKNAMED HIM Yan the Pest. He came by the bar every evening at seven o'clock on the dot. He came bearing roses and sprigs of baby's breath that were missing their white tips.

"How can baby's breath compete with the ocean breeze?" Yan said.

He offered the roses to Adele and she blushed. "Perhaps you haven't wrapped the wax paper tautly enough." Adele demonstrated how to wrap roses properly, folding the wax paper corners and rolling it just so.

"You had better tell him you're not a virgin," Rachel said, after witnessing Adele's saucy demonstration.

"But I am." Adele blinked.

"Well, you shouldn't be," said Rachel, walking away from the counter and into the kitchen, where for a second or two she thought she might faint from disbelief. Rachel's husband, Dean, had been struck down by lightning one morning on the boardwalk within a few feet of his bar. *Ah, you should have seen the lightning move*, the vendors told Rachel. Now why, just why, would she want to see a thing like that? Everyone had thought she would remarry and let someone take over the business. When Rachel smiled at customers it was easier to forget just how much she had loved Dean, to forget that she was terrified and did not know what she was doing or how she would survive. She had told herself that she was not the only woman to open a bar every morning with a baby suckling on her breast or to retreat into the back room for regular feedings. All these years and the child was now a woman. How could Adele be a virgin, working the bar all these years?

Adele was twenty-nine and giddy by nature. She was, after the liberally poured bottom-shelf drinks, the biggest draw at Dean's Beachside Bar & Grill. Rachel regaled her customers with sarcasm and honesty. Adele promised them the sunshine sailing over the horizon, sometimes on the coattails of a storm. It was the kind of good news a workingman appreciated at the end of a nine-to-five day. And Dean's Beachside Bar & Grill had the fringe benefit of being color-blind. Everyone was welcome.

"I love to paint," Adele said. "I take art classes in the city every Thursday."

"Ah, a woman who is married to her art." Yan smiled. "I must see—may I see your masterpieces?" He winked at Rachel. "What a good mother you are to raise a girl who has saved the best for herself."

Adele gave Yan a private tour of Dean's, pointing to the mural on the wall that ran the length of the bar. There were mermaids with locks threaded ruby gold and strong men with shoulders Atlas could somersault across. There were midgets dressed like Marie Antoinette and clowns on walking sticks that frolicked above the Wonder Wheel. There were starfish in hula hoops and acrobats walking upside down on tightropes juggling exotic fruit: mango and papaya and prickly pears. And fat women with verve.

Jolly Mazie
Weight 450 lbs
B511-A2

ADELE'S HANDICRAFT delighted Yan. He asked for a stepladder and climbed atop it to take the mermaids' measurements.

"You are precise." Yan nodded appreciatively.

"Yan does not waste time," Rachel noted.

"He owns several buildings in Manhattan," said Seth, sensing his own bit of sunshine on the horizon.

"Several?" repeated Rachel. "Well, that's all fine and well. But is he kind, Seth? Is he decent?"

SUMMER TICKLED AUTUMN. Yan asked Rachel in Russian for Adele's hand in marriage. And Rachel answered in Yiddish. Yan asked again in Yiddish. And Rachel responded in Russian. They both agreed in English. After Dean's death, Rachel had fallen away from religion, but in honor of Adele's father, Yan and Adele were married in the synagogue. After the wedding, they threw a big party at the bar that lasted all night and even a fraction of the morning.

Yan was surprised to find virgin blood on their marital sheets. He poured warm water into a metal bin and soaked her feet in Epsom salts, rosewater, and lavender.

"It's from standing behind that counter," he said. "Tell your mother from this day forward—no more." He gave Adele an allowance and told her to invest in the best art supplies money could buy.

"But what will she do without me?" asked Adele.

"You can be replaced, Adele," Yan said. "It's menial work. Do you want to be an artist, or a counter girl in a dive bar?" He pinched her cheeks.

Adele liked the customers at Dean's Beachside Bar & Grill. She was an only child and they were her extended family. She had grown up around them. They came from the Coney Island projects or the sliver of Italian neighborhoods tucked behind Neptune Avenue to nurse their miseries away over bottles of Budweiser. They carried on about the dreams they had the previous nights and the numbers some dead relative had encouraged them from six feet under to play. They came from Brighton Beach to order the hot dogs, which was the sole item on the menu that Rachel kept kosher. It didn't matter that Nathan's was two blocks away or that the buns at Dean's Beachside Bar & Grill arrived on their plate stale and soggy. And there was no better spot in the world for a hot cup of tea after a dip in the freezing Atlantic Ocean. Adele would embellish the tea with a shot of bourbon to raise the blood temperature of the brave soul who longed to be a polar bear instead of a man. The regulars called her *girl*, even though Adele had known for some time she was on the cusp of becoming an old maid. She decided to put off telling her mother until after the honeymoon—for Rachel worked to live and lived to work.

Adele and Yan honeymooned in San Francisco, where Yan owned two commercial buildings and conducted business near the Mission District. They swerved down along the Pacific Coast Highway to Big Sur and took early-morning and late-afternoon walks along winding trails in the forest. A sign there mesmerized Adele: *Beware. Children intrigue mountain lions.*

When they returned to New York, Yan went to work and Adele settled into painting. They moved into a three-bedroom post-World-War-II-era apartment on the twelfth floor of 85th Street and West End Avenue. The co-op building had a courtyard at its center with linden trees and grass. Every cat in the building seemed to loiter beneath the trees, and Adele came across the random remains of a squirrel or a bird that had not flown away fast enough or avoided the grasp of a sharp claw. Adele visited her mother on Fridays. She walked down Fifth Avenue to 42nd Street and took the Q over the Manhattan Bridge. She had always liked the subway but recently had premonitions about being underground. She preferred now to peer out the window of the Q at the murky East River and the vast Manhattan skyline. Just when she thought she had a handle on the city, there would be a new building made of chrome and steel.

ADELE WAS A married woman now. Rachel listened. It was Adele's decision to quit, but her mother couldn't resist needling: "A girl should always have a little money of her own, especially a married girl."

"But I have money."

"Adele," Rachel said. "Money you've worked for."

"But my art is work too."

To this, Rachel could say nothing. She did not possess an artistic temperament. She was a businesswoman, plain and simple. She looked around the bar, which was by anyone's standard the epitome of rough-and-tumble, with its slanted sawdust floors and oscillating ceiling fans and benchlike tables, one or two missing a leg and suspended on a walking cane some drunk had left and not bothered to retrieve. In 1969, Coney Island's heyday was over. But even in a dirty, lackluster village, she knew where the bargains were. The handful of times Rachel had traveled with Adele to museums in the city, she was always aware of her hair and her dress and her shoes and her Sheepshead Bay accent. After a few minutes in a museum, she would want to return to her bar and her boardwalk.

"Yes, my daughter," Rachel murmured. "I suppose it is."

DETERMINED TO TAKE her work seriously, Adele enrolled in a Pictorial Interpretation class for professional artists. The first week in class, the art instructor skewered Adele's watercolor of the ocean. "What about this ocean is significant?"

Adele looked at the painting. It was little more than a muted collage of Coney Island in pastel colors. Indeed, it could have been an ocean setting anywhere. The second week in class she painted over the ocean and made a frothing sea with a fresh bolt of lightning and a shadow roaming above.

"Promising," said the instructor, a man whose belly carried the bulk of his weight. She had seen his work at a gallery downtown with Yan and thought it dreadful, but she did not yet have the vocabulary to critique art, especially her own. Perhaps, Adele reasoned, her instructor's work could be dreadful but he could still teach her, or inspire her to teach herself. Yan had paid big money for her to attend the bulky man's class. A man of reputation. And if that meant repainting the ocean every week, then so be it.

"*Promising* is a polite word for *beginner*," Yan said.

Adele had moved on from the painting of the ocean to abstract sketches of the courtyard cats, as part of an exercise on animals in their habitats.

Adele dripped oil into turpentine. She liked to paint in the living room with the windows thrown open. "Yan, what do you think?"

Yan rose from reading the newspaper, which was his habit at the top of the morning and the end of the day. He studied the Siamese cat Adele had painted prone, ready to pounce on a pigeon in the courtyard. "Why don't you draw dogs?" he said.

"I like cats."

"With cats, you don't know where you stand." Since marrying, he had grown a beard. Adele thought it made his face seem less defined and somewhat severe.

"Depends on the cat."

"They are out for whatever they can get. Cats." Yan crossed his arms.

"Dogs wait for table scraps."

"Cat's meow."

"Well, we don't own a dog or a cat," Adele said, noticing the edge in Yan's tone. "What are we bickering about, really?"

"If you must know the truth, Adele, I think cat drawings are beneath you. They are not to be taken seriously. They are provincial."

"Why don't you take it up with my instructor? You seem to know more than he does."

"Perhaps so."

"I'm entitled to my opinion, Yan. And I suspect you're wrong."

"I pay for your lessons."

Adele remembered Rachel's words. "I'll find a job waiting tables. I know my way around a bar."

Yan coiled his fists. They made fine stones. Adele did not even have time to put down her paintbrush. The stones met her face, and her nose broke instantly. She heard the bones cracking. Adele had always liked her nose, her Barbra Streisand nose. There were six Streisand songs on the jukebox at Dean's Beachside Bar & Grill and she knew every single one. She could not get the titles of the songs out of her head as blood leached down her face onto the V of her blouse.

That evening, Adele called Rachel and told her she couldn't drop by that Friday. She no longer worked at Dean's, but she still went in once a week and sat down like a customer. Sometimes she could not resist wiping the counter with the worn, tricolored dishrags.

Yan escorted her to the doctor. He was so sweet and apologetic, holding a napkin to stem the flow of blood. Yowling like it was his nose that had been broken.

"We must be careful not to bump into walls," he said.

"Silly me!" Adele told the doctor. "I bumped into a wall."

"It won't happen again," Yan said. "It mustn't."

ADELE BOUGHT Barbra Streisand albums at Colony Records and played the music around the house on Yan's vintage phonograph player, but the phonograph player was a poor substitute for the jukebox at Dean's Beachside Bar & Grill.

The following week she showed up at the bar and Rachel said, "What happened to your nose?"

Adele waved her mother away to avoid further questions. "Well, I can fix it now!"

Rachel shouted for Seth. Seth had coaxed an engagement ring onto Rachel's finger the week before. They had no wedding date, but a wedding vow. Seth worked at the company that supplied the bar's booze. He came out of the kitchen and put down the box he was carrying. They were stocking the bar for the boisterous Friday night crowd.

Seth considered Adele. "What's this?" It was a source of pride for Seth that he had served in the Army during World War II and fought the Nazis. He had been among the troops to liberate his brethren from Dachau. As a boy, Seth had idolized the heavyweight champion Max Baer and grown up to become a professional middleweight before an injury ended his career. He was an excellent fighter, agile and graceful, even meeting old age. "I'll not have Yan treat you like a slap fool."

"As God is my witness, Seth," Adele said, "it was an accident."

Seth felt his fighting juice diminish. God had entered the room, and when God entered the room, everyone was his patient.

ADELE DID NOT fix her nose. She let it heal and returned her heart to painting. She painted cats in compromising positions and left them around the house. She painted cats with broken noses and paws. She painted vivisected cats and cats with jackrabbit ears. Her instructor was intrigued but challenged Adele to stretch. She painted cats stretching on the windowsills about her house and finally a cat that was half cat and half woman.

"Ah, a delightful sphinx," the instructor said. His saucer belly jiggled with honest mirth and admiration for her newfound confidence and style.

"Adele." Yan shook his head. "You must stop this." Yan hated the paintings. The sight of them burned holes into his eyes. He was a man of strong opinions and the cats were an affront to him.

Seated on the sofa, Adele said, "If they burn holes into your eyes, then you cannot see, and if you cannot see, then what exactly is the problem?"

She heard the shuffling of Yan's hard shoes and rose quickly, abandoning the comfort of the couch for the safety of the front door. She caught the Q train and went to her mother's house. She needed to rest her nerves before facing the crowd at the bar.

This time Adele did not lie to her mother. When Rachel and Seth came home, they found her waiting in the dark kitchen. They sat on either side of her at the kitchen table and listened.

"The son of a bitch," cried Rachel.

"This man is a child," Seth said. "There is only one way to deal with such children."

Adele held out her arm to stop Seth, who had already thrown on his overcoat. "You'll be arrested if you hurt him." She cherished her mother's happiness. It was a good-luck talisman for the happiness she still believed within her grasp.

For her part, Rachel had dreamt of fish. Five days running she dreamt of fish jumping over the moon and leaving schools of dazzling fishes in their wake. They ate up the night sky, these fishes did, and became night stars. She waited until Adele had retreated into her old bedroom to follow and ask her, "Well, are you pregnant?"

"Are *you*?" Adele said sheepishly.

"Save the saltiness for the sea." Rachel shrugged. "I am too old."

Adele and Rachel and Seth retired to their beds. The phone rang at two in the morning.

"Come home," Yan said.

"No," said Adele. "I am leaving you."

"Leaving me?"

Rachel came into the room and took the phone from her daughter's ear. She could hear Yan repeating *leaving me* repeatedly. "Yes. You."

Adele took the phone away from her mother. There was silence on Yan's end of the line. And heavy breathing.

"Veins cut deep," he said.

THEY FOUND YAN at Columbia Presbyterian with a knoll of pillows propped behind his back. He was busy disdaining the potato sack the nurses dared to call a nightgown. His right wrist wore bandages.

"Next time I will do it. I swear to God, I will."

"Send him to a sanatorium." Rachel stomped her feet.

"Kill himself? Kill himself?" Seth fumed. "With all the people in this world who have wanted to live? Let him die!"

"I do not want the guilt of his death," Adele said. She might have added that she loved him, but in this regard, she was ambivalent. But there could be no ambivalence about her mother's dreams of the fish. She left the hospital with her husband.

Six months later Adele gave birth to their son, Maximilian. Twelve months after Maximilian's birth, out dropped their daughter, Freya. Desire had found its way into Yan and Adele's bedroom again. They were proud parents and, in the way of new parents, both tired and happy.

———

ADELE CONTINUED to paint. She progressed from painting kittens to an intensive anatomical workshop with acrylics and oils. The workshop was limited to a small group of select students. She was astonished to receive a partial scholarship. She drew nude women, trapeze artists, in a blazing sky.

"Your paintings will give the children nightmares," Yan said. "They'll grow up daft and dense."

Adele looked at her canvas. She saw bodies defying gravity. "Or, perhaps, they'll grow up strong-willed and curious."

Was she imagining it or had Yan coiled up his fists? Adele fell silent. And in her silence, she began to notice the revolving door of maids and housecleaners who were hired and then, without warning, quit. Yan had not to say a word for the women to pick up their pace or for their bodies to tense in his presence. He respected their boundaries and gave good tips when he was in the room, but in his presence, she wanted to ask them—or was it just her?—why the world seemed to shift.

She painted an apartment building with giant mangled hands reaching into it. "Magnificent," said her art instructor.

"Adele," Yan asked. "Are you trying to kill our children?"

Adele stopped painting altogether.

WHEN MAX WAS three and Freya was two, Rachel married Seth. The reception was lovely. They asked Adele to keep the bar and look after the house while they were away on their honeymoon. Adele arrived at the house and she found as a thank-you paintbrushes, an easel, and a collection of paints and canvases. They were not the good stuff, but they were what she needed to get started again.

Adele carried Max and Freya to the beach in the morning and let them pack sand into plastic pails. While they napped, she sketched. Adele relished the texture of the no-fuss pencils and paintbrushes in her hands.

For several years, the children quelled something in Yan. He cut back on his murky business and keened his ears to the padding of their small feet across the hardwood floors. Their laughter made him bashful in an endearing way. The children rolled trucks through his storms and dressed up as fairies. Yan would race up and down the 86th Street platform with Max and Freya in their double stroller, sometimes skidding just short of the yellow line and the white light of the approaching train. A good spell, it was a good spell, until the black moods came. And when the black moods returned, Adele and Max and Freya spent their days and evenings and long weekends at Baba and Bubby's house on Coney Island.

"What do the children want?" Yan often asked Adele.

Was this a trick question? An explosion waiting to corrupt her face? Adele chose her words carefully. "Their parents."

Yan shrugged. "We can't save them, you know."

"Yan, we live in America. Our children are the safest children in the world. Our children are *very* safe." She thought this vital to say and vital for Yan to hear.

FIVE YEARS BECAME seven years. Seven years became nine. Adele and Yan's children grew older. Maximilian and Freya were strong-willed and curious. They noticed that Yan never mentioned his mother or his family or anything about his childhood. And he bristled if they or Adele inquired or asked. The siblings did not know what was more unnerving: that they had to live with Yan or that he had no past.

Maximilian and Freya turned eighteen and seventeen. They graduated from high school and both moved to San Francisco to attend Berkeley. Freya had skipped a grade and was glad to escape with her brother. Adele and Yan offered to drive them cross-country, but Maximilian and Freya declined.

"Come visit," Freya said to her mother.

"We want to do our own thing," Maximilian said to Yan.

Adele did not let them see her tears but when they left, she keened. Yan put a hand on her left shoulder. "You see what you have done? You've run our children away from us."

"I? I?" Adele slapped Yan so hard across his face that the chandeliers looked down and shivered.

———

THE SIGHT OF Adele on crutches was too much. Rachel told Seth, *"End him."*

Seth had come to rue the day he had introduced Adele to Yan. He waited for Yan to show up in front of his apartment building. He caught Yan before he turned the corner on 85th Street and West End Avenue. Yan had been expecting Seth and waved a naughty finger at his old friend.

"Hit me and I will tell Rachel that you snicker other women on the side."

Seth struck Yan anyway and rushed home to tell Rachel that he was occasionally unfaithful. Rachel laughed. "So what? Me too. Yan is a dangerous man, Seth. End him."

Seth returned that very evening to end Yan. This time he caught him outside the poker house in Hell's Kitchen where they had first met. Seth gave Yan the works, a boxer's pound, systematically beating him in the torso and face in a way that did not betray his age. Seth intended to kill Yan but discovered that in addition to being a fine boxer, he was also a fine referee. He left Yan bleeding on the cracked sidewalk.

"Did you do it?" This Yan business was turning Rachel's hair gray. She now looked twice her age.

"Rachel," Seth said. "Think of what you ask me to do."

Adele was on the sofa. In the bar, Rachel noticed that her daughter had begun to drink. This daughter who danced around the drunks now finished the dregs from the bottom of the glass. She slurped other people's saliva.

"We need God," Rachel declared.

"Or a good rabbi," Seth said.

IN PREPARATION FOR her talk with the rabbi, Adele abstained from drink for several days. She liked Kamikazes, a mix of lime juice, triple sec, and vodka. And martinis. Yes, martinis were her favorite. Not at the bar. At home, where she sometimes consoled herself with the good stuff. She would not tell the rabbi this, of course.

"There are conditions to every marriage," the rabbi said. "What are your conditions?"

"The shower faucet."

The rabbi was confused. "The shower faucet?"

"The dishwasher," Adele mumbled.

"The dishwasher," the rabbi repeated. He was small, pensive with owl-shaped glasses that he adjusted constantly. "It is my understanding that your husband makes a comfortable living. Surely, you have someone? Hired help."

Adele nodded. "Of course." And then continued to construct her list. "The bathroom mat, the folding of clothes. The washing machine. His footsteps around the house, with and without slippers, in search of something prowling, prowlers that never arrive. The unfolding of the clothes you've folded. To probe is to grasp is to ask, What will happen now? What will happen next? A swirling around the corners of the house followed by relieved laughter or quietness. A smile that is like a mask when Yan comes through the door, a good morning that has no good in it, a hello that is an ice pick in the chest, the silent disapproval of a meal that was all day in the making. Lemonade poured into a glass. Before his mouth touches the glass, before the glass is returned to the table—*Too much sugar*, his mouth says. But you know you've not put any sugar in the lemonade because last time you put in sugar he screamed there was too much. It's a tone that makes you touch your hemline to see if the slip you are wearing shows or the disapproving way he reaches out to touch you."

"And do you love him?" asked the rabbi.

How many times had Adele asked herself this question? The answer was like the drink she wanted, a Kamikaze. Kamikazes fly to their own deaths. Every time she turned this question over, she told herself she was complicit for having stayed with him.

Out of the blue, Adele shouted at the rabbi, who leaned forward to gauge her anger. "A single orchid left in a glass vase! A box of truffles from our favorite chocolate store, Evelyn's! Some small token that reveals a whole world of thought and beauty that eclipses every bit of ugliness that preceded it! The sway of ripe wild straw-berries offered fresh in the green carton that holds them!"

Perhaps there is hope, the rabbi thought, but to Adele he said only, "I would like to meet your husband. I have not seen him since your wedding."

Adele's wedding day was a blur. She looked away. "We are not observant. He might not come."

"You must convince him," the rabbi said.

ADELE RETURNED TO the apartment. It was the first time in their marriage that Yan had not called or come to Rachel and Seth's to retrieve her. His face was black and blue from Seth's sound beating. He had redecorated the entire apartment with new modern furniture. Everything was white.

"I'd give anything," Yan said. "To be a different person." Adele almost believed him. She was grateful that Yan had done nothing to alter his veins.

"I have rented a house for the weekend on Long Island," he added.

Adele wanted to tell Yan about the rabbi. Perhaps he would hear her better with rest and relaxation.

WHILE BROWSING the *East Hampton Star*, Adele noticed that the Pollock-Krasner house was now open for tours. Jackson Pollock and Lee Krasner were both dead. The year was 1988. The house was a fifteen-minute drive from their vacation rental in Amagansett.

"Him," Yan whispered, as they walked about the farmhouse and paused before Pollock's *Untitled (Composition with Red Arc and Horses)*. "A genius? They call him a genius. The emperor is in the woods and naked."

"Her," Adele said, moving through the modest rooms and gasping when she came upon Krasner's screen print *Free Space*, its intense blue and green swerving colors defiantly abstract and buoyant. Adele fought the urge to climb on top of the artist's bed for a more intimate view of *Rose Stone*, Krasner's hot-pink lithograph. Yan waited patiently while Adele lingered over every photograph and, engaging, scribbled illegible notes in an old Mead notebook, for she hadn't thought to bring a camera. When she asked to see Pollock's studio a second time, Yan came along and knelt beside her as she touched the permanent paint blotches on the wood floor. Krasner had taken to working in her husband's studio after his death and Adele saw evidence of her everywhere. "I like her strokes. The bold display of color. Yan, I think both of them are brilliant."

That night, their bodies linked together, Adele fell asleep before she could mention the rabbi to Yan. She did not sleep for long. She woke up to Yan sitting on the edge of the bed.

"We did not succeed, you know. Our children have everything, but still, they are not safe. Why can't we keep the children safe?"

Your children hate you, Adele thought. *Our children pity me*, she mused. But to Yan she said, "You might ask the rabbi."

"NO," THE RABBI SAID. "You cannot keep the children safe. We are God's children and even He could not keep us from eating the forbidden fruit. It's human nature to know degrees of suffering, but suffering should not last a lifetime."

Yan appreciated the rabbi's unchecked response. "What can I do for you today, Rabbi?"

"Not what can you do for me, Yan. What can you do for yourself? And Adele."

"Adele and I are fine, I think. Better than most."

The rabbi owned a house on Manhattan Beach near Sheepshead

Bay. He came from a long line of clockmakers. He heard ticking even when there was no tock, and tocks when there was no ticking. The loud noise of time eased briefly when he read the Torah and the Talmud. The rabbi studied Yan. "This is not so."

"But it *is* so, good rabbi," Yan insisted.

"You beat your wife."

"From time to time," Yan admitted.

"Adele does not deserve such treatment."

Yan said nothing.

The rabbi asked Yan if he considered himself a good Jew. Yan said he did.

"Then stop beating your wife. You are being a bad Jew," he warned.

Again, Yan said nothing. Something resembling a smile played across his lips. Yan's eyes scanned the rabbi's study with more than a passing interest. Books were stacked everywhere. If they were mountains, Yan would ascend them.

"If you do not love Adele," the rabbi said, "you should divorce her."

"But what other woman would tolerate me? She is a glutton, and I am her punishment."

The rabbi asked Yan which village his people were from in Russia. Yan shrugged. The rabbi waited. But Yan would not name the village where he was born. "What does it matter?" He shrugged. "After Stalin."

The rabbi told Yan that his people were from Vitebsk in Belarus. He called out the names of his mother and his father and his grandparents and great-grandparents. Saying their names also eased the ticking and the tocking in the rabbi's ears and steadied him in the presence of Yan, who gazed into his eyes without blinking. The rabbi was a scholar but also a firm believer in the presence of demons. In the forty years since the war, he had heard many stories and witnessed demons masquerading as depression and sorrow and blunt anger in the souls of men. The rabbi wove the conversation back to Adele, by way of mothers. "Think of your mother."

"I never liked my mother," Yan said.

Truly? Was Yan joking or in earnest? Yan's expression gave away nothing. The rabbi wondered why Adele had not known better than to marry a man who did not love his mother. But then his heart went soft, for Adele had never known her father.

Later that night, the rabbi explained the situation to his wife, Lydia, who pointed out that she had never liked the rabbi's mother; his mother had been a buttinsky.

The rabbi sat up in their sleigh bed. "You never said this before, Lydia."

"Me? Complain about the rabbi's dear mother to the rabbi? Come. Surely, you knew this, Isaac? Only God could love your mother."

"*I* loved my mother."

The rabbi's wife turned her back to him. "Not every day."

"Well, I loved her as often as she would permit. The war did things to her."

"Why do you make excuses for people? The war did things to all of us. It's doing things still."

The rabbi did not sleep well that night. He waited three weeks before calling Yan.

"HAVE YOU STRUCK Adele recently?" asked the rabbi. They were in the study. Yan sat with his hands between his knees. Like a kid.

"Not recently," Yan said.

"Perhaps, this is progress?"

Yan smiled. "Call it what you want."

"You are a successful businessman, yes?"

"I own a business that owns another business."

"And your specialty?"

"Liquidations."

"I imagine there are stresses. We men have stresses our wives don't understand." The rabbi opened the Talmud. "But the Talmud forbids a man to unjustly beat his wife."

Yan laughed. "What beating is ever just?"

"So, we agree, as it is written in the Talmud, that you should not raise your hand against your wife?"

"The Talmud is open to many interpretations, good rabbi," said Yan. He had recently cut the beard he grew on and off occasionally. The trim he gave himself was anything but neat. "As we both know. We might sit here and argue one way and then come upon a reading that sets us back. Do you think I do not know the Talmud? I know the Talmud better than anyone."

The rabbi was sure he heard a challenge in Yan's words. The rabbi had been the best student in his class at rabbinical school. Pride tempted him to accept Yan's challenge, but his humble service to God propelled him the other way.

"How do you know the Talmud so well?" asked the rabbi.

"My father was a rabbi."

"And yet you do not follow the path of a rabbi's son."

Yan rose suddenly, as did the color in his face. "It has been a pleasure, but I think we are done." This was the first hint of emotion the rabbi had seen in Yan.

The rabbi's wife had come in during the meeting with tea, for even she could not curtail her curiosity. When she caught sight of Yan strutting away from her husband like a dandified peacock or a pimp, she yelled after him.

"If you want to be a bully, carry yourself to Harlem and lay the fists on there!"

The rabbi came behind his wife. "Shush, Lydia."

"See how long he lasts up there among the savages!"

"I do not know you, Lydia. These things that come out of your mouth lately." The rabbi added, "Do you suppose his father was really a rabbi?"

HARLEM. YAN WAS intrigued by the possibilities of Harlem. Yan was intrigued by the angry challenge of the rabbi's wife. Intrigued enough to take a train to 138th Street and Lenox Avenue on a hot Friday afternoon to see what lay in wait for him there. Unlike the rabbi, Yan could not resist a challenge.

The year was 1988 and hip-hop was in vogue. Yan set up station outside the Pan Pan Diner, the chicken-and-waffles breakfast joint on 135th Street. He tapped even though he wore no tap shoes. He bade the black people of Harlem, including the winos and the crackheads, to come out on the sidewalk and dance with him.

But the black people of Harlem would have none of it.

Yan put on a riotous show and assailed the black people of Harlem with a fine current of racial slurs and expletives. They pointed and laughed or looked away, all but one little boy in a blue blazer who yanked away from his mother to regard Yan and, in the process, dislodged one of the gold buttons from his blue blazer. When Yan came toward the boy to pick up his button, the boy's mother warned, "Man, there are limits. Don't you come near me or my son."

They seemed to think it was a setup. That Yan was an undercover cop. And a billy club lay in wait for them. Or that he was crazy. They could not know that Yan's late uncle Moishe had owned warehouses in Harlem and the Bronx. When Yan first immigrated to America, his uncle Moishe would take him to the piano factory in Mott Haven and let him glide from piano to piano plucking at random keys.

YAN MADE HIS WAY back to Brooklyn to report his adventures to the rabbi that same evening. He refused to leave the rabbi's house, even though the rabbi's wife insisted that her husband had retired for the night. The next morning when Lydia took pity and led Yan to the study, he drank two cups of coffee and ate half the rabbi's babka.

"I've come to let you know that I was a perfectly fine bully, but the black people of Harlem have bigger problems than me. I saw it with my own eyes, good rabbi. That poverty. And I can tell you this: the black people of Harlem should never stop singing or dancing. People who stop singing and dancing go quite crazy, over time. Tell me, good rabbi, isn't this so?"

The rabbi asked Yan what village in Russia his family was from again. Yan ticked off a long list of villages. And then he began to rock from side to side. "Somewhere in Harlem, there is a little black boy with a blue blazer missing a button. I carry his gold button in my pocket, because the city is as small as it is large. We might run into one another eventually . . ."

The rabbi asked Yan if he could recall which rabbinical school his father had attended in Russia.

Yan kicked over the serving tray with the babka and the coffee. The hot liquid swirled from its metal pot and splattered on the plush Turkish rug that had been a wedding gift from the rabbi's great aunt, Sabine. Tick. Tock. Tick. Tock. Tick.

"Who wants to fuck with a red diaper baby?" Yan said. "Who wants to fuck with me?"

The rabbi told Yan that he needed to find a good therapist. And urged him to depart before Lydia called the authorities.

SINCE AMAGANSETT THERE had been no friction. Yan had steadfastly avoided Adele. She had reenrolled in art classes at the Art Students League on 57th Street. She had even taken out canvases and easel and paintbrushes and paints. She had just started the borders on a new painting when Yan strolled into the apartment. It was eleven o'clock in the morning. She knew from the padding of his feet on the hardwood floor that there would be an argument.

Adele had been drinking steadily, and the drink gave her courage. Yan circled around her in the living room. The living room windows were open. Adele had once again set up her studio before them. Yan watched the borders on her painting become broad strokes. He watched the broad strokes materialize into a Cheshire cat. Adele had not drawn cats in a long time. Yan picked up a brush and painted over Adele's Cheshire cat.

"You are no Lee Krasner," Yan said. He dripped paint all over her canvas.

"And you"—Adele smiled—"are an autocrat."

"Ah, so we've learned to turn the pages of the dictionary. At long last."

"You," Adele said, "are a tyrant."

"What do you know of tyrants, Adele? What do you know of anything?" Yan could tell her of tyrants, if he so pleased. He could tell her of winters when the cold spoke. Said *you will die here in this room today*. He could tell her of the rabbi's prayers, the man who was his father, and the room where they were gathered, under Stalin's orders, though for a time Stalin seemed, if not their champion, then certainly their friend. He could tell her of rooms the size of closets and being suspended between sleep and dreams, of black nights that turned brilliant with a sharp glare of flashlights and the padding of feet that you learned to count and the sniffing of dogs who were held tight, then less tight, then less tight still on a leash, and the men, the old rabbis like his father and then the women making a wall to protect the children. Who had protected the children? *I have*, Yan could tell her—if he chose. *I have protected them as I was protected*. But Yan would never tell.

"I am leaving you, Yan," Adele said.

"Good. *Leave*. Ask me do I care?"

"You have taken everything that matters from me," Adele said.

"Says the woman who has never wanted for a meal. Who has always slept well."

"Everything."

Yan stepped away from Adele and told her that he would take one thing more.

Adele was amazed. "What can you possibly take that you haven't robbed me of already?" she said.

"Your peace of mind." Yan put down the turd-colored paintbrush and dashed for the living room windows. He jumped, taking glass and the tops of windowpanes and aloe vera plants that sat on the windowsill with him. He fell twelve floors below to his death.

IT WAS A SHIVA without tears. Only Adele's and Yan's children, Maximilian and Freya, wept for the man who had terrified them.

After Yan's death, Adele's drinking gained momentum.

"There is nothing worse than an old drunk," Rachel said.

"Now that he is gone," Seth said, "this is a gift. Your time to live."

Adele burped in Rachel and Seth's faces.

Maximilian and Freya said nothing. They skirted around Adele while she cursed them for living out west. They cleaned Adele's apartment and mounted the paintings she had kept in hiding for years. They took a perfunctory inventory of their father's accounts and were astonished to find that he had named them joint executors of his estate. Yan had amassed a small fortune in real estate and private investments.

Adele sat up when Freya and Max told her she owned a house in Amagansett. She resumed her art classes. And tempered her drink. One evening, on the fourth anniversary of her husband's death, Adele bumped into her old art instructor. His belly was still a jaunty saucer and he had cataracts in both eyes that he was afraid to have removed.

"Your art teacher can't see!" he exclaimed. He invited Adele to a party, a fund-raiser on the Upper West Side for a local public school. Adele typically avoided Manhattan parties, but a small voice said: *Go, go.*

Adele went but monitored her drink. She sipped and did not slurp. She left her martini on a table and visited the ladies' room. When she returned, a handsome man with silver hair was sipping from her martini.

"No, no, that is *my* martini," Adele said. She pointed to the lipstick stain on the rim.

"Forgive me. The eyes are the first things to go," he said.

He drank her martini anyway and sat down on the Shelton sofa. Adele sat next to him. His name was James Samuel Vincent. He was a lawyer, he told her: divorced. With a son, Rufus, at Columbia University. He'd just met his son's new girlfriend—Claudia—the night before. I think, James said, it's pretty serious. My Ruff's not a boy anymore. He told Adele this while asking one of the party servers to bring them a second round of martinis.

"Yes," Adele said, thinking of her beloved art teacher, of blindness in general, but listening to James Samuel Vincent recount the joys and travesties of his life before she turned to him and laid hers out on the table.

"It's the little cruelties that get you," she told him. "Never the big hurts, the pains you can point to, and say, 'Oh, I see this bruise,' but the wounds that you can't even tell are there until one day you are eating a bowl of fennel soup or sunbathing on the deck of the pool and you can't move, you can't do anything, because you think, *Well, something is dead in me, what has been done to me, and why did I allow this to happen?* And now, and now, and now . . ."

HANK NOTES

2010

NOW THERE WAS A NEW ITERATION OF COUSINS AT THE Camphor family compound. One day, Hank told himself, the blade would loom large and he would not hesitate to snip, snip—sever ties and cut these people off forever. Yet here he was enduring another Memorial Day weekend on Sunset Beach, the gated island community of his youth. In the Camphor way, the festivities began on Friday evening, when relatives from as far off as Spokane, Washington, and as near as Duchess, Georgia, filed their vehicles and motorcycles into Seamus Camphor III's double driveway. They brought with them newborn babies in designer baby strollers and old grandmas who still used Avon talcum powder and Maybelline pressed crème to cover their liver spots. It was taken for granted that the more distant cousins would stay at the Southside La Quinta or the Holiday Inn. Hank Camphor had spent a hefty chunk of his childhood in this very house—he was Seamus Camphor III's second cousin—and thus obliged to stay on the family compound in the bedroom that had once belonged to him. Hank's old bedroom had been remodeled to look like a boutique hotel with a bidet and urinal in the guest bathroom and geometric bedspreads and triangular pillows and a large flat-screen TV mounted to the wall that could be activated to sing you to sleep if you were the least bit blue or lonely.

IN THE COMPANY of his multitude of cousins, Hank luxuriated in his own biases. He shared the trait of vanity with his mother and father (Barbara and the late Charles Camphor). He could tolerate just about anything in another human being except poor hygiene and obesity, which seemed like two things in this world a person could control: his weight and his stink. Hank never accompanied his wife, Susan, to feed the homeless at the local shelter, and he avoided fast food with a zeal that sometimes made Susan say, "I married a sweet vain man."

"I HAVE MARRIED a sweet vain man." Hank repeated Susan's words in his childhood bedroom. The flat-screen TV kept Hank company, talked to him, asked Hank would he prefer Fox or CNN? Porn, he muttered. Now alone and away from Susan and Tess, their three-year-old daughter, Hank thought he might indulge. He was pleasantly surprised when the TV switched automatically to a restricted channel with an impressive selection of adult programming. Hank preferred Golden Age porn, the rough and raw old school classics like *The Devil and Miss Jones*, *Deep Throat*, and *Inside Seka*, predilections he had acquired from raiding his father's basement as a boy. Hank said, "Seventies porn," and startled when a list of options lit up the screen. He chose Johnnie Keyes and Marilyn Chambers's *Behind the Green Door*.

HANK CAMPHOR HAD never cheated on Susan née Weatherby Camphor, but occasionally he dabbled in minor deceptions. Strolled the aisles of Rite Aid or CVS in search of some cheap, vibrant perfume (the more floral notes the better) to irritate his wife's aquiline

nose and kick her imagination into high gear. His personal favorite
was Lucky Me.

"Hank, what's that smell?" Susan would say, sniffing.

"I don't smell anything," Hank would say, massaging his jaw.

Susan was the vice president of human resources at Duke University. She was not a woman to doubt herself, but Hank could see
flecks of uncertainty in the irises of her brown eyes. It primed her
not to cling, but to take better care of herself than most women. Susan's doubt made for unpredictable sex. Hank had learned the value
of unpredictability from his parents. His actions shamed him, but
not enough to modify the bad behavior when it was working.

SATURDAY, MEMORIAL DAY WEEKEND

Camphor family getaways included a mandatory Saturday romp on
Sunset Beach. Barbecued pork ribs and deviled eggs and buttermilk
fried chicken and flat string beans were stuffed into red-and-white
coolers for the day. This outing was the highlight for Hank, who
loved the beach. He watched the children build sand castles or ride
the waves on boogie boards between chasing after a Jack Russell
terrier named Stella. The dog belonged to Seamus Camphor III,
the son of Seamus II, who was Hank's father's first cousin. Stella
roamed the beach barking at seagulls and tearing through garbage
bags in search of bones. Stella reminded Hank of nothing so much
as a top-heavy cheerleader who might steal her best friend's man.
Hank did not own a dog, nor was he inclined to, but as a boy—it
stung him now to remember this—he had asked for a basset hound
for the briefest time.

Come evening there was an oyster roast and low-country boil
with crabs and shrimp and potatoes and andouille sausage in pre-
packaged seasoning salt. Hank let the other Camphor men reach
for nylon beach chairs with deep pockets to hold their soft drinks.
He was more than happy to roll a beach towel out on the flat sand
and gaze at the perfect sunset. Every time some middle-aged man
strolled by with a soft body shot to hell, Hank would revel in the

tautness of his torso and the Herculean firmness of his own ass. He was forty but looked thirty and not a day older. The Camphor men shared Hank's height but had lost their youthfulness and agility.

THE CAMPHORS TOOK a four-hour drive to the Georgia country-side on Sunday to pay respect to their dead. Hank's father and Big Seamus, Seamus III's dad, were interred in St. Matthew's Cemetery. The modest Methodist church could no longer hold its offspring. Seamus III set wooden pews around the church lawn and installed speakerphones so that everyone could hear the old rheumy-eyed reverend give his annual sermon on the prodigal son. The reverend shook a Grover tambourine against his hips to keep the preaching zesty.

Hank never placed flowers on his father's grave. He brought a Spalding golf ball in honor of the sport Charles Camphor had loved. Charles had died in a boating accident during Hank's senior year in college. At the repast, in the annex of the modest church, Hank's mother had gripped his arm and said, "Charles is not your father."

Hank had seen so much of himself reflected in Charles Camphor's eyes that he was certain that Barbara was playing a cruel joke on him or temporarily out of her damn mind over the sudden death of a good husband. He had stood in the annex looking past the burgundy chairs and the big white countrywomen laying out the mourning food he would allow himself to eat for comfort. Hank was studying to be an orthopedic surgeon at the time and had learned that if you waited long enough a path would become clear to you, and, in this way, irreversible mistakes might be avoided.

"I met James Samuel Vincent at a conference a long time ago. We had a moment," Barbara said. "That moment included you. I'm sorry, Hank."

Whore. Hank had wanted to say to his mother: *As God is my witness, I will never marry a whore.* Instead he cried out bitterly. Tears those around him assumed were for his dead father.

Barbara walked away and went to the front of the serving line. Hank followed and, together, they pantomimed the grieving wife and son while the reverend blessed the food and friends and family formed a queue and gave their condolences one last time. Later, after the mourners took their leave and the annex room emptied out, Hank found his mother outside the church on the side where the blue grass had grown tall despite recently being cut. Her sandy-blond hair was swept to one side and she had slipped out of her black pumps and was smoking pot with his father's first cousin, Big Seamus.

"Hank," Big Seamus said. "I could not refrain from the blessed herb on this sad day."

Charles Camphor had not cared for pot or coke or drugs at all, though he placed a high premium on good whiskey, gin, and bourbon. Hank eyed his mother's red manicured nails and their expertise at holding the joint.

Barbara looked at Hank defiantly, unapologetically. "Just a toke or two and then I'll stop."

She took a long drag and allowed the smoke to filter out of her nose and mouth, and she looked at the joint like it was an intimate friend before offering it to Seamus. Hank stole the joint from his mother's grasp and toked on it himself. Big Seamus patted him on the shoulder.

"I am sorry for your loss," Seamus said. How many times were those words tossed at Hank today? One hundred. Two hundred? His father's funeral had been well attended. Jerome Jenkins, the only black friend Hank had been permitted to have as a boy, flew in from Denver. Before he left, Jerome had asked after Hank's childhood neighbors. "Whatever happened to the family who lived next door to you? That friend of yours, Gideon, with the pretty sister whose nose was always in a book? Lord, she was fine. I'd love to see her now!"

"The Applewoods moved away a long time ago," Hank said.

CHARLES CAMPHOR'S ESTATE was settled a year after his funeral. Even before Barbara was ready to put the house on the market, she began receiving inquiries from Big Seamus.

"Barbara, that's a lot of house for one lady," Big Seamus said. "Surely, with so much space, you'll be swimming in memories."

It was Hank's first year of medical school at Duke. He and his mother spoke infrequently, but Hank had also begun to feel an inkling of curiosity about his biological father. Barbara sent him a Polaroid of James Samuel Vincent at a Yankees game with Hank's half brother, Rufus. Hank studied the Polaroid in his sparsely furnished one-bedroom apartment. He marveled at genetics, the two faces that bore a striking resemblance to his. The photograph was at least a decade old and his half brother looked sixteen or seventeen at most. Did this mean Barbara had not seen James Samuel Vincent in recent years? Hank did not care to take up this subject with his mother again. When he met Susan Weatherby at a homecoming party, Hank threw the Polaroid in the trash. *A man makes his own family. A man cleans his own plate.*

They survived their rough patch, Hank and his mother. Barbara asked him to take the reins selling their old house.

"Name your best bid," Hank said to Big Seamus.

Big Seamus had never mooched off Charles Camphor like the rest of his relatives. Hank had always regarded the fireman with a degree of affection. He gave Big Seamus a good deal on the house. It seemed fitting somehow to pass the keys to his father's first cousin.

THEY WOULD NEVER figure out how the dog Stella maneuvered the Smith & Wesson from the metal box underneath Seamus III and Maxine Camphor's Queen Anne bed. The metal box weighed at least three pounds. But now, half past three in the afternoon, while everyone was happy and feeling no pain, Stella sat cross-legged on a Smith & Wesson. The barrel of the gun extended out toward the amused crowd, some of whom had started drinking before breakfast.

"Well, it's not a party till someone breaks out a gun," Hank heard Seamus III say. At that moment, all Hank could think was, *Thank God I left Susan and Tess behind in Raleigh.*

Hank's relatives laughed every time Stella fidgeted on the gun. With each jerky motion of her body, the gun, a silver-and-black nine-millimeter revolver with a seven-round gauge, seemed to spin around like the wheel on a Russian roulette table.

"Are there bullets in that?" Hank said, stepping through the tanked group of onlookers and into the bedroom doorway. Outside, on the great front lawn, Hank could hear the children playing. At least they were out of harm's way.

"Hell, yes, there's bullets, but the safety's on," Seamus III said, lifting the glass of scotch in his thick scarred hands. Seamus was a fireman who wore trophies on his body from forthright battles with fire.

"Stella, get off the gun and get on the treadmill," Maxine said. She turned to their guests. "Stella knows how to use the treadmill. If you go on YouTube, you'll see her working out. You'll see Stella running."

Hank was sure he heard kids on the stairs. He thought he heard Tess's voice. He kept reminding himself that his three-year-old daughter was safe at home in Raleigh, North Carolina.

"We need to get that gun." Hank turned to Seamus III. "Seamus, let's do this."

"It's just a fat little dog," Seamus laughed, sipping his glass of scotch and winking at his wife, who wore a diaphanous white dress that Hank thought evoked a Greek goddess. An Olympian. Aphrodite. *Venus.* It frustrated Hank that he should find Maxine so goddamned attractive. Hank had married not only for beauty—his Susan was lovely enough, in a modulated way—but for kindness and intelligence.

"Hank, if you're done ogling my wife"—Seamus III smiled—"how 'bout grabbing hold of Stella from the front while I take the rear?"

In deference to the bullets that Seamus III acknowledged the gun held, Hank and Seamus ushered guests out of the master bedroom, which was larger than a modern art gallery. When Hank and

his parents had lived there, the bedroom walls were off-white, not
salmon-colored, and the bedroom was half its current size. Big Seamus and Maxine had torn down walls in favor of cutting-edge ren-
ovations, enlarging what had already been a worthy five-bedroom,
three-bathroom house. Both men moved for Stella, whose tail
wagged and stiffened. The dog nudged the gun with her muzzle and
the Smith & Wesson made another bicycle wheel spin.

"You sure the safety's on the damn thing?" Hank said, feeling
the Southern twang he had pressed out of his voice wrinkle the corners of his lips.

The gun went off at the very moment Seamus's barrel-chested
thirteen-year-old son, Fat Seamus IV, came elbowing his way up
the great hall stairs on his hands and knees, knocking guests to his
left and to his right, determined to be alongside the adults, where
the action was. The bullet ricocheted off the antique molding on the
salmon walls and grazed the upper right corner of Seamus IV's face.
Almost instantly a crimson-colored hickey took form.

"I'm dying," Seamus IV said. "Help me, people. I'm dying!"

"You all right, Seam." Seamus III rushed over to his son, picked
him up, and cupped the boy's generous face in his hand. "Why, it's
no more than a blush."

The close-range crack of a bullet expelled from its chamber
scared Stella. The dog rushed out the bedroom door and down the
stairs. Hank, desperate for a cigarette and weary of his relatives, lit
up and followed.

The front door was wide open and there were half a dozen kids
playing with porcelain tea sets, or swiping croquet balls. Hank
noted that there was no adult supervision. One little girl with freck-
les and an astonishing carpet of red hair was rolling in a crying jag
on the front porch.

"My bubby is dead!" she wailed. The child reminded Hank of
Tess. He guessed she was three years old. Hank leaned over the
child, letting the ashes from the cigarette that he hid behind his
back drift toward the front porch floor. He could not remember the
child's name.

"Seam. Seam," the girl sobbed.

Her name came to him: Penny. She was Seamus III and Maxine's daughter. Hank wanted to say, *Penny, that idiot brother of yours still has the stuff of life.* Instead, he patted her on the cheek. "It's madness in there. Stay outside."

Hank put out his cigarette nub on the front porch of the family compound. When had his childhood home become a compound? He hadn't foreseen this when he sold the house to Big Seamus. Ash from the tobacco darkened Hank's clean hands. Surgeon's hands, they were: steady. Penny with the carpet of red hair tugged at his pants leg.

"That's not the way to Stella's shithole," she said.

"What?" Sometimes, Hank thought he would benefit from therapy, but he didn't believe in therapy as a long-term solution to anything. He didn't believe in therapy at all.

"Come back here, Stella!" Penny shouted, trying to explain in her three-year-old tone that Stella always ran away and wasn't allowed outside or in the yard except to potty in her shithole. Hank asked to see where Stella's shithole was, and Penny led him to the rear garden and marsh. Hank looked at the shithole, jammed with mulch and newspaper. It was in the spot where he had buried Tipper, more than twenty-five years ago. Salt filled his eyes.

Penny looked up at Hank. "Stella likes her shithole. *Don't cry.*"

"You'll have to excuse me, Penny," Hank said, backing up and running to catch up with Stella, who was busy leaving anxiety-ridden mounds of dung on an otherwise pristine sidewalk. Stella turned a corner. And so did Hank, picking up speed and reaching out to grab her stiff tail. He caught the whole of Stella as she wiggled and trembled in his arms, not for one second abating her baptism of shit. As if by some mercy, it began to rain. Hank sprinted through the rain past the Camphor family compound for the safety of his Mercedes. He threw the door open and shoved the dog on the floor of the passenger seat. The keys found their way into the ignition and his feet found their way on the gas and he was off, pulling away from Sunset Beach.

A WEEK LATER

Hank sent Seamus Camphor III a thousand dollars for the Jack Russell terrier. Seamus had called Hank repeatedly since Memorial Day. When Hank finally had a mind to pick up the phone, Seamus said with quiet rage, "Let me get this straight. You're paying me one thousand dollars to keep my children's pet?"

"I could go up five hundred more."

"Their *dog* that you ran off with?"

Hank was on the golf course waiting at the first hole. "You can always drive up to get her."

"Or maybe you could have Stella flown back to us."

"Trust me. She's a wreck. She wouldn't make it."

"Buddy, what's wrong with you?" Seamus coughed. "It's a damn good thing our dads were cousins. That's all I have to say on the subject."

"Nothing's *wrong* with me."

After a beat, Seamus said into the phone. "It's the little one, isn't it? Tess?"

Hank was glad Seamus was not there to see him flinch. It was true. Tess and Stella were now inseparable. The terrier slept at the foot of Tess's bed and sat in the bay windows of their Oakwood Victorian in downtown Raleigh like a sentry, until Tess came home from preschool.

Hank had not wanted children. It was Susan who had reminded him five years into their marriage that children were part of the deal. But Hank had treasured their scuba diving trips to Turks and Caicos and skiing in Telluride.

"One child, Hank, at the very least."

"They'll slow us down."

"They'll keep us young."

"What if I'm a lousy father?"

"You are an exquisite man. Our progeny will be beautiful."

They tried for two years to get pregnant. And went to several fertility specialists. When Hank's mother learned they were having trouble, she whispered to Susan during a performance of *The Marriage of Figaro*, "Well, aren't there any human resources conferences you can attend?"

Susan stood up during the opera and asked, "*Who* is this imposter, Hank? Do we know her?"

That night, Hank took Susan home and laid her out on the hood of their Mercedes in the garage. He lifted her flaring skirt and pulled down her underwear and made love to his wife with exceptional persistence and tenderness. When Susan bore him a daughter nine months later to the day, the child had his steel-blue eyes. Hank knew Tess was his.

Shortly after Tess was born, he took up golfing.

"Let me tell you something, Hank," Seamus said. "People need firemen more than surgeons." Seamus returned the check Hank had sent him in the mail with a note scribbled across it in red ink that said the same thing.

"I'll see you next May, Seamus." Hank was astonished to hear himself utter these words, and to realize, on some primal level, that he meant them.

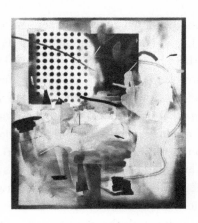

COLOR LAND

2010

T WO MONTHS AFTER MEMORIAL DAY WEEKEND, HANK
Camphor received an email from his half brother, Rufus Vincent, saying that Rufus and his family were headed back from
Georgia and wanted to stop by Raleigh on the way home to New
York. Perhaps meet some place "neutral" for coffee or lunch. Hank
liked that Rufus had put "neutral" in quotes, as it reflected an understanding of appropriate boundaries.

THEY MET IN the lobby of Color Land, a renovated four-story
arts and crafts laboratory in downtown Raleigh that catered to the
budding Picasso in every child. Each floor was devoted to its own
activities—graffiti walls and buses; burst-of-color fashion and home
accessories; booths to design, paint, or stencil belts and wallets; and
lava lamp shades to take home or have delivered as birthday presents and Christmas gifts. The showstoppers were a large gurgling
Liquid Fountain that squirted liquefied washable crayons into plastic molds that kids could take to the Color Land laboratory and

solidify. Parents and children alike were required to don rain slickers because the Liquid Fountain was known for its Niagara Falls–like mist; the other showstopper was the third-floor jungle gym, a maze of collapsible walls and geometrically shaped tubes that shifted colors as kids crawled, tumbled, rolled, or walked through them onto swings that doubled as ladders and jumping boxes and bouncing balls and, for the brave of spirit, an indoor zip line that zipped right past the gift shop, where professional thespians dressed as paintbrushes and markers and pieces of paper sang and danced and carried on for the kids. A bright red number two pencil with a rich baritone voice was much loved by the children at Color Land. He was forever flirting with the piece of paper. "I am wood that writes," he would often say. "Who needs a pen?"

Hank surveyed the lobby. The scene struck him as unbearably loud and he began to second-guess Susan's choice of venue.

RUFUS VINCENT AND his wife and children came with presents for Tess: a bagful of books from Books of Wonder, their favorite bookstore in Manhattan. They were academics. Of course they would bring books. Hank was glad that Susan had thought to regift two of Jerome Jenkins's prize-winning toys. Hank and Rufus were the same height, which Hank noticed immediately, but Rufus slumped, a casual posture that gave Hank the illusion of a slight height advantage. Rufus's relaxed manner was reflected in his clothes—clean, carelessly thrown on, rumpled clothes that were expensive.

In the perfunctory emails Hank had traded with Rufus, he could not remember Rufus mentioning that his father—*their* father—James Samuel Vincent would be joining him for the trip. But here he was. Hank's mother had chosen a perfect stand-in for Charles Camphor, a lover with whom she could produce a son Charles Camphor would never doubt was his. Both his late father and this biological father were handsome blue-eyed men, except James Vincent's hair was dark and Charles Camphor's hair had been sandy-blond.

———

"WELL, WELL!" James Samuel Vincent pulled ahead of Rufus in the lobby and offered Hank his hand. He did not seem to realize that he was blocking Hank's view of his half brother and his half brother's wife, Claudia. Hank stepped slightly to one side, shaking his biological father's hand but taking note of the simple pale green smock dress and tan sandals Rufus's wife wore. She clutched her children's hands, seeming almost to hold them back. Hank's daughter, Tess, ever the shy one, stood behind her parents. Susan and Hank were trees that gave Tess shade.

"I hadn't expected Color Land to be so crowded."

"Put an *ed* on it and it would be Colored Land," Rufus Vincent noted. He turned to Claudia and they both burst out laughing. Hank felt his face grow warm with embarrassment.

"Winona and Elijah have been looking forward to it all week," Claudia said. She offered Hank her hand.

Hank nodded. "Pleasure, Claudia."

Hank was glad that Susan had the foresight to order priority status tickets. They were able to move to the front of the long queue and enter immediately. Upon admission, every parent had to sign a waiver saying that if your kid was injured or perished at Color Land, the company was not responsible. They were given Color Land wristbands.

Susan said, "I thought Claudia and I would take the kids upstairs to the jungle gym and let you gentlemen catch up in the coffee shop."

Claudia smiled. "That sounds like a wonderful idea."

Hank tried not to show his disappointment. He watched Rufus kiss his wife before she left. "No dairy," she said. Susan guided Claudia and the kids through the entrance. Susan was the one who usually brought Tess to Color Land. She knew the ins and outs of the place. *If you add an* ed *to* Color, Hank thought, *it would be* Colored Land. He had forgotten to kiss Susan with all the hustle and bustle. His wife had forgotten to kiss him.

———

THE COLOR LAND coffee shop resembled a 1950s diner with black and white tiles and red vinyl chairs and booths. The coffee they ordered was watery like piss, which Hank could remember tasting as a boy when his body was changing and growing and curiosity would not let him do anything else but reach down to touch himself.

Rufus sat staring into the cup of coffee. "I just have to say, *this* is strange."

Hank stood up immediately. "Well, why don't we find another place? I'll text Susan. And we can *all* go to our place or somewhere else."

"No," Rufus clarified. "To have a brother and not know. One so close in age too."

"It must be stranger for our mothers," Hank said.

"Well, my mother didn't know until recently." And Rufus cut his eyes at James Samuel Vincent. "I mean she always suspected there were women, but *this*, when I told her, Mom did not know."

Hank had brought up the wrong subject. Normally he was more tactful. "I'm sorry," he said.

"What are *you* sorry for?" Rufus shrugged. "You didn't do anything."

James looked out a window onto a parking lot. It was a hot summer day. Even as a boy, he had hated Southern humidity. He had flown down as soon as Rufus told him he was meeting his half brother. He had wanted to be present. A facilitator. A mediator. It pleased James to know he had sired two healthy sons.

"What kind of doctor are you, Hank?"

"I'm a surgeon. My specialty is sports medicine."

"You operate on anyone famous?"

Hank smiled. "I could plead doctor-patient privilege, but oh, what the hell." Hank leaned forward and told James and Rufus about two NFL players who kept injuring themselves because they took too much juice and got themselves in compromising positions on the field and in the bedroom. Hank noticed, as he recounted the story, that he and Rufus had similar hands, long, almost delicate fingers, but Rufus's hands were in constant motion, circling the rim of his coffee cup, dropping in sugar and milk, picking the cup up and putting it down before taking a sip. Rufus seemed bored, despite Hank's attempt to reel him in. Hank's mother had been, after all, the other woman and, if Hank had done the math correctly, he was older than Rufus by five months. He fought the temptation to call Rufus *little bro*.

"Do you have a favorite sport, Rufus?" Hank smiled.

"Well, baseball," Rufus said. "When I was a kid, Dad and I went to a lot of Yankee games."

"*My* father"—and then Hank paused here—"Charles Camphor, the man who will always be my father—went to Clemson. He was a running back. In the South, football is *the* game."

"I've never understood football. Unless it is football as in soccer. That's a sport that makes sense," said Rufus, chewing up his stirrer.

"Did you play football in college, Hank?" James asked.

Hank looked at Rufus. "Some people find football engaging because it's so strategic. And complex. There's a good deal going on and not everyone can keep up with it all." Hank then addressed James Vincent. "I run. Six miles every day. I didn't have the frame for football. I was on the track team at Duke."

"I run," Rufus laughed. "From one lecture hall to another."

James threw his arm over Rufus's shoulder. "Rufus is a James Joyce scholar. Maybe the leading Joyce scholar in the country." James Vincent spoke with such assurance and pride that Rufus put down his coffee cup and looked momentarily stunned.

"Why Joyce?" Hank said.

"I don't know. I suppose I read him at the right time."

"My people grew up picking potatoes," James Vincent said.

"I didn't know that." Rufus's long fingers kept circling the cup.

"Sure you did."

"There's a lot that I don't know," Rufus said.

James Vincent shrugged. "Maine. Good for fishing. Bad for land. One of four boys. Your grandfather. My old man. At least that's how he'd tell it when he'd had a few drinks in him. People back then, sometimes, had to choose a daughter or a son. They picked sticks to see who would be the one to go to college. My father got the longest stick. He went to Boston and never looked back. He became a fireman."

"Huh. My people were firemen also," Hank said.

"So, there's continuity," James Vincent said, looking at Hank Camphor but nudging Rufus. "In Joyce. Joyce is land."

Rufus sat back in his seat. "What the fuck, Dad. . . . You're a Joyce expert now?"

James turned to Rufus. "A hot potato will heal a stye. A raw potato under the arms works better than deodorant. Put a potato in your shoe and kiss a cold good-bye. That's the farm boy's dictionary right there."

For a moment, Hank was reminded of the camaraderie he had had with his father, especially in high school and as an undergrad. He missed his father.

"You boys need to get along," James said.

The counter was an oval with a variety of cupcakes and giant lollipops on display, the kind with swirls and splotches of color. Hank had told the thespian pencils and pens and pieces of paper to keep back. He had given them a healthy tip on the sly to leave them alone. Rufus stood up. "Does anyone want a lollipop? I want a lollipop."

Hank burst out laughing. He thought Rufus was joking. "No," Hank said. "I'm fine."

"What's so funny?"

"I don't know. Nothing," Hank said, apologetically.

"Get yourself one." James Vincent turned to Rufus. "Get one for all of the kids. Winnie and Elijah and Bess."

"Tess," Hank corrected.

Rufus leaned in. "Hank's kid's name is Tess, Dad."

"Yes, Tess," James agreed. "She would like one too."

Rufus looked at Hank. "There was an accident. He hit his head and sometimes his hearing gets fuzzy."

Rufus walked off.

"Tell me about your head injury," Hank said.

James Vincent slurped the last of his coffee. "How's your mother: Barbara?"

"Happily married in Europe."

"What does her husband do?"

Hank thought there was urgency in the way James Vincent asked. "He's a breeder of British hounds."

"I would never have imagined Barbara on an animal farm."

"How would you have imagined her?"

"Not abroad."

Now it was Hank's turn to bristle. He did not like that James had inquired about Barbara behind his son's back, though he would've been disappointed if his biological father hadn't asked after his mother at all. "Well, it's my understanding that you only met a few times a year, so maybe your perceptions were limited."

James Vincent looked at him. "All perceptions are limited."

Hank took out his cell phone and showed James Vincent a picture of Barbara Camphor. She sat in front of a Christmas tree in an ugly Christmas sweater with her husband, Trevor, and a new litter of dogs.

"Barbara," James said, touching the cell phone.

"It's a lost cause," Hank said. "Don't get any ideas."

"I'm happily married," James Vincent said.

"Why isn't she here?"

"Would you want to be here if you were the second wife meeting your husband's son from an extramarital affair during his marriage to his first wife?"

"So, you told her?"

"After she guessed," James Vincent said. "Adele guessed first. Smart women guess."

When Rufus returned to the table, Hank whispered to him, "I'm sorry for what our father did to your mother. But I suppose without him, neither of us would exist."

THE COLOR LAND excursion lasted an hour and fifteen minutes and the kids got on famously. Tess and Winona and Elijah ran around the jungle gym and played at the Liquid Fountain until sensory overload snuck up on them and made them cranky and tired and they all broke down crying when it was time to say good-bye.

"Winnie wants to meet Stella!" Tess bellowed as Hank picked her up and tried to quiet her. His heart was delighted. His daughter had given him the excuse he needed to turn the afternoon into an evening.

"Well." Hank laughed, more comfortable and confident. "I have some crazy relatives and, frankly, Susan will tell you, we weren't sure what to expect."

Rufus nodded. "Neither were we."

Hank noticed how Rufus's kids hung on to James Vincent. He felt a tinge of something that he wanted to push away. He looked at Claudia and thought fleetingly of Lonnie Applewood from so many years ago. "If you are up to it, maybe later, after the kids have napped, an early dinner at our place?"

"That would be great," said James Vincent.

But Hank had pitched the question around James Vincent to Rufus and Claudia.

"Claudia?" Rufus turned to his wife.

"It's your call," she said. They were clearly working through something. Hank could pick it up in their body language. Temperature taking. Warm but not hot but not cold.

AND HERE'S HOW it goes with dinner. At some point that same evening after the children have eaten and are playing in the playroom, Hank takes them around the block to walk Stella, who makes him love her even more because she is so good with Winona and Elijah, who abuse the little dog with affection. It is after Susan changes Tess into her unicorn pajamas and her cousin Elijah reads the story "The Funky Snowman" from his favorite book. And before Tess and Winona braid and unbraid the hair on the Kaya American Girl doll, and Winona says she is not allowed to have an American Girl doll and Tess asks why, and Elijah looks at Winona in a way that says, *Be quiet*. And it is after James Vincent has his third round of martinis and Hank asks where they are off to next, and Claudia says they are headed home to New York after an impromptu visit to her sick mother in Georgia. And James says he will be flying back to New York tomorrow. That he came down expressly to see his other boy. And it is before Rufus rocks back and forth on tiptoes admiring the beautifully bound leather books Hank does not read—he has never been a big reader but collects them for his retirement years—and after Claudia sings Winona to sleep in an off-key voice like her mother's, planning for Rufus to pick Winona up and let her sleep the rest of the way in the car. Grateful that Winona sleeps, for the most part, peacefully these days. And it is before Hank excuses himself for a cigarette and James Vincent snoozes off with the glass in his hands and after Claudia makes her way to the bathroom and Hank, who has drunk beyond his limit tonight as well, spies Claudia walking toward the bathroom through the sliding patio door and puts out his cigarette and goes into the hallway.

IT IS AT this moment that he watches the sway of the yellow dress Claudia changed into for the evening and wants to elope with time, turn the moon on its head and the sun on its stomach and reverse time so that he is a thirteen-year-old boy again standing at the entrance to his neighbors' house. It is in this moment that Hank convinces himself that he will walk straight to the library and sit down and talk with Rufus now that the old man is dozing but somehow Hank finds his feet gravitating toward the bathroom door, where he stands waiting for the door to open and Claudia to come out. The toilet flushes and sounds like an ocean, the water runs and sounds like a lake, and Claudia opens the door and the current of a river might as well have come out to greet him and, in his tipsy, fumbling state he leans over and attempts to plant a kiss on her lips, which she averts.

"Well," Claudia says, watching him lean against the wall. "Someone's had too much to drink."

Hank says, "You remind me of someone I know. Knew."

Claudia tilts her head to the side. And for a second, Hank's sure he's staring into Lonnie Applewood's face and hearing Lonnie Applewood's voice. "Dear man, don't we all?"

He cannot decipher if Claudia is amused or annoyed. She steps around him and returns to the study. Hank gathers his composure and makes his way along the dimly lit hallway to the study, where Rufus is mouthing the words to a book and Claudia has helped herself to a drink and Susan has put on classical music and James Vincent is snoring and Rufus looks up and says to Hank, his nervous fingers slowing their run up and down the spines of the fine books, "I'm glad we could make this happen."

Hank watches Rufus lace his arms firmly around Claudia's waist. Rufus's action prompts Hank to do the same with Susan.

"Yes," Hank agrees quietly. "I hope we haven't been too much of a disappointment."

Bundesarchiv, Bild 183-0121-598
Foto: o.Ang. | 1932

ELOISE TAKES FLIGHT
(PART TWO)
1970 1978 1988 1989 1999 2010

DOWN THE STREET FROM THE FRIEDRICHSHAIN APART-
ment where Eloise Delaney inhaled her last breath, a dance
club now exists. The dance club is housed in an old refrigerator warehouse within walking distance of the Berlin Wall. Through
random windows on nights (like this one), silhouetted bodies can
be seen dancing, swaying—moving like mist and shadows beneath
lights that flash and dim and strobe hot invitations to the young.

AMONG THE YOUNG bodies is a group of American soldiers, mostly
black and Hispanic. They have traveled from their Army base in
London, checked into the Berlin Marker Hotel, and ventured out
in the December frost in search of music, nightlife, and German
women. The soldiers disperse from an overcrowded cab and join the
queue of clubbers. The smell of marijuana is everywhere. One soldier, of slight build and sporting a holiday goatee, is from Buckner
County, Georgia—the same town where Eloise Delaney was born.
They are cousins, twice removed, though he does not know this.

When the soldier was a boy of two, Eloise Delaney bounced him gingerly on her knees, but she is dead now—several years gone. As far as this world is concerned, neither fragment nor memory.

IN 1972, ELOISE DELANEY attended King Tyrone's wedding wearing crutches. Her only respectable male cousin married (at fifty) a fastidious woman named Sarah Braun who would bear him a daughter nine months later. The wedding was held on the Tybee Island pier with the Atlantic Ocean behind them and a small group of guests before them. The reception that followed was a no-frills affair with generous samplings of shrimp, oysters, scallops, and grouper for dinner. You were out of luck if you didn't like what the sea had to offer.

ELOISE RETURNED HOME from a war that many Americans were beginning to disapprove of, though most would remain in favor of Vietnam until its conclusion. She was twenty-five, and for the first time since her deployment, she read the American newspapers and watched the news. It is a hard fact in a war that for some people to live, others must die. Vietnam plagued Eloise when she was alone at night. And since she was currently without a lover, this was a good deal of the time. She thought of Jebediah Applewood saying none of this shit was real. If he had been in Buckner County, she would have loved to bump heads with him over a beer or two or three, just to have a different perspective. She wondered if any of her former comrades—almost none of them stayed in touch—shared her deep sense of betrayal and confusion. Eloise would dial up Agnes from time to time. And Agnes, almost despite herself, would hang on the line, sometimes responding to Eloise's questions, sometimes content with long silences: just because you couldn't stand someone didn't mean you no longer loved them.

TO LIFT ELOISE'S SPIRITS, Flora Applewood came for an afternoon visit to Tybee Island and drove Eloise to a "new spot" on the outskirts of Buckner County. The new spot was the Magnolia Lake Inn, a former hotel on a man-made lake. In its heyday, families would come to the B&B for barbecues and picnics and pony rides and while away the afternoon drinking cocktails and sipping sweet iced tea or nibbling on deviled eggs and delicate crab cakes. The new proprietor had stripped the paint and the lead beneath it and renovated the hotel to resemble a Hollywood movie set. On weekend nights, a DJ came in to spin LPs and on the first Saturday of every month, a live jazz band played. It was a dress-up, dress-down establishment where a man could bring his mistress or his boyfriend. And a woman could bring both and it was perfectly fine to take off your clothes and go for a midnight swim in the lake. Eloise was astonished to see the women drinking and smoking cigarettes and slow dragging arm in arm in the open. But then she looked more closely at the heavy curtains and the dusky hour of the day, and thought—for she did not want to take away Flora's joy or thunder—*We are still mostly hiding*. She slow dragged on one leg with Flora and let everyone in the Magnolia Lake Inn sign her cast. Then Eloise told her dear friend that she was moving to Germany.

"Eloise," Flora said, "when I told you to leave Buckner County, I didn't mean permanently."

But how to tell Flora that Buckner County slaughtered her heart with memories. Memories awaited her at every corner: her drunken ma, her disappearing pa, Sister Mary Weeping ducking out of the nunnery, and, of course, Agnes: the one that got away. And stayed away.

During Eloise's six weeks in Buckner County, she signed up for accelerated flying lessons at Southeast Aviation, the same engineering firm where the late Claude Johnson had worked. The flight instructor, a middle-aged white man, looked at her application and asked her why she wanted to learn to fly a plane.

Eloise lit a cigarette. "I want to hover above everything." And then, in anticipation of any questions that he might spring at her, she added. "I'm sure you've heard of Bessie Coleman?"

The flight instructor searched his memory and responded with an answer that made Eloise rethink disliking him. "Vaguely."

The first thing he taught his new students was how to categorize and inspect a plane. Eloise memorized the control panels and endured the tediousness of ground school, which included daily four-hour classes and a flight journal. She was the only black face in the room. She was also the first student the flight instructor taught to fly above the airfield and over the marsh and wetlands, where she spied alligators sunbathing below on the banks with their eyes closed.

"Well, how does it feel, Ms. Delaney?" her instructor asked.

Eloise laughed out loud. "As long as I don't crash this baby and turn us into alligator bait, it feels all right."

She soared five hundred, seven hundred, a thousand feet in the air with nothing around her but pillow clouds and sky. "Light as a feather. I'm thinking, right about now, I could do damn near anything."

She left for Germany with a recreational pilot's license.

IN THE 1970S, 60 percent of the American military bases in Europe were situated in West Germany. Eloise Delaney knew of Bessie Coleman's exploits in Friedrichshafen and Berlin. But she did not know of Germany's long and complex history with African Americans. Dr. Martin Luther King traveled to East and West Germany in 1964, and, of course, there were the Negro soldiers who had en-

listed during World War I and World War II to serve their country and fight the Germans. In France and Germany, many experienced freedom that would elude them forever when they returned home.

SHE WAS STATIONED for sixteen months at Ramstein Air Base, where she was encouraged to work in the race relations department and composing strategies to allay tensions between black GIs and white GIs on American military bases throughout Germany.

Dear Flora,

I do not like living on the base. I sit in a cubicle pushing papers. Being a glorified secretary is not for me. I didn't bust my ass doing military intelligence in Vietnam to sit in anybody's office doing data entry or, for that matter, anybody's conflict resolution or recruiting. Would it be selfish to pursue an advanced degree?

Yours, Eloise

Dear Eloise:

I've never really understood the word: selfish. Would pursuing an advanced degree make you happier? Happy?

Yours, Flora

Dear Flora:

After a year at the Logistics Headquarters, I don't think I'm going to reenlist again. I've decided to move into the public sector and enroll in classes at the University of Berlin. The future is in computers and satellites and surveillance technology. Maybe I'll study cryptology.

Cryptology Eloise

Dear Cryptology Eloise:

Well, that's all fine and well, but it bothers me that you don't say how you're living. How *are* you living, Eloise? Do you have a special friend? Life goes so fast. And loneliness is its own disease.

Curious, Flora

P.S. You must explain this cryptology business to me.

Dear Curious Flora:

My first month in my apartment in Berlin was miserable as hell. The Germans are cold. I knew they were cold, but a lot of them are colder than I expected. I was crossing the street and I crossed against a light and almost got myself killed by a driver, who yelled at me. I don't think it's a race thing. They're not what I'd call warm and fuzzy with each other either. I still cross the street against traffic, though. I just can't see the point of standing on the curb and idling when there's no cars approaching. If you don't hear from me, it means I've been run over by an impatient German.

Jaywalking Eloise

Dear Jaywalking Eloise:

Go out and meet people. The Germans can't all be impatient or bad. Go out and do and see more things and when you do them, think of me. I am old now, Eloise. Dear God, I am older than I want to be.

Tired, Old Flora

Dear Tired, Old Flora:

I am mailing this present for you to take out to King Tyrone for his baby daughter Deidre. They sent me pictures and she is the most darling thing. I heard something in that last letter of yours like self-pity. If you are feeling old, Flora, then it might not hurt to hold a new something in your arms. A baby. People say they come into this world innocent, but I think they come into this world knowing all the wise stuff we've forgotten. It's just a simple baby rattle. The Germans are good with simple things. If you hold that baby, I'll go out and meet a friend. Though I must confess, for my tastes, the German women are a bit pale. I like to dip my hands in chocolate.

Chocolate Dipping Eloise

Dear Chocolate Dipping Eloise:

Your letter left me speechless. I don't have much to write or say. Holding little Deidre did much to reset my mind. And you know your cousin Tyrone quite well. That rattle fits with everything. An *octopus* rattle, how did you ever?

Back on track, Flora

Dear Back on Track Flora:

I've gained fifteen pounds since I've arrived in Berlin. For the first time in my life, I've got a little round behind. It's a behind even Diana Ross—or Agnes—might envy. I think about her, you know? Maybe that's why I've eaten so much. Or maybe it's just the goddamn bread and pastry here. The Germans seem to like their food hearty. Pork knuckles and schnitzel and bratwurst. It's not a stretch from some of the food we grew up on. And the bread! That's what did a job on my behind. Flora, I can eat a basket of bread in one sitting. The bread makes me think of Gottlieb's Bakery and Lady Miller's cakes and, yes, Agnes. There I go again. But, true to my word, I've put myself out there and done a little exploring. It's like the Wild West here. I can barely keep track of the people coming and going. For a while the city was depopulating. But that's over. It's government subsidized—and there's this opening—this energy, being on the west side of a walled city. The Germans who stayed and the ones who are settling here now seem to want to be here. It's a very affordable place to live, especially if you're up for a certain level of everyday craziness. I'd be lying if I called Berlin a beautiful city. Berlin is no Paris, baby. There are vacant lots and abandoned buildings and the scale of things, coming from Buckner County, gets downright overwhelming. Some of this has to do with me picking up the language. I do best when I take things in a little at a time. What I like most about Berlin, for now, is that I can step outside my door and be anything. I master the language and I could start my whole life over again. Let's just say I'm free—to be distracted. I've managed to find some lovely and brazen German women friends. There's a vibrant lesbian nightlife here—with a little something for everyone. And you don't have to work hard to go to bed at night or wake up in the morning alongside a pretty face. I've met a woman named Greta—like Greta Garbo. She's in the history department at the University of Berlin and she's quite the radical. She and her ex-girlfriend share a squat house with seven other students over in Kreuzberg. Two doors down from her is the only gay squat house in Berlin. When the cops show up, the men put on their best costumes and make a grand exit. Flora, I wish you could be here to cheer them on—to see them. Words cannot do them justice. I've learned a fashion statement can become a way of life. And a way of life can mobilize a movement. Old places are getting torn down for newer modern buildings. The squatters' attitude is—why should we let you tear it down when we can fix it up and move in? *Everything* feels youthful and politicized in Berlin. Honey, these students are always protesting. I think they're taking inspiration from the '60s in the States. Greta works part-time at Café Berio in Nollendorfplatz. A spot I go to on Saturdays to people-watch and eat marzipan cake. We were flirting when she spilled hot coffee on my lap. You know I nearly killed her. We've been dating ever since. She likes to drag me along with her to rallies, and it's been good, because I'm picking up German much faster than I did on the base. Recently, we went to hear Angela Davis speak. I stood there thinking, there is so much I don't know. If I lived a lifetime, I wouldn't know it all.

New Girlfriend, Eloise

Dear New Girlfriend, Eloise:
   I'm jealous.

Jealous, Flora

Dear Jealous Flora:
   Don't be jealous, Sweet Flora. I've only ever loved two women. And you are one of them. Greta is lovely. Greta is kind. She bears the brunt of my shit when I feel like doling out punishment. The other day we were making sausages in her apartment and something about stuffing the casings with the raw meat brought back memories of my ma and pa picking crabs at the crab factory. Greta and her roommates and I were laughing and having a good old time. We'd had our share of beer and when we finished stuffing those sausages, don't you know I burst out crying? And when they asked me what was the matter, I put a royal cussing on them. And Greta told

everyone to clear out and she asked me what she could do to make the situation better. And I fucked her because, Flora, and you know this is true, sometimes that's the only thing that makes sense. And Greta had the nerve to ask me if she was my fetish? I didn't know what to say to that. She's a young history student and history students weigh everything. I told her the truth, which is that I don't waste a moment's time wondering when she runs her fingers through my natural hair, if I am *her* fetish. That's not an honest answer, she said. I wish you could see Greta. She's flaxen all over. We went down to the pub after and I told our friends a story. Get enough drinks in me and I can spin a good yarn. I've developed a reputation that way.

Yarn spinning, Eloise

Dear Yarn Spinning Eloise:

Such silence. Four months now. I haven't heard from you in a while. All well in Berlin?

Flora, Still Here

Dearest Flora, Still Here:

Greta graduated from the university. She took a teaching position in a Turkish neighborhood one stop away from her old neighborhood. We've decided to live together. It looks like I'm officially domesticated now. How do these things happen?

Shacked up, Eloise

Dear Shacked Up Eloise:

If I knew the answer, we'd both be rich.

No regrets, Flora

Dear No Regrets Flora:

Love—and happiness.

Your Eloise

———

ELOISE COULD NOT know this at the time, but the 1970s and early 1980s were to mark one of the happiest periods in her life. It was a good decade after an ugly war to work and travel and be carefree and oblivious. Bowie was living in Berlin and recording *Heroes*. Iggy Pop was shooting up heroin. Eloise avoided the drugs and went for the sex. Her relationship with Greta came to an end when Greta woke one night in their Kreuzberg apartment and overheard Eloise talking on the phone with another woman.

"*Love*," Eloise said into the phone.

"Who is she?" Greta wanted to know, after Eloise hung up the phone.

"Just someone I have my own history with."

"You can't. You shouldn't."

Eloise and Greta broke up but remained occasional lovers and close friends. Eloise tucked her clipping of Bessie Coleman away in a bureau drawer and forgot about her and flying. She continued to spin her yarns but everything else about her past she was content to forget.

"ON MY MOTHER'S side are hell-raising people," Eloise said at the pubs. "They all died violently: guns, machetes, and knives. More than a few of my people have been hanged, though I don't know if that violence should be called theirs. The violence started in the low country out in the rice fields where my great-great-great-somebody used to slave and toil, and my great-great-great-somebody's daughter, Matilda, had a chance to work in the Big House 'cause she had bright color. But at the last minute the fickle-minded mistress of the house said, *No, not that one, this one*, which enraged my great-somebody so much she slapped the mistress and the slave girl chosen to take her daughter's place. As payback, the master sold Matilda away. They say my great-great-great-grandma fought something terrible over that and was lashed within an inch of her life. When she recovered, she wouldn't work and neither would her seven able-bodied sons, despite the beatings and the whippings forced on them. They took up arms and fought so that the master hanged all but one, who managed to survive the noose without his neck getting broke. The master realized that some fights could not be won, and upon scanning his ledger, he saw that he had lost close to ten thousand dollars trying to domesticate prime property. The youngest slave, having seen his brothers killed for no good reason, didn't have regard for life anymore. He roamed the plantation waiting for death to take him. And, after all that, the brighter-colored girl the mistress had brought into the Big House dropped dead fetching eggs, and the mistress miscarried four of the master's children, and the master, being Southern and God-fearing, determined that there was a plague on his house. He bought back my great-great-grandmother Matilda. Matilda changed her name to Daisy when she saw the limp daisies pushing out of her mother's and her six brothers' graves. The loss of all of her people (her mentally addled brother being the exception) stretched her soul toward evil. If the loose branch of a tree touched her the wrong way, she'd take an ax and chop it to the ground. The master and mistress did not bother Daisy, though she broke the dishes and let the slop jar overflow and left the door of the chicken coop open for the foxes and threw the fresh pails of water in the backyard as soon as the water boy delivered them from the well. And when she spat in the master's food in the kitchen, no one uttered a word, not even the Aunt Jemimas and Uncle Toms, for they were afraid of her wrath. The master thought it part of God's mercy to see the sun rise. He would look at Daisy at the start of each morning and ask, "Daisy, are you going to poison me today?"

"No, sir," she would answer. "Tomorrow, most likely."

Daisy never poisoned the master or the mistress and when they died, they set Daisy and her dimwitted brother free, but free to do what and go where? They say General Sherman and his Union soldiers came marching up to the plantation one afternoon. (Eloise would pause here and sip her beer in front of her German friends for dramatic effect.) Sherman was always marching up on something or someone during the Civil War. When he caught sight of Daisy placing conch shells over seven well-tended graves, he listened to her story and offered her his torch.

"Young lady, *burn everything*," he shouted, for Sherman was as thirsty and calculating in his quest to win the war as Daisy was clear-headed and mean.

ELOISE WAS IN the lovely medieval town of Lucca, Italy, when the Berlin Wall fell.

She woke with a sharp pain between her legs, in a house she did not recognize and in a bed with torn sheets. She could not remember where she had been or what she had done the previous night—although she could remember a bar and carousing and copious amounts of red wine. She had rented her Kreuzberg apartment for three times its price because as momentous as the opening of the wall was going to be, she did not relish the large crowds. The prospect of freedom was thrilling but also a source of suspicion and fear too. Some of her friends had surprised her—perhaps no one more so than Greta—by their stubborn refusal to believe that reunification would happen. The wall had divided East and West Berlin and now its people were revisiting their past and using the wall to document milestones in their lives—marriages, deaths, births—in a way that made Eloise realize that Berlin was not hers. She was an American, an expat. She did not want to wrestle with the reality that the Berlin she knew was about to change. Thousands of U.S. soldiers—many of them African Americans—would be shipped home, some leaving behind girlfriends, wives, and children—within weeks of the wall coming down. But she would be okay. She worked in the public sector. She had grown accustomed to not seeing people who looked like her every day. But not seeing them and knowing they were there—well, that was an entirely different thing.

A WOMAN WITH dark hair and a distinctly Roman nose and wearing jeans and a shirt thrown haphazardly over her svelte frame came into the bedroom and kissed Eloise good morning. The woman said in a broken Italian accent that Hans was making coffee, but she thought they would do better to go out for breakfast. Eloise sat up in the bed, which she realized was gurgling beneath her—a waterbed—and stared at the yellow walls and the leaf-green Italian tiled floor. Her clothes were scattered across the green floor, everywhere. In recent years, she had fallen into the habit of waking up with strange women and drinking heavily.

"What time is it?" Eloise asked the woman in Italian.

"Past noon," the woman said, and kissed Eloise again before sauntering out of the room. Eloise could not for the life of her recall the woman's name and was relieved after sorting through her things to find her passport and wallet and everything in it still there.

IT WAS THE man Hans who caught Eloise totally off-guard. She came into the kitchen with all her clothes on and found him cooking in the buff.

"An encore?" he said, stirring egg whites into a cast-iron skillet. The previous night came to her clearly now—canoodling with the woman, Victoria, at the *enoteca* and Hans, Hans from the Netherlands, who was housesitting for a friend. Eloise saw her reflection in the glass window overlooking what in the summer months must be a splendid garden. At that moment, she bore a striking resemblance to her mother. Her head ached and her pussy hurt and her pride hemorrhaged from the loss of something precious. It was November 9, 1989, the day after the fall of the Berlin Wall. She was in her forties and smoking a pack of unfiltered cigarettes a day, but her years of drinking and picking up strange women were officially over.

———

DURING THE 1990S, Eloise traveled home once a year. The woman who had rejoiced over Claude Johnson's violent death now sought out his next of kin. She found Claude Johnson's people struggling and poor and not without their demons—the crack epidemic had trickled south toward them. She was not a rich woman but she was a hard worker, even during the partying years. Eloise sold her two-bedroom apartment in Kreuzberg for a one-bedroom apartment on Simon-Dach-Strasse in Friedrichshain. She consulted a financial advisor and set up modest trust funds for Claude's poor relations. Because that is what a sober aunty, with no children of her own, will do. During long walks on the beach with King Tyrone and his wife and their daughter Deidre, she noticed the child's knowledge of birds, fish, and seashells. From then on, she sent books on coral reefs and marine life from around the world along with maps and canisters of chocolate-covered pretzels. When Eloise's supervisors at the American embassy in Berlin offered her a much-deserved promotion, she accepted. *Buckner County will always be home*, she told Flora, *but Germany is where I live.*

IN 2006, SHE LAID flowers on Flora's grave and cried much. In 2009, she laid flowers on her mother's grave and cried less. Eloise purchased a plot beside her mother for her own interment.

TWO DAYS AFTER her mother's funeral, Eloise ran into Agnes Christie on Main Street. It was their first encounter in years.

"Agnes," Eloise said.

"Eloise." Agnes nodded and continued walking. Eloise put out a hand to stop her.

They stood on the sidewalk on a crisp autumn day with people moving about them. Eloise was suddenly aware that she had aged, but Agnes, well, Agnes still looked like Agnes, after all these years.

"What are you doing here, Agnes? In Buckner County, I mean?"

"I might ask you the same thing."

"My mother died."

"Well, well, well," said Agnes. She burst into tears, and Eloise thought this odd because, aside from dropping off shrimp to the Miller house, Delores Delaney had never said two words to Agnes.

"Eddie," said Agnes, taking out her husband's old red handkerchief. "Cancer took him."

Eloise gave her condolences and, this time, they were sincere. "I'm so sorry, Agnes."

"He was a good man."

"I didn't know him, but I'm sure he was."

"How? *How* do you know, Eloise?"

"Because I know you, Agnes. And you wouldn't marry a bad one."

"But a good man might marry a bad woman."

"Well, now you're getting into contradictions, Agnes. And I can't talk about contradictions on an empty stomach. I was about to step into one of these cafés for lunch. Would you like to join?"

The two women sat down at a coffee shop.

"Why aren't you dressed like yourself?" Agnes asked. There was just the hint of disapproval in her voice. Eloise was wearing a dress instead of pants in deference to her mother's passing.

Eloise took hope from Agnes's question. "Would you like to see me in pants, Agnes?"

"I'm just glad to see you," said Agnes, batting her lashes that were as thick as they had been when they were children.

Eloise felt emboldened enough to postpone her flight home to Germany. She invited Agnes to dinner the following night—and cocktails beforehand at the boutique hotel she had checked into on the Buckner County Riverfront.

"That sounds like fun." Agnes showed off photos of her two grown daughters, Beverly and Claudia, and all of her grandkids. Eloise could barely feign interest.

"My younger girl, Claudia," Agnes said, "is a Shakespeare scholar."

Eloise smiled. "Well, wouldn't Sister Mary Weeping just love that!"

"Who?" Agnes wrinkled her nose. She returned both the photos and the wallet that held them into her leather handbag.

"*Sister Mary Weeping*—the young nun who taught us Shakespeare at St. Paul's," Eloise said, lighting a cigarette.

"My daughter Claudia learned Shakespeare from Eddie—her father." Agnes shrugged. "Why would I tell my girls about a place like St. Paul's? Why would anyone want to talk about *that*?"

"You still run hot and cold."

"Hot, mostly."

BUT AGNES WILL not show up for dinner or cocktails at Eloise's hotel the following evening. And Eloise will sit on the double bed in a room overlooking the polluted river that leans toward beauty anyway. She will watch the white moon sail over the water and wonder if the short stout man she had seen in Nam performing Shakespeare really made Agnes happy.

And she will say, "I knew she would not come." And she will tell herself that it is probably for the best because it is one thing to trade small talk in a café and another to find herself getting old and turning gray. *I look young but Agnes looks younger.* She will light a cigarette and give in to a few wallowing hours of self-pity, wondering what she has forgotten. Has she forgotten something? She has closed her heart to love. She has become a waiter. Waiting for someone who will never ever feel the same way. *How could you leave me to lay myself bare like this? What are you so afraid of, Agnes? Really, what can happen that hasn't happened already?*

EN ROUTE TO Germany, she will remember Bessie Coleman. When she returns home, she will rummage through the bureau drawer in her bedroom for the clipping she loved so much as a child. The clipping will have faded, but Eloise Delaney will still be able to make out Bessie Coleman's face and a few sentences. Eloise will enroll in flight school in Berlin that same week and in her sixties regain her love of flying. From time to time, she will invite her more intrepid girlfriends to join her. She will continue to fall in love or in like with a number of women and they, in varying degrees, will love her too. But there will always come the inevitable moment when one of them will say, "I wasn't expecting..."

And Eloise will roll her eyes and make it easy for them. "It's not you, baby. I'm not cut out for long-term relationships."

She will walk to one of the neighborhood pubs in Friedrichshain while they pack their belongings, but return in enough time to make sure they don't pack anything that doesn't belong to them.

WHEN SHE GOES out in her little plane, Eloise will not miss them. Or anyone. Or anything. And for sheer amusement, she will study the airplane engine and mentally assemble and reassemble its parts like a chart of the female anatomy: vagina, labia minora, labia majora, cervix, uterus, and ovaries. . . . And she will think, *Eloise, you are the epitome of a dirty old woman.*

She will continue to smoke a pack and a half of cigarettes every day: her only vice. And she will not stop, even when the doctors advise her to quit. *Who are you to tell an old woman she can't have her cigarettes? I live in Berlin.*

SHE WILL COME down with a cold. In the hospital that cold will become pneumonia. She will recover just long enough to return to her one-bedroom apartment in Friedrichshain. Her German friends will call her family in Buckner County, Georgia, when she falls ill a final time. At this point, she will be sixty-three, not historically old—but hardly young.

"WHERE IS MY MA? Where is my pa? Where is King Tyrone? Agnes? Agnes? Oh, dear Lord? *Where* is Agnes?" She will look up from her deathbed at the face of King Tyrone's daughter, Deidre, who has come in his place since he is too sickly and old himself to travel across the Atlantic.

ELOISE WILL CLUTCH Deidre's hands and ask after the oceans. Deidre, to her delight, has become a marine biologist. Deidre will name the oceans for her aunty Eloise: Pacific, Atlantic, Indian, Arctic, and Southern. Eloise will nod and squeeze Deidre's hands tighter and, because it is her way to fight until the bitter end, she will utter all the ugly hateful thoughts that cloud her head. *Aunty,* Deidre will whisper: *Release these things.* She will glance over Deidre's shoulder, where she will spy Flora and her ma and pa and Sister Mary Weeping. They will drift toward her and gather her up like pallbearers out of the sleigh bed. They will laugh and make dead chatter that hums in Eloise's ears. And Eloise will cuss them out in English and in German.

"Get me out of this fucking box. What's wrong with you? Where are you carrying me? Where's Agnes? Get me out of this box! I want to be cremated. I changed my mind. Don't bury me, you hear?"

But the dead will keep perambulating with Eloise, and Eloise—or that thing that's called a soul—will fly from the bedroom window in outrage, past the tricolored flag flapping in the wind and the warehouse down the street inhabited by new squatters who move like shadows beneath lights that flash and dim, depending on how well the electricity has been jerry-rigged. Eloise's soul will pause a split second to register faint music. But there is no music.

Hello
Good-bye
Kiss my black ass

There is only her voice drifting toward the sky to greet the elements.

THE WEIGHT OF AN ALLIGATOR

2010

HER DAUGHTERS WERE SURPRISED WHEN AGNES TOLD them she was returning to Georgia, joining a tide of retirees from Northern cities who had sold their homes or foreclosed on them or were on the run from dysfunctional children and grandchildren or simply hoping to reconnect with loved ones and die in the place of their birth. For Agnes, it was less sentimental and complicated. She suffered from crippling bouts of rheumatoid arthritis. Sometimes, when she left her apartment on Riverside and 155th Street, the wind would sing harrowing songs throughout her joints. And now, with Eddie two years gone, there were no familiar hands to soothe her aches with Chinese tiger balm. During the winter months Agnes often felt like a shut-in—too intimidated by the cold to venture outdoors. And so, she passed her apartment on to Beverly and her four children and sought out the warmer climate of Georgia and the sprinkling of friends and family who still lived there. A shocking number of her friends were now fat, or blind and diabetic, prone to walkers and canes. They regarded Agnes with suspicion. "What fountain of youth did you happen on?"

"Fountain of youth," Agnes said, staring down at her edged-down Aerosole sneakers. "I lived in New York for half my life. At this point, I think I was born to walk." In those moments, she was glad that she had rented a small one-bedroom apartment within walking distance of her neighborhood library. She was glad that she had bought the secondhand forest-green Saab and could, when necessary, drive to the Whole Foods or to the weekly farmer's market and run errands for herself. She was not a religious woman, but on rising each morning, she always said a silent prayer. "God, let these limbs be blessed."

AGNES CHRISTIE VOLUNTEERED at the local library three days a week. Twice a week she taught English as a second language to some of the Mexican immigrants who had come to Buckner County to work at the nearby chicken-processing plant. It was Beverly's idea that Agnes sign up for ESL certification before heading south. "Mommy," Beverly said. "I could see you going down there and getting depressed if you don't do something with yourself." But it was her younger daughter, Claudia, and Claudia's husband, Rufus, who registered and paid for Agnes's ESL certification class, also picking up the expense for her flight and moving expenses as part of their going-away gift.

A TEN-YEAR-OLD BLACK boy walked into the library and asked for a book called *The Maganetic Stone*. At first Agnes checked the online science catalog, thinking perhaps it was a stone she was unfamiliar with. But on the third try, she scanned the general catalog and the title *The Magician's Stone* came up. She turned the computer monitor around to face the boy and pointed to the title: "Do you mean *The Magician's Stone*?" The boy blinked. He had an angular face and his eyes, she thought, were far too small for his head. "Yeah, that one," he said. Just for curiosity's sake—Agnes did not like to think of herself as cruel—she dropped two quarters, three dimes, and a penny on the vinyl floor. She watched the coins roll and waited to see if the boy would have the home training to retrieve them.

"And how much do we have here?" she said cheerfully. The last coin warmed the palm of her hand. The boy stood at the information desk and counted eighty-one cents, mouthing the words as he counted. Agnes looked at him and tried to have compassion in the same way that she tried not to brag about her beautiful grandchildren Elijah and Winona, children who, as early as two, could read, subtract, and add. When Agnes considered this boy, a sour note played in her throat like when you eat a piece of kiwifruit that's gone bad. His stupidity made her thoughts turn to her more precarious grandchildren: Minerva, Peanut, Keisha, and Lamar. On a bad day in the library, when the kids were loud and unruly and she had to call the security guard to escort them out or quiet them down, Agnes often held her breath and wondered what would become of her daughter Beverly's children. She hadn't seen them since Christmas.

"How old are you, sweetie?" Agnes asked.

"Ten," the boy said.

She had guessed right. Agnes told the boy to keep the coins and slipped him a crisp dollar on the sly. After work, she walked five blocks to the Buckner County post office and dropped a *Missing You* greeting card in the mail as a kind of penance. The card contained forty dollars, ten for each of Beverly's kids.

TWO DAYS AFTER the boy checked out *The Magician's Stone*, he returned to the library and asked Agnes to buy a chocolate bar for the school fund-raiser. She bought four milk chocolate bars and told him not to bother her again. Purvis Middle School sat directly across the street from the Buckner County library. Three times a week, about forty minutes before closing, the school principal always stopped by to stake claim on the nonfiction stacks. Wilson Tart would take his sweet time browsing the sports section before approaching the information desk with one or two sports biographies, mostly of old Negro League players like "the black Babe Ruth," Josh Gibson. Agnes shared Principal Tart's fondness for nonfiction, but her interests ran more to native flora and fauna, the coastal wetlands and the wildlife that took refuge there.

SHE DID NOT think there would be a man after Eddie. Agnes did not want one. She thought that if Wilson Tart knew her age, he would surely back off and tilt younger. She declined his first invitation to the Buckner County Jazz Festival—jazz festivals made her heart ache—but she said yes to brunch at the all-you-can eat Longhorn Sunday buffet. Sunday brunches soon became a habit with them. Over heaping plates of stuffed tilapia, a fish they both agreed had next to no taste, Wilson asked if Agnes felt the young people nowadays were perhaps more than lax, asked if perhaps something in them was permanently soiled.

"Agnes," he said, spooning the stuffing off the tilapia, "sometimes they get buck wild and I have to break their asses all the way down." Wilson was a clean-shaven bald man in his early sixties. He had lost his hair at twenty-nine. His hair had been his pride and joy, a halo of natural curls that did not require Dudley's Waving Wax or Jheri Curl activator. Sometimes he still reached for the curls that were no longer there.

The breaking, he explained, was mostly verbal, but when the occasion warranted, he would drag a student into his office out of camera's sight and pummel him upside his head.

"Who are you talking to like that, son?" Wilson reenacted shaking a student. "My dear beloved grandmother would have flayed me for less."

"One of them reports you," Agnes warned, "and that's the end of a long, distinguished career."

Wilson shifted in the upholstered booth. "No one's reported me yet. These young fools need discipline."

Agnes had never been disciplined as a child. Nor had she spanked Claudia and Beverly. She left the spankings to Eddie, who did not trust himself to dole out spankings but sparingly. And their two girls had turned out right. The first child was her needy child. Beverly had come into this world needing something that Agnes had never been able to give: a rock-bottom love that burrowed into everything she looked at or touched. She demanded love with a happy disposition that wore down Agnes's energy as a young mother who had just escaped Buckner County and was getting acquainted with human feelings again. Her other child, Claudia, arrived when she was in a better place. When there was enough distance between what had happened on Damascus Road and the person Agnes thought she could be. Agnes held a light up to Claude's memory by loving Claudia like Claude would have if she had been his.

"Time," she said to Wilson, "sometimes, the young people need time instead of discipline."

Wilson Tart considered Agnes. He was always considering Agnes. "There's a matinee at the mall. We might make it if we skip dessert. Or we could watch a movie at my place."

Bless his heart, Agnes thought. Wilson Tart wanted her. Men and women had always wanted her. It did her vanity some momentary good to see the hopeful look on Wilson Tart's bald-headed face. Companionship in old age was a good thing.

"Next week, Wilson," she smiled. "I've got a cell phone date with my youngest, Claudia, at eight. I'd hate to have to rush home."

QUESTIONS, QUESTIONS, QUESTIONS.

"Mom, how do you love someone enough? How did you love Dad enough?" Claudia had awakened Agnes in the middle of the night recently.

Agnes, sitting up in her plaid monogrammed nightgown, was relieved her daughter's midnight call was not news of someone's death.

"My dear," Agnes said, eyes adjusting to the darkness of her bedroom and the blue light emanating from the cell phone. "We didn't have time to ponder such things. And neither should you."

But when she hung up the phone, Claudia's questions would not let Agnes sleep. This idea of loving someone *enough* instead of loving him, or her, in the moment and sticking to the truth of that love because you never knew which day would be your last. Her Eddie had spent the formative years of their marriage in Vietnam. He had hated that war, but for reasons mostly unbeknownst to her, he had reenlisted. Her Eddie was a going-off, wandering kind of man, even when standing right in front of her. It was just his temperament.

When Claudia raised the subject with her again, she asked her daughter what precisely was wrong. "Do you still love Rufus?"

"This thing with Winnie," Claudia said. "She's better. We're working on it, Mom, but sometimes it feels like we don't know each other at all."

"That's nonsense—"

"No," she said. "It isn't, Mom. Did you ever feel like you and Dad had grown apart?"

"*What* do you want to know each other for?"

"That's what couples do."

People nowadays think they need to know everything about their partners, Agnes thought, but to Claudia she said, "Some things we just aren't meant to know. Tread carefully. Don't strangle the mystery out of love."

IT WAS QUITE natural when Eddie was in Vietnam for Agnes to stroll into a bar at night and order a cosmopolitan. She would arrange for the girls to spend the night with Eddie's mother and take a break for herself. Alone she'd sit in a barebones chair taking in the scenery until another woman approached her. Agnes never had to wait long before some gal did. She would rise and the zigzags on her patterned wrap dress would swirl with her. "I've been sitting here waiting for a friend to show up," she would lie. And if a woman attempted to draw her into conversation or halt her sudden urge to flee, Agnes would laugh, shrugging away their offer to pick up her tab.

"I think my friend was trying to tell me something. Inviting me *here*. She must have been trying to tell me something." She would adjust the strap on the waist of her wrap dress, never losing sight of the women dancing fork knife fork knife fork knife to the Staples' "I'll Take You There" on the dance floor, or gathered in clusters around the red velvet pool table.

AND SOMETIMES, much less frequently, though more frequently than memory allowed Agnes to admit, she sank deep into the bar chair and asked the bartender for another drink. "Why don't we switch it up a bit? I'll have a sidecar this round. Eloise should be here any moment now."

"What does she look like?" A conversation would spark with the woman to her right or to her left.

"Oh," said Agnes, resting her bangled arms on the edge of the bar. "She's about five foot six, skin soft caramel, what the Spanish call *dulce de leche*. I'm guessing she'll be wearing a ribbed vest and tapered pants and a fedora of some kind."

Agnes described, between sipping the Cointreau, lemon juice, and cognac that went into her sidecar, how she first met Eloise. How Eloise had been for all intents and purposes an orphan left on her parents' doorsteps. How they had shared a bedroom well into their teen years before drifting apart. The cigarette smoke in the bar provided a thick enough screen for Agnes's half-truths and ready-made lies.

"People get lonely and do stupid, stupid things," said Agnes. "Like pick up the phone to call old lovers better left alone or friends who weren't their friends in the first place."

At random times the phone would ring at Eddie and Agnes Christie's house in the South Bronx: random months, days, and hours. You'd almost think the instrument had a mind of its own. Of course, there were fingers looping through the hole in the rotary dial or pushing the touchtone buttons. Agnes knew it was Eloise, even before the first words were spoken.

"I know someone's there," said Agnes, covering the receiver, looking over her shoulder to make sure her daughters weren't in earshot. More breathing.

"Who's there?"

"No one that matters," Eloise Delaney said. "Hang up the phone."

"I would," Agnes said. "If I understood why some people persist."

"Love," Eloise whispered.

"I don't know the first thing about it."

"Yes, I suppose love's just my burden to carry."

"Eloise, you're wrong to call me at home."

"Where should I call you, Agnes?"

"No. Where."

"When can I see you?"

"You see me every day," Agnes said. "Reach out. In the thin air."

THERE WAS ALWAYS a point in the night when even the most determined suitor would regard Agnes with tired eyes and stand up to pursue other options. At Hazel's, a racially mixed lesbian bar in the West Village in 1972, Sandy Simmens sat listening to Agnes for a solid forty-five minutes before dipping her hands into her pockets to fetch a nail file and nail clippers. This was the way Sandy had learned as a child to curtail her anger when someone called her a butch or a dyke. Or Jasper. She would calmly clip her nails before a fight began. So that her adversary had a moment to back down and she had a moment to consider if she would be the victor or the victim.

"Listen," Sandy Simmens said to Agnes. "Nobody wants to hear this bullshit. You can sit here by yourself or come home with me and get fucked."

Sandy Simmens's no-nonsense approach appealed to Agnes. As did the close-cropped 'fro and starched white shirt tucked into buckled, musk-colored Halston jeans. She stopped short of telling Sandy Simmens how much she reminded her of Eloise.

AS A RULE, Agnes never slept with the same woman twice. But Sandy kissed her. And sucked her. And humped her. And teased her, playing notes on her body not unlike the jazz musicians who jammed in the restaurant on the second floor of Hazel's, the restaurant that Agnes never stepped foot in because jazz made her heart ache and because the aroma of the chicken, shrimp, and fish that the owners dappled in cake flour for lightness wafted down the stairs and mingled with the menthol cigarettes at Hazel's, so that the odor clung to her clothes and she had to run them through the wash once, twice, three times to erase the burnt-oil smell.

"Whoever she was, she taught you well," said Sandy, leaning across the full-sized bed to grab a box of Morton salt matches. Street noise could be heard through the windows that opened onto the terrace of Sandy's tidy studio apartment.

"What makes you think anyone had to teach me anything?" Agnes, suddenly shy, coiled sheets around her naked shoulder.

"Relax," said Sandy, propping her elbow on a flat pillow. "We should do this again. Dinner. Or something."

She knew of men down south who abandoned their wives and children. *Poor Eloise.* Of children who stood waiting and staring out of draped windows for a mother or father, almost always a father, to come home. Eloise had been one of those children, though at the time, she, Agnes, had been too self-involved to really notice. Yes, yes, Agnes knew of men who would show up every now and again to see their offspring, buy them a bag of popcorn or pick cookies out of a corner store bin. Agnes had not been one of these children. She was a deacon's daughter, an altogether different thing.

Agnes assaulted Sandy with kisses and then took the round-about way home to the Bronx, which is the say, she went south toward Brooklyn before traveling north to the Bronx and taking a gypsy cab on Arthur Avenue. She would see Sandy on three more occasions and then shut herself down again.

SHE MET EDDIE CHRISTIE in 1967. They were attendees at a belated wedding reception for Agnes's first cousin, Charlotte Applewood, a Sunday afternoon lunch hosted by Agnes's parents.

"You've got a cloud above your head," said Eddie Christie. He jumped up and down on the long green lawn trying to knock the clouds away. Agnes craned her long neck toward the heavens but saw nothing but blue skies.

"A bright cloud of sorrow."

"Go away," Agnes said. In truth, she was putting the best on the outside. She was not in the mood for anyone's lunch or party.

"Knock, knock," he said, moving in circles around the patio tables and chairs, viciously swatting at clouds. Agnes stifled a strong impulse to knock him sideways into yesterday, tomorrow, the middle of next year.

A month earlier, Edward Christie had stood as best man and witness for Charlotte and Reuben Applewood in Las Vegas. Now the short brown man corrupted the Miller family's lush grass with his shiny military shoes and gold-buttoned Navy suit. Agnes thought he resembled a midnight-blue penguin.

"You're a nuisance," she snapped.

Eddie reached to claim another cloud on her behalf, but halted midgrab when he noticed a queue forming around the punch bowl. Agnes watched as his heels touched ground and he pivoted in a northwest direction, abandoning her altogether and making his way from table to table to take orders from the seated church ladies. It was spring and pink azaleas were blooming everywhere, but none more so than those on the church ladies' floral print dresses. Eddie leaned over and listened attentively as the old biddies whispered into his ear. Agnes could guess what they were saying. *Where did you say you were from again, darling? Now, isn't he just the sweetest thing. See if you can take this envelope over to the bride and groom. Not much in it, but maybe enough for a Corningware set.* Eddie Christie did not seem the least bit bored or put off by their lollygagging, but Agnes knew, *just knew*, the old biddies' breath was hot and damp, an unpleasant mix of saliva and the herbal throat lozenges they favored over spearmint chewing gum.

Agnes gravitated toward the dessert table. At its center was a lovely three-tiered wedding cake. She had stayed up the night before to help her mother, Lady Miller, frost the cake with rich lemon butter frosting. Lady Miller had a good side business baking cakes for members of her church. Sometimes she made cakes weeks before a wedding and stored them in the garage freezer. But this cake for Charlotte, her only niece, was made fresh.

"You've been sleeping a bit much lately," Lady Miller said, sprinkling the cake froster with warm water so the cake wouldn't meet the frosting and gather crumbs.

"I've been tired."

"You're sure that's all?"

Three weeks before, Agnes had broken up with Claude Johnson. Since then, her mom had been fishing for an explanation.

"Mama," Agnes said. "Rest your nerves. I'm not pregnant."

"Is it her?"

Agnes stuck her finger in the frosting. Something she knew her mother did not approve of. "Give her a name."

"Eloise," Lady Miller said. It was her mother who had asked Eloise to leave.

"Eloise Delaney is the least of my concerns," said Agnes. She had loved Claude Johnson more than anyone. Maybe, possibly, even more than Eloise, but this was something her mother could not understand. And Agnes lacked both the stamina and the wherewithal to make her.

EDDIE CHRISTIE FINISHED serving drinks and followed Agnes to the cake table eating clouds like a fire-eater eats fire. Agnes spun around and stared into his mouth. For a split second she saw cloud smoke on his breath. He bowed, a gallant gesture, swallowed hard, and swayed in such an exaggerated manner that Agnes smiled. It was her first smile since Damascus Road. She was smiling because he was short and ugly and reminded her of the Negro writer whose works they'd read in English Lit at Buckner County College: James Baldwin. Except Baldwin, from what Agnes gathered, was slight. Eddie Christie, if he didn't watch himself, might grow thick. But what was it? There was something endearing about him.

"Well, I spiked the punch," he said. "And I'm ready for cake."

A voice called for him through the crowd. *Eddie? Eddie, sweetie?*

Just as quickly as he had eaten the swirling clouds he retreated again, pulled on another errand. Agnes waited until Charlotte and Reuben Applewood linked arms and sliced their wedding cake, each offering a first bite to the other. Agnes thought the whole affair delicate, as delicate as the fashionable yellow cage dress Charlotte wore. The Miller women had sartorial flair, if not splendor. The Miller women all married well.

"Who is he again?" Agnes whispered to Charlotte Applewood, nodding toward Eddie Christie.

"That's Reuben's cousin, Eddie."

Reuben Applewood was good looking. Meticulous. Look at him from five different angles and every angle he'd look all right. Reuben and Agnes had attended the same Catholic school. Their parents worshipped the same God. She watched him glide to a table to hug his aunt Flora, who was busy hugging Eddie Christie.

"Well, they don't look the first thing alike—Eddie and Reuben."

Charlotte smoothed the folds of her yellow dress and laughed. "You know we got these cousins in blood drawn fresh and friendship cousins who are just as tight."

Ain't that the truth, thought Agnes. People had been saying all afternoon that she would be the next one to nab a husband. That she and Charlotte could pass as twin sisters. Agnes had tried not to take offense.

"Well," Agnes said finally. "He's an active somebody. And *I* don't like short men."

"Agnes," Charlotte said. "I don't recall asking you who or what you liked." Nor did she point out that Agnes had cut two slices of cake. There had always been a gulf between these two cousins because when they were girls, they couldn't play right.

"Take out the toys that you put away," Charlotte would say to Agnes. Being only children, they were taught to stash away their favorite things before friends arrived: fine china sets were put on a high shelf and plastic tea sets were laid out, last year's Baby Doll was put on the bed and the Baby Doll who could pee and cry was stored in the cedar chest. And when Agnes refused to retrieve her little china tea set, Charlotte would yank her ponytail until one of their mothers intervened.

Geographical distance brokered something like affection. Charlotte's family moved to Ohio when both girls were eight.

AT THE END of the party, Eddie and Agnes made a game of spinning, even while eating the lemon butter cake.

"Can't you keep still?" she teased him, but she swayed from dizziness more than he did. "I'm beginning to think you really did spike the punch."

Eddie smiled. "Stillness is a problem for me."

She noticed his perfect white teeth. They were one of his few nice attributes. He told her he was shipping out to Nam in six weeks.

"Next time I may need you to tear through some clouds for me."

Agnes, because she could think of nothing comforting to say, took off her pumps. Without them, he was almost her height. They moved about her parents' folding lawn chairs. The magic of what only hours before had been a sparkling party evaporated; the cicadas came out to sing.

When the chairs were folded, Eddie carried them to the little carriage house that her parents used to store the cooler, grill, and lawn furniture during the winter. Her mother watched approvingly. Lady and Deacon Miller were relieved to see Agnes doing something other than sleeping.

"SOMEBODY GOT THE grand idea to pave over our backyard in the Bronx," Eddie said. "First thing I'm going to do is dig up the pavement when I get back home. Hell, maybe I'll put down a lawn like this. And keep a spot for bocce."

Agnes had never heard of bocce. Eddie told her it was a sport in the bowling family that people played as far back as ancient Rome. He told her how the Italians played bocce in their backyards and in the neighborhood parks and he mimicked throwing a bocce ball and cussed in Italian when he missed his target. Agnes liked that he spoke Italian. And that was when they got the idea to drive to Sears and JCPenney to see if they could find a bocce set.

"You can play and think of me," Eddie said.

Sears and JCPenney turned into a lost errand—neither place carried bocce sets—but the salesclerks said they'd be more than happy to order one. The zeal of the moment dissipated but their hunger was real. They had eaten plenty at the reception, but Agnes took Eddie to a small barbecue restaurant that she swore had the best spareribs in town. It was ten o'clock when Eddie parked her in front of her parents' house. Lady and Deacon Miller's silhouettes could be seen through the bay windows watching TV.

Eddie kept the car in neutral. The old Buick belonged to his father. He had used the car to drive to Georgia from the Bronx. "I'll just have to mail you a bocce set, or maybe you'll have to come to New York."

Agnes nodded and without saying the first good-bye started to climb out of the car. Before her feet touched the curb, she burst into tears. Eddie, who had not had time to get out and open the door for her, leaned over and put his hand on her shoulder.

"What's the matter, Agnes?" he asked

Her mouth opened, but Agnes did not have words for what had happened to her on Damascus Road. She wanted to tell Eddie how she had looked to her left and to her right at the trees tilting for sunlight away from the swamp. How—were her eyes deceiving her?—there seemed to be black snakes dangling from the branches. How she looked at the sky and the sky seemed endless. And her heart leapt, ran out of her chest through her mouth to Claude Johnson. What, she wondered, was that officer doing to him? And where was God. Was God hoarse that night? Or maybe, maybe He just had too much sleep in His eyes? The animals, the things that roamed the swamps, they took God's place and bore witness. Yes, yes, she wanted to tell Eddie Christie all of this, but the most she could say was that clothes gave her pleasure: a fine piece of fabric, the way silk brushed against her skin, how beautiful tulle and lace, a pleated wool skirt, a summer dress, pure cotton, billowing out, carried by a breeze, snagged on wind. As a young girl, she had collected patterns—*Redbook, McCormick, Simplicity, McCall's*—and laid them out on the rug in her bedroom, sank to her knees, felt the heft of fabric scissors in her hands as she traced a pattern's outline, then cut, giving shape to something formless. But what were clothes really but an afterthought, false cover. There was no real protection in flimsy things. An officer turns around and says, *Miss, if you don't take it off, I will. Better you do it, than me, miss? That dress must have cost you a small fortune.* And in truth, it did, plucked off the rack at Fine's for the jazz festival she and Claude Johnson would attend. "Look now, Agnes," Lady Miller had said. "This one. Isn't it lovely?"

EDDIE HANDED HER a red handkerchief from the glove compartment. He let her sit there quietly in the passenger seat, half in, half out of the car, her feet grazing the curb. He could not judge if he should reach out, perhaps, make a gesture to console her. He did not want to put her off in any way. He did not understand the whole of what she had said, but he understood that something awful had happened to Agnes Miller. He began to perspire, wishing he could erase this thing from her memory.

"There's some things you need to know about the Bronx," Eddie said finally, after what seemed like a long while. "The Bronx is ugly. But it can be a beautiful place to live."

Agnes thought the short man might as well be describing himself. Her first impulse was to slip away, to flee, but she could not, for all the world, let go of Eddie Christie's handkerchief.

EVERY THURSDAY AFTERNOON in Buckner County, Georgia, Agnes Christie and Charlotte Applewood pulled weeds from the graves of elders they had never known but now found themselves caring for in the afterlife. The two senior citizens shared between them the loss of two good husbands, neither interred in St. Andrew's Episcopal Cemetery. Agnes's husband had died two years before of liver cancer. Charlotte's beloved, Reuben, had died suddenly from an aneurysm. And so, these two women, who could barely tolerate one another as little girls, were now sometimes acquaintances and dear friends. They walked the mall on rainy days to keep their blood pressure in check and diabetes at bay. They tended to St. Andrew's Cemetery at first to provide structure to their days, and later, because the more times they ventured there, the more they found out about the ancestors buried in the graves.

THE CEMETERY TOOK UP space with one of the oldest black Episcopal churches in the South. A church built by former slaves. Agnes and Charlotte had not known about St. Andrew's as girls because their mothers folded into their men's houses of worship, abandoning the dryness of Episcopal worship for more lively Methodist and Baptist services. Agnes and Charlotte had married men who kept the Catholic faith, but Agnes would attend no one's church. Still, she never opposed Eddie taking the girls to mass on Sundays (if they wanted to go). Children needed something to believe in, Agnes thought, for the times when they believed in nothing.

"How are your girls?" Charlotte asked Agnes.

"Fine," Agnes said, "as far as I can tell." She held back from telling Charlotte that she was worried about Claudia's marriage. And that she hadn't heard from Beverly since she'd dropped forty dollars in an envelope. It seemed to Agnes that Beverly could have the decency to pick up the phone and thank her. Or have the kids call. She was a senior citizen on a fixed income. Money was not something she readily had to give.

"And Gideon and Lonnie?" Agnes asked after Charlotte's grown children.

Charlotte paused between pulling out weeds. "I wish they would call more or at least visit."

"They like to do their own thing, Charlotte," Agnes said, but some part of her was gleeful to hear that Charlotte's beloved children did not always reach out to her in a timely fashion either.

"Gideon and his partner are adopting a little girl from Nairobi,"

Charlotte announced. "The child is six or so, around Lonnie's son's age."

Agnes searched Charlotte's face for some hint of how her friend felt about Gideon being gay. Was Charlotte disappointed not to have a daughter-in-law? How often had Charlotte and Reuben stayed up at night talking about their son's habits? How much sleep had they lost? And living in San Francisco, no less.

"Can't they adopt a baby? Who knows what kind of problems a six-year-old orphan might have," said Agnes.

The countryside surrounding St. Andrew's was once a haven for back-to-earth hippies. On some lots, people still grew pot as well as zucchini, mustard greens, and tomato plants. But lately, new houses had started popping up in the area, identical middle-class houses that looked like they would blow over as soon as a good wind hit them. It was not uncommon to see a black man in a cowboy suit trot by on his white horse or hear the whistle from the freight trains that came by in the afternoon.

"A baby comes with its own worries," said Charlotte, rising suddenly.

Normally, Charlotte would have helped Agnes up, because of the arthritis that sometimes locked her cousin's joints in place. Today she was inclined to let Agnes climb onto her own two feet. They had been circling one another all their lives, she and Agnes, and this circling made Charlotte sad and tired. Charlotte had given her husband a boy, and though Agnes could not articulate the why of it, she was certain Eddie had also wanted a son. Agnes felt that she had failed Eddie in this and other ways.

"And think on it!" Charlotte said. "Deacon and Lady Miller took in your friend Eloise Delaney. What would have happened if they had *waited* for a baby? For a while she was like your sister. Better, really? A best friend?"

Agnes stood steady on her feet. Charlotte was giving today just as good as she got.

"I haven't seen or thought of Eloise in years," Agnes lied. She had seen Eloise a year ago. It was not even six months after she had arrived in Buckner County. She had even joined her for lunch on Main Street. Their lunch had gone surprising well, but later that night Agnes had backed out on her promise to meet Eloise for cocktails at her hotel. Instead she stayed in her apartment and took every stitch of clothing she owned and pressed and ironed through the night. She was too old to be bringing up stuff. And Eloise was a suitcase full of stuff.

Now, it was Charlotte's turn to search Agnes's face for truth or evasion. Charlotte put a handful of weeds in the black garbage bag and willed her voice to soften. Could it be that Agnes really didn't know?

"I guess you didn't read the paper this morning, Agnes?" said Charlotte. "Eloise Delaney's obituary was listed."

"This morning?" Agnes repeated.

"I'm afraid so, cousin. Yes."

Agnes took in air, sucked it down her windpipe.

As soon as Agnes arrived home, she fell into bed. Her body bristled and burned: the pricking of a lifetime, so sharp and piercing that she could not go to work the next morning, nor could she reach for the phone to call in sick. There were a thousand needles coursing through her body, pinching her joints and her skin, and yet she would not give pain the pleasure of seeing her cry. At one point, she managed to turn onto her side and thought—*for a second*—that Eloise Delaney was there in bed with her, looking at her the way she had when they were stupid, foolish girls.

"I'm so sorry," Agnes screamed. "I'm so sorry, Eloise."

It was Wilson Tart who came by the apartment to see about Agnes when she didn't show up at the library. He rapped on the door and was met with silence. A silence he crept away from because Wilson did not want to see a woman he had grown to like dying or decomposed. He remembered that Agnes had a cousin in town and called Charlotte Applewood, who showed up ten minutes later with the key Agnes had given her in case of an emergency.

Charlotte phoned Beverly and Claudia immediately.

———

IN THE HOSPITAL, they put Agnes on an IV drip and released her the same day. Her vitals were normal. Whatever was ailing Agnes, the doctors confirmed prior to Beverly and Claudia's arrival, was not physical.

"You got to get out of this bed," said Beverly, sweeping the covers away from her mother when she and Claudia arrived twenty-four hours later in Buckner County.

"Sometimes when senior citizens get the blues," the doctor had said, "they don't eat. They don't sleep."

In Agnes's apartment, Beverly was firm. "Beds are the enemy of old people. You stay here a day or two longer and Moses himself won't be able to get you up."

"Claudia?" Agnes said, looking past Beverly to the daughter she had always loved. The one she had thought might be an engineer. But she supposed a scholar was good enough.

Beverly backed away and said to Claudia, "She's yours."

The shock of seeing her mother in bed was too much for Claudia.

"You've got to listen to Bev," said Claudia.

"You girls don't need to be here," Agnes said.

"Well, Mom, what are we supposed to do?" Claudia put hard tones in her voice like her sister's. "Let you stay down and die?"

Agnes looked around her bedroom. She realized for the first time that she had not done much of anything to make the bedroom or her apartment feel like home. She would have to put up pictures and whatnots. She couldn't continue living in limbo.

"By myself? No, I've had a friend or two to keep me company."

Claudia looked at Beverly. The two sisters had waged war over their father, but now Beverly put a hand on her sister's shoulder and asked, "Mom, what year is it?"

"2010."

"How old are you?"

"Too old for my liking."

"Who's the president?"

"A black man. Married to Michelle."

"Obama. His name is Obama," Claudia added.

"I know the president's name, Claudia. How are my grandchildren?"

"How many do you have?" said Beverly.

"We might have stopped with the year," Agnes said.

"Rufus is driving down with Winnie and Elijah. And Chico's bringing Beverly's kids."

"All of them?"

Beverly nodded. "The more, the merrier."

"Gracious me. We've got to do something. You know I'm particular. They can't see me like this."

AND SO IT WAS that Beverly and Claudia and Rufus and Winona and Elijah and Minerva and Peanut and Keisha and Lamar and Chico came down to Buckner County. In order to save money, Agnes insisted that they all stay with her, but Claudia and Rufus wanted to stay downtown in one of the boutique hotels with a view of the river. They stayed in a deluxe family suite and, after they'd walked the riverfront with the kids, Rufus looked up Hank Camphor's profile on LinkedIn and emailed him that he and his family would be driving back to New York but might stop by Raleigh on the way home—if that seemed amenable to Hank? *Some place kid-friendly and neutral*, Rufus said in his email. In his mother-in-law's apartment earlier that day, he had seen several irons on display on the mantelpiece. He had taken the irons as a good omen and wondered if the research he had recently resumed on Celtic folktales in Brittany was making him superstitious. Claudia said she thought not, between brushing her teeth and donning a slip. Rufus was predisposed to be superstitious anyway—and a little neurotic.

Like her mother, Claudia had never been one for negligees. Slips framed her figure. They were her nightgown of preference. She started to tell Rufus how much it had bothered her that there were no pictures of them in her mother's apartment. The place had seemed so empty, the way her mother was living out of boxes, but then Claudia recalled what Agnes had said about choking the mystery out of love. Maybe, she and Rufus could go one night without problems. Or complaints. *If Winnie sleeps through the night*, said Rufus, looking up from the computer to admire Claudia's off-white slip. *Is that new?*

AND BEVERLY, Beverly and the kids stayed at the Marriott. They also shared a suite, but Beverly kept the doors open because Minerva had started dating a boy who lived in their Washington Heights building. The boyfriend, Julio, came along for the trip. Beverly was not about to leave Minerva alone in an apartment by herself to get pregnant like she had as a teenager. The drive had worked out for the best, because now Beverly could hear Minerva and Peanut in the next room arguing about what they would watch on television. And Julio was trying to broker peace. Beverly thought, as teenage boys go, Minerva could do worse. She turned to tell Chico as much, but the drive to Buckner County had been a long one for her boyfriend. Chico had driven solo and was already fast asleep. He had fallen asleep before the twins. It would have made Beverly angry, except she needed the quiet. It occurred to her that one day she would be the matriarch of the family. And that thought was sobering.

AGNES CHRISTIE GAVE her daughters and grandchildren and their partners a tour of St. Andrew's Episcopal Cemetery. They walked the grounds and made their way to the stairs of the white nineteenth-century church and the parish that had once been a one-room school for freed slave children. Minerva and Peanut kept saying, "Wait, our ancestors built this? Our ancestors built this?" The smaller children—Elijah, Winona, Keisha, and Lamar—were just happy to run around and play on the grass in front of the church since it was one of the rare occasions they all played together.

THEY WERE HEADED back to town when the children's stomachs began to growl, and their parents were eyeing destination signs for a quick spot to eat that might offer something more than fast food. The children caught sight of the big brightly painted bird, a Georgia woodpecker, on top of a Log cabin–style restaurant. The woodpecker held a sign in its mouth: *The Great Byrd Lodge. Come one. Come all.*

Agnes was the first one out of the minivan. If she hesitated, she told herself, she would talk herself out of entering the restaurant. She walked inside the Great Byrd Lodge and made her way to the oak counter, where former officer William Byrd held court in a red-and-white checkered shirt. The red in the shirt matched the red flame of his hair. The retired officer's hair flickered at seventy in the way it had not at twenty-five. Agnes wondered if he held his color naturally or did he use dye, for she was sure he had once been blond. His legs formed a bow in old age; one seemed slightly shorter than the other. This was from the stroke he took at fifty-five.

BEVERLY AND CLAUDIA followed Agnes into the restaurant. Her grandchildren were there too. They were messing around on Minerva's cell phone and arguing. Normally, Agnes would have minded the noise her grandchildren made in a restaurant. Normally she would have questioned their *home training.* But the Great Byrd Lodge did not seem a place where home training mattered. All things considered.

"I'd say he was about ninety-nine pounds in his prime," said Agnes, looking past former officer Byrd at the dead alligator mounted on the wall. She did not wait for his response. Agnes went and sat down at one of the rustic booths. She waited there for her complimentary piece of pie.

Officer Byrd looked toward the table where Agnes sat. Something lit up in his brain but that something was muddled, wedged as it was between everything he had ever done and been and longed for or hoped to forget.

"Well," he said when Beverly came to the counter. "The lady nailed it. You folks from these parts?"

Beverly reached for a menu. It was a quiet afternoon. The restaurant had a sprinkling of people. Beverly was focused on getting food for her kids before moods struck them.

"My mom was born here," she said.

"Welcome home," he smiled. "She just won a free piece of pecan pie."

"MOM, ARE YOU all right?" Claudia took a seat in the booth along-side her mother. Winona and Elijah and their cousins piled in the booths directly behind them. Claudia shot Rufus and Chico a look, and Rufus motioned that they had the kids covered. Beverly came and sat opposite Agnes. Beverly also took note of her mother's si-lence.

"Mom?" Beverly asked.

Agnes was trying to imagine the life the alligator had lived be-fore it wandered out of the swamp. It was a male alligator, she knew from reading about it in the paper, which was how she had guessed its weight. But there were things she could not guess so easily. Like what the alligator felt before the man with the red-flamed hair pointed his gun. Had the beast had an inkling of what was to be-come of him? Had he lunged or acted on instinct?

The former officer William Byrd brought over the pecan pie, fa-voring his limp leg. Agnes shut her eyes and clutched Beverly and Claudia's hands tighter than she had when they were crossing the street as kids. She waited a second before she opened them. The former officer William Byrd had retreated into the kitchen.

"I am glad you came to see after me, girls. I'm glad you brought the kids." And then Agnes smiled and batted her long lashes at them. She might have been young again, in her prime: so many lives and selves in one body.

"Pecan pie is entirely too sweet for me. But you all enjoy it. We're *here*. Dig in."

ACKNOWLEDGMENTS

I WOULD LIKE TO THANK my editor, Alexis Washam at Hogarth; her assistant, Jillian Buckley; and the publicity and production team at Crown, who put their hearts and souls into ushering *The Travelers* into the world. I would also like to thank Molly Stern. I am greatly indebted to my agent, Ellen Levine at Trident Media, for championing this novel from day one (along with Claire Roberts, Alexa Stark, and Martha Wydysh). The Iowa Writers' Workshop provided me with invaluable time to write and to study with professors who value the written word: Ethan Canin, Samantha Chang, Charlie D'Ambrosio, Kevin Brockmeier, Allan Gurganus, Paul Harding, Margot Livesey, Ayana Mathis, and Marilynne Robinson. For their sharp feedback and support, here's to my Iowa workshop mates Jen Adrian, Mia Bailey, William Basham, Charles Black, Jackson Burgess, Moira Cassidy, Yvonne Cha, Christina Cooke, Tameka Cage Conley, Susannah Davies, Amanda Dennis, Mgbechi Erondu, Jason Hinojosa, Maya Hlavacek, Eskor Johnson, Jade Jones, Aleksandro Khmelnik, Afabwaje Kurian, Maria Kuznetsova, Claire Lombardo, Lee Yee Lim, Paul Maisano, Magogodi Makhene, Daniel Mehrian, Melissa Mogollon, Grayson Morley, Derek Nnuro, Okwiri Oduor, Karen Parkman, Jianan Qian, Sergio Aguilar Rivera, William Shih, Kevin Smith, Lindsay Stern, Keenan Walsh, Dawnie Walton, Monica West, De'Shawn Winslow, David Ye, and Michael Zaken. My thanks to Joan Silber, Marcus Burke, Garth Greenwell, Van Choojitarom, Connor White and poet Ryan Tucker, Kelly Smith, Connie Briscoe, Jan Zenisek, and Deborah West.

Robin Christianson and her family made the Historic Phillips House a sanctuary during my two years in Iowa. The Rae Armour West Postgraduate Scholarship enabled me to do research when I returned home. Tin House's Summer Workshop scholarship gave me the opportunity to workshop with Jim Shepard, and the Jentel Artist Residency in Wyoming provided a stunning mountain setting for rewriting and tackling edits.

Thank you to Daniel O'Rourke for sharing invaluable experience and knowledge about the Navy and Vietnam; historian Allen Steinberg for letting me attend "The Vietnam War in Film" class at the University of Iowa; Gregory and Michelle Owens, two of the smartest people I know, for their friendship and feedback; Tim Cockey (whose feedback I also relied on much) and Julia Strohm; Nosquia Callahan for research tips and her scholarship on African Americans in Germany; and Dr. Linda Brown, Dorothy Roberts-Truell, and Xavier Gunn for granting me interviews about their time abroad in the military. Thank you Brigitte Morel, Anthony Baggett, and Andreas Mertens, who walked down memory lane with me in Berlin and introduced me to Chuck Root. Thank you to Jake Schneider, Ben Robbins, Bennett Sims, and Carina Klugbauer for a private tour of the Schwules Museum. Jean Morel was my cultural and aesthetic consultant on farm life and all things Brittany. Francena and Robert Edwards explained the daily routine of life on a small family farm. Thank you to Vicki Mahaffey for sharing her knowledge of Joyce, Christopher Dennis for sharing his knowledge of Shakespeare, and Allie Croker for a great tour of Shakespeare's Globe theater. I pause here to thank Margot Livesey, Paul Harding, and Magogodi Makhene again for reading multiple drafts of *The Travelers*. De'Shawn Winslow, Monica West, Claire Lombardo, Sasha Khmelnik, and Mia Baily (with whom I took every workshop class and traveled from Paris to Berlin) are now lifelong friends.

Elizabeth Hadley Freydberg's *Bessie Coleman: The Brownskin Ladybird* and Gail Levin's *Lee Krasner* brought Bessie Coleman and Lee Krasner (pioneers in their respective fields) home to me. John Darrell Sherwood's *Black Sailor, White Navy: Racial Unrest in the Fleet During the Vietnam Era* helped me put flesh and blood on Eddie Christie and Jebediah Applewood. Major General Jeanne M. Holm and Brigadier General Sarah P. Wells's "Air Force Women in the Vietnam War" and the Vietnam Women's Memorial shed light on the history and contributions of American female soldiers during the Vietnam War.

Last but not least, my deepest gratitude to family and friends for their support: my daughters, Nuala and Gaby, and their father, Brendan Mernin; my late uncle Robert Booker; my siblings, Ronald, Jackie, and Michael; and my niece, Tamala. Thank you to Drew Reed, Heather Gillespie, Bridget Battle, Gale Mitchell, Cassandra Medley, Janice Bennett, Steve Garvey, Vernell B. Jenkins, Liz Lazarus, Crystal and Martin Beauchamp, Tim Sanford, Lynn Connor and the Lost Lit crew, Kareem and Yuka Lawrence, Evan Smith, Tony Scott, Gaby Starr and family, Lynn Nottage, Karen Duda, Julie and Matt Greenberger, Lynn Holst, and Lucinda Williams.

PHOTO CREDITS

PAGE 1:   Delano, Jack, photographer. *Unloading potatoes at a starch factory in Van Buren, Maine.* Oct. Photograph. Retrieved from the Library of Congress, www.loc.gov/item/2017792377.

PAGE 4:   Delano, Jack, photographer. *Aroostook potatoes of the Green Mountain variety grown on a farm near Caribou, Maine.* Oct. Photograph. Retrieved from the Library of Congress, www.loc.gov/item/2017792173.

PAGE 9:   Foltz Photography Studio. *The Hermitage Plantation; Outbuildings.* Savannah, Georgia. Date Unknown. Photograph. Courtesy of the Georgia Historical Society.

PAGE 27:   *Entrance to Columbia-Presbyterian Medical Center, West 168th Street.* New York, NY. 1928. Photograph. Retrieved from Archives & Special Collections, Columbia University Health Sciences Library.

PAGE 33:   Foltz Photography Studio. *New Solms Hotel.* Tybee Island, Georgia. 1938. Photograph. Courtesy of the Georgia Historical Society.

PAGE 45:   Lazarus, Liz. *Bronx Front Porch.* Bronx, New York. 2016. Photograph.

PAGE 46:   Schomburg Center for Research in Black Culture, Jean Blackwell Hutson Research and Reference Division, the New York Public Library. *Ira Aldridge as "Othello."* 1887. The New York Public Library Digital Collections, http://digitalcollections.nypl.org/items/510d47da-72e5-a3d9-e040-e00a18064a99.

PAGE 59:   Front cover of *Rosencrantz & Guildenstern Are Dead* by Tom Stoppard (1967), reproduced by permission of Faber & Faber, Ltd.

PAGE 61:   USS Oriskany *(CVA-34) Catapulting an A-4 Skyhawk during operations off Vietnam, 30 August 1966.* Official U.S. Navy Photograph. Courtesy of National Archives, photo#: USN 1117395.

PAGE 63:   *Piano Factory Workers, circa 1916.* Collection of Stereograph Cards. Courtesy of The LaGuardia & Wagner Archives, LaGuardia Community College/The City University of New York.

PAGE 71:   *Two sailors press pants during the ship's second Vietnam cruise* (USS Intrepid Cruise Book, 1967). Retrieved from the Collection of the Intrepid Sea, Air & Space Museum.

PAGE 73: *Programme for the 1995 production of* Rosencrantz and Guildenstern are Dead *at The Lyttelton Theatre.* sjtheatre/Alamy Stock Photo.

PAGE 75: Porter, Regina. *Bronx Basement.* Bronx, New York. 2016. Photograph.

PAGE 90: George Arents Collection, the New York Public Library. *George Washington Bridge.* The New York Public Library Digital Collections, http://digitalcollections.nypl.org/items/510d47e2-3624-a3d9-e040-e00a18064a99.

PAGE 93: *Golferinos.* ca. 1905. Photograph. Retrieved from the Library of Congress, https://www.loc.gov/item/2002705510.

PAGE 121: *Craftsmaster of YFU-74, Vietnam,* 1969. Official U.S. Navy Photograph. Courtesy of National Archives, photo#: USN 1139720.

PAGE 126: *E.O.D. Team member searches for Mines, Da Nang, Vietnam.* 1966. Official U.S. Navy. Courtesy of National Archives, photo#: 428-K-31466.

PAGE 128: Schomburg Center for Research in Black Culture, Manuscripts, Archives and Rare Books Division, the New York Public Library. *The Negro Motorist Green Book: 1950.* 1950. The New York Public Library Digital Collections, http://digitalcollections.nypl.org/items/283a7180-87c6-0132-13e6-58d385a7b928.

PAGE 130: Trikosko, Marion S., photographer. *MEMPHIS, TENNESSEE. Lorraine Motel.* Photograph. Retrieved from the Library of Congress, www.loc.gov/item/2017646278.

PAGE 133: *TV Dinner circa 1955: Still-life of a three-hold aluminum tray, "TV dinner".* Hulton Archive/Getty Images.

PAGE 140: Vachon, John, photographer. *Aberdeen vicinity, Maryland. Truck drivers having coffee at a diner along U.S. Highway 40.* Feb. Photograph. Retrieved from the Library of Congress, www.loc.gov/item/2017846238.

PAGE 147: *Bessie Coleman, the first African American licensed pilot shown here on the wheel of a Curtiss JN-4 "Jennie" in her custom designed flying suit (circa 1924).* Courtesy of Smithsonian National Air and Space Museum, photo: NASM92-13721.

PAGE 151: Schomburg Center for Research in Black Culture, Photographs and Prints Division, the New York Public Library. *Negro school children, Omar, W. Va.* The New York Public Library Digital Collections. http://digitalcollections.nypl.org/items/510d47df-f8f3-a3d9-e040-e00a18064a99.

PAGE 154: *Group Photo of Fire Company No. 16 with Steam Engine.* 1875. Courtesy of the Missouri Historical Society, St. Louis. https://mohistory.org/collections/item/resource:141351.

PAGE 161: *Bessie Coleman, Aviation Pioneer* (Public Domain). Courtesy of Smithsonian National Air and Space Museum, photo: NASM-980-12873.

PAGE 170: *Lyndon Johnson signs HR 5894.* 1967. Photo courtesy of the U.S. Army Women's Museum.